I0732750

The Dark Winter

The Dark Winter

ELENA GRAF

PURPLE HAND PRESS

Purple Hand Press
www.purplehandpress.com

This is a work of fiction. Names, characters, places and incidents are the product of the author's imagination or used fictitiously, and any resemblance to actual persons, living or dead, businesses, institutions, companies, events, or locales is entirely coincidental.

Trade Paperback Edition
ISBN-13 978-1-953195-06-7
Kindle Edition
ISBN-13 978-1-953195-07-4
ePub Edition
ISBN-13 978-1-953195-08-1

Cover photo by: Arthur Villator / Shutterstock.com Used by permission. Extended rights courtesy of Arthur Villator.

03.12.2025

PART I

HIGH OCTOBER

Chapter 1

Before she opened her eyes, Olivia Enright knew that her bedroom was filled with pellucid, golden light. She'd forgotten to close the blinds again, although it only required a few taps on her phone. Last night, when she was being undressed by an excited lover, she didn't care where her phone landed, but looking for it now would only wake the woman sleeping against her shoulder.

The sun teased up the red highlights in Sam's chestnut hair. The sparse grays, that she liked to complain and brag about, shone like they'd been polished. "Good morning, my dear girl," Olivia murmured, glad that she was sound asleep and wouldn't protest. Whenever Olivia used that term of endearment, Sam reminded her that she hadn't been a girl for decades. Lately, she'd been emphasizing the point by adding that her sixtieth birthday was only a few weeks away. Were the casual mentions a sign of anxiety about a milestone birthday or a hint to plan a celebration? She doubted that Sam, who was basically shy, was hoping for a party, but Olivia had been secretly planning a gathering of their closest friends.

Carefully turning her head, Olivia glanced at the clock. As tempting as it might be to wake Sam with lovemaking, she had to get up. Her appointment with Mother Lucy began at eight, and Olivia despised being late. She hated it so much that she'd been known to exile people from company meetings for tardiness. That was before her son's trading scandal, when she was still the chair of the Enright Fund. When she became the town manager, she tried using that trick in meetings, but the laid-back Mainers were unimpressed. She'd since learned to live with them straggling in whenever they pleased.

Olivia finally eased her arm out from under the sleeping woman. As Sam turned away from the sunlight, Olivia admired her long, elegant neck. Sam might tramp in dirt from her construction projects, but everything about her was refined, from her patrician features to her long-fingered, graceful hands.

"Later, you," Olivia whispered, kissing her softly. Sam's eyes, the warm brown of strong tea, briefly opened. A moment later, she was asleep again. Olivia took Sam's deep sleep as a sign that their lovemaking had been satisfying. The bed smelled of female sex, briny, like the salt marsh after the tide went out.

Olivia found her pants under the bed. Fortunately, her phone was still in the pocket. She keyed in the command to activate the motorized blinds before closing the bedroom door.

While she waited for the coffee to brew, she browsed *Bloomberg*. Since giving up her controlling interest in the Enright Fund, she no longer needed market intelligence to guide its investments, but reading the financial news was an ingrained habit. Besides, the article on the inversion in the bond markets was a welcome distraction from the morning's real business—preparing for the video meeting with her granddaughters.

She hadn't seen the girls in years. Fortunately, Amanda had sent some photographs. "They've changed so much. I don't want you to be shocked when you see them." Olivia had been known on Wall Street as having a heart of steel, but when she saw the pictures, she burst into tears. Since then, she'd looked at the photos many times, studying their young eyes for signs of damage from their father's sexual abuse. Amanda had said they were at a delicate stage in their therapy, which was why Olivia was so glad that Lucille Bartlett, rector of St. Margaret's Episcopal Church, had agreed to act as an intermediary.

Olivia's lawyers had worked out the arrangement. She'd been shocked at first that her daughter-in-law was willing to speak to her after years of silence and helping her son shield his assets during the divorce. But there was money involved, a lot of money. What a greedy thing Amanda was! She'd taken Jason for everything she could in the settlement. The child support payments he'd had to pay were beyond ridiculous. Protecting his money from Amanda was Jason's motivation for putting the title to the Hobbs house in his mother's name. A smart move, as it turned out, especially after the Feds started poking around in his trading practices.

Olivia took out the cream for her coffee and discovered it was a few days past the best-buy date. Olivia sniffed it to make sure it was still good. She ignored the few clots that floated on the top of the dark liquid. As she was about to put the cup to her lips, tanned arms came around her waist and gave her a hug.

"Morning," Sam murmured into her skin and nibbled it. Olivia gently swatted her away.

"I'm too old for hickeys in visible places."

"How about in invisible places?" Sam asked with a chuckle. "Thought you can sneak off like that?"

"I tried to be so quiet, but you have sharp ears."

"Thank you for letting me sleep, but Liz and I have a project going over at Erika's."

Olivia put down her coffee and turned into Sam's arms. "Can't you even stay for a cup of coffee?"

"Not really. I'm already late. Can I take some with me?"

"Of course." Olivia pulled Sam closer. "Will you come back for dinner?"

"Probably not tonight. I've been here for days. I need some time at home."

"Sam…"

"I'm not promising." Sam opened a cabinet and took down an L. L. Bean thermal cup from the top shelf. Olivia often envied her height and long arms. Olivia needed to stand on a stool to get things from the topmost shelf. After preparing her coffee, Sam bent to kiss her. Playfully, she added a kiss on the tip of her nose.

Olivia knew it was sentimental, but she followed Sam to the front door and waved as she drove away.

After Sam left, Olivia finished reading the article on bond inversion while her bath filled. As she settled into the tub, she realized how much she treasured it, not only because she loved a hot bath, but because it had brought Sam to her door.

The scene replayed in Olivia's mind like a movie. She'd been expecting a man when Sam had replied to her inquiry about a bathroom renovation, but a tall, attractive woman appeared for the appointment. Her business card showed her full name: Samantha McKinnon, followed by a long string of initials, including the coveted fellowship in the American Institute of Architects. Looking back, Olivia couldn't decide which had impressed her more, the long list of credentials or Sam's well-developed biceps. They'd gotten off on the wrong foot with an argument about wearing masks, but under Sam's attitude of forced patience, Olivia had detected a spark of sexual interest. She couldn't help but fan it until it burst into flames. It had taken time, but it had been worth it.

She turned off the spigot and gingerly descended into the bath. The hot water was delicious, but she usually cut herself off at fifteen minutes, which she timed on the clock on the wall. "You're the only person I know who has a clock in the bathroom," Sam had said when she'd taken it down to prepare for the renovation project.

Olivia put on a full complement of makeup. There were very few people Olivia would allow to see her bare face. She had a good rapport with Lucy, so she might be one of them, but the rector always looked put together, a holdover, Olivia assumed, from when she was an opera singer.

The bathroom clock indicated Olivia had enough time for another cup of coffee, maybe even some breakfast. She brought her Scandinavian yogurt topped with blueberries and sliced almonds to her office. When her Mac woke up, a string of email notices popped up from overseas financial agencies. Olivia tapped them away because it was Saturday and didn't really matter. She managed to finish her yogurt before Facetime rang for her meeting with Lucy.

That smile! Lucy was wearing a deep-red lipstick that instantly drew the eye to her radiant smile. Anyone seeing it felt warmly welcomed. She was wearing her red hair back today, which put the focus on her features. Even in her late fifties, the woman was stunning. Lucy modestly wrote it off to good genes. Her mother had been a model.

"Good morning, Lucy! I see you're in your rectory office."

"I had to get out of the house. I can't hear myself think. Erika has Sam and Liz working on some project. She says I have too much junk, and we need more storage, so they're finishing the loft in the garage."

"You can never have too much storage."

"But don't you think it's insulting to call my stuff, junk?"

Olivia laughed. "As a marriage counselor, you should know that couples often value things differently." Olivia's eyes swept Lucy's image in the box on the screen. "No collar today?"

"I'm experimenting. The collar is so formal, especially when I meet with young people."

"I like the formality. I'm not sure I approve," said Olivia.

Lucy looked surprised. "Do I need your approval?"

"Well, maybe. I am a member of your vestry. I prefer the collar but, I do like your scarf, and that sweater. Green is your color, Lucy. Matches your eyes."

"Thank you, Olivia. You look pretty good yourself today. Beautiful cardigan."

"All right then," said Olivia, getting down to business. "Enough preening for the camera. Before we talk about the meeting with the girls, has Abbie passed along the proposal for the endowment?"

"Yes, and I gave it to Tom to review." Lucy frowned slightly. "Olivia, are you sure you want to give us all that money? You've already been so generous to St. Margaret's."

"Yes, I do. An historic building like St. Margaret's costs money to maintain. You should have an endowment for it like you do for the summer chapel. I don't approve of you and Tom taking salary cuts to keep the place going."

"You don't need to worry. The bishop put a stop to it."

"And so he should. You both more than earn your keep. No, I am determined to get the endowment in place before Amanda tries to get her claws into my money."

Lucy's face remained neutral, but Olivia could detect the faint disapproval in her green eyes. Few people would even have noticed, but Olivia had learned to read facial expressions from many years of business negotiations.

"You didn't like that comment, Lucy."

"I wish you would keep an open mind about Amanda."

Olivia affected a contrite expression. "All right, Mother Lucy. I'll try."

"Please just call me, 'Lucy.'"

"Really? I thought you liked that title."

"I do, but I've spent the last few days at a conference of female priests, and the subject of what people call us keeps coming up. Using "Mother" is associated with Roman Catholic nuns. Most of the other women use only 'Reverend' or their first names."

"Well, I'll say it again. I don't approve of all this informality, especially where children are concerned. They should be brought up to respect their elders. Why has it never bothered you before?"

Lucy shrugged. "I don't know. I guess because I was brought up Catholic, and we always called our priests, 'Father.' It seemed right to claim 'Mother' for female priests, but maybe not."

"I like the idea of calling you 'Mother.' You are a mother to your flock, Lucy, and you do it well."

"Thank you. I'm sorry, I'd love to continue this conversation, but I have another meeting at ten, so let's figure out the logistics for this call."

They agreed that Olivia would listen in without video while Lucy opened the meeting and drew out the girls' feelings about seeing their grandmother again.

"Amanda will also be able to observe the entire meeting," Lucy said. "That was a condition of allowing it."

"I understand," said Olivia. "I would probably insist on it too."

"I think Amanda is a good mother," Lucy said. "I don't know her well enough to say for sure, but let's give her the benefit of the doubt."

"What's that old saying? The best defense is a good offense. I've always lived by that."

Once again, Olivia saw the subtle look of disapproval in Lucy's green eyes.

"Olivia, you've made so much progress. Every human relationship doesn't have to be transactional. Your son loved Amanda enough to marry her. Let's look for the good in her."

Olivia's experience of Amanda didn't incline her to tolerance, but she decided not to argue with Lucy because she could never win. Not only did Lucy's instincts about human nature always give her the advantage, she also had the Almighty on her side.

Chapter 2

From down the street, Sam could see the big, gray F-150 already parked in Erika's driveway. "Damn you, Liz Stolz. You always make me look bad." Sam smiled because she really didn't mean it, despite the friendly rivalry that went back over twenty years. And Sam would have beaten her to the job site, if Olivia hadn't kept her up half the night.

For a woman who seemed so rigid and buttoned-up on the surface, Olivia was a free-range animal in bed. Sam considered herself adventurous, but Olivia had managed to teach her a few things. She tried not to worry about where this was going and just enjoy the amazing sex, but she kept feeling an undercurrent of expectation. Clearly, Olivia was looking for more than a great lay. The question was, could Sam provide it?

Sam gulped down the rest of her coffee and hopped out of her truck. She unwrapped a new dust mask, intending to use it for double duty. Cutting the sound-proofing blocks made clouds of lung-clogging dust, and the COVID mask mandate was still in effect. The KN95 mask was rated for both.

Grabbing her tool bag, Sam headed into the garage. Before going upstairs, she stopped for a moment to admire the ingenious return she'd designed to maximize the parking area in the garage. She wondered if Lucy had even an inkling of what her wife was planning.

Erika intended the finished room over the garage to be a Christmas gift for Lucy. When she'd shared her concerns about Lucy walking alone on the beach in the dark, Sam had suggested creating a soundproof practice room over the garage. Before Lucy had married Erika and still lived in the rectory, she would sing her vocal exercises in the empty church before heading out for her morning walk. Now that autumn was upon them, it was dark when Lucy rose, and Erika was pushing them to finish early.

The only problem with the project was fitting it in with all the other jobs Sam was working on, which meant working on weekends. Fortunately, Liz had agreed to help, and she was giving her time for nothing. She said it was because Erika was an old friend, but Sam knew the real reason. Liz was doing it for Lucy.

Nearly everyone in Hobbs loved St. Margaret's rector for her natural warmth, her brilliant smile, and her kindness, but Liz loved her differently, which was obvious to her friends, and even more obvious to Maggie, her wife. The situation had come to a head last summer. Liz had tried to kiss Lucy when they were alone on the boat. Maggie had figured it out and confronted Lucy. For a while, the situation had been tense, but since then, things seemed to have settled down. At least, Sam hoped so.

The pneumatic nailer's familiar *whap, whap* sound meant that Liz had finished installing the soundproofing and was already nailing on the paneling strips. Sam's footsteps on the stairs were drowned out by the compressor running to refill the tank. To get Liz's attention, Sam switched it off.

Liz pulled off her earmuff hearing protectors. "Well, well. Look who finally showed up."

"I was busy."

Liz rolled her eyes. "Yeah, I bet you were. Olivia looks like the kind of woman who can never get enough."

Sam grinned in reply, realizing that it confirmed Liz's assumption, but she didn't mind Olivia being thought of as sexy because she certainly was. Oh, was she ever!

Liz had already installed most of the ceiling boards. She was even taller than Sam, which made working overhead easy.

"Not bad for an amateur," Sam said. "You even managed to put the right side up."

"Of course, I did," said Liz, looking indignant. "You think I'm stupid?"

"I wouldn't expect stupidity from a surgeon."

Liz grunted. "You'd be surprised how stupid surgeons can be. Basically, we're nothing more than highly trained plumbers and mechanics." Liz kicked the box of leftover insulation blocks. "Are you sure this stuff will block the sound? Lucy sang at the Met. Her voice is incredibly powerful."

"The reviews of this product are pretty good. If it docsn't work, Lucy will just have to go back to practicing in her church."

"You mean you don't guarantee your work?"

Sam shrugged. "Oh, I do. Once the surface materials are installed, Lucy can scream her bloody head off, and no one will hear her."

"In that case, this would be a good place to commit a murder."

"You have someone in mind?"

"You, maybe, if you don't wipe that shit-eating grin off your face. You don't have to rub it in that you're getting laid."

"And you're not? You can't tell me that studly Liz Stolz isn't getting attention from her lady." The expression on Liz's face changed abruptly, which is how Sam knew she'd said something wrong. "I was just kidding. I'm sorry."

Liz shrugged, but Sam had the feeling she would have said more if the circumstances were right. After twenty years of knowing Liz, Sam's instincts about her were pretty reliable.

"What's going on?" Sam asked. "Not getting any?"

"Nope."

"Want to talk about it?"

"I'll tell you another time. Now, let's get back to work." She turned on the compressor. The clatter of the pistons pounded on Sam's eardrums until she threw the switch and there was blessed silence again.

"Let's go to the diner for breakfast, and you can fill me in."

"Erika wants this job done."

"I know, but an hour won't make a difference. We're nearly done." Sam yanked on Liz's arm. "Come on. Let's go." She headed out the door and down the stairs.

Behind her, she heard Liz disconnect the nailer from the hose with a blast of air. When Liz had taught a safety class at their woodworking club in New Haven, she'd shown some stomach-turning photos of air gun accidents. The lesson had obviously left an impression. The grisly images formed in Sam's mind every time she shut down the compressor.

"Let's take your truck," said Sam, when Liz came down. "Mine has all my tools in the back, and I'd rather leave them in Erika's driveway than in the diner parking lot, especially with all the leaf peepers in town."

The door of the screen porch opened as they headed to the truck. "And where do you two think you're going?" Erika called in her British-accented English. Darts of disapproval shot from her pale eyes. "Sam, you just arrived!"

"We need to pick up something!" Sam called back.

"Will you return soon?" asked Erika, hands on hips. When she was annoyed her German inflections were more prominent.

"Back in an hour." Sam replied, grinning in Erika's direction. "We're hungry."

"I could make you breakfast," Erika offered.

"Nah, your breakfast would be too healthy. We want a real diner breakfast. You know. Fried eggs and bacon…lots of grease. We'll be back soon. Promise." Erika still looked doubtful. Sam gave her a friendly wave before shutting the door.

Liz watched Erika through the windshield. "She's anxious to get it done. She really doesn't like Lucy walking on the beach in the dark."

"Oh, for fuck's sake, Lucy did just fine before Erika moved back to Hobbs. What did she think she was doing before she got here? I mean, Lucy has a brown belt in Jiu Jitsu. She can take care of herself."

"It's that protective thing."

"Erika thinks she's going to protect Lucy? Lucy, who could break someone's neck if she wanted to? Have you ever seen her do her martial arts moves?"

"She always does a demonstration fight for the church festival. She took down a man twice her size. Scared the shit out of me. I would never want to get on the wrong side of that woman."

"And she's so tiny. What? Five three…maybe?"

"Small but tall. Amazing that she could sing Wagner. But gosh, did she do it well."

"Oh, Liz, you've got it bad. She's even trained you not to take the Lord's name in vain."

Liz frowned. "I guess she has. God damn it!"

They both laughed.

Liz pulled into the parking lot of the Hobbs Diner, a town landmark beloved by the townies and tourists alike. Usually, the line would be out the door, but the pandemic had kept the leaf peepers away.

Sam stifled the queasiness that came on whenever she stood on the diner's uneven floor, which had been patched with four different patterns of linoleum and sagged toward the back. The architect in Sam found the old structure more than unnerving, but the owner had resisted her suggestions for improvement. Pat insisted that her customers loved the out-of-kilter floors as much as the tubular furniture, circa 1950. Supposedly, the tourists associated the shabby, old-fashioned feel with Maine. The idea, she'd explained, was to defy the expectations the décor suggested with the diner's home-cooked Maine specialties like their signature lobster pie.

The counter waitress waved to them and pointed toward the back. "That table's been lonely for you, Doc. Where you been?"

"Trying to practice what I preach, Paula. Eating in public may be allowed now, but it's not necessarily a good idea."

"Well, it's good to see you," Paula said, leaning over the counter to speak confidentially. Sam noticed that the part in her hair, dyed a bright red that never would occur naturally, was completely white. "It's been dead in here this morning," Paula confided. "I hope they don't cut our hours again."

The customer at the end of the counter was paying too much attention, so Liz waved Paula down to where the waitresses picked up their orders. "How's the foot?" she asked.

"Much better. Wearing that strange shoe at night helps a lot."

"Good," said Liz, patting the counter. "Keep it up."

"Why would you wear a shoe at night?" asked Sam as they walked to their table.

"I'm not ignoring you, Sam. I can't tell you because of privacy laws," said Liz, sliding onto the bench seat.

"Oh, come on. You already let on there's something wrong with her foot."

Liz looked annoyed, but she answered. "Speaking in general, people with plantar fasciitis sometimes benefit from wearing a brace that keeps their foot from pronating at night." Liz glanced around the mostly empty dining room. "We're living dangerously, coming in here to eat, but this place has been observing all the guidelines."

"I read in the paper that they shut down for two weeks when they had a case."

"Like I said, they're being careful. As a doctor, I don't like setting a bad example, but if we don't support the local businesses, they'll just die."

The Saturday waitress approached with a coffee pot.

"'Morning, Lois."

"'Morning, Sam."

Lois glanced at Liz. "You're looking peaked this morning, Doc. Pandemic got you down?" Lois poured Liz's coffee into an indestructible, white mug that was probably original to the place.

"I'm working her too hard," Sam explained.

"I see," said Lois. She gave Liz another critical look and shook her head, obviously not buying Sam's explanation. "I already put in your order. Should be out in a few minutes."

"Good, because I could eat my arm," said Sam.

"Wait for the bacon and eggs," Lois advised dryly. "It will taste better."

After Lois headed off, Sam said, "Try to smile, Liz. You're the town doctor. Everyone knows you. They'll worry if you look sad. You know what they say, 'If Liz ain't happy, ain't nobody happy.'"

That garnered a chuckle from Liz, but her face instantly became serious again. "Everyone knows my mother just died. I love Hobbs, but it's like any small town. Everyone knows everyone else's business." Liz peeled open a single-serve creamer and dumped the contents into her coffee. She opened another and did the same. The coffee needed at least three servings to modestly change the color.

Sam studied her friend. In the six months since the pandemic had officially begun, Liz's hair had gone from dark-iron gray to mostly silver. The

October sunlight, streaming through the window, made it brilliant. Liz was serious by nature, but her blue eyes seemed sadder than usual, and Lois' observation was spot on. Liz looked tired.

"Not sleeping?" Sam asked.

"Not much. Lots of people are having trouble sleeping. I've written twice as many scripts for sleep aids as usual. Lucy said it could also be a symptom of grief."

"But you said you were relieved when your mom passed."

"When your mother is almost ninety, losing her mind and pissing on the floor, thinking she's sitting on the commode, death doesn't seem like such a tragedy. Yes, I'm relieved. But I keep waiting for a big emotional hit."

"When my father died, it took me six months for it to sink in."

"Maggie says I'm not dealing with the grief, and that's why I don't talk to her. The fact is, it's the other way around."

"Why isn't Maggie talking to you? This isn't still about that stupid kiss last summer?"

Liz slouched in her seat. "It's hard to know. We haven't talked about it lately. Maggie is what I call, 'a saver.' She saves up her grievances and then, *wham!*" Liz punched her fist into her other hand. "She hits you with them when you least expect it."

"I hate that."

"Me too," Liz agreed. "And she's full of shit. We do talk. You know, the information exchange—what's for dinner? When are the grandkids staying the night? What happened in the Rotary meeting? That kind of stuff. Nothing too deep. Maggie doesn't like to talk about the pandemic or politics. It gets her too upset."

"It's pretty upsetting," Sam agreed.

"But after seven years together, what do you talk about? You already know everything there is to know about each other."

"Why do you think I never tied the knot?"

"You've been pretty close a few times."

"That's when I know it's time to leave."

"I never expected to get married. Jenny and I talked about it to protect our assets, but we never got around to it. When we split up, I was glad we didn't."

"Yeah, that could have been a big mess."

"It was messy enough with that house in Guilford. I thought she'd never get the money together to buy me out."

Sam kicked her gently under the table. "Must be hard to have so much money."

"Says the trust-fund baby," said Liz, grabbing Sam's knee and squeezing it to get her back for the kick. "I probably would never have asked Maggie to marry me except for the damn cancer. She was so scared."

Sam frowned. "You married her because she was scared?"

"Sounds like a dumb reason, but yes. I've seen what it's like for women whose partners dump them because they have breast cancer. It sounded so romantic. Two lovers reconnected after forty years of separation. Plus, we were in the throes of new romance and fucking like rabbits."

"But not now?"

"Rarely." Liz glanced out the window into the parking lot. "Let me amend that. Never. We had sex after we patched things up after the kiss, but then it stopped completely. It's been months."

"That's not good. Why bother to be married if there's no sex?"

"There are other reasons…financial…legal."

"Then form a corporation."

Liz shrugged. "That's what people used to do before they legalized same-sex marriage."

Lois returned and put plates of bacon, eggs, and home fries in front of them. The food was exactly as Sam imagined it. The stack of buttered toast glistened with melted butter. The bacon was fried to crispy perfection.

"Anything else?" Lois asked brightly.

They both asked for more coffee, and Lois left to get the coffee pot. Sam dipped the corner of her toast in an over-easy egg. As Lois walked away, Sam's eyes followed her. "It's criminal that a woman her age needs to wait tables to make ends meet."

Liz looked up from her plate. Her eyes trained on Lois chatting with the customers at a nearby table. "Fortunately, she's still healthy enough to do it. So many people think they're going to work in their retirement and aren't physically able. Single women get screwed by social security. Many never make enough money in their jobs and don't benefit from a husband's bigger salary."

"How old is Lois?"

Liz looked thoughtful for a moment, and Sam realized she was mentally scanning her medical records. "Seventy-eight, I think."

"And still working. Wow," said Sam.

"Yeah. Wow."

"What are you going to do about Maggie?" asked Sam and bit into a piece of toast. She wiped away the extra butter that remained on her lips with her fingers.

"I don't know. Talk to her, I guess. I don't intend to live the rest of my life as a celibate."

"Too horny for that."

"Wouldn't you be?"

"I don't know," Sam said, gazing out the window at the trees across the parking lot. The tops were just beginning to turn orange. In a week or two, the leaves would be brilliant. "My sex drive has changed. I still really like sex, but I was doing okay before Olivia seduced me."

"No, you weren't. You were crabby. Normal people need sex."

Sam gave Liz a firm look. "Liz, in case you haven't noticed, we're not normal."

"Sure, we are. Who set these rules anyway?" Liz gestured to Sam's plate. "Eat up. Erika will be wondering what happened to us."

Chapter 3

Before her next meeting started, Lucy slicked on a fresh coat of lipstick. Chewing on her lower lip was a nervous habit she'd never been able to break. By now, she'd eaten off most of her lipstick.

Her prenuptial couple, Brenda and Cherie, were good friends, and they wouldn't give her appearance a second thought, but Lucy always liked to look professional in therapy sessions, or when she was in her official capacity as the rector of St. Margaret's. She felt vaguely guilty about not wearing her collar. She'd always seen it as a signal to others that she was available to minister to their needs, but she knew other priests felt differently. During a recent meeting of the women's clergy forum, they'd discussed collars. "People act differently with me when I wear the collar," one woman said. "They apologize for saying things they think will offend me. They don't see me as one of them. They act like I'm special, someone set apart."

But you are special. You're an ordained priest, thought Lucy, which took her back to her ordination day. She'd felt different when she'd been vested in the splendid red vestments. She'd been awed when she stood by the bishop to consecrate the bread and wine for the first time. She'd felt transformed by the experience.

The parish admin knocked on Lucy's open door, interrupting the memories. "Mother Lucy, your one o'clock appointment is here."

Lucy waved toward herself. "Jodi, come in for a moment. I want to speak to you."

Jodi's eyes widened and she looked instantly anxious.

Lucy smiled. "It's nothing bad. I promise."

Jodi approached but stood well clear of the masking tape Liz Stolz had run along the floor to mark off the safe zone for social distancing.

"From now on, I want you to call me by my name, just 'Lucy.' Okay?"

Jodi frowned. "Sure, Mother…I mean, Lucy, if that's what you want. I was just trying to be respectful."

"Yes, I know, but we've been working together for almost a year. There's no need for us to be so formal. Don't you agree?"

"Sure. If that's what you want," said Jodi, but she looked doubtful.

"Good. I'm glad we agree. Now please bring in Ms. Bois and Chief Harrison."

Lucy was used to seeing Brenda with her blond hair up or tied back, which the Hobbs police dress code required, but she wore it over her shoulders today. Out of uniform, Brenda was like a different person. She looked relaxed in a polar fleece zip up and jeans. Her fiancée, Cherie, who was usually the more dressed up of the two, wore a sweater dress accented with an artsy scarf.

By October, everyone's tan had faded, but Cherie's biracial heritage had blessed her with year-round warmth to her complexion. Her perfect features, blond hair, and stunning blue-green eyes caused people to turn around on the street to look at her. If Lucy was the kind of person to be jealous of another woman's beauty, Cherie would definitely be on her radar.

It was sweet to see how Cherie glowed when she looked at Brenda. Lucy suspected their dreamy smiles were an extension of post-coital bliss. She was glad to see them looking so happy. Their relationship was barely six months old, but they had been through challenges that would have ripped apart a less-devoted couple.

Cherie had infected Brenda with COVID-19, nearly ending her career as Hobbs' police chief. Now, Brenda was a COVID "long hauler." Fortunately, her heart issues were now under control. Cherie had also passed on the virus to her father. Compromised by COPD, he had been one of Hobbs' first deaths from the coronavirus. Cherie said her final farewell to her father through Facetime, when Lucy had gone to the hospital to administer the last rites.

The ritual had apparently meant a great deal to Cherie, who had been a faithful member of Lucy's congregation since she'd moved to Hobbs to become Liz's physician's assistant. When Brenda's interest had forced Cherie to reckon with a horrible incident in her past, she'd chosen Lucy as a therapist. As a college student, Cherie had witnessed a state trooper shoot her obviously black sister to death. She had come a long way in overcoming her fear of police officers and guns.

Over the summer, Lucy had gotten to know the couple on a more personal level. Liz's "Thirsty Thursdays" on her big, wrap-around deck had provided all of them with much needed socialization and cemented the bonds. When Cherie had asked Lucy to officiate at her wedding, Lucy was touched, but not surprised.

"Are you really sure you want to move up the wedding?" Lucy asked to open the conversation. Cherie was also a licensed therapist and practiced at controlling her face, but Lucy read the fleeting doubt in her eyes. "Cherie? You look unsure."

"You know I wanted a big wedding with all my Louisiana relatives. Of course, when they find out I'm marrying a woman, they might not want to come."

"You haven't invited them yet, so you don't know that for sure." Brenda's tone sounded slightly accusing. "Plus, it would cost a heck of a lot to come all the way to Maine. At least in Zoom, they can see us get married without all the expense of travel."

Lucy turned to Cherie. "Last time, you said you were going to tell your family about Brenda."

"I did. I said I was marrying the police chief. Of course, they all assumed I'm marrying a man, but I didn't say anything to change their mistaken ideas." Cherie glanced away and focused her gaze out the window. "I'm afraid. It's not only coming out as gay. Some of them disapproved of my mother marrying a white man, and Brenda's white."

"Racism works both ways," Lucy observed.

"They know how much I hated cops after that trooper killed my sister. They won't understand."

"You could use your training to help them understand," suggested Lucy. "From what you say, most of them are religious people. You could talk about forgiveness being one of the greatest gifts anyone can give."

Cherie looked perplexed. "It's been a long path for me. And while I forgive Brenda because I know her and love her, I'm still not sure about other cops. When I see that black flag with the blue stripe in front of people's houses, I know it's code for hating blacks."

Lucy inhaled a deep breath. "There are a lot of assumptions being made in these crazy times. Let's give people the benefit of the doubt." She glanced at Brenda. "You need to be especially sensitive now, Brenda. You heard what Cherie said."

"I'm really trying, but I'm afraid she'll forget that I'm not the bad guy, like when the Black Lives Matter protests began."

"No, I forgave you. I won't forget. I know you now. I've seen how hard you're working against police brutality and racism. I hear you speak out against it on national TV. But sometimes, I wonder if you'd still love me if I looked more black."

Brenda's face crumbled in pain. "I love you. I don't care what color your skin is. Yes, I was attracted to you because you're beautiful, but I never thought, 'I wish she was whiter.'"

"That's because when you met me, you thought I was white. I had to tell you I'm half-black."

Lucy felt a fight coming on. "All right. We know it takes guts to confront your own racism, so let's give Brenda some credit. You've seen the training videos she created for the NYPD. Right, Cherie?"

"Yes, I've seen them," she said, frowning as if she wondered where this was leading. "That was her job."

"It was my job, but I did it because I believed in what I was doing. I took a lot of heat from other cops for my position."

"None of us truly knows what it feels like to be in another's skin," said Lucy, trying to lower the temperature. "We can only keep trying. God loves us for the very act of trying. She knows we're not perfect."

Brenda exhaled a long stream of air. "Maybe we should hold off on the wedding until we figure this out."

Cherie gave her a sharp look. "It was your idea to move it up!"

"It was a real scare with my heart. If I'm going to die soon, I want to die as your wife." She frowned. "Then you'll get my police pension. Someone ought to benefit from it."

Lucy tried not to sigh obviously, but she was discouraged. "Sounds like you two still have some talking to do before you get married. How can I help?"

Cherie's beautiful eyes filled. "Oh, Lucy. You can't help. I need to pray for faith. I know Brenda loves me, and she's doing the best she can. I have to learn to trust her."

"You do know your distrust has nothing to do with me?" asked Brenda. Cherie nodded sadly.

"Then forget that I'm a cop and love me—Brenda."

"I do love you, and I'm trying really hard."

"You're right, Cherie. Pray for faith, and while you're at it, hold the image of Brenda in your mind and surround her with the light of your love. Repeat it until you see your love surrounding her. All the sexual attraction in the world isn't enough. You need to find the faith and love that can sustain your marriage."

Lucy was relieved when the conversation turned to the logistics of a Zoom wedding.

Brenda and Cherie finally headed out. Lucy took a minute to recharge her batteries and say a little prayer. The Zoom meeting with Olivia and her granddaughters was less than ten minutes away, and the situation was so fraught with distrust.

Olivia's daughter-in-law, Amanda, had accused Jason, her husband, of sexually molesting their young daughters. Lucy desperately hoped the allegations were untrue, but there was strong evidence supporting them. When Jason had been caught for insider trading, the FBI had seized his laptop and found a large cache of kiddie porn, not conclusive proof, but it certainly didn't look good for Olivia's son.

Lucy was no stranger to sexual abuse. She'd been raped by the man she'd trusted to help her at the Met. Only years of therapy and the support and love of a dear friend had helped her recover. She was glad that Olivia's granddaughters were in therapy and their mother was supportive. Many parents refused to believe their children's allegations of sexual abuse.

The cell phone chirped to remind her it was time to open the Zoom meeting with Olivia's daughter-in-law. Lucy crossed herself before waking up her computer and navigated to the meeting app. Her settings allowed people into the waiting room before the meeting. She felt a flash of guilt to see Olivia and Amanda already there. Then she glanced at the clock and saw it was two minutes to three. She wasn't late. She wondered if it was a good or bad sign that they were both so eager to start the meeting. Then, Lucy remembered Olivia was a stickler for punctuality.

Lucy took a deep breath and smiled her warmest smile as the other participants appeared on the screen.

"Hello, Olivia. And hello, Amanda. Welcome. I'm really glad to hear that you've been meeting on your own. I hope your conversations have been productive."

Olivia, who liked to dominate every conversation, jumped right in to answer first. "I think any conversation is productive after such a long silence. Amanda and I have a lot to talk about."

Lucy saw Amanda nod in agreement. She was an attractive woman in her late thirties, a bottle blonde. Her features were so perfect as to be nondescript, but she put herself together well.

"You know I'm always here to help," Lucy said in a cheerful voice, although she actually dreaded having to join more of their meetings.

"Thanks, Mother Lucy, but we're managing at the moment," said Olivia. "Just get us through this introduction to the girls, and I think we're good."

"Amanda, the girls' therapist is aware of this conversation and my involvement?"

"Yes, and she's glad you're here. She volunteered to join the call, but I told her it wasn't necessary."

"That would have been fine too, but it might have made it more difficult to schedule. Let's see how this goes. You may not need me in the future."

"The girls have become very attached to you, Mother Lucy," Amanda said. "Let them down easy, please."

"Of course, and I hope I'm able to meet them someday."

"Oh, you will," said Olivia. "You can count on it!"

Lucy smiled genuinely this time. "Okay. Are you both ready? When the girls come on, Amanda and I will turn off our video feed. But we'll be here, Olivia, if you need either of us."

"I'm sure I can manage, thank you," said Olivia, looking slightly insulted. It was rare for her to show any emotion, so Lucy was surprised. As always, she was groomed and made up perfectly. The colors in her scarf exactly matched her top. Every dark hair was in place. Her blue eyes were penetrating. Lucy could see how Olivia had easily intimidated her business associates. She hoped she would show a softer side to her granddaughters.

"I'm going to allow Sharon and Jessica into the meeting now. Are they in the same room with you, Amanda?"

"No, they're on their iPads in their own rooms. They wanted privacy."

"Do they know you'll be on the call in the background?" asked Lucy.

Amanda looked momentarily flustered. "Yes, I told them. Maybe they forgot that part."

"Then leave your video on until I ask you to turn it off. I want them to see you when they come into the meeting, both to reassure them and so they know you're not trying to eavesdrop. It's important that we maintain their trust. Okay?"

Amanda nodded. "Sure, Mother Lucy."

"Please, just call me 'Lucy.'" In the other video window, Lucy saw Olivia give her a sharp look. "I'm trying for a more relaxed atmosphere," Lucy explained to Amanda, who also looked curious. "Let's get started. Olivia, time for you to go dark for a couple of minutes. All right, here we go!"

The video windows showing two pretty girls opened on the screen.

"Hello, Sharon. Hello, Jessica," said Lucy, nodding to each of them in turn.

"Lucy!" squealed the younger girl.

"Hi, Lucy," said Sharon, her sister, smiling from ear to ear. "How are you?"

"Wonderful! I'm so glad to see you both. I have your mom on this call, as you can see. And your grandmother. Your mom and I are going to listen in, just in case you need us. Do you understand?"

Both girls nodded.

"And Jessica, don't be afraid to talk and ask questions. Okay?"

"Yes, Lucy," replied the freckle-faced, blond child. "I need to speak up…like you said." In past conversations, ten-year-old Jessica had seemed cowed by her older sister. Lucy always made a special effort to draw her out.

"Okay, Grandma Olivia, I think you can join us now," said Lucy cueing her.

Olivia's video window opened. When Lucy saw the tears glistening in Olivia's eyes, she knew that all the careful preparation had been worth it.

Chapter 4

Sam groaned as she lifted her heavy tool bag. "Jeez, I need to clean this thing out. Will I see you tomorrow?" she asked in a hopeful voice.

"Tomorrow's Sunday. Lucy will give us hell for working on the Sabbath." Liz bent to unscrew the valve cap under the compressor tank. The air escaped with a blast followed by a slow hiss.

"Lucy won't even know," said Sam. "She'll be busy all morning at the worship services at the outdoor chapel."

Liz raised a brow. "You're not going? I thought Olivia had you converted."

"Not even close, but Olivia thinks Lucy walks on water."

"That surprises me. Olivia's a pretty savvy judge of character."

"What are you trying to suggest? That Lucy's not as holy as she seems? Liz, you need to be careful what you say. Lucy's a priest, and her reputation is important. She didn't ask you to kiss her."

"When a woman is as beautiful as Lucy, she doesn't have to ask."

Sam rolled her eyes. "Liz! It's bad enough men say shit like that. Don't be a pig!"

"What? It's not as if I forced myself on her. When she said, 'stop,' I did."

"She's married to Erika, your friend," said Sam. "How could you do that to her?"

Liz shrugged. "Erika always had other lovers. This is the first time she agreed to be faithful to one woman…and only because Lucy insisted they get married."

"But she is married, and so are you. You need to stop looking at Lucy that way. Look at the mess you made."

"Thanks for the unsolicited advice."

"You're welcome," said Sam, but she sounded disgusted. Liz was about to defend herself, when Sam changed the subject. "If we come back here tomorrow afternoon, we could finish the job."

"Lucy won't like us working on Sunday. She won't say anything because she's tolerant of other beliefs, but she won't like it. I'm off Monday. I'll help you then."

"I guess it will have to keep until Monday," said Sam and headed down the stairs. "Don't forget to lock the doors when you leave," she called after her.

"I won't," Liz said mostly to herself, knowing Sam was already out of earshot. She was annoyed with Sam for being so blunt, but that was also why she valued her friendship. She could always count on her to tell her the truth, and Sam meant well, even if it was none of her damn business. Of course, Liz had made it her business by telling Sam about the kiss when it happened. Ordinarily, she'd go to Erika when she had troubles with women, but for obvious reasons, she couldn't talk to her about Lucy.

Liz wondered how she'd managed to make such a mess of things. Trying to sort them out had only made them worse. She'd been staying away from Lucy, so Maggie wouldn't be so jealous. In fact, when Sam had first asked Liz to help her, so she could get the job done quickly and keep down the labor costs, Liz had almost said, no.

Lately, anything Liz did for Lucy made Maggie suspicious. "Lucy needs something, and you jump," Maggie had said. Her wife had never been jealous of the favors Liz did for other people. If Liz had the time and could help someone, she did. That's who she was. Now, Maggie was suspicious of anything to do with Lucy, and even things she did with other friends. Before the kiss, Maggie never asked Liz where she was going, mostly because Liz told her. Now, Liz kept her plans to herself because all the suspicion was driving her crazy.

Liz's eyes traveled the room. When it was complete, it would be a comfortable space. Most of the work was behind them now. Erika's plan to give this soundproof practice room to Lucy as an early Christmas present looked like it would really happen. With any luck, they would be done with the project before they left on their annual Acadia camping trip. Of course, with the bad blood between Maggie and Lucy, Liz wasn't looking forward to what had been for years an anniversary celebration. It had once been such a special event that Erika and Lucy had married in October, so they could spend their honeymoon in Acadia with their friends.

Liz carefully rolled up the compressor hose and set it on the motor. She emptied her nail gun and pneumatic stapler before putting them in their cases. Like Sam, she always brought her tool bag home with her in case she needed something from it. For the same reason, she still carried a medical bag even though most doctors didn't anymore.

Liz heard a rustle of gravel. She looked out the window to see who had pulled into the driveway and saw Lucy's car. By the time she located her keys, which she'd thrown in her tool bag, there was a knocking on the window. She turned and looked into Lucy's green eyes. She waved in greeting, hoping to get away without a conversation. Lucy knocked on the glass again, so Liz had to roll down the window.

"And where do you think you're running off to?" Lucy demanded, hands on hips.

"I need to go."

"No, you don't," countered Lucy. "You have time for a glass of wine. I hardly see you anymore. Now, get out of there."

There were very few people Liz would allow to speak to her in that way, but Lucy always got away with it. Obediently, Liz opened the door and got out. "Here, take this in, please," said Lucy, pulling a supermarket bag full of empty plastic containers out of the backseat of her car and handing it to Liz. "Erika told me if I want more lunches, I have to bring back the containers. Imagine that?" Lucy slung the strap from her computer bag over her shoulder and grabbed her purse off the front seat. "Come in and tell me what you've been up to."

"Oh, you know. I've been working with Sam on your storage project. Erika says you have too much crap."

"That's pretty insulting, don't you think?"

Liz shrugged. "Everyone has crap, even the sainted Rev. Bartlett."

"Because I'm a priest, and I can land anywhere, I tend to travel light, but of course, I have my important stuff…like everyone. I'm glad I kept all my theology books, now that I'm back in school." Lucy reached for Liz's hand and gave it a squeeze. "How are you, Liz? I haven't seen you much lately."

"I'm good. Except Sam just insulted me by calling me a pig. Do you think I'm a pig?"

"No, but sometimes you act like an adolescent boy."

By now, Lucy's blunt assessments seldom surprised Liz, but this one pulled her up short. "It's from growing up with all those brothers," Liz protested. "It could be pretty raunchy in those days. My parents' vendors still gave away girly calendars with naked women. Men said all kinds of things they wouldn't dare say now."

"And neither should you. I think you picked up some bad habits from men," Lucy said, giving her a penetrating look. "You're not a man, Liz. You're a woman."

"Ouch, Lucy. You don't always have to be so honest."

"You asked, Liz, but you don't have to act like a naughty, little boy to get my attention." Lucy tapped Liz's chest over her heart. "Remember. I see you. The real you, and I love you." She tugged on Liz's arm. "Come in and talk to me."

"Shouldn't you be studying?" Liz asked.

"Yes, but I never see you anymore, and you're more important."

Lucy opened the door to the screen porch with her shoulder. She handed Liz her laptop bag while she searched in her handbag for the front door keys.

"A shame we have to lock all the doors now. People are so crazy with this election coming up."

Liz frowned at the political signs across the street. "That's why I carry a gun."

"Well, you know what I think about that." Lucy finally got the door open. "Erika! I'm home and I brought a guest."

Erika bounded down the stairs. "Liz, I was hoping you would stop in after you were done. Can you stay for dinner?"

"I was going to heat up some leftovers. Maggie is up in Scarborough watching the kids. This is Alina's weekend to be on duty at the news desk."

"Her loss, our gain," declared Erika. "Your leftovers can wait." Her pale blue eyes twinkled with a canny look. "How's my *storage* project going?"

"Pretty good. We're resting for the Sabbath." She glanced at Lucy, who nodded in approval. "We'll pick up again on Monday when I have off. I'll finish the wiring. Sam can't because she's a real contractor and would need the inspector to sign off on her work."

"Not that we'd ever tell on her," said Erika with a wink.

"Yes, but Sam is pretty by the book. I don't blame her. She wants to keep her contractor's license. She's not old enough to retire. Not like us." She handed Erika the bag of empty plastic containers. "A gift from your wife."

"About time she brought these home," said Erika, looping her blond, nearly white hair over her ears. She gestured to the sofa in the living room. "I'll get you something to drink. *Bier oder Wein?*"

"Oh, Liz, try the new wine I bought," said Lucy, pulling on her arm. "It's wonderful." She smiled that brilliant smile that could make Liz do anything.

"Okay. I'll try it."

When Erika left to get their drinks, Lucy sat down beside Liz and took her hand. "What's going on with you, friend? You look sad."

Liz heaved out a sigh. "Well, there's been a lot of death in my life lately. Mom, my uncle, my cousin. Because of the pandemic, I couldn't get to any of their funerals. Never mind my patients dying from COVID. I'm up to here with death." Liz measured to her hairline. "I'm at the point, where I'm numb."

Lucy was too practiced a therapist to frown, but Liz could see the subtle change in her eyes. "That's not good, Liz. You need to let yourself grieve, especially your mother. That's a big one."

Liz nodded her agreement. "I know it is, but I'm sort of relieved. Her last year was really difficult. Her last hospitalization accelerated her dementia. She said some pretty nasty things to me."

Lucy had been gently stroking Liz's hand while she spoke. "I'm sorry, Liz. What can I do to help?"

Liz coughed up a cynical chuckle. "Funny you should say that. Maggie has been begging me to see a shrink, but I won't."

"Why not?"

"A holdover from when you could lose your medical license for evidence of mental illness."

"Liz, you know it hasn't been that way for decades!"

"I know, but I don't really believe in therapy."

Lucy made a face.

"It's nothing personal. Just a surgeon's contempt for those airy-fairy disciplines." She grinned.

"Liz, you keep digging yourself in deeper. Don't you know when to stop?"

"Sorry, Lucy. I know you're legit. In fact, Maggie said she would even go along with me coming to you for help. She says she can't stand seeing me so depressed anymore."

Erika came in with two glasses of wine and reached them over the back of the sofa. "Lucy, you can't really take on Liz as a client, can you?"

Lucy turned to answer her wife. "No, but I can talk to her as a friend… if that would help."

"I don't know…" Liz said uncertainly.

"Liz, I have a client who graduated from therapy last week," Lucy said. "That means I have an open spot at four o'clock on Thursdays. I'll come home early, and I expect to see you here."

Liz turned to Erika for support. "How do you live with this woman?"

Erika laughed. "I go along. Resistance is futile." She saluted with her glass of wine. "Try it. It's really quite good. Lucy must be listening to your wine lectures."

"I don't lecture. You, Professor, lecture."

"At least, I come by it honestly."

"Are you still thinking of retiring this year?"

"If the current president isn't re-elected maybe. I've certainly enjoyed all the attention being the expert on political discourse, but after four years, it's beginning to wear thin."

Lucy stroked her wife's arm. "Honey, what's for dinner that smells so good?"

"That's Liz's chicken cacciatore recipe. A classic."

Lucy visibly brightened. "Liz, did you know that was the first dinner Erika cooked for me? You know I'm a slob when I eat pasta and spattered the tomato sauce all over my favorite summer top. She used it as an excuse to take off my shirt."

"Oh, Lucy, how you embellish!" Erika protested. "You took off your shirt voluntarily. I had nothing but the most honorable of intentions in offering to treat the stains."

"My wife is so virtuous," Lucy said, miming an angelic look.

Liz instantly came to Erika's defense. "Lucy, Erika is German, and therefore, extremely literal. If she says her intentions were innocent, they probably were."

Erika gave Lucy a sly look. "Well, not completely innocent, but in that case, practical."

"That's another German trait…practicality," Lucy explained, as if Liz, who came from a German family needed an explanation. Lucy put her wine glass on the coffee table. "Mind if I change into my jammies? It's been a long day, and I just want to relax."

Erika patted Lucy's thigh. "No, go on, dear. Make yourself comfortable. We have at least half an hour until dinner. I'll put out some snacks while you're upstairs."

"Good. Because the good smell from the kitchen is making me really hungry."

"Come into the kitchen, Liz, while I find something for us to eat."

Liz leaned against the counter while Erika composed an elegant charcuterie tray with soppressata, bresaola, an assortment of cheeses, and olives. "You do that as well as your mom."

"She was a very good teacher. She would have loved it if Papi had let her open her own restaurant."

"So many women of her generation went along with what their husbands wanted and never got to realize their dreams."

"So many women of every generation never get to realize their dreams," replied Erika, popping an olive into her mouth. "I think Mutti always hoped that she might have more children."

"I'm sure you were more than enough for both your parents."

"It had nothing to do with me, per se. It was simply horrible in the GDR at the time, shortages of everything. We were lucky to have our tiny, cramped apartment in Berlin. And we only had that because Papi was world famous as a Maths professor."

"Do you ever wonder what your life would have been like if you and your parents hadn't escaped?"

"Often. Although the Iron Curtain fell so long ago, hardly anyone ever thinks about it now. Most of my students weren't even alive when the Berlin Wall came down. When I mention it, they stare at me like I have ten heads." Erika picked up the tray. "Come. Lucy will be looking for food when she comes down and hunger makes her ornery."

Liz laughed. "She has such a sweet nature. I have a hard time imagining her being ornery."

"Believe me. She growls at me when it's time to feed her." Erika nodded toward the wine bottle. "Grab that, will you?"

Liz had to admit that Erika made her cacciatore recipe better than she did, maybe because she hadn't made it in years and her friend had more recent practice.

Liz finished her dinner before Erika and Lucy and patiently waited for the others.

"I still don't know how you can eat that fast," Erika said, glancing at Liz's plate.

"It's from my hospital days. I'd sit down with my food in the doctor's dining room and my beeper would go off—in the days, when we still used beepers. I learned to snarf down my meal in case it was interrupted."

"But, Liz, you're such a good cook," Erika said. "Why would you put all that work into preparing a meal and then gobble it down? I don't understand."

"Erika's right. You should take time to enjoy life, Liz. You're always in such a hurry."

"I can't help it. Old habits die hard."

"Life is short, Liz," said Erika, sitting back. "Take some time to enjoy it while you can."

"Uh oh, I feel a philosophical lecture coming on," Liz said.

"Never mind," said Erika. She sat back and watched Lucy finish her dinner before getting up to help clear the table. "Liz, would you like to sit with me on the deck while Lucy cleans up the kitchen?"

"Don't you think it's a bit nippy out there?"

"I'll give you a jacket."

"I have a sweatshirt in the truck. I'll get it."

When Liz rejoined Erika on the back deck, the last glow of twilight was beginning to fade, spattering the inland rivers in the salt marsh with color.

"This is my favorite time of the day," Erika said. "A shame the days are getting shorter, but I adore autumn."

"Enjoy it quick. High October won't last much longer."

"It's supposed to be warm tomorrow for Lucy's Eucharist service at the outdoor chapel. Will you come?"

"I don't think so."

"Of course, you'll come. The faith thing intrigues you in the same way it intrigues me. You don't understand it, so you can't stay away from it. Is that why you're attracted to Lucy?"

"Among other things," Liz admitted.

"I know exactly what you mean. She has so many amazing qualities, but most of all that smile. That's what hooked me."

"I remember," said Liz.

"Liz, I want to thank you for sending me to Olivia Enright for financial advice. I know how hard it was for you to admit you didn't know what to do in the downturn."

"No matter how much you trust me, you need to protect your retirement…and your legacy."

"But I do trust you, Liz. That's why I made you my executor. I know that you'll always do the right thing. If something ever happened to me, I know you'll take care of Lucy and my father."

Liz gave Erika a critical look. "For God's sake, you're not even old enough for Medicare. Do you know something that I don't?"

"No, it's just that there's so much death lately. Even without the virus, none of us has any guarantees, do we?"

"No, we don't." Liz finished her wine in two gulps. "Good wine."

A moment later, Lucy came out, bundled in a polar fleece. "I brought some more wine," she said brightly, insinuating herself between the two of them. "Who's ready for a refill?"

Chapter 5

Sam could hear her phone ringing from the shower. "Oh, for God's sake, give me a break!" She lathered her hair and dialed back the hot water to warm for the rinse. Finally, she switched off the faucet and sighed. That feeling of being clean after a hard day's work never got old. Refreshed, she stepped out of the shower and wrapped a thick bath towel around her torso. She dried her short hair with a smaller towel, worked some gel into it before combing it out.

In her bedroom, Sam thrust her legs into her boy shorts and pulled on a pair of sweatpants. Shirtless, she headed into the kitchen to put her leftovers into the microwave to heat. Her cooking was more pedestrian than Olivia's, but it was tasty and nutritious. She decided to shut the blinds in the kitchen even though the only other house on Jimson pond was a New York couple, who hadn't shown their faces since the pandemic began. If it weren't for them, Sam wouldn't mind going naked.

She shrugged on a sweatshirt before heading to fire up the pellet stove. She couldn't understand why Liz still burned firewood instead of pellets. Sam had lectured her on the efficiency of renewable fuels. "Bullshit," Liz had replied bluntly. "It takes energy to compress the sawdust into something that looks like horse food and transport it on trucks from Canada. Meanwhile, the guy down the road cuts up trees the power company has to clear anyway. Then, I split it in my backyard on a reconditioned, 2-cycle splitter that burns very little gas. Now, that's efficient."

"Liz, you're a dinosaur."

"And at sixty-five…very much aware of it." Since she'd passed that milestone, Liz had been mentioning her age more frequently.

Sam smiled at the memory of the conversation with her friend. Liz was proud of being old-fashioned, of burning wood, not pellets, of carrying a medical bag, of doing house calls and physicals instead of only relying on tests. Sam had to admit that most of Liz's old-fashioned values had merit.

She didn't have to be completely "woke," as the kids said, but it would be good if Liz unstuck herself from the misogynistic, butch culture of her past because it got her into so much trouble.

Sam's phone rang, interrupting her thoughts. "Oh, not again!" It had to be someone in her contacts because other numbers were blocked. The screen flashed the name without a photo because Sam hadn't gotten around to adding one yet—Olivia, of course. Sam debated for a moment. She was tired and really not up for more conversation after talking to Liz all day. She could silence the ring and let the call go into voice mail, but right before the last ring, Sam swiped the screen to open the call.

"Samantha! I was wondering where you were. I called earlier." Sam could hear in Olivia's voice that she was trying to hold back the edge of impatience.

"I was taking a shower. Then I was downstairs filling the stove." Sam was annoyed to hear herself accounting for her actions to her girlfriend. They were dating, not married.

"I was really hoping you would stop by after work."

"I didn't say I would, did I?"

"No, but I was hoping you might. I wanted to tell you about the conversation with the girls."

Sam muted her phone and sighed. How could a woman as confident as Olivia be so needy? Sam unmuted the call. "Okay. I'll throw on some clothes and come over."

In the kitchen, the microwave pinged.

"I could come over to your place. I made some veal stew for dinner. I could bring you some," Olivia said in a tantalizing voice.

"Veal? Who eats veal anymore? The way they treat those baby calves—"

"Oh, please Samantha. I will not feel guilty about what I eat. It was absolutely delicious. If you tasted it, you would agree."

Sam thought for a moment. If Olivia came over, she would stay the night. If Sam went to Olivia's house, she could leave if she'd had enough of her company.

"I just heated up my dinner in the microwave. Let me eat it and throw some clothes on. Then I'll come over."

"Okay. I'll see you soon." Sam could hear Olivia smile because that had been her plan all along. Olivia always said she enjoyed staying at Sam's house, but she really preferred to stay in her huge Gull Island castle. Olivia's bedroom on the third floor had an expansive view of the ocean. Her sprawling king-sized bed was more comfortable even for someone who liked to entwine herself with her lover.

The accommodations at Sam's house were quite different. Sam had built the bed frame for her queen-sized bed from solid cherry. The live-edge headboard came from a tree taken down in her parents' backyard. She wouldn't give up that bed for anyone. She'd renovated the house by Jimson pond herself, but it could be damp and chilly despite all the modern climate control she'd installed.

Sam sensed that Olivia's preference to be in her own house had less to do with comfort and more to do with territory. Olivia liked having everything on her own terms, and if possible, on her own turf.

She glanced at the clock. Six-forty-five. She refused to be rushed by Olivia's wants and needs. There was a reason she was still single. No one was going to tell her what to do or when to do it.

She took out her dinner of green chili from the microwave. It was a perfect, slow-cooker meal for days when she was going to be late on a job site. It took all of fifteen minutes to brown the ground meat, usually turkey, along with chopped green pepper and onion, and dump in bottled green salsa, canned jalapenos, and white beans. When she came home, she could walk in the door, the delicious smell greeted her.

At Olivia's, dinner was always a production. The table was set perfectly with china and silver, the place mats and cloth napkins always matched. The dinner was usually something gourmet. It could be simple, like a salmon fillet over a bed of wilted spinach, but the presentation always looked like a photo out of a food magazine.

Sam, as an architect, loved elegant design, but everything at Olivia's had to be just so. It reminded Sam too much of growing up in her parents' home where the décor, the table settings, and the food had to look like it belonged in *Town and Country*. Sam wondered as she spooned a dollop of sour cream onto her chili what her mother, who deplored the nouveau riche, would think of Olivia.

After she ate and cleaned up the kitchen, Sam headed upstairs to dress and pack a bag in case she decided to stay the night. She'd leave the bag in the car to avoid giving Olivia any ideas. Olivia had given her a drawer to keep a change of clothes, but Sam only kept the bare necessities—a change of underwear, socks and toiletries. Olivia probably had no idea what a big statement Sam had made when she'd left a toothbrush at her house.

Sam put a dressy top, jacket, and pants on a hanger, knowing that if she stayed the night, Olivia would probably insist on going to church in the morning.

She drove to the barrier island thinking about how she let Olivia call the shots. Was it always true that one person in a relationship decided what to do, where to go? Sam considered the relationships of her friends. Liz let Maggie think she was in control, but she put her foot down where important things were concerned. When Liz didn't want to do something, she ignored Maggie and did what she wanted. Sometimes, she disappeared into her wood shop or to her boat to escape her company. Brenda was still in the stage of catering to Cherie, but she'd been equally accommodating to her first wife, who'd tragically died in a traffic accident. Erika was unique. She lived in her own world, and Lucy's magnetic personality could induce anyone to do anything. Erika was no exception. "Resistance is futile," Erika often would say, quoting the Borg queen. Where Lucy was concerned, that was the damn truth.

Sam arrived at Olivia's Victorian, the biggest house on the block, thinking it was a perfect example of what her mother called, "ostentatious displays of wealth." Old money, her mother had explained, was quiet, restrained, even a bit shabby. The older the wealth, the shabbier it was.

There was nothing shabby about Olivia's house because it was less than ten years old, built by her son, Jason, as a waterfront retreat from the pressures of Wall Street. It was a "smart house" with all the technology that existed at the time it was built—doors unlocked, lights came on, and blinds closed to the command of a cell-phone app. But Sam knew technology aged and couldn't always be upgraded. That's why Sam seldom installed smart technology in the homes she designed unless the client insisted.

All the front lights were on, a display indicating that Sam was expected. Olivia opened the door for her. As soon as she closed it, she pulled Sam into a deep, sensual kiss. "Welcome back," she said with a seductive smile.

"Do you want to go straight to bed? Or can I hang up my clothes first?" asked Sam, trying for irony.

Olivia laughed. "No, I can wait until later. I want you to taste my stew."

"I told you I was going to eat before I came over," said Sam, trying not to sound as irritated as she felt.

"I know, but one little taste, please?" Olivia pinched her fingers together to show how little she was willing to accept.

"No, I'm full now. Maybe tomorrow."

"Please…"

"You won't be happy until I eat your baby cow."

"You eat beef, don't you? All commercially raised animals are treated inhumanely."

"I know, but those calves in those little huts, shut off from the sun, barely able to stand up. That's just cruel."

Olivia rolled her eyes. "You and your friends are so damned virtuous! Sometimes, I don't know how you stay alive."

"Sometimes, I forget that you are one of those conservative types who can't stand people with a social conscience."

Olivia put her hands on her hips. "I have a social conscience. I'm just not a bleeding-heart liberal."

"Nice, Olivia. Keep it up. What a way to get me into bed."

"That's nonsense. You're not really insulted."

Sam chuckled. "No, I know what you do is mostly for show. You're contrary like Liz."

Olivia waved dismissively. "Go, get your bag out of the truck and bring it in."

"How do you know I have a bag in the car?"

"See? I know you too. You always come prepared. When you come back, I've got a fire going and a bottle of wine open." She gave Sam a firm look. "Go on," she said, urging her on with a nudge.

Sam gave Olivia a quick kiss. "I'll be right back."

When she returned, she found Olivia in a movie-star pose on the couch, manicured feet with painted toenails up on the sofa, her arm stretched across the back, a hand-blown, perfect wine glass in her hand. The bright-red, painted toenails made Sam smile.

"Do you block your scenes, or do they come naturally?" Sam asked, picking up the glass of wine waiting for her on the coffee table. She sat down on the sofa opposite Olivia.

"You've been spending too much time with theater people," said Olivia in a disparaging tone.

"Well, Maggie Fitzgerald always has the gang from the Webhanet Playhouse or the State Theater at their parties. Lucy Bartlett is a refugee from the opera. Yes, I guess, I do hang with theater people."

"Those people worry me. They're always acting."

Sam almost spat her wine. "And you're not?"

"It's different. I don't pretend to be fake."

Olivia sat up and slipped her feet into a pair of mules.

"Everything is different for you, isn't it?" Sam observed in a completely neutral tone. "You have your own standards."

"I don't want an argument, Samantha. It's been a difficult day."

Sam sat back to indicate that Olivia had her attention. "I'm listening."

Olivia poured herself another glass of wine. Sam had noticed that Olivia never overindulged and knew her exact limit when it came to alcohol. The ability to "hold her liquor" had probably been critical to being the female wolf of Wall Street.

"As you know, Lucy has been working behind the scenes with my ex-daughter-in-law and the girls' therapist to prepare for me to meet my granddaughters. That woman is amazing, so unassuming and authentic."

Bet you could learn from her, thought Sam, while she continued to smile pleasantly.

"Good thing Amanda sent photos of the girls. It was shocking to see how much they've changed since I last saw them."

"Remind me. Whose idea was it to end contact?"

Olivia gave her a sharp look, but then looked contrite. "Mine, I'm afraid. You may recall that I sided with Jason in the divorce. Amanda retaliated by keeping my granddaughters away from me. What did she expect? Of course, I would take my son's side. Family loyalty is important to me."

"Your granddaughters are also your family," said Sam, sitting back.

Olivia sighed. "Yes, and now, the only family I have left."

"Well, that's not completely true. You could look up your brothers and sisters and their kids."

Sam carefully watched Olivia's face, but she saw not even a flicker of emotion. "I don't know if I'm ready to stir up that hornets' nest." Olivia's eyes pleaded. "Can we discuss this another time?"

"Of course. But don't keep me in suspense. What happened with the girls?"

"They were very sweet. Well behaved and polite. They want to know when they can visit. Amanda said they keep talking about coming up this summer…when it's safe to travel, of course."

"Sounds like they have happy memories of visiting Maine. Nothing about their father and the abuse?"

"Oh, good God, no! And Lucy warned me not to address that topic. She says I should wait for them to bring it up. I hear the girls' therapy is in a delicate stage, especially because they're going into adolescence."

"I've read that survivor memories of abuse can be unreliable. That victims can be subject to suggestion by the therapist or an attorney trying to draw them out. They can imagine abuse that never happened and think it's a blocked memory."

Olivia smiled warmly. "You really took the time to look it up?"

Sam shrugged. "After you told me about Jason, I did a little research. Lucy suggested some articles. She looked at me funny when I asked, but I didn't let on why I was asking. Neither did she."

"No, Lucy is the very soul of discretion."

"You're such a Lucy fan."

"Isn't everybody? Besides, what's not to like?"

"Nothing, I guess," said Sam, shifting uncomfortably.

Olivia gave her a hard look. "You know something, Samantha. What is it?"

There was no way in hell, Sam was going to tell Olivia about the secret kiss between Liz and Lucy. "Nothing. Lucy is wonderful, but she's just a woman like all the rest of us."

"Ah. Something sexual."

"Nobody's business but hers."

"You know I'll get it out of you."

"No, you won't. I don't tell on my friends."

"We'll see." Olivia sat back and arched a brow.

Chapter 6

Maggie Fitzgerald switched off the microphone before quietly plucking the strings of her guitar. Luckily, it was still in tune. Except for compositions intended to be sung a capella, she always preferred live accompaniment to pre-recorded music. Without an organ available, she usually accompanied herself on the guitar. It brought back memories of singing what they called "folk Masses" in her youth. She was still a Catholic then, before she divorced, and the Church turned its back on her. The old pastor had been kind about it. He'd known her since childhood. While he didn't exactly condone leaving her husband, he knew why. Not only was Barry cheating on her, he'd been verbally abusive, and sometimes, he'd threatened her physically.

Maggie had been shocked the first time Barry raised his fists to her. He'd never been anything but chivalrous when they were dating in high school, always a perfect gentleman, opening doors, allowing her to go first in a restaurant, giving her his jacket to wear when it was chilly at an outdoor party. Confessing her college affair with Liz Stolz seemed to have flipped a switch in him. At first, he was so kind and understanding. They'd married quickly, barely three weeks after she'd graduated from the local college her parents had insisted she attend after Maggie told them she was involved with a woman.

The memories played in Maggie's mind, brought back by the simple sound of a plucked guitar string. It also brought back happy memories—the abject adoration of a young, gangly, and too-tall Liz Stolz in the audience during a folk Mass or in the campus coffee house. Could that really have been almost half a century ago? And here they were, reconnected after a separation of forty years, and married—something no one could even imagine when they first met.

Waiting for her cue to sing the offertory hymn, Maggie glanced at the celebrant standing behind the stone altar in the outdoor chapel by the sea.

The granite altar had been standing in that place since the late nineteenth century. On days when the sea was rough, one could hear the sound of the waves pounding on the rocks below. Ocean wind and rain had worn down the stone, so it had been replaced in the 1980s. Even the Maine granite couldn't withstand the power of the sea.

Maggie admired Lucy's perfect features. Lucy's mother had been a model, and her daughter had obviously inherited her perfect features. Liz had found a see-through mask to comply with the mask mandates. She'd searched the internet for it for hours. The governor still wanted masks worn in public, even outdoors. Lucy was probably safe, of course. Liz tested everyone in their circle every other day, Lucy every day before a public worship service.

The morning sun played in Lucy's red hair making it seem to glow with otherworldly light. From a theatrical point of view, it was perfect lighting for the scene. Lucy, a former opera star, knew all about scene-setting, but this was clearly an unintended effect.

Lucy looked so natural in full vestments, but she could carry any costume, whether portraying a nineteenth century courtesan or a Wagnerian heroine of a time lost in the mists. The green chasuble fluttered in the strong wind from the ocean below. The liturgical calendar was in the "ordinary time" between Pentecost and advent. The vestment color complimented Lucy's red hair and green eyes. In every aspect, Lucy cut the figure of the perfect priest. She had a brilliant, welcoming smile for everyone she met. "The most radical thing in the world is God's love for us. If I can just show people that love, even in a small way." Maggie hated herself for wondering if Lucy was sincere when she'd made that statement. Of course, she was. Despite all her training to sing on the operatic stage, Lucy was the realest person Maggie had ever met.

She missed her friend, the generous woman who'd brought her back to the Church. Granted, it was a different Church from the one in which she'd grown up. Even more than the spiritual influence, she missed being "girls" together. Maggie especially missed their spa days. While they had a pedicure, a massage, or a mud pack facial, they kept up nonstop conversation. Since they'd first discovered their common love of shopping, they'd spent hour upon hour together hunting through the many thrift shops in Hobbs for unique treasures. Maggie was so happy to have a companion for those "girlie" things that Liz loathed. She hated to shop. She'd impatiently wait outside, playing on her phone, while Maggie browsed.

The idyllic friendship Maggie used to share with Lucy was one of the biggest casualties of the kiss. Maggie knew her wife had instigated it. Liz considered herself quite the ladies' woman. She claimed it was a holdover from when she was training as a surgeon and encouraged to be just like the men—to wear man-tailored worsted suits and little silk bow ties in the same patterns as men's neckties, to swear, to crack dirty jokes over the operating table, even to make disparaging comments about other women. Yes, it was another time, but it was no excuse. Maggie had worn those suits too when she'd worked in public relations at Barry's engineering firm. The rest of the world had moved on, but Liz was stuck in the male-dominated world in which she'd come of age. She herself was a pioneer in the field, one of the few highly successful female surgeons of her generation, but the progress of her gender had passed her by.

Maggie could see from the moment they met that Liz adored Lucy. Liz was a rabid opera fan, who would pay ridiculous sums of money for tickets to performances featuring her favorite singers. When the new rector turned out to be a Met star, Liz instantly became her biggest fan. The religious part had turned her off. Liz was an atheist, but she'd happily turned a blind eye to that small flaw in the perfect package.

Lucy had put up with Liz's relentless flirting and gave as good as she got in a teasing, good-natured way. Fortunately, Erika, who'd been Liz's friend for decades, knew all her foibles and took it in stride. "You know how Liz is," she would say and roll her eyes. At first, Maggie wrote it off to Liz's penchant for little-boy mischief, acting out for naughtiness-sake. Why couldn't it have stayed that way? Why did Liz have to ruin it by making it serious? Why did Lucy have to respond? Maggie knew why. The attraction was real, and it was powerful. In their company, anyone could feel it like an irresistible magnetic force.

"The offertory hymn will be 'My Song is Love Unknown,'" said Lucy in a loud voice, staring at Maggie. Evidently, Maggie had missed the first cue. Maggie smarted with embarrassment. Her pale complexion would make it obvious. Even more so now that she had let her hair go completely white.

Maggie snapped to attention and began the hymn. As she listened to Lucy read the Eucharist rite, she wondered again why Lucy still read it from the *Book of Common Prayer*. After she'd had to memorize whole operas, she must have the Communion rite memorized too. Lucy had smiled and explained, "It's to let people know it's the words of the Church and not my words."

After the service, Maggie waited as Lucy greeted her parishioners with a little bow, sometimes an elbow bump, which since the pandemic had replaced a handshake. There was no fellowship after the service on guidance from the bishop. Maggie missed socializing with the other people in the church, especially with the choir and musicians under her charge. Across the path, Maggie saw that Erika was also waiting and headed in her direction.

"Can you let Lucy know that I'm heading home? Tell her she should come whenever she's ready."

"She has her own car, and she'll be a while, talking to people," Erika said. "I'll come with you. Let me just tell her I'm leaving."

Maggie picked up her guitar case and started toward the parking lot. As she drove home, she wondered if Liz had thought to put the casserole into the oven. She'd meant to leave her a note, but then she'd forgotten.

When Maggie got home and opened the refrigerator, she found the casserole on the shelf, ice cold. She took it out and set it on the counter.

"Liz!" she called, but there was no answer. Where was she? Her truck was in the driveway, and the Audi was in the garage. Maggie called upstairs and into the basement. Silence. Then she remembered Liz saying she wanted to work in her shop.

Erika came in. "How can I help?"

"I'm trying to find my wife."

"Yes, I heard you calling for her."

"I think she's down in her shop." Maggie glanced out the kitchen window to the building at the end of the gravel walk. There was no machine noise, but the building was soundproof to avoid disturbing the neighbors. "It's hard to tell if the light's on with the sunlight reflecting in the windows."

"I'll walk down and tell her we're here," Erika volunteered.

"I'll go," said Maggie, mainly because she wanted to see what Liz was doing. She turned on the oven to preheat. "If I'm not back by the time the signal goes off, would you put the casserole in? And the bread?"

"Certainly, Maggie. Meanwhile, I'll help myself to some coffee, if you don't mind."

"Please," said Maggie gesturing to the coffee pot. "You know where everything is here." She had no reservation about leaving Erika to fend for herself. During the lockdown, Erika and Lucy had been quarantining in the apartment over the garage. They'd all been living together, as Erika's father always put it, "cheek to jowl." For all this chaos the pandemic had caused, that time of living with a crowd in a tiny, tight-knit community in Liz's sprawling house was one of the happiest times of Maggie's life. Alina and her girls were living with them, Stefan, Erika's father, Emily, Lucy's daughter. Their common meals at the huge dining table that Liz had built were boisterous, but cheerful. Their epic talent nights were broadcast on the local station. Their life together was like living in a tiny, happy village.

When Maggie tried the doorknob of the shop, she was relieved to find it unlocked because she hadn't thought to bring the key. Liz often locked it when she worked alone to prevent someone from entering the building while she was distracted by the noise and running machinery. Maggie could hear the high-pitched grinding of some machine working as she came into the shop. Maggie flipped the light switches up and down, their signal to announce her arrival.

Liz shut off the machine and the dust collector. She pulled off her earmuffs. "Hey," she said. "What's up?"

"You forgot to put in the breakfast casserole."

"Oh, shit. I meant to do that." Liz glanced at the wall clock shaped like a circular saw blade. "I'm sorry. I was so involved here I forgot the time."

"Of course, you did."

"Maggie, I didn't do it deliberately. You have to pay attention when you do woodworking, or you cut off your fingers!"

"What are you doing?" Maggie asked, glancing at the strips of wood on a wheeled cart.

"Routing the panel grooves for Olivia's project."

"I thought Sam was making that armoire."

"She is, but big case pieces aren't her thing. Look at this. I figured out how to make it knock down using screw dowels hidden by faux pegs, so we can get it in and out of the house easily." Liz grinned and held up a piece of bronze plated hardware. She took it apart and put it back together to demonstrate its ingenuity.

"Very nice," said Maggie, although one screw looked like another to her.

"And here are the panels Sam carved for the door and the bracket feet. Aren't they amazing?"

"They are." Maggie tugged at Liz's arm. "Come on. Your girlfriend will be here in a few minutes."

"Girlfriend? What girlfriend?"

"You know. Lucy."

Liz's face darkened. "Maggie, you have to give up this resentment and needling. It was a stupid mistake. I'm sorry. I told you I'd never do it again. I haven't, and I won't. Now let it go."

"Come in soon," said Maggie in a cool voice. "I could use some help. That is, if you can tear yourself away from your project."

Chapter 7

Erika was searching for something very specific. In season, the florist department in the supermarket sold live rosemary plants pruned into Christmas-tree-shaped topiary. Usually, they were trimmed with red satin bows and decked with tiny, foil stars. But Halloween was the next holiday on the calendar, so the floral offerings all featured pumpkins, witches, and black cats.

There wasn't a store employee in sight. If Erika was to find the rosemary tree she sought, she'd have to locate it herself. Finally, on the bottom shelf in the back, she spotted a tiny rosemary tree. It had a small void in the back, but it was the only one. She put her fingers into the soil. Dry. She'd have to water it when she got home. Guarding her treasure, she picked up the red tote containing the ingredients for eggnog and headed to the checkout.

The gathering was an impromptu celebration, but Erika had just found out that she needed to go up to Waterville for a few days for faculty evaluations. The chairman of the department had come down with COVID after visiting her adult children over Labor Day. She was still in the hospital, and Erika, as assistant department head, had been filling in. She supposed the little party could have waited, but this weekend, they were heading to Acadia for their annual anniversary camping trip with Maggie and Liz.

Erika glanced at her phone. Almost four o'clock. She had to hurry. The vestry meeting would be over by five, and Olivia was in charge of getting the guest of honor to the party in time. As Erika drove down to the beach house, she wondered if she had an extra bottle of rum stashed somewhere. If not, she certainly had some German brandy, and that would do in a pinch.

Liz had parked precariously perched at the edge of the salt marsh. Erika supposed she was trying to leave room for the others to park. Her new truck was ridiculously big. At least, Liz didn't see it as a phallic symbol like so many rednecks in Maine, who flew confederate flags from the beds of their trucks. What ignorant fools! So many Maine volunteers had lost their lives during the Civil War, accounting for some of the highest losses in the Union army. American schools failed to teach history properly. What did they teach? From the quality of the students she'd been getting at Colby, she really had to wonder. Thank God, she'd be retiring soon!

Erika hurried in with her grocery bags, the flimsy, thin plastic kind. In Maine, reusable bags had been banned since the pandemic began. She managed to get everything in the door before the first bag ripped. Fortunately, the container of cream was undamaged in the fall. She took out the stuffed mushrooms she had prepared and the platter of raw vegetables, arranged in a rainbow fan by color. She arranged the cheeses on a tray and put out some olives and spiced nuts.

Despite all her planning, she felt stressed. Her utensils in their crock by the stove side were tangled, but she finally found her favorite whisk and got to work on the eggnog. The eggs tempered beautifully, and the custard was magnificent. She tasted it, but wasn't sure, so she poured some into a juice glass and brought it out to the garage.

"Liz!" she called up the beautiful, new stairs Sam had built. "Elizabeth! Are you up there?"

"Present!" Liz called back.

Erika ascended the stairs and found Liz sitting squaw-style in front of an electric outlet.

"Liz, I need you to taste something."

"I'm kind of busy at the moment."

"Please. I made eggnog to put us in the Christmas spirit."

Liz turned and gave her an irritated look. "You've got to be kidding." She sighed to indicate she was being very patient, but she accepted the glass. She tasted the eggnog and frowned. "Needs something."

"Liquor?"

"Yes, that too. But it's not sweet enough. Did you put in some sugar?"

"Just a pinch."

"Needs more. Try making a simple syrup, or it will never dissolve."

"Good idea. I knew you would know." Erika looked around. "Why are all the receptacles and switches still hanging out of the wall?"

"So Sam can check them before I install the plates. Technically, we might not be violating code by me doing the work, but I don't want your garage burning down."

"Neither do I."

"At least if Sam checks everything, I'll feel better. Now, remember, if anyone asks, you did the work. I had nothing to do with it."

"As per usual. I understand."

"Sam said she'd try to get here early after grouting that bathroom she's working on." Liz glanced at her watch. "Doesn't look like she'll make it on time. Do you think Lucy will mind the wires hanging out of the wall?"

"I rather doubt it. Lucy completely appreciates everything anyone does for her. She will be ecstatic when she sees this practice room, despite dangling switches and outlets." Erika watched Liz's face. "I'll tell her how hard you worked on it."

"That's not necessary. I just want her to be safe. You're not the only one who worries about her walking alone on the beach in the dark." Erika knew that Liz worried about everyone, her patients, her friends, the townspeople, but she especially worried about Lucy.

"I invited Maggie," said Erika, "but she said she was busy with a rehearsal."

Liz compressed her lips. "What did you expect?" she picked up her pliers and went back to work.

Erika downed the rest of the eggnog. "Yes, it does need sugar." She watched as Liz deftly created a loop in the copper wire. "Liz, I remember when you said you were going to marry Maggie. I thought, well, that's not the best thing. It was clear that you were only marrying her to reassure her. Now, I know we had a philosophical conversation about it, and you parsed your reasons at the time. But really, Liz, did you marry for the right reason?"

"Does it really matter now?"

"Yes, I think it does. Are you happy?"

"No."

Erika sat up straight. She hadn't expected that. "Well, that's a definitive statement. Oh, Liz, I wish you had listened to me." She put aside the glass and got up to give Liz's shoulder a squeeze. "What are you going to do?"

"I don't know. Everything I say is wrong. We fight constantly. She complains that I don't talk to her. She complains she never sees me."

"Well, that's probably true. You're always off at your hunting club or your chamber of commerce meetings, or the Rotary, or some other damn thing that you're involved in."

"Maggie knew I had a busy life when she hooked up with me." Liz pinched her finger with the pliers and swore under her breath.

"Oh, dear," said Erika with a big sigh. "You must come over and drink with me soon. One night after Lucy's gone to bed. But now, I need to get this party off the ground. Let me go make the simple syrup. I shall return soon."

"Add more vanilla. It can't hurt."

"Good idea."

Erika returned to the kitchen and found some superfine sugar to make the simple syrup. She heard feet scraping on the floor mat in the living room.

"Hello?" Sam's voice. "Am I too early?"

"I think your friend wants you to inspect her electrical work."

"I'm going right over. I parked at the municipal lot down the street, so my truck won't give away the surprise."

"That was unnecessary. Lucy knows you're working on my 'storage' project."

Sam laughed. "Yeah, right. Let me see what Dr. Stolz is up to. I'll be back soon to help if you need any."

Erika decided the taste of the doctored eggnog was much improved. It was handy to have a friend who took equal pleasure in cooking, and Liz had a discerning palate. She could figure out the ingredients in a dish simply by tasting it. The only other person besides her mother, who had that knack, was Maggie Fitzgerald, but she was professionally trained. She'd taken the La Varenne course when she was a bored housewife in the eighties.

A glance at the clock told Erika she had just enough time to string the tiny lights she usually used on the outdoor Christmas wreath around the rosemary topiary. She'd found them not long ago flung in a drawer, probably put away in haste after the other outdoor decorations had been taken down. The blue of the multi-colored LED lights was so intense it made her vision vibrate, but she decided the way the colors reflected in the gold foil stars was absolutely perfect. Now, if they only had some pine smell to get them in the Christmas spirit. She remembered the balsam sachets they'd brought home from Acadia last year. They were probably still in their plastic bag and smelled wonderful.

She was racing against time now. Her eyes fell on the kitchen clock. Ten minutes before liftoff. She wondered how fast Liz and Sam could get the wiring stuffed into the boxes. They worked well together, as if they'd worked on the same crew for an eternity.

Erika's phone lit up with a text message from Lucy: *Running a few minutes late. Sorry. I know it's my turn for dinner.*

Erika smiled. *Little do you know, Lovely Lucy, that we're dining at the Thai restaurant after our little party.* She blew a kiss to the screen before turning on the broiler. The stuffed mushrooms didn't have to be hot, just warm.

When she headed back to the new practice room, Erika grabbed another bag full of CDs to put on the shelves Sam had built into the eaves. She balanced the little rosemary Christmas tree in the other hand.

She wasn't surprised to find all the switches and plugs where they belonged, but Liz and Sam were racing to install the cover plates.

"Back again?" Liz asked in a testy voice.

"Yes, last-minute inspection. They'll be a few minutes late."

"Thank God," said Sam, breathing a sigh of relief.

"Should I turn on the heat pump?" asked Liz. "It's a little nippy tonight. It will be a good test to see if it works, or I can turn on the electric fireplace."

"Yes, the fireplace will provide nice ambiance. I'll put my little tree on the mantle."

She heard the sound of shuffling coming up from downstairs. "Hey! Are you guys up there?" Erika identified the familiar voice as Brenda's.

"Get up here before they see you!" Sam called back in a veiled shout.

Brenda came up the stairs, bringing two bottles of Champagne. "A toast for the new place."

"Oh, my! I hope my Champagne flutes are clean," said Erika anxiously.

"I'll go down and rinse them," Cherie volunteered.

"In the china cabinet in the dining room," Erika called after her.

"I parked in the municipal lot and we walked." Brenda put the Champagne bottles on the table.

"My friends are so clever," Erika said. "Fortunately, the guest of honor and her escort are slightly delayed."

Sam mimed wiping sweat from her forehead. "God always provides where Lucy is concerned."

Lights flashed on the side of the garage facing the street.

"That will be Lucy and Olivia," Erika said. "Let's all find a seat and turn down the lights." She switched on the colored Christmas lights on the rosemary tree.

"Where is everyone?" Lucy's voice called into the garage.

"Liz and I are upstairs looking over the new storage," Erika called down. "Would you like to see?"

"Sure!" As Lucy came up the stairs, she gave Erika one of her brilliant smiles. "Does it really have room for all my junk?"

Erika laughed. "Come up and see."

"May I come up too?" Olivia asked.

"Please do."

Erika moved aside so she could see Lucy's face as she took in the room. Their friends sat on the modern-style chairs and sofa.

"Surprise!" they called in unison. A moment later, Cherie came up the stairs with a tray of Champagne flutes.

"What's this doing up here?" Lucy asked. She went to the corner where her electronic keyboard stood.

"This is a place for you to practice singing," Erika explained. "It's soundproof."

"I meant to test the sound system," said Liz. "That was the trickiest thing to wire. Lucy, can you connect to the Bluetooth speaker to see how it sounds?"

Lucy took out her phone and streamed the accompaniment for *"Un bel di."*

"Wow!" exclaimed Lucy. "What great sound! Who picked those speakers?"

"Liz, of course," said Erika.

Lucy shot one of her solar-flare smiles in Liz's direction. She went around the room taking in the details—the large, triangular windows in the gables, the ship-lapped walls and ceiling, her annotated scores and CDs on the specially designed shelves built into the eaves. "You found room for all my junk, and it's beautiful," she murmured. When she turned, there were tears in her eyes. "Absolutely beautiful."

"Sam designed it," Erika explained. "She and Liz built it."

Lucy reached up to kiss Sam. "Thank you. It's wonderful." Sam blushed.

Lucy took Liz's cheeks in her hands. "And you! What a gift you are!" She stood on her toes to kiss her, but Liz turned her face so the kiss landed on her cheek. Lucy wasn't satisfied with that. She touched her fingertips to her lips and placed them on Liz's. The tears continued to flow. Lucy tried to brush them away with the back of her hands. "I can't believe this. It's all so wonderful. So thoughtful. So perfect!"

Olivia put her arm around Lucy's shoulders. "You are much loved, Mother Lucy."

"I guess so."

"I wonder if I can have some volunteers to bring up the refreshments," said Erika in a hopeful voice.

Cherie jumped to her feet. "I'll help."

"Me too," volunteered Olivia.

"Thank you. Everything is on the island in the kitchen."

Erika watched Lucy go to the electric fireplace to admire the tiny Christmas tree. "Yes, it's Christmas in October," Erika explained. "Don't expect more presents under the tree."

"Oh, my word! This wonderful gift is enough for all the Christmases and birthdays yet to come." Lucy caught Erika around the waist and hugged her tight. "Thank you!"

Chapter 8

Give her another few minutes, thought Lucy, watching the time tick away on the top of her computer screen. Then her phone rang. *This will be her saying she's not coming.* Lucy stifled her disappointment as she tapped open the call. Here she was skirting the bounds of professional propriety by offering to talk to a close friend about her grief, and Liz couldn't even bother to be on time.

"Oh, my God, Lucy," said Liz in a harried voice. "I'm so sorry. I had a patient who wouldn't stop talking. With the restrictions, people who live alone are so lonely. I set an alarm, but I put my phone on mute for a meeting, and..."

Lucy could imagine Liz looking all flustered, her face slightly red, her blue eyes wide. Liz was usually the calm sort, not by nature, but because it had been trained into her. After more than four decades in medicine, few things could ruffle Dr. Stolz's feathers. Not keeping her agreements was one of them.

"It's okay, Liz. Come over now. I'm upstairs in that beautiful practice room you and Sam built. I thought we'd have privacy here."

"Sure you're not busy? I have things to do just like you do. I know you set aside this time for me, but…"

"Liz, this is important," said Lucy firmly.

"So are dental appointments."

"Well, no one's ever compared talking to me to going to the dentist. You don't have to come, Liz. You can just go on being miserable, but I wish you wouldn't."

"I'll be right there," Liz replied without enthusiasm. Usually, when she said she was coming to see Lucy, her tone was full of smiles and eager anticipation.

Not long after, Lucy heard footsteps on the stairs. Liz had probably raced down beach road as usual. She was even worse about speeding during the off-season, when the roads were mostly deserted.

She arrived wearing a polar fleece because it was a bit chilly, but she still hadn't given up her "summer uniform." She'd switched from hiking shorts to cropped pants of the same high-performance material and exchanged her rafting sandals for casual mules. She looked more like she was ready for a walk in the estuarine preserve than for office hours as the senior doctor of Hobbs Family Practice. Lucy knew that once they came back from their camping trip, Liz would finally acknowledge that fall had arrived and switch to chinos, a button-down shirt, and real shoes in the office.

"How do you like your new practice space?" asked Liz, giving the ceiling a careful inspection. "I see I could have been a little tighter with the boards there." She pointed to a slightly larger gap than the others.

"Oh, Liz, don't be so critical. I love it! And look, Erika moved in an old folding desk, so I can work here if I want to. I just love this view of the ocean."

Liz leaned over and kissed Lucy on the cheek. "Sorry, I was late. Thanks for giving me your time."

Lucy grasped Liz's shoulder before she could get away and looked into the earnest, blue eyes. "Of course, I would give you my time, Liz."

"No using your shrink tricks on me," said Liz, wagging a finger as she moved to the sofa opposite Lucy. "Promise?"

Lucy laughed. "Sorry. It's second nature by now. What if I said, 'no using your doctor tricks on me?'"

Liz dropped into the sofa and regarded Lucy with a raised brow. "On that subject, I still think you should switch to Cathy Pelletier as your doc." Liz crossed her arms and put one ankle on the opposite knee. Eventually, she perceived that Lucy was reading her body language and didn't approve, so she uncrossed her arms and put her feet flat on the floor.

"And I still think you should see another professional, someone who doesn't love you the way I do, but this is what we've got, so let's see how it goes."

"It's hard living in a place where everybody knows everyone," said Liz.

"Not only is Hobbs Family Practice the only game in town, but I know many of my patients through the Rotary, the Chamber of Commerce, my gun club. The police chief is my fishing buddy, and Olivia gives me financial advice. We all have to do our best to remain professional."

"It reminds me of how life used to be when we were young, and everyone had a social relationship to the town doctor and the parish priest."

"It's not necessarily a bad thing," Liz agreed. "It just makes it harder for us to maintain our objectivity."

"Sometimes, I think objectivity is overrated. I have to spend so much time drawing out people to define the context for their psychological issues. When I know my clients, at least I have the basic facts."

"Exactly. Epidemiological context is meaningful."

Lucy gave the woman sitting across from her a stern look. "Do you see what you did, Liz? You drew me into a conversation about ethics and social boundaries. Good thing I know you. You're like Erika. You'll use any excuse to engage in a philosophical debate rather than talk about your feelings. How are you?"

Liz pursed her lips and nodded. "I'm okay."

"I can see from your face that you're not. What's going on?"

"Well, let's see. An entire generation of my family died this year. One of my dear friends, someone I've known for decades, died of cancer last week. I knew that one was coming, but I couldn't go see her because of the travel restrictions. There are so many losses the numbers don't reflect. So much damage to the social fabric. When this is over, the long-term effects on physical and mental health will be staggering."

"I'm afraid of that too." Lucy realized Liz had succeeded in diverting her into another theoretical discussion to avoid talking about herself. "Let's stick with you, Liz. How do you feel about your mother's death?"

"Relieved."

"I can understand. She had a lot of health issues."

"The pneumonia she had the year before nearly killed her, but my brother yanked her out of the hospital and nursed her back to health. Now, he says maybe he should have let her go then. It was like that Stephen King book, *Pet Sematary*. She came back from the dead, but she was never the same. The dementia had really kicked in. That's not uncommon. Hospitalizations often accelerate mental decline in the very elderly."

"But you told me she was doing better."

"She was. She was even able to go see her great grandkids for Thanksgiving that year. The long drive was hard on her, but she made it. She was doing pretty well until she fell again."

"But you were there for her, Liz. From what you told me you were always there for her."

"I was. By anyone's standards, I was a good daughter."

"Tell me about your response to your mother's death? Have you cried?"

Liz shrugged. "I shed a few tears. I expected to have a bigger reaction. So far, nothing."

"What did you expect to happen?"

"I don't know. I used to dread my mother's death. I put so much effort into protecting her and keeping her alive. We used to talk every day before she became too deaf to hear me."

"That must have been hard."

"The forced silence turned out to be a gift. It broke the habit of hearing her voice every day."

Lucy heard the slight catch when Liz spoke. She cleared her throat and started again.

"We had a period of silence after my brother died, and she told me she'd disinherited us. We didn't speak for a few months. But I just couldn't spend the rest of her life without speaking to her."

"I admire you for being able to do that. Someone else might have told her to go to hell."

Liz looked slightly surprised to hear Lucy use those words. "It was partially selfish. I didn't want to feel guilty when she died."

"Do you feel guilty?"

"No, but I wish I could have been there for her at the end. I could have gone if I really wanted to go. By then, the travel restrictions had been lifted."

"Liz, I know how you like to be a hero, rushing in like the cavalry to save the day, but you can't save everyone. After all these years as a doctor, you should know that by now."

"I do. Up here." Liz tapped her forehead with her finger.

Lucy let out a long stream of breath. "We all have regrets about how we handle things with other people. None of us is perfect. You and I are professionals, and even we make mistakes."

"You can say that again."

"And because we're trained, we often hold ourselves to a higher standard, but we also need to forgive ourselves for our imperfections, just as we would forgive other people. You, especially. You seem to think you have to be superhuman all the time."

"That's pretty much what surgeons are trained to be…to make difficult decisions under the worst circumstances, to turn on a dime, if necessary… to stand for hours at an operating table, even when your feet get numb and your back aches and your eyes begin to glaze over."

"I'm sure your training taught you grit, but what you do in your professional life doesn't necessarily apply to your personal life."

"Kind of late for that. It's like military training. Once it gets into your blood, it's hard to get it out again."

"Liz, you're always taking care of everyone else. Maybe it's time to take care of yourself for a change. Give yourself a break. Love yourself as much as you love other people, and let people love you and take care of you."

"I'm not sure I know how to do that." Liz compressed her lips and turned away.

Lucy realized Liz was trying to hide her tears. If this were a real therapy session, Lucy would wait respectfully for her client to recover control, but Liz was her friend, someone she loved. All she wanted to do was put her arms around her to encourage the tears to flow. The only reason she didn't was the fear that she would be pushed away.

Chapter 9

Maggie watched Erika and Liz laughing together at the water's edge. After decades, they still found one another's lame jokes funny, even when no one else did, partly because their humor was so esoteric, no one else understood it. They'd been friends since Liz was a surgical resident at Yale New Haven and Erika was a graduate student. They spoke German together and debated philosophy into the wee hours of the morning. They teased and poked at one another mercilessly, yet they never got on the other's wrong side. A friendship like that was to be treasured.

Lucy, sitting on the other side of the picnic table, gazed at them with a little smile, enjoying their high-toned silliness almost as much as if she were a participant. Maggie wondered why she was the only one not having a good time.

Camping over Columbus Day weekend was something they did every year, a ritual like birthdays and holidays, first on their honeymoon, now to celebrate their anniversary. It was Lucy and Erika's anniversary too. They had planned their wedding around the annual weekend in Acadia, where they'd spent their honeymoon.

"I'm glad we were able to come this year," said Lucy, as if she'd been hearing Maggie's thoughts. "It didn't look like we could at first, so I'm glad it worked out."

Liz had done all the research to make sure it was safe. On arrival, she'd insisted on sanitizing all the surfaces with disinfectant cloths, despite the assurances of the campground personnel that it had already been done. They'd brought their own towels and bedding, remade the beds and returned the campground linens to the office.

"We'll be stuck eating campfire meals all weekend," said Maggie. "Except for the diner in Hobbs, Liz still won't eat in restaurants except outside in tents or takeout."

"I don't mind. Eating campfire food is part of the fun," said Lucy. "I'm a city girl. We never camped when I was young."

"What about her 'living off the land' thing? You'll eat the fish Liz caught? Skin and all?"

"I ate plenty of strange things when I traveled as an opera singer. Game and wild caught fish were fairly common, so I'm not squeamish about them."

"I was, at first," Maggie admitted, "but I've learned to like it."

Erika waved in their direction, and Lucy waved back. "I'm so glad to see Erika relaxing. She's been so anxious about this election. Here, she can get away from it all. Liz too. She's been working way too hard since the pandemic started. At least here, she gets to read."

"Do you know what she's reading?" asked Maggie, staring at Lucy.

"Fun stuff, I hope."

Maggie shook her head. "She's reading the medical bulletins and reports. She reads for work at least an hour every day. Keeping up on medicine is like being a college student for the rest of your life, especially now, with all the new COVID information coming out minute by minute. She's always reading. It's not easy being married to a doctor."

Lucy gazed in Liz's direction. "Even I gave myself a break from studying, and I *am* a student."

"You're a PhD candidate, that's a little different."

Maggie felt herself being evaluated by Lucy's practiced eyes. "Are things better between you two?" Lucy finally asked after a long, thoughtful silence.

Maggie shrugged. "As good as they can be, I suppose."

"What does that mean?"

"I still don't trust her."

Lucy's eyes clouded with pain. "Maggie, you have my word. It was one time, and it's never happened again. Never."

"Oh, I trust you, Lucy. I just don't trust Liz. When we first got together, she was still involved with her ex. She slept with her while I was in the house. She said they didn't have sex, but how do I know?"

"You've been suspicious of her all this time?"

"Pretty much."

"But why marry someone you don't trust?" asked Lucy, looking puzzled.

"We'd just gotten back together. It was all very romantic. United after forty years. A second chance to make it right. How could I resist?"

Lucy's penetrating gaze was unnerving. "It does sound very romantic."

"It was, but we rushed into the marriage. We thought after forty years, hell, what were we waiting for? Now, I know we got married because I was afraid. The cancer terrified me. My mother died of it. And there was Liz, like a rock through the surgery and the treatments."

"She's very devoted to you."

"She is. And for most things, I couldn't ask for a better partner. She's attentive and responsible. She takes care of the house, manages my finances. She's great with my daughters and the grandkids. She always supported my career."

Lucy reached out for her hand. "So what's wrong?"

"It's hard to trust someone who cheats on you."

"But she didn't cheat, Maggie. It was just a kiss, an impulsive kiss."

"You think a kiss isn't cheating?"

"Technically not. I acknowledge my role in it, and I'm truly sorry, but don't make it into more than it was. It was a moment in time, over, and done."

"Easy for you to say."

Lucy looked uneasy. "Maybe we should drop this conversation. I don't want an argument to ruin our weekend." She glanced toward the shore where Liz and Erika had been sitting. "And they're coming back."

Erika looked at the two women sitting at the picnic table, studying their faces. "Well, don't you two look the picture of good cheer? What's the matter?"

"Nothing," said Lucy. "Maggie regrets that we can't go out to a restaurant instead of eating camp food every night."

"And miss Liz's lovely fish dinner?" said Erika. "She would be crushed if we spurned her prize trout."

"What's this I hear that you don't want to eat my fish?" Liz said, looking from Maggie to Lucy and back again. "Believe me this will be the tastiest lake trout you'll ever eat. I'm grilling corn on the coals. I made a bean salad. All yummy stuff."

"That's enough, Liz," said Erika. "You're making me hungry."

"Then I guess I should clean the fish and get dinner going," said Liz, heading toward their cabin.

"I'll get some salsa and chips to hold us until dinner," Erika volunteered.

Liz came out of the cabin, holding a huge lake trout by the gills. She headed to the water's edge. Meanwhile, Erika appeared with homemade black-bean-and-papaya salsa and a bag of local corn chips. "I see we have a front-row seat to watch the savage butcher her kill."

Lucy laughed. Even Maggie had to smile. Erika's hyperboles were legendary.

"It's a splendid evening for your sing along tonight. Warm even for High October," said Erika, scooping some dip onto a chip. It crunched loudly as she bit into it. She chewed thoughtfully. "Needs a bit more lime juice. Unfortunately, I didn't think to bring any, so we'll have to rough it."

Lucy sampled it. "Tastes fine to me."

Erika glanced at Maggie as if pleading for sympathy, two cooks commiserating. "I'm sure it's fine, Erika." She reached for a chip to try it. Like everything Erika prepared, it was excellent. "It's delicious. Doesn't need a thing," Maggie pronounced.

Liz returned with the fish fillets wrapped in newspaper. "I'm going to season these and wash up. I'll be back!"

"Take a shower while you're at it," said Maggie under her breath after Liz headed toward the cabin.

Erika and Lucy both stared at her, but Maggie merely shrugged.

The fish was, as Liz had predicted, delicious. The entire meal, including the corn, seasoned perfectly and dripping with butter, was outstanding. Liz had taken a shower before dinner to get rid of the fish-guts smell, so she was pleasant to sit beside as she told the story of how she'd almost lost the catch.

The sun set over the mainland. Erika got up to snap a photo with her phone. The campers in the neighboring cabin approached with sling chairs. The eyes of everyone at the table turned to Lucy, who shrugged. "It was part of my job, when I was a curate, to get out the word about events. I put up posters around the campground about the sing along and the worship service tomorrow."

Another couple approached with folding chairs. Erika and Lucy started to clear the table.

"I'll get the wine," said Liz. She returned with two boxes of wine, one red and one white and a bag containing a stack of plastic wine glasses.

"I hate boxed wine," said Maggie, getting up to collect the remaining dishes.

"It's good enough for something like this. Besides, after a few glasses no one cares." Liz frowned. "Why are you in such a bad mood? We're supposed to be having fun."

"You go off fishing and leave me with Lucy and Erika."

"I always go fishing when we come up here. What's changed?"

Maggie shrugged and smiled in the direction of the new arrivals. "I'll get my guitar." She headed towards the cabin. "You should get yours too."

When Maggie returned, she saw that Liz had moved the picnic table aside to create a stage on the stone patio. She was building up the campfire.

"Get your guitar," Maggie said.

"I will. I will. It's you they're coming to hear. I'm singing backup."

Maggie sat down on one of the benches Liz had set in the center of the patio. She plucked the strings of her guitar to tune it. "This is my favorite part of camping…our sing-along night."

"I know," said Liz. "Any chance for a performance."

Maggie heard the faint disapproval in Liz's voice, but she ignored it. She smiled at the couple, who'd settled in sling chairs at the edge of the patio.

"We come back every year. We so look forward to your little concert," said the woman. "We've especially looked forward to it this year because we've been shut inside so much. Just seeing other people is so wonderful!"

The little concert was everything Maggie had hoped for. She and Liz sang folk favorites from the 1960s to encourage the audience to sing along. Lucy occasionally joined in but mostly sat in the audience with Erika's arm around her.

The first two boxes of wine went quickly, and Liz got up to replace them. Maggie could see her policing the crowd to make sure everyone was wearing a mask and observing social distancing. Instead of common snacks they usually had, they'd brought along individual bags of cheddar corn, chips, and peanuts.

Liz took a break while Maggie and Lucy sang Broadway songs, including some of the duets they'd perfected for the Webhanet Playhouse benefit nights. The moon rose and Liz asked Lucy to sing Dvorak's "Song of the Moon."

As Lucy sang, Maggie watched Liz. The adoring look on her face never used to bother her because she knew how much Liz loved opera, but now it infuriated her. When Liz asked Lucy to sing "Marietta's Lied," Maggie got up to excuse herself. She listened from inside the cabin and then used the bathroom when the aria finished to justify her absence. She hated herself for envying Lucy's magnificent voice and the effect it had on Liz, but she couldn't help herself.

She returned to the gathering to sing some good-night songs for the finale. The crowd melted away with words of gratitude and wishes for a good night.

"I'll build up the fire and clear away the mess," Liz volunteered. Erika gave her a pat on the shoulder. Lucy stood on her toes to kiss her on the cheek while Maggie watched with a frown. Liz busied herself with collecting the wine glasses and snack bags while Maggie went in to get ready for bed. She was reading when Liz finally came in.

"That took you a long time."

"I was sitting by the fire listening to the tide come in. That's my favorite sound."

"I thought your favorite sound was Lucy's voice."

Liz shot her an irritated look as she headed to the bathroom to brush her teeth. A few minutes later, she slipped into bed. Maggie put aside her book and turned off the lamp.

There was the sound of heavy footsteps overhead. "Sounds like the raccoon is back," said Liz, rising on her elbow to listen. "Probably smells the fishy newspapers in the trash." She pounded on the wall and there was the sound of scampering on the roof. Liz rolled over with her back to Maggie. "Good night."

But Maggie wasn't sleepy. A performance always energized her and afterwards, she found it hard to sleep. She listened in the dark and heard a soft moan. She wondered if Lucy and Erika knew that the cabins weren't really soundproof. She wondered if they really cared.

Evidently, Liz had heard it too because she rolled over and spooned Maggie. She kissed the back of her neck. The press of her lips was warm and exciting. "It's our anniversary, you know," Liz reminded her as if she didn't know. Her hand reached over to cup Maggie's breast. Through the nightgown, Liz teased the nipple with her fingertips, then pinched it gently. Maggie felt mildly aroused. Then, Liz slipped her hand under her nightgown and caressed her gently. For two people who hadn't had sex in months, it was too much too soon. Maggie moved her hips away from Liz's touch.

"Please, Maggie," Liz begged softly. Listening to her plead was painful, as painful as on all the other nights when she'd begged to make love. Paradoxically, it only pushed Maggie further away.

"I'm really not in the mood."

"You're never in the mood," growled Liz and rolled over. When she punched her pillow to fluff it, Maggie could feel her anger and disappointment in the blows.

Maggie listened in the dark. She could hear a little giggle from next door and Liz sigh. She wished she could give Liz what she needed, but she just couldn't.

PART II

THANKSGIVING

Chapter 10

Lucy wasn't looking forward to this prenuptial session, especially not after Cherie had appeared in her office in tears two days before. She'd finally come out to her aunt in Louisiana, and her reaction had been hurtful. Aunt Simone was the last member of her mother's generation still alive, and Cherie had very much wanted her to attend her wedding. Lucy had spent over an hour trying to calm Cherie, but she wasn't sure when Cherie had left her office that she was in a good place.

So many people of their parents' generation had done so much damage to the people they professed to love. Lucy wondered what her own mother, now dead for years from ovarian cancer, would say if she knew that her daughter was now married to a woman. When Liz came out, her mother had disowned her. Maggie's mother had broken up their relationship. Maggie was yanked away from Liz and forbidden to even write to her. When they'd reconnected, they hadn't spoken for forty years. Maybe they would have broken up anyway, as so many youthful romances did, but they never even had a chance at a future together.

Lucy bowed her head and said a silent prayer for all the LBGTQ people who'd been rejected by their families. She thought of the non-binary priest in the neighboring parish, who'd made a special ministry of outreach to people whose sexual identity didn't conform and wondered if there was some way to support her…them…she now remembered to call her. Who knew that pronouns could be so difficult?

Jodi knocked on the open door. "Chief Harrison and Cherie Bois are here for you, Mother Lucy."

Lucy gave the admin a firm look. "Jodi, I thought I asked—"

"I know, but it's hard to break the habit. Besides, that's how I was trained, to be formal when announcing people…to show respect."

"Okay, it's fine. You can call me whatever you want."

Jodi laughed. "You might come to regret that statement."

"Never mind." Lucy gave Jodi another stern look, then smiled to let her know they were on good terms. "Let them in."

Jodi waved into the waiting area outside Lucy's door, and the couple came in. Jodi closed the office door behind them.

Brenda and Cherie pulled the visitor's chairs closer together before they sat down. That was a good sign, Lucy decided, but she looked them over carefully to assess where things stood from their expressions and body language. Brenda was wearing her police uniform today, so she must be coming from duty. Lucy remembered how difficult it had been to convince Cherie to look past the uniform to the woman beneath. She smiled to herself at the memory of Cherie's face when she'd suggested taking off Brenda's uniform as part of their foreplay. She'd been pleased when Cherie admitted that she'd tried it and it had worked.

"How was your week, ladies?" Lucy asked cheerfully as they took their seats. "Things better with you, Cherie?"

Cherie nodded. "I spoke to my aunt again. She says she doesn't approve, but she loves me, so she's going to try to be more understanding."

"It's not easy to come out to people of our parents' generation," said Lucy in a sympathetic tone. "They were brought up to think same-sex love is a sin, especially religious people. Marriage between two women or two men was unthinkable when they were growing up."

"It was unthinkable when *we* were growing up," said Brenda.

"Did you come out to your parents, Lucy?" Cherie asked.

Lucy shook her head. "No. Unfortunately, both my parents had passed by the time I had my first relationship with a woman."

"I'm sorry," said Brenda, looking appropriately sad.

"Someone before Erika?" Cherie asked, looking inappropriately curious.

"Yes," said Lucy, continuing to smile, although she was surprised Cherie, a therapist herself, would ask such a personal question. "But we're here to talk about the two of you," Lucy reminded her in a gentle tone, "and your readiness for marriage."

Cherie's little smile undermined her exaggerated look of contrition. "Sorry, Lucy, none of my business."

"I'll tell you sometime, but not in a counseling session."

"Now you've got me curious too," said Brenda, wiggling her brows. "Do tell. I'm all ears."

"Never mind, let's try to stay on task, all right?" She nodded toward Cherie. "It was very brave of you to tell your aunt. Now, is this the last hurdle? Are you ready to move forward?"

"We're still arguing about what I should wear at the wedding. Cherie wants me to wear a white dress," said Brenda, "but I can't even imagine it."

"Well, what do you want to wear?" asked Cherie, frowning.

"My uniform," Brenda blurted out.

"What!" exclaimed Cherie, obviously taken off guard. "You've got to be kidding!" Even Lucy, with all her training, couldn't keep her mouth from gaping at that statement. This was the first she'd heard of this plan. Cherie stared at Brenda in horror. "No! Absolutely not! I'm not marrying the police chief. I'm marrying Brenda Harrison, the woman, not the cop. That's what you keep telling me, and now you want to wear your work clothes on our wedding day? Your fucking uniform? No way!"

Lucy couldn't keep her eyebrows from shooting up. She'd never heard Cherie using the F-bomb before. "Okay. Okay. Let's talk about this," said Lucy patting the air to urge calm. She gave each of them a firm look. "Brenda, why is it so important for you to wear your uniform?"

"Well, in military weddings, which a police wedding technically is, it's considered correct to wear the dress uniform. My attendants, like my captains and the fire chief want to wear their dress uniforms."

"Are they all going to be in uniform?" Lucy asked.

"Well, not Liz. But she volunteered to wear a tuxedo so she wouldn't stick out too much."

Lucy glanced at Cherie, who was still fuming. Fortunately, she hadn't interrupted Brenda while she was talking. Instead, she'd crossed her arms and looked the other way.

"Who else is in your wedding party?" Lucy asked.

"Olivia Enright will be my best woman," Brenda said proudly. "I figured I owed it to her after she brought me back from the dead. I wouldn't be wearing this uniform if it wasn't for Olivia."

It made perfect sense that she had chosen Olivia as her witness. As town manager, Olivia had refused to accept Brenda's resignation when her heart issues were discovered. Olivia's contacts in the media had provided Brenda with the opportunity for an encore career as a spokesperson for compassionate policing.

"But knowing Olivia, I'm sure she won't be wearing a uniform or a tux," said Lucy.

Brenda laughed. "No, I'm sure she won't. She'll probably wear a fancy dress and look drop-dead gorgeous."

"So could you," said Lucy.

"No dresses or skirt," Brenda insisted. "I haven't worn one in years, and I'm not starting now."

Lucy shrugged. "Pants, then."

"I'd rather wear my uniform." Brenda folded her arms on her chest. Cherie glowered at her.

Lucy thought for a moment. This wasn't going well. She'd have to get creative. "Let's say you wore your uniform. For Cherie, that's a hated symbol of police brutality. But in the earlier times, leaders often married their enemies to form alliances. Imagine what a powerful message it would send to see a black woman and a police chief marry."

"Clever, Lucy," Cherie countered, "but that sounds like Stockholm syndrome. Identifying with the oppressor."

Lucy had to concede Cherie had a point.

"You don't have to wear a traditional bridal gown, Brenda. You could browse some wedding sites to get ideas. Maybe a tuxedo or a suit. You know how great Liz looks when she dresses up in one of her power suits. I bet she could help you pick out something appropriate that's not your uniform. Why don't you ask her?"

"Well, maybe…" Brenda said, scowling.

That sounded hopeful. Lucy breathed a sigh of relief.

"You need to decide soon, but you don't have to decide today. You can talk more about it."

"You can be sure we'll talk more about it!" said Cherie giving Brenda a stern look.

Fortunately, the topic changed to dealing with Cherie's Louisiana relatives, but the meeting ran long. Lucy found herself watching the clock on her desk. She wanted to be home when Liz got there for their four o'clock meeting to talk about grieving. As soon as Brenda and Lucy walked out the door, Lucy jumped up to pack her bag and stow her computer. She was putting on her coat, when Jodi came in.

"Lucy, Ms. Enright is here to see you."

"Please, Jodi," Lucy pleaded. "Please make excuses for me. I really have to get home. Tell her I'll call her tonight."

"She says it's really important."

With a sigh, Lucy nodded and took off her coat. A moment later, Olivia breezed into the room, all smiles. "Oh, thank you, Lucy, dear, for seeing me on such short notice."

Lucy crossed her arms, despite knowing it was a closed gesture. "What's so important, Olivia, that it can't wait until later?" she asked impatiently.

"I'm so excited, Lucy, my daughter-in-law will let the girls come for Thanksgiving."

"That's wonderful!"

"Except she wants you there."

"What?" Lucy's mind scrambled to figure out how that could possibly work. Erika had already accepted an invitation to Liz's house for Thanksgiving. Never mind that the CDC was issuing stern warnings not to gather outside of closed social networks for the holidays.

"You've made quite an impression on my daughter-in-law…and the girls. They're so excited to meet you."

"I don't know, Olivia. The COVID cases are rising again."

"Amanda says she'll have her daughters tested every day. She'll send the girls up in a limo that's been completely sanitized."

Lucy had worked too hard on arranging the reconciliation to blow this reunion. "I'll think about it, but first, I want to ask Liz Stolz if it's safe."

"Of course. I expected that. And I'm sure she'll give you helpful advice. I'm happy to tell her all the details of the plan to ease your mind."

"I'm sorry, Olivia, but I have another appointment." Lucy rose and swung the strap of her computer bag over her shoulder. "I'll think about it and let you know."

"Thanks, Lucy. You're a blessing," said Olivia, blowing her a kiss.

Lucy waited a moment to leave, so Olivia couldn't engage her in the parking lot and continue the conversation. Once she saw Olivia's black BMW drive by the window, she grabbed her coat and headed out.

Lucy almost never exceeded the speed limit, but she leaned on the gas pedal on the way home. Maybe Liz would be late for her appointment as usual, but the big, gray F-150 was in the driveway when Lucy arrived. She found Liz was sitting with the door open, her feet on the running board, as she keyed a message into her phone.

"I'm so sorry I'm late," Lucy apologized as she got out of her SUV. Liz merely nodded and continued typing her message. Lucy walked over to the truck. "Something important?"

"Always something important," said Liz, tapping hard to send the message. She slipped the phone into the pocket of her jacket. "Busy day?"

"Always busy," replied Lucy with a grin.

"Such a smart ass." Liz got up and kissed her cheek. "See? I'm being good. I never kiss you on the lips anymore."

"My noble knight." Lucy tugged on Liz's arm. "Come in. I'm sorry I'm late."

"Stop apologizing," said Liz. "I'm always late for something, but I've learned to stop apologizing because I can't help it. Besides, apologies are usually meaningless."

Lucy led Liz up the stairs to the practice room and unlocked the door.

After dropping her bags on a nearby chair, she pulled out the tab collar from her black blouse and unbuttoned the top button. "Oh, what a relief," she said, sitting on the sofa.

"Back to the collar, I see," said Liz. "Can't stay away from it."

"It's what people expect," Lucy said in a weary tone.

"Why should that matter? You're not exactly a conformist, Lucy. You're a shit disturber like me."

"Your role doesn't depend on your uniform."

"Not anymore, but there was a time when my white coat and scrubs defined me. I've tried to liberate myself from expectations."

"But I see you're back in your chinos and L.L. Bean oxford cloths."

Liz shrugged. "Summer's over. Back to looking half-way professional." She sank into the opposite sofa and stretched out her long legs.

"I enjoyed our weekend in Acadia," said Lucy, obviously changing the subject. "Did you?"

"I had fun fishing and hiking. And spending time with you and Erika."

"But not with Maggie?" asked Lucy, knowing it was a pointed question.

Again, Liz shrugged. She looked up at the ceiling.

"It was your anniversary," said Lucy to encourage conversation.

"Yes, it was. Not that it meant anything."

Lucy sighed and gave Liz her most sympathetic look. "What's wrong, Liz? Are you and Maggie still at odds?"

"No, we're at a point where it doesn't matter."

"Oh, Liz. Is it really that bad?"

Seemingly fascinated by the paneling she'd installed, Liz continued to stare at the ceiling. "It's pretty bad."

"In what way?" She waited patiently for Liz to answer.

"Maggie wants things from me I'm unable to give her. She wants me to spend more time with her. And I have. I quit surgery so I'd have more time for her. But that wasn't enough." Liz finally lowered her gaze and made eye contact. "She wants me to retire, but I don't want to quit the practice. The partners can't get enough money together to buy me out. And now, I've loaned so much money to the practice, they might never be able to buy me out."

"Liz, I know you. It's not about the money."

"Of course not. I don't want to retire. Maine needs doctors, especially now, during the COVID crisis. Doctors my age are retiring right and left to avoid dealing with it. I can't bring myself to quit. My patients need me right now."

"I understand." Lucy slipped off her dress flats and put her feet up on the coffee table, enjoying the look of mild surprise on Liz's face as she did. "We're talking as friends, right? Why not be comfortable?"

"Good idea." Liz slipped off her shoes and put her feet up too.

"What can you do to improve things with Maggie?"

Liz squinted at the ceiling. "I have no idea. I look for opportunities to spend time together. I ask her to come with me for a walk on the beach. She's not interested. She won't go out on the boat with me. She's not interested in anything I want to do."

"Do you want to continue the relationship?"asked Lucy, cutting to the chase.

"That's a good question. Maggie and I have a nice life together. Or at least, we had. We're kind of a fixture in this town. Our families are intertwined. We used to enjoy each other's company. It's gotten worse since she retired from teaching…and the pandemic, of course. Maggie is a very social person. The isolation has been hard on her."

"That's probably why she wants more of your attention."

"The irony is, the more she wants it, the less likely I am to give it. She's resentful when I read for work or take Telehealth calls at home, but it's my job."

"And you have your own issues, like grieving your mother's death."

"Oh, it's more than that. There have been other changes. I didn't just quit surgery because I wanted to spend time with Maggie. My fingers are stiff and don't have the agility they once had. Arthritis runs in the family. Sure, I can still suture a wound if I have to. I probably could do simple procedures to stay in the game, but the welfare of the patients is more important than my ego. A good surgeon knows when it's time to quit."

"Oh, Liz. I'm so sorry."

"I know. Me too. I was really good at it. When I was a surgeon, I made a difference."

"You make a difference now, Liz. You just said that's why you don't want to retire. You're a key player in the health of our community. Hobbs loves you."

"When I was chief of surgery at Yale, I was in a high-powered, high visibility role. I was a world-famous breast surgeon."

"I suspect that your identity was defined by your professional success. That's probably true for Maggie too. That's why she kept trying to make a comeback as an actress."

"She quit teaching to focus on theater work."

"But the comeback never materialized. She must be feeling a similar loss of status. You achieved your dreams and stepped back. For her, she missed an opportunity that will never return. Except for a few lucky breaks, minor actresses don't get big roles in their sixties. You can understand how that could cause a loss of self-esteem and a need to have it reinforced elsewhere. When did Maggie become more needy?"

"When she quit teaching."

"You see the connection?"

"Yes, and I don't know why I missed it before."

Lucy did some mental calculations. "You quit operating about the time you bought the boat. Right?" Lucy said, speaking her thoughts aloud. "That's also when you became more sexually aggressive."

"Shit. I never thought of that," said Liz, wrinkling her nose in disgust. "That's the kind of asinine thing Neanderthal men do."

"Why are you surprised? Weren't you trained in that alpha-dog, top-down, command, control, coerce culture of medicine? You've said how much it influenced you."

"I hadn't thought of it that way," said Liz with a reflective expression. "At least, that explains it."

"It explains it," said Lucy. "It doesn't excuse it."

"And what explains but doesn't excuse your response when I kissed you?"

Lucy felt her cheeks flame. She returned Liz's direct look. "We're talking about you, Liz. But to your point, I'm not blameless. Unfortunately, our indiscretion upset the ecology of your relationship at a time when it was fragile."

Liz shook her head. "Our 'indiscretion,' as you call it, was a symptom. Maggie and I have been drawing apart for some time. We always went our separate ways, but we were both so busy with our careers we didn't notice. After she retired, it became more obvious. Apart from some theater work, the highlight of her week was baby sitting the grandkids."

"It surprises people that couples who have been together for decades suddenly break up when one retires, but there's a reason for it. Suddenly, the distraction of children or careers is gone, and the partners have to take a hard look at the relationship. They don't always like what they see. Acting out is more common than you think."

"You mean like coming on to you on my boat?"

"Yes, or other things. Liz, forgive me, but I have to ask you this question. Have you ever been unfaithful to Maggie?"

"No."

"Are you sure?"

"I don't lie, Lucy. Since Maggie and I got back together, I haven't had sex with anyone else."

"Liz, I hope this isn't a Bill Clinton defense. There's more to intimacy than sex. And more to cheating too. You pushed hard that day on the boat, telling me about the comfortable bed below. If I'd gone along with it, we would have had sex."

Liz raised her hands in surrender. "I admit that I lust for you in my heart." She returned Lucy's intense gaze. "But I hope you've noticed that I've cleaned up my act. I've been staying away from you. I don't flirt with you. I'm trying to be more respectful. No more lewd comments. I'm trying to reform."

"I've noticed. But now it's obvious to everyone that you're staying away from me. You sat on the porch and read during my worship service at the campsite. I tried to catch your eye during Communion, but you wouldn't even look at me."

"I was busy," said Liz in a belligerent tone. "I was posting on the Yale docs' portal about my testing project."

"Right."

"I'm telling the truth," Liz said adamantly.

Lucy studied Liz's earnest face. "I trust you, Liz, but clearly, Maggie doesn't."

"So, what should I do?"

Lucy took a deep breath because she suddenly felt exhausted and needed some air to wake up. "I'm sorry, Liz. I can see the problem, but I don't have any suggestions. My stockpile of brilliant insights is depleted."

"We're all burnt out and tired of this pandemic. I'm fried myself. Let's pick this up another time when we're both in better shape." She got up and slipped on her shoes. "I appreciate having your ear." She crossed to where Lucy sat and kissed her on the cheek. "See you later."

Lucy grasped her wrist. "I love you, Liz. Please take care of yourself."

"I will. I love you too."

Lucy listened to Liz walking down the stairs. A few minutes later, she heard the big truck engine start and the sound of gravel dashing away as it drove out.

Lucy wanted to cry. She felt so bad for Liz and Maggie and her part in their unhappiness. She knew it also came from fatigue. The pandemic was taking its toll on everyone's mental health, including her own. Her limbs suddenly felt so heavy she couldn't move. The room was chilly, so she picked up the remote and turned on the electric fireplace. Gazing at the faux flames, she pulled an afghan over her legs. She thought of Brenda and Cherie haggling over a uniform, of Olivia's anxiety over the prospect of seeing her granddaughters, of Liz and Maggie growing apart, of so many people struggling to find their way. Her eyes felt heavy, so she decided to give them a rest by closing them for a minute.

"Lucy? Lucy?" A voice reached through Lucy's dream. She'd been wading in the stream near the house where she'd lived as a child and fishing with her father. When she opened her eyes, Erika was standing over her.

"I saw Liz leaving, but you didn't come down. Everything good between you?"

"Yes, fine," said Lucy, accepting Erika's kiss. "We both had a hard day. It wasn't a good time to talk."

"Ah, sometimes, it's best to hold a conversation for another day." Erika gestured with a pair of wine glasses. "I thought you might need some alcohol." Lucy focused on the table and saw a bottle of wine. She recognized it as the bottle they'd opened last night after dinner. After a bad day, one bottle hadn't been enough. "Thank you, sweetheart for coming to look for me," she murmured, sitting up.

Erika poured two glasses of wine and handed one to Lucy. They touched glasses. "*Prost!*" Erika declared.

The wine tasted good, especially because it signified permission to relax after the trying day. "Have I told you how much I love this room?" Lucy asked, gazing around.

Erika's pale eyes widened with pleasure. "Yes, but I don't mind hearing it again. I confess that I was afraid you'd think it was a silly idea. I know how much you like the acoustics in your church."

"I do, but I can come in here and sing in my nightgown and fuzzy slippers. I can sing in full voice and the neighbors won't complain. I can listen to music as loud as I want. It's not silly at all!"

Erika leaned over and kissed her. She parted her lips gently with her tongue and teased the inside of Lucy's mouth. Then she withdrew and smiled. "You can show me your full appreciation later."

"I'm so glad you didn't wait until Christmas, and I can enjoy this gift now. It's my secret hideout. My private place. All for me."

"You could move into Emily's room now that she's down at Yale."

"No, that's her space. This one is mine, and it's special. My wife planned it and my friends built it. It's precious to me. More precious than you will ever know."

Erika smiled, obviously pleased, and took a sip of wine.

Chapter 11

S am looked up from cutting her pork chop. "You asked Lucy Bartlett to come to Thanksgiving *here*?"

"Yes, the girls really want to meet her. They've become close to her during the counseling she did with them." Olivia smiled one of those overly sweet, manipulative smiles meant to calm her listener. Sam recognized it and was no longer taken in, but she restrained herself from rolling her eyes.

"But I already accepted an invitation to Maggie and Liz's place for Thanksgiving."

"Yes, I know, but they can all come here. We have plenty of room."

"No kidding," said Sam looking down the enormous dining table. It was large enough to comfortably sit a dozen people or more.

"I thought I'd make it one big party and combine it with your birthday."

"That's cheating," said Sam. "And I don't want a big party for my birthday. You can take me out for dinner if we can find someplace safe. I hear The Boathouse in Kennebunk has individual, outdoor dining spaces set up…ski gondolas retired from Shawnee Peak."

"But can't we have a cake with your friends, so you can blow out the candles?"

"That's kid's stuff. I don't need a birthday cake," scoffed Sam, spearing a piece of chop like she wanted to kill it.

"Don't break the plate," said Olivia, regarding her with a worried look. "I like these dishes. You can't get them anymore. The company's out of business."

"I'm so sorry," said Sam with exaggerated contrition. "And why didn't you warn me you were going to invite your granddaughters?"

"I just found out about it today, and it wasn't my idea. Amanda suggested it. She and her new love are going to the Caymans."

"Oh, so you're the babysitter while mom goes on vacation with her boyfriend?"

"Apparently." Olivia shrugged. "I really don't mind. I'm dying to see the girls."

"Famous last words. They could bring the virus up here, and we could both get it." Sam shook her head. "Liz will never go for this."

"Amanda says the girls will be quarantined, and she'll have them tested every day. She's hiring a car service that guarantees the passenger compartment will be completely sanitized. Now, there's a business niche I never would have considered."

"Sounds like she's thought of everything."

"Amanda was an events planner before Jason married her. She's an expert in logistics. She was so organized it drove my son crazy."

"Men aren't naturally as organized as women. They have to be taught it in the military."

"Women are organized because being a mother requires organization."

"I thought you had a nanny for your son."

"I did, but even with a nanny, getting out of the house in the morning takes planning."

"Well, you tell Liz about the change of plans. I've always gone to Liz's house if I couldn't get home for Thanksgiving. This year, I would have gone to see my mother, but only nuts like your daughter-in-law are traveling."

"Samantha, I love you, but why must you always say mean things to me?"

Sam forced her face to remain neutral. This was the first time Olivia had said those words, and it was in the middle of an argument.

Olivia looked up from her plate and realized Sam was staring at her. "What's the matter? You look like I slapped you."

"You did…in a way. I'm not sure I'm ready to talk about love."

Olivia put a forkful of salad into her mouth and chewed thoughtfully. "I've never met someone like you, Sam. You can be blunt to the point of being hurtful sometimes, but you always tell me the truth. Most of my female lovers were so obsequious. That's how I figured out they were only interested in my money."

"I'm sorry if I'm hurtful sometimes. Tact has never been my strong suit."

"Obviously not. But after decades on the Street, I know how to deal with savages."

Sam was glad she didn't have food in her mouth because she burst out laughing. "And you say I'm blunt. I'm a savage?"

"Not completely. You have refinement. I suppose I need to thank your mother for that."

"She tried. Not completely successfully. If I heard 'if you don't have anything nice to say, don't say it,' one more time…."

"There is something to that idea, you know," said Olivia, carefully crossing her tableware on her plate. She put her elbows on the table and leaned her chin on her hands. "I will speak to Liz about the girls coming, and I will invite them all."

"That also means inviting Maggie's daughter and grandkids. Maybe Liz's brother, the redneck, as well as Erika. Maybe even Brenda and Cherie. A full house."

"Yes, I expected that. Don't worry. I'm used to dealing with large dinner parties. Organization, you know."

"What if Liz says, 'no'?"

"She can't order me not to do it, only advise me."

"But you're forcing Lucy to make a choice. And I bet I know how she'll decide."

"I do too. That's why I'm not worried."

"That's not fair to take advantage of Lucy's good nature. She risked her life to give Cherie's father the last rites before he died."

"I heard about that, and that Liz went along to make sure she wore the proper protective clothing. That's why I think Liz might agree to come to dinner…to keep an eye on things and make sure everyone's safe, especially Lucy."

"Wow, you really have everyone figured out, don't you?"

Olivia shrugged. "It's essential to good management. Know your enemy…and your friends." She got up with her plate. "I'll take care of the dishes. You rest. I know you worked hard on that new renovation project today."

Sam got up too. "I'll help you. None of this role-playing stuff."

"At least not out of bed," said Olivia with a raised brow. "All right, come on. Bring your plate, please."

Sam watched Olivia's pert ass as she headed toward the kitchen and sighed. *Damn. That woman is irresistible.* She got up with her plate and followed her.

"Did you like the chops that way? It's a pedestrian meal, but this was a new twist with the seasoned panko, so I thought it was worth trying." Olivia turned on the water and began rinsing the dishes.

"You know you don't have to rinse them. Modern detergents are designed to cling to left-over food to clean more efficiently."

"Who says?"

"Bosch did research on it."

"I've always rinsed my dishes, so I'll keep doing it. So, there."

Sam shrugged. "Okay. Be that way."

Olivia turned and kissed her. "I'll try it once, but not tonight. I'm half done. And I'll only experiment because you recommend it."

"You're so open-minded." Sam smiled. Every little victory was to be savored, even winning debates over rinsing dirty dishes. Sam reached down to give Olivia's shapely ass a caress.

"Hmm," intoned Olivia, "I wonder what you have in mind."

Sam chuckled and reached around Olivia to stroke her crotch. "Dessert?"

"I made a pie."

"Please, don't get me started," said Sam.

"It's blueberry pie. Your favorite."

"My second favorite."

"You have a filthy mouth, Samantha, but I love it!" Olivia dried her hands on the dish towel hanging by the sink. "Let's go upstairs and you can talk dirty to me," she said, drawing Sam down into a kiss. She flicked her tongue over Sam's lips, which always excited Sam into being more aggressive. She pressed her lips closer and kissed her deeply. Olivia finally pulled away to catch her breath. "There's my savage. Let's go upstairs and get comfy."

"I don't want to wait," said Sam, easing down Olivia's yoga pants and lace panties. "You're all wet," she whispered into Olivia's ear as her fingers caressed her. She delicately licked the outside of Olivia's ear and then let her tongue wander in. She knew Olivia especially liked having her ears kissed.

"I've been wet since you came home," Olivia whispered back. "In fact, I couldn't wait for you to come home. I had to make myself come because I was thinking about you."

The idea of Olivia touching herself drove Sam crazy. She reached under Olivia's arms and gave her a boost onto the counter top. She was inside Olivia in seconds, enjoying her slick interior and finding her way around in this new position. Olivia leaned back against the cabinet door, allowing Sam to go deeper. She moaned and put her feet on Sam's shoulders, which aroused her even more. "Yes," she breathed into Sam's ear. "Yes, go deep."

Sam always marveled at Olivia's ability to come on the inside, how her insides grew soft and hot before they clutched her tight. Olivia came with a groan and fiercely gripped Sam's shoulders. But Sam wasn't finished. She put her hands on Olivia's buttocks to urge her forward. "I want to taste your pie. I hear it's really good."

Olivia gave her a playful punch. "You're such a smart–" Her words were cut off as Sam took her into her mouth before teasing her with her tongue.

"Hmm," said Sam. "Excellent pie. I think I'll have some more."

"You think you're so clever." Olivia flinched when Sam went back for more. "Easy, tiger, I'm sensitive after that first orgasm." Sam slowed the rhythm of her strokes to a languorous exploration. Olivia sighed and opened her legs wider. Sam listened carefully for her breaths to come faster, pacing her strokes to Olivia's excitement. When Olivia threaded her fingers in Sam's hair and pulled gently, she knew she was near. The second orgasm was more powerful than the first.

When the spasms ended, Sam stood up and grinned. "Gives a whole new meaning to eating in the kitchen."

Olivia smiled. "Oh, Samantha, your jokes are just awful."

"I know."

"Now, you."

"Are you kidding me?" asked Sam, making a face. "I'm not getting up on that counter."

"Fine. Let's go to bed. Help me down." Olivia placed her hands on Sam's shoulders and let her help her off the counter with a little lift under the armpits. She snatched up her clothes, giving Sam a delightful view of her lady parts. She was tempted to go inside, but Olivia stood up too fast.

"I knew what you were thinking," said Olivia, warning her with a look. "Come on. I can't wait any longer. I've been thinking about this all day." She gave Sam's hand a little yank. "Don't just stand there with that silly grin. Let's go!"

She chased Olivia up the stairs. Olivia finished undressing and bounded into bed, but Sam took her time. She unbuttoned her jeans and let them fall. Then she took off her boy shorts and flung them away. She peeled off her T-shirt and sports bra, preening a little to show off the muscles in her arms.

"Oh, yes," said Olivia with approval.

"Do you have another orgasm for me?" asked Sam, covering Olivia's body with her own. She pushed Olivia's legs apart with her knees.

"Maybe I do," Olivia whispered into her ear. "Fuck me hard."

Chapter 12

Liz read the email more carefully, trying to figure out why Moderna wanted her contact information. She appreciated that Russ Levin, the head virologist at Yale, was the kind of guy who'd ask before he gave out her phone number or email address.

Since test kits had been widely available, Liz had been regularly posting reports on her results in the Yale Docs message board. Today, she'd discovered that Russ had been sharing her data with someone he knew at Moderna.

"Why would they be interested in my little project? I just did it for fun," she said aloud as she typed the words into the portal.

Russ messaged back: *Maybe they'll make your Hobbs group a panel in our study. Sounds like you have everything ready to go. Your records are impeccable.*

I only shared the data because no one really knows anything about this virus. It's only a small sample.

But it's a well-defined sub-panel already set up, and it's large enough to be scientifically useful. They like your meticulous record-keeping.

Okay. Send them my email and phone number. I'll see what they want.

As she finished typing the last words, the intercom on her phone beeped. "Liz, Lucy Bartlett is here. She wants to talk to you if you have a minute."

Liz pressed the button and spoke near the intercom mic. "Sure. Send her down." Liz usually didn't allow people to interrupt her lunch break, but she always made exceptions for Lucy. There was a knock at the door. "Come on in," Liz sang out. She finished typing her message and closed the link to the portal before lowering the lid of her laptop. "Well, if it isn't the Reverend Lucille Bartlett, my favorite priest," she said, bending to kiss Lucy's cheek. "I meant to tell you I like you better in the collar. Glad you went back to it."

"That seems to be the result of my informal poll."

"Playing to expectations usually works." Liz gestured expansively to a visitors' chair. She gave Lucy a quick once over with a clinician's eyes. She knew very well that Lucy was probably doing something similar.

"You look happy, Liz. Something good happen?"

"You bet. Moderna seems interested in my little testing project."

Lucy looked puzzled. "That name sounds familiar, but I don't know why."

"Moderna is one of the companies developing COVID vaccines. They're using this new mRNA technology that's really cool. My buddy at Yale thinks we might be able to get into one of their clinical trials, which means some of us could get the vaccine early."

"But is it safe? A lot of people think the president pushed the companies to rush out the vaccine so he can be elected."

"He fucks up everything good. Yes, I think it's safe. If Fauci and Collins at NIH think it's okay, it's okay. I trust them." Liz sighed. "Except, I don't know if I can get all my test volunteers to take the shot. A lot of Brenda's guys still think the virus is a hoax. The other half think the vaccine's not safe because the president pushed it through. What a mess!"

"I'm sorry to burst your bubble, Liz. A moment ago, you looked so happy."

"It's not you, Lucy. This whole pandemic is getting old." Liz leaned back in her chair. "But you didn't come to talk about this, so what's up?"

"I have a dilemma, and I want you to hear me out before you say anything."

"So, it's something I won't like."

"Probably not."

Liz scowled but gestured with her hand for Lucy to proceed. She crossed her arms on her chest. Lucy looked disapproving, so she uncrossed them.

"That's better," Lucy said. "Olivia's granddaughters are coming for Thanksgiving, and she wants me to meet them." Liz opened her mouth to speak, but Lucy raised her hand and said, "Let me finish, please. I've been working with Olivia and the granddaughters for reasons that are privileged."

"It's okay. Sam told me about it."

"The gossip that goes on in this town!" exclaimed Lucy, looking frustrated.

"Don't worry. It's not going anywhere. Sam's not bound by professional confidence, but I am. Go on, Lucy."

"This visit is very important to Olivia. She hasn't seen her granddaughters for years, and there's difficult history. Bonding with them is important. She assures me everything will be done safely. The girls are quarantining for two weeks and coming up in a special car service that guarantees hygiene according to all CDC guidelines, but I said I would run it by you."

"Is Emily coming home from Yale?"

"No, she's worried because there have been cases in her dorm. She doesn't want us to get it because we're…you know, old people, and at high risk."

Liz chuckled. "At least, your daughter has some common sense. Not like her mother." She grinned to let Lucy know she was teasing, but Lucy's didn't smile, not even slightly. "Lucy, are you sure you're not doing this because Olivia is giving your church all that money?"

"Liz!" Lucy exclaimed. Her complexion darkened for a moment. Liz realized she was genuinely insulted that she should ask such a question.

"I'm sorry. That wasn't fair. I know you're doing it out of Christian charity, like when you risked your life to give Jean-Paul Bois the last rites. You take your job seriously, but one of these days, your luck is going to run out."

"That's my problem."

"No, it's my problem if you get sick and infect everyone. No, I don't agree. It sounds like Olivia is taking precautions, but don't bring them to my house for Thanksgiving."

"I won't, and I think Olivia wants to invite you and all your guests."

"Very kind of her, but we're not accepting. And frankly, Erika and her father shouldn't either. Stefan is at very high risk, and Erika has asthma, so she shouldn't go either."

Lucy sighed. "I forgot about that. Okay. Then I guess, I'll go by myself."

"You'd already decided what you were going to do before you walked in here. So why bother to ask me?"

"Sometimes, Liz, I just want to see your ornery face," said Lucy, getting up.

"Ditto."

"You should come by and have a drink with me and Erika after work. We never see you anymore."

"I should. Staying away from you doesn't seem to make any difference with Maggie. It's like she doesn't even care."

Lucy made a sad face. "I'm sorry. But Erika misses you, and so do I."

"I miss you too, but I can't do it today. I have a chamber of commerce meeting at five o'clock. I'll probably see Olivia there. Let's see if she invites me. If she does, I'll give her a piece of my mind."

Lucy affected an oh-so-patient look. "Liz, please don't."

Liz laughed. "You know I won't. You consulted me as a physician, and I will be completely professional." She slapped her thighs and got to her feet. "Mother Lucy, you are one stubborn woman," she said, bending to kiss Lucy on the cheek.

"So are you." Lucy gave her a quick hug. "I love you, though."

"I love you too."

Liz stood in her doorway and watched Lucy walk down the hall. She admired the little wiggle in her walk. *Stop looking at her*, Liz told herself. *She's married, and you're married. You're just frustrating yourself.*

Liz glanced at her watch. If she left now, she'd have time for a drink at Dockside before the meeting. As she drove to the restaurant, Liz gazed over the salt marsh. It looked sad at that time of year. The lush greens of summer were gone, replaced by matted, brown grass. Everyone said there would be a surge in COVID cases this winter thanks to the holidays and so many traveling to see family despite the CDC guidance. If people weren't careful, it would be a long, dark winter.

Peter Chase, the owner of Dockside, greeted her when she came in. "Hi, Dr. Liz, you're the first one here."

"I need a drink, so I came early," Liz explained. She clucked her tongue as if she were tasting a beer. "Something hoppy."

"Allagash has a new brew. Want to try it?"

"Bring it on."

Peter led her to a table with a view of the water. "Since you're the first one here, you get the best view in the house." Sitting down, Liz glanced around the deck, now enclosed with a plastic curtain and noted with approval how Peter had arranged the tables, correctly spaced, for the meeting. "We have fried scallops on special," he said, handing Liz a menu.

"Sounds good. I'll have the dinner portion."

After he left, Liz gave the menu a quick glance. All the restaurants had limited menus since the shutdown, but Peter had made a special effort to keep his diverse enough to please his customers. Liz decided to order a salad to go with her scallops and make it dinner.

In the early days of her relationship with Maggie, dinner would be waiting when she got home from a meeting. Once Maggie got involved in directing at the State Theater and began teaching at UNE, they started cooking for multiple nights and stowing meals in the refrigerator for when they got home. Liz was proud of their efficiency and independence, but sometimes, she missed coming home to a woman who couldn't wait to see her and a hot meal prepared especially for her.

Liz heaved out a long sigh at the memory. Did all relationships end up here? she wondered. Once the sexual glow died, what sustained the bond? Was it shared hardships? Raising kids? Common goals and plans? She'd yet to figure it out.

"I thought I might find you here," said a familiar voice. Liz looked up into Olivia's face.

"May I sit at your table?"

Liz pointed to the next table. "Sit there. We're both leaders in this community. Let's set a good example."

Olivia glanced around. "But there's no one else here."

Liz couldn't argue with that point. "Okay. Sit down."

Olivia looked as polished and put-together as always. Her designer scarf perfectly matched her perfect suit. Her earrings were just the right shade to blend with everything. Even her lipstick coordinated. Strange how a woman, who always managed to rub everyone the wrong way, never wore a clashing color.

"I see you're back to your button-downs and blazers," observed Olivia. "Summer must really be over now."

"Thanksgiving is just a few weeks away."

"Speaking of Thanksgiving…" Olivia began.

"Please order a drink first and then we'll chat."

"But I need to talk to you before the others come and see us violating *your* social distancing rules."

Liz ignored her and signaled to Peter, who approached with menus. "The town manager would like a glass of your best chardonnay," she said before he even reached the table. "On me."

Peter turned around and headed back to the bar for Olivia's drink.

"They're not *my* rules, Olivia," said Liz when he was out of earshot. "They're the governor's and the CDC's rule. In fact, six feet is just a random measure and spread depends on the ventilation, the surfaces involved, the number of people–"

"Oh, Liz, I know all that. We don't want to set a bad example, as you say."

Peter arrived and set Olivia's glass of wine in front of her. "Would you like a menu?"

Olivia shook her head. "No, thanks. My friend is making dinner for me tonight."

"You can have some of my scallops when they arrive," Liz offered. "To hold you until you get home to Sam."

"How kind. I love scallops. Or 'scollops' as they call them here."

"They taste good no matter what they call them." Liz leaned her chin on her hands and engaged Olivia's gaze. "No, I don't think it's a good idea for your granddaughters to come to Maine, but if you have to have them, try to limit their exposure to others for their sake too."

"So, Lucy already got to you."

"We have a hotline."

"So, I've heard."

Involuntarily, Liz narrowed her eyes. "Like you, we're in charge of looking after the people in the community." Her tone sounded defensive, so she smiled to derail any suspicion on Olivia's part. "Communication is a good thing."

"Yes, it is," said Olivia regarding her cautiously. "You're not in the best mood. Maybe I'll wait to invite you and your family and friends to Thanksgiving."

"Thank you for the invitation, but it will never happen. Not as long as the cases are going in the wrong direction, which they certainly are."

Peter came and brought Liz's dinner and an extra plate. "Fresh out of the bay this morning," he said as Liz shoveled some of the scallops onto the extra plate he'd brought for Olivia.

"Won't you please consider coming?" asked Olivia. "I've dreamed of a big Thanksgiving dinner, but we were a small family, so it never happened."

"This isn't the year for it. All the predictions say we're going to have another surge of the virus. Otherwise, I'd be happy to take you up on your invitation."

"Maybe next year?"

"Maybe. If the virus is under control."

"You think it won't be over by then? Not even by next fall?"

Liz raised her shoulders. "Who knows?"

Olivia looked concerned.

"Life is short. Drink the wine. Eat the scallops."

Olivia nodded and put a scallop into her mouth. She closed her eyes as she chewed. "Oh my God, these are delicious!"

Chapter 13

"If you knew Liz wouldn't approve, why did you bother to ask her?" asked Erika as she expertly drained the cooking water from the string beans with a pot lid. She returned the pot to the stove to allow the heat to steam off the rest of the water and cut in a knob of butter to melt. She raised the lid on the rice. Almost ready.

Lucy leaned against the edge of the counter as she sipped her wine. She was still wearing a clerical blouse, although the collar had probably long since found its way into one of her pockets. Erika knew she would find it when she did the wash.

"I wasn't asking her permission," Lucy protested. "I just didn't want to hear about it afterward."

"Oh, but you will. God help you if anyone gets sick because of this… especially *you*."

"I'll be careful. You know I will. But those poor little girls. They need to know that everyone in their father's family isn't a monster."

"Olivia's not a monster?" Erika asked with an arched brow. "Could have fooled me."

Lucy gave her a gentle punch on the hip. "Be kind, Erika. It doesn't cost anything."

Erika made a tart face. "I am kind. I'm simply not as trusting as you are. I don't believe that Olivia's actually reformed. She's used to getting her way. People like that don't change. She's more subtle about it and has turned on the charm, but she still wants to control everything, including your church, if you don't watch out."

Lucy gave her a cool look to warn her away from this topic. "How long till dinner?" she asked, obviously changing the subject.

"I was going to ask if you wanted to change out of your work clothes. You don't have a good track record with blouses and food."

"It's my big boobs. They're always in the way."

"Now, Lucy," Erika said in her arch, professorial voice, "your boobs are perfectly lovely, and I adore them. Go change into something you don't care about in case you find yourself suddenly wearing my scampi."

Erika was glad for the moment of quiet while she dealt with the last critical moments of meal preparation. Overcooked shrimp could be tough and dry, no matter how much butter, lemon and parsley she slathered on it. To help her concentrate, Erika streamed music through the small speaker on the counter. Lucy's elegant but powerful soprano filled the room. Erika never tired of hearing her wife sing her signature operatic roles.

The solitude was brief. Lucy returned bundled in a polar fleece hoodie. "Sometimes, it's weird hearing myself on a recording."

"And why is that, love?" Erika asked absently as she stirred the shrimp in the pan.

"I don't know…kind of like hearing a ghost of myself from the past."

"If you believe in string theory, it might not really be in the past. It could be occurring in one of many contemporaneous presents."

"What?" asked Lucy, looking mystified.

"In one of those alternate universes, you might never have retired from opera, and you might still be singing at the Metropolitan, which would make me happy, but then maybe we would never have met, or maybe Jeanine would still be alive, and I would be with her. Hmm. So many possibilities!"

"Oh, Erika. Please. My brain is too tired for philosophy."

"Technically, that idea belongs to theoretical physics. But it doesn't matter. Sit down. It's almost time to eat. Pour the wine, will you? I found you something special. It's in the fridge."

"Are we celebrating something?"

"Yes, as a matter of fact. The administration accepted my resignation, effective at the end of the summer term. I told them I've had quite enough of being department chair again, especially because this time, I didn't choose it. I'd forgotten how tedious the endless administration meetings can be. They've agreed to make me emeritus after I retire. In exchange, I will give a lecture on political discourse, or whatever I like, once a year."

Lucy hugged her from behind. "Oh, Erika! Congratulations! You've wanted this for so long!"

"Let's not celebrate just yet. If the current occupant of the White House gets elected, I may come to regret it. Not that I haven't enjoyed my celebrity status that his tenure brought me, but that man is bloody dangerous."

"If he gets reelected, then PBS and the news stations will want to keep interviewing you, and you'll be busier than ever. But he won't be reelected." Lucy raised her crossed her fingers. "…I hope."

"Open the wine, dear," Erika urged as she spooned rice into two pasta plates. Lucy headed to the refrigerator. "If he gets reelected," Erika continued, "this country may not survive as a democracy. Besides, I'm sick of talking about him. I know you can't understand why, but I really want to write that book on Hegel."

"No, I can understand. I really want to write that book about physical intimacy."

"My wife wants to write a theology dissertation on sex." Erika shook her head. "Of course, she does. Little sex pot that she is." Erika brought the dishes to the table. "Do you know what they've decided about residency for the winter semester?" she asked.

"No, but rumor has it, we will still be remote until the fall of 2021."

"Just think. Soon, you'll be the Rev. Dr. Lucille Bartlett."

"I'm not big on titles, so I probably won't use it much."

"But your church is. They'll even paint it on the signs. Tom has those extra initials. You have to keep up with your associate rector, after all." Erika bent to kiss her. "I'm proud of you, Lovely Lucy. I know your book will be brilliant."

The cork emerged from the bottle of pinot grigio with a satisfying pop. Erika surveyed the carefully set table to see if there was anything else they needed. She went back to the counter for the hunk of Romano cheese and the grater.

"Before we lived together, I never ate so well," said Lucy, pulling out a chair from the table and sitting down. "It's like having a restaurant meal every night."

"Thank you. Preparing good food was the way my mother showed us love. She was never demonstrative, but then, neither am I."

"Oh, you do fine…in bed."

"Enjoy the meal," urged Erika. "Never mind your lovely boobs. If you need me to take off your soiled shirt, I shall be happy to oblige."

"I bet," said Lucy, raising a forkful of scampi to her mouth. As she chewed, her look of pleasure showed her appreciation. "Delicious," she said, holding her hand in front of her mouth. She swallowed. "Will you marry me?"

"Too late. I'm already married." She picked up her wine glass and saluted Lucy. "To my lovely bride."

"I want you to know that I expect delicious meals like this for the rest of my life."

"And you shall have them, I promise." Erika smiled as she watched Lucy enjoying her meal.

Erika leaned on her hand. "Lucy, are you sure going to Olivia's for Thanksgiving is a good idea?"

"No, I'm not sure. But the girls' bond with me is an anchor in their relationship with their grandmother."

"Olivia's not the warmest person. She needs you, but Lucy, dear, you don't have to give so much of yourself to everyone. You are entitled to have a personal life."

"I know, but I'm fond of the girls. I hate that being with them means choosing to be away from my family."

Erika reached out and patted her hand. "I understand. I knew when I married a priest, I'd be signing up for some sacrifices. I'll miss you at Thanksgiving, of course, but we shall make up for it."

"That's the one regret I have about this plan…not being able to spend the holiday with you and our friends."

Erika shrugged. "We don't celebrate Thanksgiving in Germany in the same way. The mythology about the indigenous people coming to the rescue of the invaders is unique to this country. I'm surprised the holiday hasn't been overturned the way Columbus Day has been."

"Wait long enough and it will happen. The mistreatment of Native Americans is despicable, but some traditions have value. Thanksgiving was one thing we could all agree on. There aren't enough things that bind us together as Americans anymore. Stuffing ourselves and watching football in a food coma is apparently one of them."

Lucy reached for a piece of bread and mopped up the juices in her plate. "What did they say when you put in your resignation?"

"Well, I've been making noises about it for years, so it wasn't that much of a surprise. The dean isn't delighted, of course, especially because Morgan Collins is still out with complications from COVID."

"Is she any better?"

Erika shrugged. "No one knows. She was doing fine, then she developed blood clots. They have her on blood thinner, but it's evidently quite dangerous, and anti-coagulants can make it worse. When I see Liz, I'll ask her what she knows about it."

Lucy looked at her empty plate. "That was delicious. Is there more?"

"Really, Lucy, you've become a little piglet. Yes, there's more, but I'm saving what's left for our lunch tomorrow. I could throw together a quick salad. How about some veggies and dip?"

Lucy considered it for a moment. "No, that's too virtuous. I'll settle for one of those brownies you made yesterday."

Erika smiled. "A perfect solution."

Lucy got up to clear the table. "I am a little concerned that my wife thinks I'm turning into a piglet." She cocked her hip and looked indignant.

"You've put on a little weight, Lucy, but you were far too thin when we met. And the weight has gone to all the right places," said Erika, allowing her gaze to wander down from Lucy's green eyes to her full breasts.

"Down, girl. You can have some later."

Erika chuckled and began portioning out the remaining scampi, rice, and beans into two dishes for lunch. "When must you get back to Olivia about Thanksgiving?"

"She didn't set a date, but obviously soon."

Erika covered the lunch dishes and put them into the refrigerator. "I'll dry the dishes for you."

"No, you go out and sit down. You cooked. I'll clean up. I'm not great in the kitchen, but, at least, I know how to wash dishes. Go put on the news. I'll be out in a few minutes."

Erika headed to the living room and switched on the TV. As she sat down, she thought about Lucy spending Thanksgiving with Olivia instead of with her. Yes, it did bother her a bit, despite the brave face she'd worn for Lucy's benefit. When her mother and she had arrived in America after escaping from East Germany, Helga had made Thanksgiving a special holiday, complete with a big turkey and all the traditional trimmings. Ever since, Thanksgiving always made her think of her mother and being together as a family. She wondered if she should tell Lucy and urge her to decide against going to Olivia's. But she sensed that Lucy had already decided and sharing her feelings would only cause internal conflict. Either way, Lucy would feel that she had let someone down. It was so hard to keep everyone happy. No matter what one did, someone would be disappointed.

"Something wrong?" asked Lucy, as she sat down beside Erika on the couch. She picked up her arm and draped it over her shoulder.

"I'll miss you on Thanksgiving," Erika admitted.

"Oh, sweetie, I'll miss you too, but we'll be together next year. I promise."

Chapter 14

Lucy's shoulder began to itch at the injection site, but she forced herself not to scratch. Liz had said the vaccine could cause pain in her shoulder or itching. Lucy hoped that meant she'd gotten the real thing. When Liz had told her that the placebo effect could cause symptoms simply through the power of suggestion, Lucy remembered thinking that's how prayer heals.

Lucy was a woman of faith, but also a firm believer in science. She had preached in her Sunday sermon about seeing science as a gift from God and using reason rather than believing in conspiracy theories. After hearing how many of Brenda's officers wouldn't take the vaccine, Lucy hoped that a little boost from the pulpit would help convince the skeptics. Even as she preached on common sense and the common good, in her heart, she knew that she was preaching to the converted. Mostly, Episcopalians believed in science.

Her hand reached for her itchy shoulder, but she slapped it with the other to remind it to keep away. Jodi walked in at that exact moment and raised her brows. "We still have flies? I thought the frost got rid of them." The screens in the old building had gaps, and occasionally, insects wandered into Lucy's office.

"No, it's just itchy where I got the shot. I'm trying to remind my hand to stay way."

"I guess that's one way." Jodi glanced at the door. "Mother Lucy, Maggie Fitzgerald is here. She wants to know if you can talk to her for a few minutes."

Lucy glanced at the desk clock. Almost five. The truth was, she wanted to go home. She wondered why her flock always waited until the last minute to decide they needed to see her. "Sure, Jodi, send her in," said Lucy, striving for a positive tone.

She got up to greet Maggie, who was dressed to the nines, as usual, and fully made up. Sometimes, it seemed to Lucy that her friend took the actress glamour too far. Maggie wasn't a natural beauty, but she knew how to make the most of her looks. She took care of herself, watched her weight, and obviously moisturized her skin because it looked fresh and youthful. Lucy knew from accompanying her to the spa, she had more help. Usually, Maggie wore her long, white hair up, but today it hung loose around her shoulders.

"I hope I'm not keeping you from something important," said Maggie, looking contrite.

"I always have time for a friend." Lucy opened her arms for a hug, but Maggie only touched her cheek to hers and patted her waist.

"Thanks. I really needed to talk to you."

"Okay," said Lucy, drawing back to search Maggie's hazel eyes, which looked obviously troubled. "Sit down and let's talk." She gestured to a visitor's chair. She pulled the other chair closer and sat down. "What's the matter? You look upset."

"I can't stand it anymore."

Lucy reached out and grasped Maggie's hand. "What can't you stand?"

"Can you give me absolution…like a Catholic priest?"

Taken by surprise, Lucy released her hand and sat back. "Yes, but we see reconciliation a little differently. It's reserved for extreme cases when someone's feelings of guilt are too much to bear. Are you sure you don't want to talk to me as your friend?"

"No, I need you to hear my confession. Sometimes, I really miss the Catholic Church. If my conscience bothered me, I could go to confession and be forgiven, no matter what."

"It's not quite that simple. You need to be sorry for your sins. It's not like throwing clothes in the washer, and they come out clean."

Maggie looked slightly insulted at the suggestion. "I never thought so."

"If you think the formal rite of reconciliation will help, I'll get my stole," Lucy said, getting up to head to her desk.

"Yes, I want my confession to be official, and I'm glad to see you're wearing your collar again." Ironically, before Jodi had announced that

Maggie was outside, Lucy was about to take her collar off and stick it in her pocket. She had just missed getting away. *Don't think of it that way,* Lucy scolded herself. *Someone needs you to minister to her soul, someone you call your friend.*

Lucy opened her desk drawer. Susan's white stole was rolled up and ready for special occasions, but this occasion called for a purple stole. Lucy always kept one nearby in case she was called out to administer the last rites, which, in the days of COVID, was much too often. She also took out the small prayer book she brought on home visits.

"As you know, we confess our sins during worship services. Private penance rite isn't as common as it is for Catholics," Lucy explained. "There's no confessional. Just you and me sitting together in my office. Will that work for you?"

Maggie nodded her agreement.

"Hold on a moment while I tell Jodi she can go home and turn off the ringer on my phone." After Lucy attended to these details, she kissed the cross on her purple stole and draped it around her neck. She returned to the seat beside Maggie, found the place in the *Book of Common Prayer.* "We begin with you saying, 'Bless me for I have sinned.'"

"That sounds very familiar," said Maggie, looking relieved, and repeated the words.

Lucy read: "The Lord be in your heart and upon your lips that you may truly and humbly confess your sins: In the Name of the Father, and of the Son, and of the Holy Spirit. Amen." She handed the prayer book to Maggie and pointed to the text she was to read.

"I confess to Almighty God, to his Church, and to you, that I have sinned by my own fault in thought, word, and deed, in things done and left undone; especially for committing adultery…" She glanced anxiously at Lucy. "I cheated on my wife by sleeping with a man," she hastily explained.

Lucy struggled for detachment. The subject of Maggie's heterosexual past was controversial. The mere mention of Maggie's ex-husband could drive Liz into a fury. Her eyes flashed and her fists clenched. In someone so trained to self-control, the transformation was startling.

"Maggie, you don't need to say more…not unless you really want to. The details of your sin are known to God."

Maggie's eyes filled. "No, I want to confess. I need to talk about it."

Lucy sat back. "God is listening, and so am I."

Somewhere, deep in Maggie's soul, a sob broke loose from its moorings. Lucy snatched the tissue box on the table beside Maggie and handed it to her. "Why did you sleep with this man, Maggie? Did you love him?"

"No, but his interest made me feel more attractive. I certainly felt like shit after I found out my wife kissed you." Maggie's accusing tone made Lucy tense.

"I'm sorry you felt that way. What we did was wrong, and I deeply regret it. Did the affair make you feel better?"

"For a little while. He was just a young actor at the State Theater, star struck by an old broad, one who'd once been a legend…in her own mind. He was sweet and beautiful, and for a moment, I felt beautiful too. Like I was worth something, like someone valued me, saw me as special."

Lucy inhaled a deep sigh. "Oh, Maggie, why do you need someone else to make you feel special? You are special by being who you are. God sees you as wonderful and unique, a masterpiece in her eyes. After all, she made you."

"Really? I'm just an aging actress with sagging breasts and wrinkles, and white hair that's getting thin. No wonder Liz isn't interested anymore."

"What makes you think she's not interested?"

"She kissed you."

"Maggie, Liz is a flirt."

"This was more than flirting, and you know it."

If they got started on this subject, they would be diverted into debating how serious the kiss was. Lucy deliberately turned the conversation back to Maggie. "Liz loved you enough to marry you."

"She married me out of duty. She felt sorry for me because I had cancer. She wanted me to know she would stand by me."

"I'm sure there was more to it than that."

"Oh, we were in lust. And it was so romantic. Fated lovers reunited after forty years. Meanwhile, I was terrified, and she was there when I needed her. You know Liz. She's the one who takes care of everyone. I'm one of the people she takes care of. She makes sure I get all my cancer screenings on time. She makes sure there's oil in my car. She takes care of my finances."

"That's what people do when they're married. They take care of one another. There's nothing wrong with that. Human beings are meant to be interdependent."

"How could you let her kiss you?" Maggie asked shrilly. "You were my best friend, the best friend I ever had. You were always there for me. You never judged me. I loved you."

"I loved you too, Maggie, and I still love you." Lucy reached for Maggie's hand.

"I wanted to hurt you too. I felt so betrayed by both of you, especially when you kept telling me it was nothing, just a kiss, an impulsive, one-time kiss. I wanted to hurt you too, but I didn't know how."

"You did know how. My best friend left me. You avoided me. You wouldn't speak to me, and I missed you."

Maggie squeezed Lucy's hand. "I missed you too."

"How long have you been carrying this burden? When did you sleep with this man?"

"In August, when we were doing rehearsals for a special broadcast production."

"That was risky. You could have been exposed to the virus. You could have exposed other people. Liz. Your daughter. Your grandchildren. Your friends."

"I didn't care. I didn't even think about it. I know how selfish it sounds, but it's true." Maggie wiped away her tears with the back of her hand. "I was so angry. You can't even imagine how angry I was," she paused to wipe away tears. "I wanted to hurt Liz the way she hurt me."

"You had an affair out of revenge?"

"Yes! I knew that sleeping with a man would hurt her like nothing else could. When I dated men in college, it made her crazy with jealousy and rage. Claudia told me Liz nearly went insane when she heard I married Barry. She wanted to come to Syracuse and kill him!"

"I'm sure it really upset her. But she was young then, and so were you."

"It wasn't easy to be Catholic and gay in the 1970s. My parents were hysterical when I told them. They threatened to cut me off if I didn't leave college in New York and go to that little Catholic college in Syracuse."

Lucy knew the story of Liz and Maggie's past, so she didn't press her for more details. "You did it to hurt Liz, but you also hurt the man you slept with. You used him. Sex exists to express love, not to hurt people. Are you still involved with him?"

"No, it only lasted a few weeks. It was over by Labor Day, when he went back to New York."

"Oh, Maggie. Why didn't you tell me you were so miserable? I could have hooked you up with a counselor who could help you."

"I didn't want you to know how much you'd hurt me. I didn't want to give you the satisfaction. It's so obvious Liz worships you. Whenever you sing, she stares in adoration."

"That's how opera fans are. Believe me, from the other side, it's pretty hard to take."

"This is about more than being a diva. Liz loves you. She's loved you since the day she met you. She worships the ground you walk on. Me? I'm just her boring, old wife."

"Oh, Maggie, don't be so hard on yourself."

"This is such a mess. I've hurt so many people. I never realized. I thought I would feel better after talking about it, but I only feel worse. Please give me absolution. This whole thing makes me feel so dirty!"

"That's why it's called adultery. Infidelity adulterates the sacred union of a marriage." Lucy gave her a hard look. "I know you feel bad, Maggie, but are you truly sorry for hurting yourself and the others involved? The man you had the affair with? Liz?"

"I am. I truly am." Maggie wiped her face with the tissue. Her mascara had run. Lucy plucked out a few tissues from the box on Maggie's lap and dabbed her friend's face.

"So, let's let God take this sin from you and make a fresh start." She handed the book to Maggie. "Here's what you read." Lucy pointed to the text. "Start here."

"For these and all other sins which I cannot now remember, I am truly sorry. I pray to God to have mercy on me. I firmly intend amendment of life, and I humbly beg forgiveness of God and his Church, and ask you for counsel, direction, and absolution."

"Before I give you absolution, Maggie, I want to know how you intend to handle this situation with Liz. You admit that you did it to hurt her. How can you make amends for the harm you've done to your marriage?"

"Do I have to tell her? If I tell her, it will be the end of the relationship. Sleeping with a man is the one thing she could never forgive."

"You knew that, and yet you went ahead." Lucy took Maggie's hands in hers and looked directly into her eyes. "Is that why you did it? To end the relationship?"

Maggie's gaze darted away. "I don't know. I'm afraid. I don't want her to leave me."

"Do you want to leave her?" Lucy asked in her gentlest tone.

"I don't know!"

Lucy gave Maggie's hands a squeeze and released them. "Here's what I think, Maggie. I think you need to talk to a professional to help you figure this out. Not me, of course, we're too close. I can recommend someone in Portland or Portsmouth. Are you interested?"

Maggie heaved out a sigh. "I have to think about it. Can I let you know?"

"Of course."

Lucy took the book back and read the words of absolution, making the sign of the cross. "The Lord has put away your sins. Go in peace, and pray for me, a sinner."

Maggie dissolved into tears again. Lucy pulled her out of the chair and held her close. She could smell the shampoo in Maggie's freshly washed hair, feel the grip of her fingers pressing into her arms. "I thought it would all be gone," Maggie said between sobs. "This awful feeling inside. This hollowness and pain. The guilt!"

"It doesn't work that way. The ritual of absolution isn't magic. The words are only as powerful as your belief that you are forgiven, but all forgiveness starts with you. Maybe you do need to tell Liz about it, not to hurt her, but because the burden of keeping this secret is eating you up inside."

"I can't tell her. She'll leave me."

"If you're sure it will end the relationship, I would think twice about telling her until you decide what you want to do. But can you keep this secret and maintain your marriage?"

"I don't know. We barely talk to one another as it is. I stopped having sex with her."

Lucy blinked. She wasn't sure she wanted to know this.

Maggie had completely missed Lucy's reaction, despite being an astute reader of body language, which only confirmed how upset she was. "She keeps asking me for sex, but I'm not interested. I don't know if it's the guilt or what. She was always more interested in sex than I was."

Lucy held her at arms' length and studied her face. "Maggie, you have so many things going on here, we can't even begin to address them today. You need to talk to someone who can help you sort through all the aspects of this situation. Since I'm peripherally involved and we're friends, it can't be me."

"You're abandoning me?"

"No, I can still be here for you as a supportive friend and your priest, but as far as working out your marital problems, you need to talk to someone else. There's a woman in Portsmouth, I think might be right for you. She's semi-retired, but she takes on a few cases. I'll give you her name and phone number. Okay?"

"Okay. I guess."

Lucy got up and found an appointment card in her desk. She wrote down Gloria Parrish's name and phone number. "She's good people. You'll like her."

Maggie slipped the card into her pocket. Lucy gave her a quick hug and walked her to the door. Tears came to her eyes as she watched her friend walk down the hall to the public entrance. She took off her stole because it suddenly felt so heavy.

Chapter 15

Olivia decided to apply just a little more blush. Depending on the natural light through the window, the video cam tended to drain the color from her face. She wanted to look her best when she met Sam's mother, even if it was only online. This was a big step in the relationship, but it hadn't been Sam's idea. When she said she was going to video-visit her mother on Zoom for Thanksgiving, Olivia asked if she could join them. To her surprise, Sam had reluctantly agreed.

Sam poked her head into Olivia's powder room. "Are you almost ready? I'm going to fire up my laptop."

"I'm ready."

"You have the link and know how to get into the meeting?"

"Yes, I do." Olivia made an effort to sound patient. "Sam, I was the chief executive of a major financial company. I am reasonably competent."

Sam crossed her arms on her chest. "I never found the big shots to be competent. They usually let their minions do all the work. I often wondered how some of them put on their undies in the morning."

"I was never like that. I always learned all the software, so I could navigate and use it myself."

"Of course you did. You like to be in control," said Sam with a smirk. "Well, let's get started. Your grandkids will be here soon." She disappeared from view. Olivia listened to her feet running down the stairs.

She couldn't figure out why Sam was in such a foul mood. She'd been fine the night before, especially in bed. Olivia wondered if she was cranky because she felt uncomfortable around children, but she'd observed Sam with Maggie Fitzgerald's granddaughters. Then, she seemed fine. She'd taken the girls fishing in Jimson pond, kite flying on the beach, and searching for pretty stones along the water's edge. Olivia hoped she'd feel inspired to do the same with Sharon and Jessica. That is, if they were interested. They might be spoiled like many girls their age, but during their conversations, the girls had seemed surprisingly down to earth, despite their mother's annoying, entitled personality.

Olivia worried about keeping them entertained for the time they'd be in Maine. When they were small, it had been easy to keep them occupied, but now they were older. Sharon was clearly in puberty, and Jessica wasn't far behind. Of course, she would take the girls to Kittery to shop in the outlets. Adolescent girls liked to shop, didn't they? What female of any age didn't like to shop?

Sam, of course. She bought everything online. She had it down to a science and had found a few favorite retailers, whose sizing was reliable and carried styles she liked. Her favorite was a company that had once distributed a popular tool bag designed to sit in a five-gallon pail. Now, they were a purveyor of women's work clothes. Olivia had been watching their fortunes as a small cap but had decided not to add it to the portfolio, not convinced the detour would make them profitable.

Olivia went into her office and opened her laptop. As she navigated to the Zoom link, she mentally thanked Lucy for the trick of entering the meeting without the video feed. She could eavesdrop on the conversation and the other participants couldn't see her face until she was ready, but Sam caught her.

"Mom, I see Olivia has joined us. Olivia, can you turn on your video, so we can see you?"

Olivia made sure she was wearing a practiced smile before the video feed showed her face. She was so busy looking at herself, it took a moment to notice Sam's mother staring at her.

"Hello, Olivia," said Laura McKinnon. Her eyes almost imperceptibly narrowed to take in the newcomer. "Happy Thanksgiving."

"Happy Thanksgiving to you, Mrs. McKinnon." Olivia studied the woman on the screen. Although she was eighty-five, she had clearly once been a classic beauty with refined features. Her gray hair was cut precisely to her jawline. Her makeup was subtly elegant, the lipstick was exactly the right shade for her coloring. Olivia quickly pigeonholed her as a wealthy,

WASP wife, probably Junior League and a life-long member of the country club. Only her strong resemblance to her daughter engendered the slightest feeling of warmth for the woman.

"Olivia, please don't make me feel older than I am. Call me Laura."

"Thank you. It's such a pleasure to finally meet you, Laura. Samantha speaks of you often." That wasn't true, but it sounded good. "Do you have family visiting for the holidays?"

She saw a shadow of sadness pass in the older woman's eyes. "Unfortunately, no. Sam's brother and his family are staying away because of the virus. I don't blame them, but I do miss the children."

Out of the corner of her eye, Olivia could see Sam watching carefully trying to gauge the success of the introduction. What she detected was slight contempt for both of them. She knew Sam hated what she called "phoniness," especially women preening as they sized one another up.

Sam had described how her mother had vainly tried to turn her into a lady, subject to the norms of 1960s culture. "My mother told me I walked like a football player, that I needed to take shorter steps." To demonstrate, Sam had mimed the mincing steps her mother had considered "ladylike." "She was always telling me to 'fix myself up a little.' Like the face God gave me wasn't good enough and needed improvement."

Unfortunately, these revelations had come in the middle of an argument after Olivia had suggested Sam put on some makeup because her tan had faded, and she looked pale.

In the present, the three-way conversation proceeded in fits and starts, mostly with Laura asking polite questions about Sam's work and the progress on the house at the pond. Sam had to remind her that the renovation had been completed months ago.

Laura suddenly turned to Olivia and gave her a penetrating look. "My husband was a great admirer of your financial acumen. He always checked on the Enright fund when he read the financial pages."

Olivia was instantly on edge, wondering if Sam's father had lost a big sum of money after the scandal. "I hope the fund was good to him," she replied casually.

"Oh, it was. He got out before it all went south." So, she knew the firm had collapsed. Olivia wondered if she also knew the sordid details of Jason's questionable trading practices.

"All good things must come to an end," said Olivia in a philosophic tone. She saw Laura eyeing her carefully.

Sam was beginning to look bored with the conversation. She began making comments that suggested she wanted to wind it down, saying they had to get ready for the arrival of Olivia's granddaughters. That was true, but Olivia could always detect when Sam had enough of something and wanted to move on.

"Have a great day, Mom," Sam said. "I'll call you on Sunday."

Olivia saw a moment of genuine pleasure in Laura's eyes, and realized she was looking forward to Sam's call. Olivia felt a pang of sympathy when she realized the woman was probably lonely. She knew exactly how that felt. Before Sam had come into her life, Olivia had looked forward to any social contact, even Zoom meetings with town officials and the Fox-addicted old biddies in the Republican women's club.

After the meeting ended, Sam came into Olivia's office and gave her a kiss. "Thanks for being nice to my mother. She can be such a pain in the ass."

"Obviously, she was trying to be on good behavior too. Did your parents lose a lot of money when my company went down?"

Sam shrugged. "I have no idea. Dad never talked to me about things like that."

"What did you talk about?"

"Not much really. Mostly, Mom and I talked. After Dad died, I was sorry we didn't talk more."

Olivia sighed. "We all have regrets, don't we?"

Sam stared at her feet. "I suppose we do." She glanced at the clock on Olivia's desk. "We should get a move on. Everyone will be here soon."

Olivia's phone pinged and showed a video feed of Liz Stolz standing outside the front door. "In fact, your doctor friend is already here." Olivia watched Liz glaring impatiently at the front door. "And she looks like she's in a hurry."

"She has a houseful of guests on the way," Sam reminded her, as they headed to the front door.

When Olivia opened it, Liz handed Sam a stock pot. "I brought you some Hubbard Squash soup. Should be enough for everyone. It's traditional, you know. A Maine thing."

"Good morning, Dr. Stolz," said Olivia in a cheerful voice as Sam took the pot away. "Happy Thanksgiving."

"Happy Thanksgiving to you, Olivia. Your friendly and efficient COVID testing service has arrived! I've already tested Lucy Bartlett. She's negative, of course. She had to lead a Thanksgiving prayer on Facebook Live, but she'll be over soon. I talked to the girls' driver. They just got off at the Hobbs exit."

"It's very kind of you to interrupt your Thanksgiving preparations to test everyone," said Olivia, leading her into the kitchen.

"Trying to keep everyone healthy," said Liz unpacking the test kits. She laid them out on the kitchen counter. "Any reaction to the vaccine?"

"My arm's a bit sore where you poked me."

"That's a good sign. It probably means you got the real thing. What about Sam?" asked Liz, donning protective gloves.

"She hasn't complained of any symptoms."

Liz's face was impassive as she ripped open the test kit. Although the idea of a swab probing her nostril was repulsive, Olivia bravely tilted her head back. Once the hateful thing withdrew, she said, "You're getting very good at that."

"You'd think so after doing hundreds of these tests." Liz deposited the sample in the machine. "Sam!" she called. "Get down here!"

"I'm here, Liz." Sam came into the kitchen. "You don't have to yell."

"I need to get back to my turkey." The meter pinged, and Liz glanced over to read the results. "You're negative, Olivia. Next!" Liz carefully threaded the probe up Sam's nose.

The front door alert set off Olivia's phone. "That will be the girls." Her heart was pounding as she headed to the door. She took a deep breath to center herself before she opened it.

It was shocking to see how tall Sharon was, nearly as tall as Olivia. Her hair, which had been blond when she was a little girl, had suddenly darkened into a rich brown. Her sister was no longer a little girl, but a person, with intense, curious eyes. They both looked solemn and slightly frightened as they clutched their colorful wheeled bags.

"Welcome to Maine," said Olivia with overstated enthusiasm. "Happy Thanksgiving."

"Happy Thanksgiving," the girls murmured in unison.

Olivia waved to the driver standing by the SUV limo in which her granddaughters had arrived. She was pleased to see he was wearing a mask. Hopefully, all the hype about the sanitized car was true. The driver waved back and called "Happy Thanksgiving!" before getting back in the vehicle.

"Come in, girls. I'm so happy to see you."

The girls rolled their bags over the threshold and looked up expectantly. It pleased Olivia to see that they were mannerly enough to wait for direction.

"I hate to ask you to do this, but my friend, Dr. Stolz, is here to test you to make sure you don't have the virus."

"We were tested before we left," said Sharon, looking insulted.

"I know, sweetheart, but it doesn't hurt to be careful. You don't want to make Grandma sick, do you?"

They both shook their heads.

"Good girls. Now come with me." They obediently followed her into the kitchen. "This is Dr. Stolz."

"Hey," said Liz. "Ready?"

"Yeck," Jessica said.

"I know," said Liz. "I hate it too, but I'll be quick. I promise." She pointed to a spot in front of her. "Who's first?"

"I'll do it," said Sharon, rolling her eyes. Liz looked up and winked at

Olivia. "Good kids you have here." True to her word, Liz made quick work of testing the girls. To Olivia's relief, they both were negative.

"Okay," said Liz, stowing the testing gear. "Thank you all for your cooperation. Happy Thanksgiving."

"Thanks for the soup," Olivia called after her.

"You're welcome. Hope you enjoy it."

Olivia turned to her granddaughters. "I put you in your old rooms. Can you find the way by yourselves?"

They both nodded.

"After you put your bags away, come down. I need help getting our Thanksgiving feast ready. Will you help me?"

"Yes, Grandma," said Sharon. Jessica stared warily until her sister nudged her with her elbow.

"Yes, Grandma," Jessica repeated in a shy voice.

Olivia heard their chatter as they went up the stairs. Were they comparing notes? Did they think she had gotten old since they'd last seen her?

Sam had been watching the exchange carefully. "They seem like good kids."

"You look relieved."

"I am," Sam admitted with a grin. "Nothing worse than spending time with mouthy girls."

Olivia's phone pinged. She glanced at it and saw the video of Lucy at the front door. "Rev. Bartlett has arrived," she said, heading to the door. She opened it to see one of Lucy's sunny smiles.

"Happy Thanksgiving, Olivia," said Lucy, giving her a quick hug. Lucy was such a naturally affectionate person. It had to be so hard for her not to be able to hug people since the pandemic began.

"Come on in, Lucy. The girls are here, and I'm about to put them to work in the kitchen. You too, if you're willing."

Lucy made a face. "I'm happy to help, but I should warn you I'm not great at cooking."

"You'll just be chopping vegetables. It will set a good example for the girls."

"Always happy to set a good example," said Lucy with another brilliant smile. "I broadcast my Thanksgiving service this morning. That means I'm off duty for the rest of the day. I'm very much looking forward to spending time with you and your family."

"Let me take your coat," offered Olivia.

"I brought my Wellies. In case the girls want to take a walk in the salt marsh with me later when the tide is out."

"I'm sure they would love that."

Sharon came into the room. Her eyes lit up. "Lucy!" She ran in her direction and gave her a hug around the waist.

"Hello, Sharon, so nice to meet you," said Lucy hugging the girl's shoulders.

Jessica bounded into the room. "Lucy!" she squealed and joined her sister in hugging her.

Lucy raised her smiling face to Olivia. "I guess they're glad to see me."

"I guess so," replied Olivia, smiling so she wouldn't appear jealous of Lucy's popularity.

Chapter 16

"Liz, Mrs. Downey is waiting for you in three," said Cherie, standing in the doorway.

Liz looked up from reviewing the end-of-year accounts. "What's going on with her?"

"Too many toasted pumpkin seeds over Thanksgiving."

"Irritating her diverticulosis, is it?"

Cherie gestured to Liz's computer. "Look at her ultrasound and see what you think."

Liz navigated to the ultrasound library and watched. "Doesn't look like anything significant."

"I didn't think so either. Apparently, you put the fear of God in her the last time she came in for a belly ache."

"I'm good at that, they say. Putting the fear of God in people, I mean."

Cherie laughed. "Yes, you are. Should I send her home and tell her to call us if it gets worse?"

"That sounds right. Under other circumstances, I'd consider sending her in for observation, but with the COVID cases going up, there are no beds at Southern Med, or anywhere, really. Tell her to lay off the pumpkin seeds. Any seeds, even berries until things calm down. Tell her to call me if it gets worse."

"Will do," said Cherie and headed out.

Liz watched the ultrasound again to be sure. She was relieved to see nothing worth worrying about. Cherie returned a few minutes later. "She okay with the wait-and-see approach?"

"Yes. She'll call if it gets worse."

"Good." Liz lowered the lid of the laptop. "Cherie, I want to thank you for coming in on Thanksgiving weekend. I'm sure you have plenty to do with your wedding only a few weeks away."

"Everything is pretty much done. When you have your wedding on

Zoom and only invite twenty of your best friends to your catered reception in the fire station, there's not a whole lot to do."

"I'm sorry, Cherie. I know how much you wanted a big, fancy wedding with all your family here. This pandemic sucks."

"What sucks is that my honey wants to be married in her police uniform. I wish you could talk her out of it, Liz. She listens to you."

Liz sighed. "Cherie, it's your wedding too. Can't you change her mind?"

"I've given up. The more I argue, the more determined she seems to be."

"I'm familiar with that aspect of marriage," said Liz, sitting back in her chair. "I think it has to do with scent marking your territory."

"What?" asked Cherie, her blue-green eyes wide. "Did you just say what I thought you said?"

Liz laughed. "Yes, I did."

"I'm glad you think it's funny," said Cherie in an annoyed tone. "After that trooper shot my sister…and me, I couldn't even look at a police uniform. I had panic attacks every time I saw a cop. That's part of why I became a psychotherapist."

"I didn't know that."

Cherie gave her an exaggerated nod. "Truth. And if it wasn't for you and Lucy, Brenda and I would have never gotten this far. But can you imagine living your life being terrified of police uniforms and your spouse wants to wear one at your wedding?"

"I think it's a stupid idea, but that's my opinion."

"Liz, please talk to her. Time is running out. Lucy said you might be able to convince her to wear one of those sharp suits like you wear sometimes."

"Oh, you mean, like when I have to play grown-up?" asked Liz with a chuckle. "It's kind of late for that, Cherie. We'd probably have to go to Boston to find something."

"Aren't you and Brenda the same size?"

"More or less. She's a bit trimmer than I am, since she was sick with COVID. What are you saying, Cherie? You want me to *lend* Brenda a suit?"

"Something borrowed…something blue."

"What about a tux?"

"No. I don't like that role-playing stuff. And I don't want you to wear one either."

"Good. Because a tux only looks good on a flat-chested woman, which, obviously I'm not."

Cherie took a seat in one of the visitors' chairs. "Please, Liz. I really need your help. I know Brenda looks up to you. She respects your opinion."

Liz wasn't sure she wanted to get in the middle of this, especially because Cherie worked for her, but she looked desperate "Okay. I'll see if I can talk Brenda into coming over to try on some of my suits. It would probably be good if they got some wear. Otherwise, I should just put them in the consignment shop."

"See? Everyone benefits. Brenda finds something beautiful to wear to our wedding. Your suits get worn, and I'm happy. Everyone wins. Please, Liz. I can't marry Brenda in her police uniform. I just can't!"

"That means now I have to decide what to wear. You know I still haven't forgiven Brenda for asking Olivia to stand up for her." Liz made a face.

"Liz, she's not that bad. Come on, admit it. She's growing on you."

"Yes, like athlete's foot." Liz glanced at her watch. "It's noon. I guess we're not getting any more patients today. Let's pack up and go home."

"Come over and talk to Brenda. I'll give you lunch. I made gumbo," said Cherie in an enticing tone. "I know it's one of your favorites."

Liz had plans to work in her shop after she finished reviewing the practice's books for the accountants.

"Please," begged Cherie. "It will mean so much to me if you can get her off this crazy idea of wearing her uniform."

"All right. I'll meet you there."

After Cherie left, Liz took out her phone and texted Maggie: *Going to Brenda's for a while. Home soon.*

As she drove to the other side of town, Liz tried to formulate a strategy. She knew how much Brenda loved her police uniform. Brenda had never wanted to be anything but a cop. Her father had been a cop and her grandfather. All her brothers were cops. She liked to say she was "blue through and through."

Liz arrived before Cherie, but she waited in the driveway. She'd told Cherie about that sneaky back road. Maybe she didn't remember. While she waited, Liz checked her phone messages, but there was none from Maggie, which lately wasn't unusual. Even before things had gotten so bad between them, Maggie seldom checked her messages. As Liz scrolled through the others, she smiled when she saw there was one from Lucy: *Thanks for helping me be with Olivia's grandkids. Taking a hike in the estuarine preserve. Such fun.* The message was followed by a string of colored hearts forming a rainbow.

Cherie finally pulled into the driveway. She got out of her Ford Escape and waved.

"Did you forget about the shortcut I told you about?" asked Liz as she approached to help Cherie carry her bags inside.

"No, that road is a mess from the frost heaves last spring. I don't like having my insides jiggled out on the way home."

"I heard it's on the list for repaving."

"About time." Cherie scrutinized Liz briefly. "You and Brenda hear all the gossip about what's going on in town."

"It can be useful from time to time."

"You again?" said Brenda when she opened the door.

Cherie looked hurt. "Is that any way to talk to the woman you're going to marry?"

"I don't mean you, Cherie," Brenda said with a grin. "I meant this riffraff you brought home with you. Hey." She threw an arm around Liz's neck, more like a wrestling hold than a sign of affection. "What? You have to come here for lunch? Maggie's not feeding you anymore?"

"Oh, I can eat leftovers at home too. We have enough turkey to feed an army. But I never turn down Cherie's good Louisiana cooking."

"Come on in."

Liz followed Brenda into the living room.

"Beer? I always offer one to anyone who shows up because I can't have alcohol with the heart meds. Vicarious pleasure."

"Be patient, Brenda. Things may settle down with your heart."

"Dr. Stolz. Eternal optimist."

"Not really. I'm a realist, actually. I'll pass on the beer. It's too early in the day, and I want to work in the shop later."

"So, what brings you besides Cherie's good cooking?"

"Your wife wants me to talk you out of wearing your uniform for the wedding."

Brenda looked startled at first, but she then laughed. "That's what I love about you, Liz. You never mince words."

"In my line of work, I need to get in the maximum consulting time for billing purposes."

"So, is this a house call or are you just offering some friendly advice."

"I really did come for the gumbo."

"Sit down and we'll talk," Brenda said. She sat down and crossed her legs. Liz took the chair opposite her. "I came up with the idea of wearing my uniform so the guys don't have to rent a tux. Besides, I kind of like the idea of a police wedding."

"I know how important your uniform is to you, Brenda, but this is Cherie's wedding too. You've been married before. This is a big event for her. And who's more important to you, your police buddies or the woman you're going to marry?"

"Cherie, of course."

"Right answer."

"So, what should I wear? You are never going to get me into a white dress. And don't even suggest it, Liz. You didn't wear one for your wedding either."

"Hell, no. You'd never get me into one of those things. In my day, heterosexual wedding claptrap was a hated symbol of patriarchal oppression. I would never go there. But Maggie wanted to wear a white dress, so fine. It made her happy."

"What are my alternatives? A tux? I don't really go for that butch-femme thing. I'm a woman."

"Yes, and a fine-looking one at that."

Brenda looked shocked.

"What?" said Liz, staring at her. "I can't pay you a compliment?"

"Don't get any ideas. I'm taken."

"So am I." Liz sat back and took a deep breath. "Now, I know this might sound crazy, but my closet is full of designer suits that I paid good money for but never wear anymore. Even my wedding suit, which has never been out of the plastic since the day I first wore it."

"You want me to borrow your suit? Wouldn't it be weird for me to wear your wedding suit?"

"As Cherie reminded me…something borrowed, something blue. If you were a guy renting a tux, you're technically borrowing it, right?"

"I guess so. Well, we are the same size. I suppose I could try on a few of your suits."

"They'll probably fit you better since you've been laying off the brews, and I haven't."

"But I'd have to wear heels."

"Yeah, I don't think your service shoes will go with a ladies suit, but you don't have to wear spiked heels. We can find you something more comfortable." Liz measured about three inches with her thumb and forefinger.

Brenda screwed up her face.

"Brenda, it's *one day*. You're going to be living with Cherie for the rest of your life, and you need to keep her happy. Start now. Plus, then I can wear a suit too. My tits are too big for a tux."

Brenda laughed out loud. "It's all about you."

"Always."

"That's not true. If it were, you wouldn't be here. Okay, Liz, I'll take a look at what's in your closet. Can I come over tomorrow when I go off duty?"

Liz mentally scanned her schedule. "Sure, that will be fine. Around four-thirty works. I should be home by then."

Cherie came to tell them that lunch was ready.

"I'm going over after work tomorrow to try on some of Liz's suits," said Brenda.

Cherie turned her eyes in Liz's direction. "How did you manage that? I've been begging her for weeks!"

Liz shrugged. "I gave her permission not to be an asshole."

"Don't get your hopes up, Cherie," warned Brenda. "I'm only going over to look. No promises."

"Brenda, get your foot out of your mouth," Liz said under her breath after Cherie returned to the kitchen. "If she's happy, you'll be happy."

Chapter 17

As Maggie waited for her sandwich to be delivered to her car, she thought about her therapy session. She liked the woman Lucy had recommended. Gloria Parrish was a woman in her seventies with short hair and a kind, open face. She wore hearing aids, which had put Maggie off at first. Then she realized that wanting to catch every nuance of what her clients said was a good thing. It showed a caring Maggie hadn't expected, although she hadn't really known what to expect based on Lucy saying this therapist "might be right" for her.

"I'm a lesbian," Maggie had announced after introducing herself.

Gloria's eyes smiled rather than her mouth. "That's nice."

"I want you to know up front, in case you have any issues with gay people."

Gloria chuckled softly. "I don't. I'm a lesbian myself."

Maggie's face flamed. What a way to make an impression! But Gloria didn't seem to hold it against her. She waited patiently for Maggie to say more. When she didn't, Gloria said, "this session is really to see if we're right for one another. I've limited my practice to a few clients, so no commitments either way until we see if we can work together."

That was unexpected too. When did therapists start auditioning clients? "Lucy Bartlett said you could help me."

"She may be right, but let's see. Why are you interested in therapy?"

"It's a long story, but I did something I regret and I'm trying to figure out what to do about it."

"Ah, what did you do?"

"I had an affair with a man. My wife doesn't know about it."

Gloria's face remained completely impassive. What seemed so dramatic to Maggie hadn't even caused her to blink.

"Do you intend to tell your wife about it?"

"That's what I need to figure out. Why I had the affair and what to do about it."

"Is the affair still going on?"

"No, it was a fling. He's much younger. Well, relatively young…in his forties. Very handsome. An actor I worked with at the State Theater. We were doing this special social-distanced version of *The Glass Menagerie* for broadcast. It's one of my favorite plays." From the patient look on Gloria's face, Maggie realized she probably didn't care about which plays were her favorites. She reminded herself to stay on task. "I got involved with him because he was a big fan of mine. I found that very attractive."

"You're a professional actress, I take it."

"I was…or I tried to be. I had a hit on Broadway in the eighties. My husband didn't approve, so I settled for a career in academia. I went back to school and got a PhD from Yale. I taught at NYU for years before I came up here. I was hoping for a comeback by doing summer stock at the Webhanet Playhouse when I met my wife. I broke my leg during a performance, and she set the break."

"Your wife is a physician?"

"Yes, she owns Hobbs Family Practice. She bought it when she retired as chief of surgery at Yale New Haven. She used to do surgery, but she was cutting back. Then, last year when COVID forced the cancellation of elective surgeries, she quit completely. She said it was just as well. Arthritis makes her hands stiff." Maggie realized she was meandering again and telling this woman things that were both irrelevant and none of her business.

"Tell me more about your relationship with your wife," Gloria suggested.

She resolved to get back on topic. "We were college lovers, but my parents forced me to break it off when they found out. When we met again after forty years, we took it as a sign that we'd always been meant to be together."

"Fated love."

"Yes, so it seemed."

"But now it doesn't?"

"She cheated on me. She kissed my best friend." Maggie caught herself before blurting out Lucy's name. If she and Gloria knew each other, it was probably better to leave her out of the conversation.

"You consider a kiss cheating?"

"Wouldn't you?"

"It depends. Was there more after the kiss?"

"Liz says no, but I don't know what to believe anymore."

"So, the kiss broke the trust for you?"

"Yes. Liz and this woman have been flirting since they met, but everyone thought it was just a game. The other woman is very attractive, gorgeous in fact. She could have been a model like her mom. Everyone falls in love with her."

"It sounds like you had an affair with this young man in retaliation. Is that true?"

"Pretty much. I wanted to do something that would really hurt Liz. I used to date men while we were involved in college. It drove her nuts. All these years later, Liz still seethes whenever I talk about my ex-husband."

Gloria glanced out the window, obviously buying herself a moment to think.

"You did something that you knew would infuriate her. Were you *trying* to end the relationship?"

"My priest asked me that question. That's why I'm here. And to figure out if I should tell Liz about the affair, and if I do, how."

"Okay. I get the picture." Gloria thought for a moment. "Have you considered marriage counseling?"

Maggie shook her head. "Liz would never do it. She hates 'shrinks' as she calls them. Not all of them, of course. She works with them professionally as a family doctor. She tolerates them and finds them useful. Just not for her."

"Does she have a reason for her dislike?"

"She told me that when she was coming out and really needed therapy, having treatment for a mental illness could have prevented her from getting a medical license."

Gloria looked pensive, and Maggie guessed she was calculating the era when Liz would have been in training. "She's probably right about that," she concluded.

"I've tried changing her mind, but Liz is like a brick about certain things."

"Aren't we all?"

Gloria smiled, and Maggie saw a hint of her sense of humor. The remainder of the session was a review of Maggie's relationships and how they had ended. By the end of that summary, Maggie felt like an even bigger failure. "Everyone cheats on me," she concluded.

"You don't know that Liz actually cheated. She may want to cheat, but so far, it seems there's only been a kiss."

"She avoids Lucy now. Whoops. I didn't mean for that to slip out."

"It's all right, nothing leaves this room. But now I know why Rev. Bartlett sent you here instead of dealing with it herself," said Gloria with a nod. She frowned. "Does your wife know you're in counseling?"

"No. And I don't intend to tell her…at least, not for now."

"How long have you been married?"

"Seven years this past October."

"And was this her first long-term relationship?"

"No, she was with her ex for over twenty years. They were still sort of together when we met after the accident. But they were always cheating on one another."

"You mean they had an open relationship."

"Yes, although that's a nice way to put it."

"They agreed to be polyamorous. It's one way to be in a relationship. It's hard to do and doesn't work for everyone, but it works for some people. Obviously, you have strong negative feelings about the idea."

"It's not wrong to expect fidelity!" Maggie realized she sounded defensive and needed to dial back the tone. "I mean how can you trust someone after they cheat?"

"If there's an agreement to have an open relationship beforehand, it's not really cheating."

"But we got married! We promised to be the only one for each other."

"Then that's the agreement you made. Which is not to say it couldn't be renegotiated." As Gloria studied her face, Maggie forced herself to assume a pleasant expression. She felt like she was being probed and suddenly had a flashback to all the fertility exams she had early in her marriage to Barry. The doctors peering into her vagina. All the focus had been on her, when Barry had been the culprit all along.

"In kissing your friend, your wife pressed your buttons about cheating. In sleeping with a man, you were trying to press her buttons about your heterosexual past. Is that correct?"

"Correct."

"Maggie, I need to ask this question. Are you really a lesbian? Maybe you're bisexual."

"Maybe I am. I can be excited by men and respond to them sexually. I enjoy sex with men. I was married for over twenty-five years. It's what I'm used to."

"Of course. How is your intimate relationship with your wife?"

"It had been tapering off before all this happened. I had breast cancer seven years ago, and I'm positive for the BRCA2 gene. I take tamoxifen every day. It depresses the libido."

"Yes, I know. It's hard enough for older women without taking a drug that blocks estrogen."

"Exactly. But age hasn't deterred Liz. She's always raring to go. I feel bad when I have to fend her off. She doesn't always take it well."

"Were your needs always out of balance?"

"No, in the beginning, we both loved having sex."

"Not uncommon," said Gloria. She tried to be subtle about it, but Maggie could see her glancing at the clock set strategically across the room. "All right, Maggie. Let's see where the conversation we've started today takes us." Gloria picked up an appointment book. "I have Saturday mornings at ten o'clock open. Would that work for you?"

Maggie said that it did.

Lost in her thoughts about the session, Maggie jumped at the sound of someone gently tapping on the glass of her car window. "Order for Fitzgerald. Cuban sandwich."

"Thanks," said Maggie and handed the server a ten-dollar bill in addition to the tip. The restaurants had been hurt by the pandemic, but the wait staff was being crushed.

As she rolled up the window, Maggie wondered if she should have ordered a sandwich for Liz. It was one of her favorite things to eat when they came to Portsmouth. She'd introduced Maggie to this restaurant after the mammogram that confirmed her cancer. Maggie glanced at the dashboard clock. It was already past two. If Liz had headed to Brenda's as her text had indicated, Cherie would have given her lunch by now. Besides, a Cuban sandwich had to be eaten fresh. Maggie spread out the dish towel she carried to guard her clothes when she ate in the car. She closed her eyes when she bit into the sandwich to savor the taste.

She noticed two young women crossing the street and guessed they were students at UNH. Portsmouth was a college town. One had her hand in the other's pocket. Young lesbians were so bold now. When Maggie and Liz had been in college, they dared not even look at one another in public. Maggie watched the women head down the street. As they turned the corner, they linked arms.

Funny how that gesture, once so common among all women, now meant overt sexual interest. Did heterosexual women link arms anymore? They'd had a debate on this subject when they were blocking South Pacific two summers ago. Tony Roselli was arguing for a period-appropriate detail, but the director, a much younger woman wasn't interested. Could the generational divide really be that deep? Sometimes, it seemed that young women were so different. They were much more open about their sexuality and yet more moralistic at the same time. The alphabet soup of LGBTQ+ just got bigger all the time. When she was still teaching, Maggie thought she understood something about young people. Now, she wasn't so sure.

Maggie's phone rang. She wrapped up the Cubano and wiped the bright-yellow mustard on her fingertips on the dish towel. *Oh, well. It needs to be washed anyway.* She had to search through the pockets of her handbag before she found her phone. By then the call had gone into voice mail. She listened to Liz's anxious message and realized she should return the call.

"Where the fuck are you?" demanded Liz in an irritated tone when she answered. "I thought you'd died. Didn't you get my text?"

"Yes, and I meant to respond, but I was driving when I got it, and then I was in a meeting."

"Oh?"

"Nothing important," said Maggie. She knew Liz wouldn't expect her to account for her time, although if the situation were reversed, Maggie would certainly have asked where she'd been, suspicious she might be with Lucy. "I'm in Portsmouth having a Cuban sandwich."

"And you didn't ask if I wanted one?"

"Haven't you eaten already?"

"Yes, Cherie fed me some of her delicious gumbo. I'll tell you all about it when you get home."

"Okay," said Maggie. She felt so guilty when she hung up. Liz sounded so ordinary in her faux grumpiness. She had no idea anything was wrong. *If only she knew…* At that thought, Maggie felt a chill inside.

Chapter 18

Asurprising number of parishioners had shown up for the outdoor service in the churchyard. The November cold and chilly wind off the ocean made it impractical to open the summer chapel. Lucy had decided to offer the Eucharist to the intrepid souls who wouldn't mind setting up a beach chair near the graves of the town's forebears. For sanitary reasons, the Communion wine had been distributed into single-serve, plastic condiment containers. Lucy had come up with the idea when she'd ordered Chinese takeout on one of her nights to cook. Funny how inspiration during the pandemic came from the strangest places.

"Brilliant," Tom Simmons had concluded when Lucy first used the containers to bring Communion on a hospital call. "Why didn't we think of this before?"

"We never expected it to last this long," Lucy had replied, which was true. Everyone had hoped the pandemic would be over by now.

"Leave it to a woman to come up with such a practical solution," Tom said with a fond smile. Lucy knew the compliment was completely sincere. Tom was one of her biggest fans, both as an opera lover and as her associate rector. He'd given up a prestigious post as rector of a large, historic church in Connecticut to come to St. Margaret's.

She knew he had reasons other than his admiration for Lucy. At sixty-four, he finally felt comfortable expressing his sexuality. Nearby Webhanet was a haven for gay men. And there was other history to connect them. He had briefly been Erika's lover, when they were both trying out heterosexuality before figuring out it wasn't for them. Even Liz knew him from her early days at Yale. Now, their long-ago friendship had been successfully transplanted to Hobbs in a new incarnation.

Lucy watched her parishioners arrive. Over two dozen people had gathered for the churchyard service, despite a thermometer reading in the thirties. Lucy wore thermal underwear, double-weave black jeans, and a polar fleece jacket under her vestments. At the last minute, she added gloves and a black hat with a pompom on top to her outfit. It looked a little like a biretta, not that Lucy ever wore one. They reminded her too much of the Roman Catholic priests of her youth, especially the leering monsignor in her parish. Even as a girl, she knew enough to avoid him. He was later arrested for pedophilia. Newspapers all over the country carried the sordid details of the case.

Lucy was pleased to see all her regulars were there—Maggie Fitzgerald, who would gallantly lead the singing despite the cold, Olivia and Sam, Cherie and Brenda, the vestry members, of course, and a few of her elderly parishioners. Her breath coming as vapor, Lucy kept her sermon short. They distributed the hosts and Communion wine to the congregation where they sat to save time. Instead of the usual greeting line after the service, people called their hellos and good wishes to their rector as they collected their chairs and headed toward the parking lot.

When Lucy heard a voice behind her, she almost jumped. She turned around and looked into a familiar face.

"I'm sorry. I didn't mean to startle you," said Brenda, her eyes smiling above the Hobbs Police Department mask. "I tried to get your attention."

"I'm sorry, Brenda. I can't hear right with this woolly hat on, but I needed something to keep my ears warm."

"I understand," said Brenda, touching her watch cap and an embroidered Hobbs Police logo. "Thank you for doing this. We all really appreciate it. Never thought of holding a service in a churchyard except for a funeral."

"The early Christians held all their services in the catacombs, where their dead were buried. That's why cemeteries were usually next to the church." Lucy glanced around. "Where's Cherie?"

"We came separately. I'm on duty this afternoon." Lucy looked down and saw that Brenda was wearing her striped uniform trousers and service shoes. "I'm covering for one of my officers who came down with a bug."

"Not COVID, I hope?" Lucy asked anxiously.

"No, thank God, just a stomach thing. I think they left their turkey out too long." Brenda collapsed the chair Lucy had been using during the service. "I'll carry this for you. You already have enough to carry." She nodded to the plastic washtub containing the lectionary and cloths for the makeshift altar. "Where are we going with this?" Brenda asked.

"Into the church. I need to take off my vestments."

"Do you have a couple of minutes for me after you do?" asked Brenda with a smile. "See? I had an ulterior motive for wanting to carry your chair. I wasn't just being chivalrous."

"You don't have to barter for my time, but I do appreciate that you've continued to tithe while we weren't holding live services."

"Oh, I've got it on autopilot now."

"That's how I know. I can see who contributes."

Brenda pulled open the heavy church door and held it back for Lucy to enter.

The old building felt so empty and cold from lack of use. The parish was saving on the heating bill without holding services indoors, but the ancient wood dated back to colonial times. Sometimes, dampness made it smell its age. "Have a seat in one of the pews while I take off my vestments. I'll just be a minute."

After she took off the layers of vestments, Lucy felt the chill in the old church. She was glad she thought to wear a black polar fleece and her collar under her vestments. At least, she looked like a priest. When she'd dressed that morning, she hadn't anticipated any official duties after the Eucharist, but she should have known better. A priest, like a doctor, was always on call.

When she came out of the vesting room, she saw Brenda, gazing reflectively at the rose window in the front of the church. Lucy genuflected to the altar and slid into the pew in front of her. "You look deep in thought. Is everything okay?" she asked, leaning on the back of the pew.

"Yes, fine." Brenda said with shrug. "Pretty much fine, I mean."

"Do you want to go to the rectory or talk here?"

"I don't have much time, so here works better."

"A lot of people find this a good place to talk," said Lucy, glancing at the altar.

Brenda's eyes took the measure of the chancel. "I miss coming to this old church. Marcia and I renewed our vows here before she died."

"Is that what you were thinking about before I came?"

Brenda nodded. "I really miss her, and that's why I'm worried. I'm not sure I can go through with this wedding."

"But I thought you and Cherie had everything worked out."

"We did. It has nothing to do with the wedding itself." Brenda sucked in a huge sigh. "I'm afraid." She pursed her lips. Admitting fear must be difficult for a police officer, Lucy reasoned, especially one who'd been decorated for bravery in the line of duty. "When Marcia died it was the worst pain I ever felt. It was like that car had hit me instead of her. Everything was dark for months. I was lucky they gave me leave from the force because I was a fucking mess." She glanced anxiously at Lucy. "Sorry for the language."

Lucy shrugged. "I've heard that word before." She reached out for Brenda's hand and gave it a squeeze. "Are you worried you'll lose Cherie?"

"No, I'm worried she'll lose me. I love her so much! I can't even think about her bearing that awful pain I felt when I lost Marcia."

"But Brenda, your heart problems are under control. Liz thinks you'll eventually heal completely. I've heard her say it."

"Liz is an optimist."

"I don't want to argue with you, Brenda, but I've always found Liz to be honest and direct. If she tells you there's a good chance for a full recovery, I'd believe her."

"My heart function was dangerously low. I could have died."

"Yes, many people have died from COVID. Many more will. It's a terrible disease. But you lived, and you're healthy enough to go back to work. Look at you, sitting there in your uniform, ready to pitch in and cover for a member of your team. Your recovery was a gift."

"Yes, I know, and I'm grateful, but who knows what lies ahead. Liz says they're discovering new complications all the time…brain disease…blood clots that can kill you, even after you recover and seem healthy."

Lucy took a deep breath and let it out slowly, so she wouldn't sound impatient. "Brenda, we all die. We don't know when, which is lucky for us. If we did, we might never get out of bed in the morning. Not only do we die, but people we love die. Grief is the price we pay for loving people. But the joy of love is more than worth the pain of grief."

"The only reason I want to get married now is so that Cherie will get my pensions if something happens to me."

"You've said that before, but you know in your heart that's not why you're marrying her. Now, tell me the real reason."

"Because I love her and want to spend the rest of my life with her."

"That's right. Because you love her and want to be with her. All the other reasons, no matter how good and how practical, don't really matter."

"But what if I die?"

"Then you'll die having loved Cherie as much as you can for as long as you can. You'll die as her spouse."

Brenda frowned. Then her face looked thoughtful as she considered Lucy's words. "Thank you for not bringing in all the religious stuff. I mean, I believe but sometimes, it sounds like just words."

"I know what you mean. I don't like hearing empty words either." Lucy got up to sit in the same pew with Brenda. "Let's just sit here together for a little while."

"You mean and pray?"

"You can pray if you want. I just want to sit in your presence and you in mine. I just want to be in this beautiful church with you next to me."

Tears suddenly came to Brenda's eyes. "That's the kindest thing anyone has ever said to me."

"Sometimes, the greatest kindness is to be quiet with someone who's struggling or in pain." She reached for Brenda's hand. "I'm here for you, Brenda." She smiled and faced forward. "Now, let's just be quiet together."

They sat without speaking for about five minutes before Brenda began to get fidgety. She released Lucy's hand and wiped hers on her pants because it had become sweaty. Lucy resisted the impulse to do the same because it might seem like a rejection. "How are you doing?" she asked in a tender voice.

"I'm better. How do you do that?" asked Brenda with a grin.

"I didn't do anything."

"It must be magic."

"It's not magic," Lucy assured her. "Anyone can do it."

"I wish I could sit here and talk to you more, but I've got to get to work. Thank you, Lucy, for your time."

"Time is the greatest gift you can give anyone. Give Cherie your time, however long or short it is. Give her your love."

"I will," Brenda said, getting to her feet. Lucy got up too. Otherwise, Brenda would have to crawl over her. Brenda leaned down to give her a hug. "Thanks. You are the best priest we ever had and the only reason I come to church."

Lucy laughed softly. "Tell the truth. You come to church because Cherie makes you come."

Brenda rolled her eyes and affected an innocent look. "I also come because of you. What you say always makes sense."

As Lucy watched Brenda head to the door, she reflected that of all of her jobs as a priest, listening was the most important.

As she drove home, she thought about Brenda and Cherie, both survivors of a virus that had already taken so many. How many of those people would have imagined only a year before that they'd be dead of a yet unknown illness? No, there were no guarantees. Living life joyously and fully was the only way to thank God for the gift of life.

"You're looking solemn," said Erika when she met her at the door. "Didn't your frigid worship service go well?"

"Oh, it went extremely well. More people showed up than I ever expected. I had a parishioner who needed my time afterward. That's why I'm a little late."

"I'm so sorry I couldn't be there to root you on."

"I know you're busy with all those end-of-the-year faculty evaluations."

"I hated personnel duties when I was department chair, and I hate it filling in for the chair. Fortunately, the provost's office has decided to give me a big bonus for my volunteer duty. I was surprised because the college is apparently losing a great deal of money without the students on campus."

"At least, they're showing you some appreciation," said Lucy, reaching up to pull Erika down into a kiss. "And they should. You're wonderful. And if anyone doesn't know, I'll tell them."

"My fan club."

"Oh, you have other fans. Like your friend, Liz."

"Yes, what's wrong with Liz? We never see her anymore."

Lucy shrugged although she knew the reason for Liz's absence.

Erika gave her a canny look. "Lucy! Don't you dare use ethics as an excuse not to tell me. You're talking to her as a friend, not a therapist."

Lucy shrugged, but couldn't stop herself from smiling. "I don't tell my friends' secrets. It has nothing to do with professional ethics. If you're so curious, why don't you call Liz yourself? I'm sure she'd love to hear from you, and she might even bring along some of that single-malt scotch you like so much."

"Hmm. That's not a bad idea. I might just call her."

"But not tonight," said Lucy, running her hands up from Erika's waist to give her breasts an affectionate caress. "I have plans for you."

"Before or after dinner?"

"Oh, afterwards, I think. Once I get you into bed, I won't want to let you go." Remembering her talk with Brenda, she drew Erika down into a kiss and fervently willed her to feel all the love she felt in her heart.

Chapter 19

Olivia glanced across the room and caught Sam admiring her legs. The slit in her dress showed only a hint when she stood with her legs together, so Olivia adjusted her stance to improve the view. Sam's eyes grew large. Olivia cocked a warning brow in Sam's direction, but she was enjoying the attention. It almost distracted her from the speech she was about to give honoring Brenda.

She'd found the idea of a wedding reception in a fire station odd at first, but now, she had to admit it had a wonderful, small-town charm. A year ago, she wouldn't be caught dead at such an event, but now she was proud to share it with her friends. Liz, who was acting as the AV technician, had installed an amazing audio system, complete with chest-pounding bass. She approached and handed Olivia the microphone she had just sanitized.

"Hello, everyone," Olivia began in a perfectly modulated voice. She was used to addressing a crowd. "Thank you for coming out today to honor Cherie and Brenda on their special day. Let's all give them a hand."

The guests, sitting at carefully spaced tables in pairs or groups depending on test status and household arrangements, applauded enthusiastically.

"Now, it is my solemn duty to speak as Brenda's 'best woman.' I'm also her boss, but that doesn't count today, when her only real boss is her new spouse." There was a murmur of laughter, but Olivia saw Sam roll her eyes and realized she should probably back off that kind of talk. "I know it's traditional to roast the bridal pair, especially the groom, but since this is an unconventional wedding, I can take some liberties." She paused for effect and noticed that even Lucy looked anxious about what might follow that remark. Olivia loved to keep people guessing. "Sorry to disappoint. To parody the Bard, I come not to roast Brenda, but to praise her." People in the audience were making faces. Maybe the literary references weren't landing well. "We all love Chief Harrison. Not only is she, by general acclaim, the best police chief Hobbs ever had, but she is a brave woman. She worked homicide on the NYPD for twenty years in some of the toughest neighborhoods in Brooklyn. She was decorated for bravery twice and received the mayor's award for a video training series, that is still used many years later by police departments all over the country."

She paused to allow the crowd to applaud. Brenda glanced at Sam who was giving her the thumbs up.

"I bet most of you didn't know that your police chief was such a celebrity. Well, maybe you've seen Chief Harrison on Fox News and News Center Maine, explaining the best way to handle volatile racial situations and promoting compassionate policing. Sometimes, I'm a little jealous she gets so much attention from the press, but she certainly deserves it because…she's the real deal. On a personal note, I want to say how honored I am that Brenda chose me as her witness on the day she's marrying the lovely Cherie Bois. I am even more honored that Brenda calls me her friend. There is no one braver, more loyal, and kinder than Brenda. Congratulations to both of you on your marriage." Olivia raised her glass. "Hear, hear."

People jumped up from their seats to applaud. Brenda's captains and officers whistled and cheered. Olivia saw a single tear run down Brenda's check. She touched her fingertips to her lips and threw Brenda a kiss.

Olivia returned to her seat. "Well, how did it go?" she asked.

"Sounded like you were giving her the award for police chief of the year instead of a wedding speech, but it worked. People liked it." Sam put her arm around Olivia. "You looked really hot up there."

"I could see how much you like my dress." Olivia ran her hand along the inside of Sam's thigh. "You look pretty hot yourself in this silk suit. You clean up well."

The official wedding photographer came by to focus a picture. "Smile, ladies!" Olivia snatched her hand back from Sam's leg.

"That will probably be in the paper," murmured Olivia with a frown. "If everyone didn't already know the town manager is gay, they will now."

"Oh, stop worrying. People in Hobbs are pretty cool. They won't hold it against you."

"Why not? They won't let me get away with anything else!"

An oversized TV flashed on, showing Cherie's aunt beaming warmly at her niece. She was dressed in a wide-brimmed hat that matched her dress and coordinated with the beads in her necklace. She spoke warmly of Cherie and told stories of when her niece was a girl in Louisiana. "I'm so proud of you. And Cherie girl, your mama is looking down from heaven, and I know she's proud too."

"Well, that's amazing," said Sam.

"What do you know that I don't know?" asked Olivia with a frown.

"Cherie just came out to that aunt. She's old school. Cherie wasn't sure she would even come to the wedding, but there she is, and she looks happy."

Olivia leaned closer so she could speak discreetly, not that anyone was close enough to hear with the social distancing. "Cherie looks so happy. She is absolutely beautiful. And Brenda looks so chic in that suit. Was it really Liz's wedding suit?"

"It was. I was there."

Olivia glanced across the room and saw Maggie sitting alone because Liz was so busy with the technical details. Maggie's smile looked completely fake. Olivia always recognized a plastic smile when she saw one, because she knew the effort it took to hold that pose. She studied Maggie's eyes and saw sadness. Olivia scanned the room for Liz and found her chatting with one of Brenda's captains in the bridal party. For someone who could be so blunt, even grumpy, Liz certainly knew how to work a room. She appeared to be having fun, while her spouse sat, looking miserable.

"I'm going to go over and say hello to Maggie Fitzgerald," Olivia said, patting Sam on the knee.

"I'll come with you."

Olivia was half-way across the dance floor before Sam caught up to her. She took one of the chairs set six feet away and moved it closer. "Hello, Maggie, are you enjoying the wedding?"

Maggie shrugged. "All wedding receptions are pretty much the same, aren't they?"

"Not always." Olivia gave Maggie a critical once over. She was wearing her white hair in a dramatic upsweep and was made up glamorously. Olivia assumed that was for the entertainment that had been planned for later. She glanced over and saw that Lucy had changed out of her cassock into an elegant, green dress, probably for the same reason. "This wedding is certainly unique, a same-sex wedding between a police chief and a mixed-race woman who hates the police. That's pretty sensational. I'm sure it will make the papers."

"Probably. Brenda is a big deal in this town." Maggie narrowed her eyes. "It's strange seeing her in Liz's suit."

"I bet it brings back happy memories."

"Not really. We argued so much about what she would wear. Of course, a white wedding gown was out of the question."

Olivia laughed. "I don't know Liz as well as you do, but I could have told you that."

Maggie gave her a long, pensive look. "A lot of people think they know Liz, but they really don't."

Olivia wasn't going to touch that one. "I'm looking forward to your entertainment with Mother Lucy."

Maggie's face brightened. "I'm looking forward to it too. I hardly get a chance to be on stage anymore. The theaters are all shut down. Hopefully, the Webhanet Playhouse will have a season this year. Tony Rosselli wants to revive the production of *Mamma Mia*. Maybe this time, I'll make it through the run of the show."

"What do you mean?"

"Oh, you must have heard the story of how I broke my leg in a trampoline accident."

Olivia shook her head. "No, I never have."

"That's what brought me and Liz back together after forty years. She set my leg in her office." Maggie made a snapping gesture by twisting her fists. "Just like that!"

"That was brave. No one does that anymore."

"Well, you know Liz. She's an old-fashioned doctor."

"Yes, that's what I like about her. I hope she never retires."

"I hope she does. Soon."

Olivia tried not to look surprised at that remark.

"We always talked about traveling," Maggie explained, "and we did the first few years we were married. We traveled through Europe, Japan, India, Morocco. It was fun. But Liz doesn't have time for such things now. She's so involved in everything."

"Yes, she is a busy girl, your wife. Keeps her young, I think."

"It's that damn boat. It's her new, favorite thing."

"Don't you enjoy the boat?"

"I get seasick."

"Oh, I'm sorry to hear that," said Olivia in a sympathetic voice, but even she could hear how fake it sounded. "Sam really enjoys fishing with Liz and Brenda. I wouldn't mind going along, but it seems to be their thing, if you know what I mean."

"I do. Unfortunately."

Maggie perked up. "There's Lucy signaling to me. I suppose it's time to start the show." Maggie got up. "Excuse me, Olivia. I'll catch you later."

Olivia nudged Sam. "Let's go back to our table. The view from there is better." As soon as they sat down, Olivia asked. "What's going on with Maggie? She looks so unhappy."

Sam shrugged.

"Sam, you know something!"

"It's her business."

Olivia huffed. "What good are you?" she said and dramatically folded her arms on her chest.

"You should be glad I keep my friends' confidences, including yours."

"I value discretion, so yes, I do." She gently stroked Sam's thigh. "You are so honorable."

"I try," said Sam, grinning.

Liz dimmed the lights and counted down the cue to the recorded accompaniment. Maggie and Lucy came out on to the dance floor holding hands. "We know that female friendship can be complicated, so we're going to sing some of our favorite duets from Broadway," Maggie announced. "The first song is 'For Good' from the musical, Wicked."

Olivia sat back to enjoy the show, wondering if the wedding guests had any idea what talent they were witnessing—a retired Broadway star, and a principal soprano at the Metropolitan Opera. Their singing and stage moves were perfect. Clearly, Maggie was in her element, transformed from the woman who'd looked so depressed only a moment ago into an enthusiastic musical actress. They sang more Broadway songs, sometimes separately, sometimes as duets.

Lucy stepped forward, "Each of our newly wedded ladies has asked me to sing an aria. If opera isn't your thing, this might be a good time to head out for a pit stop or to get a beer from the bar, but I hope you'll stay and listen."

Olivia watched the crowd, expecting a few departures, but not a single person moved. The introduction to the piece began. Olivia sat up straight, completely attentive. She had never heard the famous soprano, Lucille Bartlett, sing opera live. The hair went up on her arms as she began to sing "*Casta Diva*" from *Norma*. Everything she'd read about Lucy's singing was true. What power and beauty that voice had! How could this talented woman ever give up singing professionally? Then she stopped thinking about it and listened.

When the aria ended, there was silence. Olivia glanced around the room. She would be furious if these Maine yahoos refused to appreciate such an outstanding performance. Then Paul Duvaney, the fire chief, jumped up and began smacking his hands together. "Brava!" he shouted at the top of his lungs. He whistled shrilly through his teeth. *That ham-handed oaf was an opera fan?* Olivia stared in amazement. The audience continued to applaud. Erika, clapping modestly, regarded her wife with a sweet look of love and pride. Finally, the applause died.

"All right," said Lucy, who had no need for a microphone to project her voice. "Which partner in our newly-married couple chose that aria? Come on. You have a fifty-fifty chance of being right."

Liz raised her hand. "Cherie."

"Right! You know your people, Dr. Stolz."

"Okay. One more, and then Maggie and I will take requests. Now, you know by process of elimination that Brenda chose the aria I am about to sing."

"I had a little help from a friend," said Brenda, vigorously pointing at Cherie.

"For Cherie from Brenda," said Lucy, throwing a kiss in their direction. She signaled Liz to start the accompaniment and began to sing *"Un bel di Vedremo"* from *Madame Butterfly*.

Olivia was stunned. This woman was a priest in a small town in Maine? All this time Olivia had been locked up in her big house on Gull Island, she'd had no idea this level of culture existed in Hobbs. She looked around at the others in the room, scrutinizing their faces. They were ordinary people, mostly police and fire officers. They were just as taken with the performance as she was. In the back of the room, Liz Stolz was watching the singer with a look of abject adoration. Olivia followed her line of vision and realized Lucy's eyes were locked on Liz's gaze.

So, that was Mother Lucy's secret!

Part III

THE LONGEST NIGHT

Chapter 20

"I must admit that no one knows how to throw a party like Liz and Maggie," said Erika taking off her coat and hanging it in the hall closet. She took Lucy's coat from her and hung it up too. "They were mostly on good behavior, except for that little spat in the kitchen, when they thought no one was listening, but the tension in that house was palpable!" She turned to Lucy and scrutinized her face for a reaction. As usual, when anyone spoke of their friends, Lucy's expression was completely neutral. "You can't fool me with that deadpan look, Mother Lucy. Remember I know you!"

Lucy raised her auburn brows. "Then you know I never tell anyone what my friends tell me. Liz and Maggie can both talk to me because they know I'll keep their confidence. I want to keep it that way."

"But Liz is my dearest friend. I trust her with my life. She knows all my deepest secrets."

"All of them?" One of Lucy's brows now arched higher than the other.

"Well, she doesn't know about the extensive collection of dildos you have amassed."

Lucy eyes grew wide. "It's not 'extensive' and 'amassed' is a dramatic word."

"You know how I enjoy hyperbole. Next to sarcasm, it's my favorite verbal tool."

"So I've noticed."

"How about some of that lovely Bordeaux we had with dinner last night?"

"There's some left?" asked Lucy with surprise.

"Good God, no! I opened another bottle after you finished the first one."

Lucy gave her "the look," which caused Erika to smile. "Apologies for taking the Lord's name in vain," she said, "but you really bent your elbow last night. I shall open another bottle to breathe in anticipation of another thirsty night."

"Don't bother. I had enough wine at the holiday party."

"I was thinking of myself, dear. If that's allowed…"

Lucy gave Erika a light punch on the arm.

"Careful, love. It's still painful from the shot."

Lucy instantly looked sympathetic. "I'm sorry, baby. I forgot." Lucy kissed the spot where she had punched Erika. "There. It should be all better now."

Erika laughed and kissed the top of Lucy's head. "You are so childlike sometimes. It's adorable. Let me see to the wine."

Erika went into the kitchen to open a new bottle of the Bordeaux and poured two glasses from the previously opened bottle. She always liked to use the stem wine glasses, having a ridiculous number of fancy wine glasses from when Jeanine decided that being an oenophile was something she'd like to add to her list of affectations. There were sturdy burgundy glasses as well as delicate glasses with a curve for concentrating the vapors of pinots and cabernets, even German Riesling glasses with green, ringed stems. And that was only part of the collection. Erika smiled at the memory of her departed lover and her amazing zest for learning new things. It was one of the things she had treasured about her.

"You're not having any reaction to the vaccine this time?" asked Erika as she returned to the room.

"My arm is really itchy where I got the shot, and it hurts a little."

"Liz says that means we got the real thing and not the placebo."

Lucy reached for the wine glass Erika offered. "She told me they'll probably unmask who got what now that the vaccine is so near approval. That means those who didn't get the vaccine will likely go to the front of the line for the real thing."

"Does it worry you that we've been guinea pigs?" asked Erika.

"No. I trust Liz. She wouldn't give us anything she didn't think was safe."

"Especially not you," said Erika.

"Stop. We've both been on good behavior."

"I gave you permission to sleep with her whenever you want." Erika affected nonchalance, but out of the corner of her eye, she watched Lucy's reaction carefully.

"I took a vow to give my body to you, and to you alone, and I will keep it. 'Till death do us part.'"

"Such a loyal wife," said Erika with a smile, "but we can renegotiate, if you wish." She took a sip of wine. "Always better when it breathes a little."

"Brenda was telling me she still has many officers who refuse to get the vaccine. She can't order them to be vaccinated, but she's disappointed."

"I'm sure they're the same people who grumbled about wearing a mask. That orange man told them it's a hoax, so of course, it is. Then that stupid stunt—ripping off his mask after he had COVID as if he were some kind of superhero! Right-wing men have their masculinity wrapped around the virus, and their president is setting the worst example. Thank God, he was defeated."

When Lucy sighed, Erika realized she'd taken the Lord's name in vain again. This time, she didn't bother to apologize. It was pointless. Lucy would never reform her.

"That's why Tom went over to be vaccinated with the police and fire-fighters. He's such a good guy. I'm so lucky to have him as my wing man."

"Yes, Thomas has some virtues, I admit."

"Was he a good lover?"

Erika shot Lucy a stern look. "Lucy, there are some things you don't talk about, and some things, I don't. But since you ask, he wasn't bad. I already knew I preferred women, so it was a foregone conclusion that he could never be adequate. Fortunately, he was very sporting about it. We parted without hard feelings."

"Now, there's a man who's confident in his masculinity." Lucy leaned against Erika, resting her head against her shoulder. "It was a wonderful party, but it's nice to be home alone with you."

"Lucy, that's my bad arm."

She sat up straight. "I'm sorry. I keep forgetting." She kissed the spot again. "Maybe I should bless it too?"

"Oh, Lucy, I think you've had too much to drink." Erika put her arm around her wife. "Maybe this will keep the tender parts out of range."

"Oh, I like that." Lucy snuggled closer. "I so look forward to a time when everyone is vaccinated, and we can all get together. Let's throw a party!"

"We can plan it, if you like, but I think that will be far in the future. Liz says it's more likely to get worse before it gets better."

Lucy sighed and burrowed into the crook of Erika's arm. "Oh, dear God, I hope not."

Erika glanced down at the silken, red hair of the woman snuggled against her. "Now, why isn't what you said wrong?"

"Because it was a prayer."

"You bloody priests have all the answers." Erika pulled Lucy closer. "I think I'm about good for one more glass of wine. What about you?"

"One's good for me. It's almost two AM."

"I'll put the cork in the bottle when we get up. I feel like listening to Christmas carols."

"Put some on. I'm sure you can stream some. They're everywhere this time of year."

"No. I want you to sing some for me."

"Oh, Erika. I'm sooooo tired."

"Please."

Lucy sat up. "Okay. But in my natural voice. Not fancy."

"Anything you sing will be lovely."

Erika was transported when Lucy began to sing the original German version of "Silent Night." It brought her home to singing it with her parents in their little apartment in Berlin while they lit the candles on their scrawny Christmas tree. Erika's mother had a far better voice than her father. They sang softly because, even though the GDR never came down as hard on religion as the Soviet Union, it wasn't encouraged either. People who still believed in the "opiate of the people" were looked down upon as retro-grades. Sometimes, Erika looked down on Lucy's faith because that's how she was brought up. Now, she realized how unfair she'd been. Lucy never pushed religion on anyone, especially not her wife. She always invited her to services, which Erika attended to show her support, but Lucy had never tried to convert her.

Lucy finished the carol. "More carols in German?"

"Please. It brings back such wonderful memories of my childhood."

Lucy gave her such a loving look, it almost brought Erika to tears. "What would you like me to sing?"

"*Geistliches Wiegenlied.*"

"Good. That's written for a mezzo. My voice is tired after singing so much tonight."

Erika reached for Lucy's hand and held it while she sang, thinking how perfect Lucy was for her. Her voice could excite her like nothing else. Her smile could brighten her darkest night. But it was her womanly beauty, not on the outside, but the inside that could make her swoon. Lucy could have quite a temper, but otherwise, she had the sweetest nature Erika had ever encountered in a woman.

When Lucy finished singing, Erika said, "Finish your wine and let's go to bed."

"I thought you wanted me to sing to you."

"I do, but now that you've gotten me all excited, I need to make love to you."

Lucy's green eyes grew wide and Erika worried she might reject her overture.

"Okay, but can we take our wine upstairs with us?" Lucy asked with childlike enthusiasm.

Erika smiled. "Why not? We might want refreshment afterwards."

In the bedroom, Lucy shimmied out of her black skirt and rolled down her black tights. She had come to the party straight from a bereavement group, so she'd pulled a silly Christmas sweater over her clericals. They came off together, but she waited to get Erika's attention before unhooking her lacy black bra. The sight of those creamy, perfect breasts with their pale nipples springing free never failed to arouse Erika. She couldn't wait to get her lips around them. But Lucy laughed softly and turned her back to pull down her matching lace panties. She jumped into bed and pulled up the covers.

"Hurry up, Erika! Now that you've got me going, I can't wait!"

To draw out the excitement, Erika took her time. She pulled her sweater over her head, carefully folded her wool trousers over the back of the chair. She unbuttoned her blouse slowly.

"Is this your idea of a strip tease?" asked Lucy, rolling her eyes. She leaned up on her elbow and mocked a leer. Finally, she grew impatient. "Come on, Erika! It's cold in here. I need you to warm me up!"

Erika quickened the pace of undressing, but she still couldn't bring herself to leave her underwear where she'd stepped out of it like Lucy had. She folded it and put it on the chair.

"Hurry up or I'll have to start without you!"

Erika could see the motion under the covers—Lucy touching herself, which sent a flash of excitement straight to Erika's crotch.

"Go ahead. I'll watch."

"I bet you'd like that."

"I would."

"Forget it. Just checking to make sure I'm ready for you." Lucy opened her legs and Erika lay between them, pressing gently. Lucy's eyes closed in pleasure. "Mmm, keep doing that. It feels so good."

"Can you come this way?"

"Probably not, but don't stop." Lucy pulled Erika's face closer. "I love you with all my heart." Her lips, still lush with dark lipstick, parted, a clear invitation to a kiss. Her mouth tasted sweet from all the cookies she'd devoured at the holiday party and the rich wine. Her tongue gently teased Erika's.

Erika rolled off so she could caress Lucy's breasts. With a hand at the back of Erika's neck, Lucy pressed her closer. Erika savored her sighs of appreciation as she sucked gently. Such perfect breasts deserved more than pleasure. They deserved adoration, and Erika sucked each one in turn, hard enough to hurt a little because she knew Lucy liked that. Finally, she reached between Lucy's legs and found she was, as she had predicted, abundantly ready. She caressed her lightly on the outside before moving inside, where it was so warm and silken. Erika often envied Lucy the ability to come so fully on the inside, but she always felt slightly inadequate. The more excited Lucy became, the more her body opened.

Erika rolled over to open the bedstand drawer where they kept their toys, but Lucy pulled her back by the shoulder. "No, not tonight. Just you. *Only you.*" Lucy ran her fingers gently down Erika's cheek. "Come back. I need you inside me," she whispered into Erika's ear.

Chapter 21

When Lucy opened the rectory door, she saw that the afternoon's pleasant flurries had accumulated into several inches of wet snow. She glanced down at her black flats, wishing she had thought to bring the L.L. Bean duck shoes that Erika had given her on their first Christmas, insisting every Mainer needed to own a pair. She also wished she had paid more attention to the weather report that morning.

Now, she had no choice but to walk through the cold, white carpet to get to her car. She raised her eyes towards heaven imploring God for patience. The snow was just one more aggravation in a day full of them. The warden had reported that the cantankerous old boiler in the church had finally given up its ghost and needed to be replaced. Olivia's endowment was still under discussion, so they would need to find the money elsewhere. Jodi had come down with the virus, which had created a ripple of fear through the parish.

Jodi's illness also meant that Lucy had to field the phone calls and emails her admin handled so efficiently. After the first few hours of rings and pings, Lucy just wanted to scream, "Stop! Please stop!" Finally, she turned off the office phone on her desk and let everything go into voice mail. Thankfully, the warden's daughter, who was off from school for the holidays, had volunteered to pitch in tomorrow.

Lucy felt cold water seeping into her shoes as soon as she stepped outside. She hated wet feet with a passion. Even when she'd played in the snow as a child, she'd demand that her mother give her dry socks when her feet got wet. She said a quick prayer of thanks for having such an understanding mother, followed by the prayer for acceptance of things she couldn't change.

When she finally reached her car, her feet were numb. Her vaccinated arm hurt when she reached over the console to deposit her bags on the passenger seat. Feeling sorry for herself, Lucy rubbed the sore spot before starting the engine. She couldn't wait to get home to Erika, who would hug her and assure her that everything would be all right.

As Lucy turned on to Beach Road, she noticed blue lights flashing behind her, so she pulled into the parking lot of Hobbs Family Practice and watched in her side view mirror as the officer approached.

"License, insurance card, and registration, please," said the young man with a high-and-tight haircut. Lucy didn't recognize him. He was probably a new patrolman, right out of the military. Brenda had been hiring a lot of MPs lately. He was wearing a blue Hobbs police mask, which reminded Lucy to put on hers too. She snatched it off the dashboard and pulled the loops around her ears.

To Lucy's surprise, her hands were shaking as she opened the glove box. She always kept her registration in the enormous envelope of paperwork and manuals the dealers always provided with a new car. Now, she had to rifle through the random papers and receipts for oil changes to find it. Fortunately, her insurance card was in the little plastic pocket designed to hold it. She handed the card and the registration to the officer while she searched in her purse for her wallet. Meanwhile, the policeman's flashlight was shining right in her eyes. He was staring at her collar, looking a little sheepish. Finally, she wiggled her driver's license out of the sleeve in her wallet.

The patrolman directed the beam of light on her documents and frowned as he scrutinized them. "Do you know why I stopped you, Rev. Bartlett?"

Lucy shook her head. "No, I'm afraid not."

"You didn't stop at the red light before making your turn. You're supposed to come to a full stop before turning."

"I'm sorry. I guess I wasn't paying attention."

He handed back her documents. "I won't write you up this time, but be careful. The roads are starting to get icy. We don't want anyone to get hurt. Please pay attention."

"Thank you, officer. I will."

The young man touched the brim of his hat. "Drive safely, Ma'am. G'night."

Lucy waited for the policeman to turn around in the parking lot and drive away before starting the car. Her lights shone on the windows of the offices where Liz worked, but at this hour, all was dark inside.

Lucy was still shaking as she pulled out into traffic. She needed that hug from Erika even more desperately now. She was so grateful when she pressed the button on the garage door opener, and it opened. She pulled her car into the bay, especially careful, as always, to avoid the clever and beautiful staircase Sam had built.

She took off her wet shoes inside the door. Usually, Erika heard her come in and came to greet her, but all was quiet when Lucy stepped into the house. A delicious smell emanated from the kitchen. Lucy sniffed the air and identified it as barley soup with oxtails, a recipe from Erika's mother. It was a special treat because Erika had to drive all the way to Biddeford to get the oxtails. Unusual cuts of meat, sold in ethnic communities, weren't popular grocery items in Maine. The aroma of the soup made Lucy hungry. After she hung up her coat, she pulled off her black tights and walked barefoot into the warm kitchen, glad that Sam had insisted on radiant heat under the tiles. The soup was boiling very hard, so Lucy turned it down a little. At least living with Erika had taught her that much about cooking.

"Erika?" she called. "Erika, I'm home!"

"Oh, Lucy," said the sleepy woman coming in from the family room. Erika's hair was in disarray. She rubbed her pale eyes and yawned. "I'm sorry, dear. I didn't hear you come in. I was having a quick laydown."

Lucy made a sad face and reached up her arms. "I need hugs. Lots of hugs. It's been an awful day."

"Oh, Lovely Lucy, I'm so sorry. Here. Let me hug you." Erika gathered her up into a strong embrace. "You're home now. Now go upstairs and change and your dinner will be ready when you come back."

"It was boiling hard, so I turned it down a little."

"I see. Thank you." Erika gave Lucy a quick kiss. "Now, off with you and put on something cozy. Meanwhile, I'll put the bread in the oven to crisp." She nudged Lucy aside. "Go on."

"Another kiss."

Erika gave her a quick kiss. "I love you."

"Love you too."

Lucy headed upstairs. She was grateful to take off her suit and clerical blouse. She tossed the collar into the laundry, knowing Erika would rescue it later. She put on heavy sweatpants and her thick hoodie. She found a thick pair of woolly socks and pulled them on her frigid feet. Her toes were so cold she almost couldn't feel them.

She returned to the kitchen to find Erika ladling soup into bowls.

"What can I do?"

"Put the breadboard and knife on the table, the butter too."

"I love this soup," said Lucy, hurrying to follow Erika's instructions because the good smell was making her ravenous. "It's my favorite. Can you teach me how to make it?"

"I've started writing down my mother's old recipes in that notebook by the fridge. Although I'm sure Liz knows them all." Erika looked reflective. "For some reason, hers never tastes like this. And mine doesn't taste like my mother's. It's strange how two women can cook from the same recipe and yet it never tastes the same."

"I want to learn how to make this soup, and the pea soup. I love that too."

"Then, Lovely Lucy, I shall teach you." Erika gingerly tasted a spoonful of soup. "Hot. Be careful!"

"I'll let it cool a little," said Lucy. She cut two pieces of bread and buttered them. She handed one to Erika. "You don't usually nap. Didn't you sleep well last night?"

"I always sleep well after we make love." Erika raised a blond brow.

"Hmm. Me too."

"But I have this headache. Right here." Erika tapped her forehead above the bridge of her nose. "It's very odd. I so seldom get headaches."

"Maybe it's a side-effect of the vaccine. You should call Liz."

Erika raised her shoulders. "It's nothing. Just a headache. Probably sinus congestion with the weather coming in."

Lucy smiled. "I never heard a storm called 'weather' until I moved to Maine. Thar's weather comin' in," said Lucy, lowering her pitch to sound like what she imagined to be the voice of an old fisherman.

"Yes, Mainers have a unique way of speaking."

Lucy blew on her soup, then cautiously tasted it. "Delicious. I definitely want to learn how to make it."

"Next time, you can cook, and I'll watch…to advise you."

Lucy smiled. "Perfect." She reached for the knife to cut them each another piece of bread.

Lucy told Erika about Jodi, and the boiler, and being stopped by the young police officer who looked straight out of boot camp. Erika told her that there was good news from Colby. "Morgan is feeling well enough to come back after the Christmas break."

While Lucy listened to her wife describe how relieved she was to have the burden of department chair off her shoulders, she wolfed down two bowls of the rich, thick soup full of vegetables and mushrooms. She ate half a loaf of roasted-garlic ciabatta slathered with butter. After that, she was finally content.

Erika glanced at her empty bowl. "Evidently, you were hungry."

"I'll clean up," Lucy said, jumping up from her seat. "You go out and turn on the news, and I'll be right there."

Erika stared at her, looking suddenly dazed, as if someone had flashed a bright light in her eyes. "I think I shall go upstairs and lie down. This headache simply won't quit!"

"You should call Liz."

"It's nothing." Erika waved dismissively. "A headache. Nothing more."

"Okay. I'll clean up. Then I want to watch some news. I was so busy today I have no idea what's going on in the world. You don't mind?"

"Of course, not." Erika leaned down and kissed her. "Thank you for cleaning up. I tried to be neat, but the prep for soup is so messy…all those vegetables to chop."

"Don't worry. Go lie down. I'll be up soon."

Lucy carried the pot out to the screen porch, thinking how clever it was to use the outdoors as a second refrigerator. As a city girl, she never would have thought of it.

Erika was right about the cleanup. Lucy found carrot peelings, bits of onion, and wisps of celery shoots everywhere. There was a trail of barley to where the soup pot had cooked. Cleanup took longer than she'd expected. She was more than relieved to hang up the dish towel and turn on the light under the cabinet. She took her glass of wine out to the living room, happy to find that PBS news had just started, and she hadn't missed much. She stretched out on the couch. With Erika upstairs, she had it all to herself.

When Lucy opened her eyes, the program had changed to a rerun of Masterpiece Theater from Sunday. They'd already seen it, so she switched it off. She glanced at the clock and saw that it was after ten. Maybe her fatigue was a side effect of the vaccine instead of the fallout from a difficult day.

Before switching off the Christmas tree lights, Lucy noticed a new addition to the decorations. A scarlet, satin bra was draped from a branch. Lucy took it down and carefully put it under the tree with the other gifts. After checking the doors, she switched off the downstairs lights.

Erika was all bundled up under the duvet when Lucy came into the bedroom. She decided to give her wife a good-night kiss, so she wouldn't wake her when she got into bed. She bent to kiss Erika's forehead, and found it cool. Usually, Erika stirred and smiled and turned to give her a kiss, but she didn't move.

"Erika," Lucy called softly, but she didn't move. Anxious, Lucy shook her arm. "Erika? Are you okay?"

No response, not even a sigh.

Now, Lucy was in a panic. She rolled Erika on her back and patted her cheek. "Erika! Wake up!" She felt for a pulse in her neck, panicking while she tried to locate it. It took a few desperate moments to feel the beat, and Lucy sighed in relief. She watched her chest rise and fall. She was still breathing. "Erika! Wake up!" said Lucy, shaking her shoulders, but Erika's eyes remained closed.

Lucy grabbed her phone out of her pocket and dialed Liz's number.

"Lucy? What's up?" asked the sleepy voice when Liz answered on the other end.

"Erika won't wake up. She went to bed with a headache, and now she won't wake up!"

"Is she breathing?" asked Liz, clearly alert now.

"Yes," asked Lucy, growing more worried by the moment.

"Call 911. I'll be right there. Don't go anywhere. With COVID, they won't let you ride in the ambulance. I'll take you to the hospital."

"Okay," said Lucy, surprised to hear the urgency in Liz's voice. She was even more surprised when Liz hung up on her. Lucy's fingers trembled as she tried to dial 911. It took two tries until the call went through, and the dispatcher finally answered.

"This is Lucy Bartlett. My wife went to bed with a headache and now, she's unresponsive."

"Is she breathing?"

"Yes. And she has a pulse."

"Okay. I'll dispatch an ambulance. Tell me your address."

Lucy forced her voice to be steady while she gave the dispatcher her address, cell phone number, and Erika's details.

"And what is your relationship to the patient?"

Lucy momentarily hesitated because it still sounded so new and so strange. "I'm her wife."

"Would you like me to stay on the line with you until the ambulance arrives?"

Part of Lucy was afraid to let the friendly voice go, but she knew she would be taking the dispatcher away from someone else who might really need her.

"No, my friend is coming. She's Erika's doctor. Dr. Stolz."

"Oh, good, so you'll have someone with you. The ambulance is leaving now. They should be at your location within ten minutes. Call back if you need us."

"Thank you," said Lucy. The call clicked off, and Lucy stared at the phone. She felt so helpless. Shouldn't she do something? She kissed Erika and shook her again. "Please! Please, Erika. Just wake up!"

She tried to focus her thoughts, but she just couldn't think. Then a singularly clear thought formed in her mind. I can pray for her. I can say the prayers for the sick. Lucy found the black bag which contained her kit for giving the last rites. She kept one in her night stand in case she was called out to attend a dying soul. Many people waited until the last minute to call the priest. The bag held a small bottle of blessed oil, a purple stole, and a compact *Book of Common Prayer*.

Lucy's fingers were shaking as she thumbed the tabs to the prayers for the sick. She could barely get the bottle of oil open and almost spilled it on the sheets. She made the sign of the cross with the oil on Erika's forehead. "For the sake of your Son, Jesus Christ, have mercy on us and forgive us; that we may delight in your will, and walk in your ways, to the glory of your Name…"

Lucy heard the downstairs door slam and feet running up the stairs. She knew it was Liz, who had a key to the house. She took in the scene in a glance, but she hesitated when she saw Lucy wearing the purple stole.

"I'm sorry to interrupt your prayers, Lucy, but may I examine her?"

Lucy stepped aside. "Of course."

Liz took a flashlight out of her pocket, lifted each of Erika's eyelids, and flicked the light over her eyes. The pupils were unresponsive. Lucy tried to read Liz's face, but it was inscrutable. She took a stethoscope out of the pocket of her leather jacket, yanked up Erika's nightshirt, and listened to her chest.

"You should get dressed, Lucy," said Liz in an unnaturally calm voice, "so we can follow the ambulance to the hospital."

Lucy didn't want to leave, but she returned the items to her last rites kit and went into the walk-in closet to choose clothes to wear.

"Dress warmly," Liz called to her. "They might not let us into the ED. Maybe me, because I have privileges, but they won't let you in. No visitors of any kind are allowed."

Lucy chose a heavy polar fleece jacket and put on thermal bottoms under corduroy pants. On the other side of the door, she heard the murmur of male voices and Brenda's voice giving orders. "Make sure the driveway is clear for the ambulance!"

Lucy dashed into her clothes. When she came out, she saw one of the EMTs doing an assessment, while the others brought in a stretcher. Brenda approached and put her arm around her. "Don't worry, Lucy. We'll take good care of her." Lucy wanted to put her arm around Brenda's waist and return the hug, but she just couldn't move. Brenda gave her shoulders a little squeeze. "It will be okay," she said in a reassuring voice.

Across the room Liz leaned against the wall, arms folded on her chest, while she talked to the paramedics with a frown. Was she also feeling the frustration of not being able to do more? The paramedics got into position to lift Erika on to the stretcher. "One! Two! Three! Lift!" One of them arranged an oxygen canula in Erika's nostrils.

Brenda and Liz were speaking in hushed tones on the opposite side of the room. Lucy went over to join them. When Liz saw Lucy, she tried for a pleasant expression, but her brows were knit in a frown. "We should go, Lucy," Liz said.

"Do you need me to come with you?" asked Brenda.

"No, thanks. I've got it," Liz replied, patting her arm. "Thanks for coming over."

"Of course, I would come. As soon as I saw the dispatch come over my phone screen, I jumped into my clothes and came." Brenda reached down and gave Lucy a hug. "I hope everything is okay. Love you, Lucy."

Brenda's strong hug brought tears to Lucy's eyes. "Love you too, Brenda."

"Cherie and I are praying for Erika…and for you."

"Thank you," said Lucy. Tears finally escaped as she watched the tall, blond woman head down the stairs.

"Did you dress warmly like I told you?" asked Liz. Her voice sounded gruff until Lucy realized it was thick with emotion. "Bring gloves and a hat. We might be stuck in my truck for a long time."

By the time they got downstairs, the ambulance, flashing all its lights, was heading down the road. The police cars were already gone.

"I brought the truck because the cab is small and easy to keep warm," Liz explained as she clicked open the doors.

Lucy found the ring over the passenger door and hauled herself inside. Liz seemed so intent on backing up that Lucy was almost afraid to ask any questions. Finally, she couldn't stand it and had to ask, "Is Erika going to be okay?"

"I don't know," said Liz.

"What happened? Is this from the vaccine?"

"It could be, but I doubt it. More likely a cerebral event."

"You mean like a stroke?"

"It could be a stroke. An aneurysm. A mass we didn't know about pressing on part of her brain. You say she went to bed with a headache?"

"Yes. She said it was unusual because she doesn't usually get headaches."

"We'll have to wait and see," said Liz.

The roads had been plowed since Lucy had gotten home, but she gripped the armrest as Liz sped down Route 1 on the way to the highway. Liz always drove too fast. Usually, it didn't frighten Lucy, but tonight, it did.

"Liz, can you slow down a little? The roads are slick."

"I want to be there when they unload the rig," Liz explained. "Don't worry. You know I'm a good driver."

Once Liz got onto the highway, she drove even faster. "Liz, I'm anxious enough as it is, please don't drive so fast. You're scaring me."

Liz glanced at her with annoyance, but she slowed down to the speed limit. Lucy tried to focus on something else for distraction.

"What did you see when you looked in her eyes?" Lucy asked.

"Her pupils were unresponsive to light."

Lucy stared out the window while she tried to process the words. "Is that bad?" she asked, even though she knew it was.

"It's not good. I suspect a brain event, but we won't know the cause or the extent without a scan."

Liz knew all the back roads to Southern Med. When they arrived, she swung into an empty parking space in the doctors' lot and jumped out of the cab. "Stay here," she ordered, snatching a mask off the dashboard. "I'll be right back." She slammed the door. Lucy watched Liz hurry in the direction of a parked ambulance. She banged on the door. The driver got out and talked to her for a few minutes. They walked to the rear of the ambulance and knocked on the door. The EMT in the back hopped out. The two of them began to unload the stretcher. Lucy jumped out of the truck and crossed the parking lot.

"I thought I told you to stay inside," Liz said irritably.

"If they're not going to let me inside, I want to give her a kiss."

"You really need to stand back, Ma'am," said the EMT, blocking her path with an extended arm.

"This is my wife."

"Yes, we know. We need to get her inside."

"Just a minute, please."

Liz motioned with a wave for the EMTs to back off. They stood by respectfully while Lucy kissed Erika's forehead and smoothed her hair. She was still warm. That was a good sign, wasn't it? She felt a hand gently pulling her shoulder. "Come on, Lucy. They need to get her inside. Her vitals are deteriorating. She needs treatment as soon as possible."

"I love you, Erika," said Lucy as Liz tugged on her arm. Lucy stopped resisting and allowed Liz to lead her back to the truck. Liz opened the door on the passenger's side, but Lucy was distracted, watching the EMTs wheel the stretcher inside. "Get in, Lucy. I'm going to go in and see if I can pull any strings. Do you have Erika's ID and health insurance cards?"

Lucy climbed into the passenger seat. "Oh, my word, I didn't even think of that!"

"It's okay I can get into the office system through my phone and send it to them. They may have it on file from when Erika had that appendicitis scare last summer." Liz handed her a ring of keys. "Lock the doors, and, please, stay put this time. I'll be right back either way. You can start the engine and crank up the heat if you get cold."

Lucy had been to Southern Med many times as a chaplain or to bring Communion to her parishioners, but she had never been there as a terrified spouse of a patient. She watched Liz heading to the emergency entrance. Her lanky walk gave her a familiar point of reference in the bizarre, out-of-focus world where she had suddenly found herself. The lights were too bright, but the sounds were muffled. She could hardly hear.

Fortunately, Liz returned quickly. She opened the passenger door. "Let's get in the back. I keep an old quilt in case I break down in bad weather. We can bundle up in it and sit close for warmth."

"Won't they let you in?"

"No, they won't let anyone in except patients. No exceptions. All the people who could help me get inside are home asleep at this time of night. Like we should be. And they have a full house, so they'll have to transport Erika to another hospital once she's stable."

"Where will they take her?"

"I have no idea. All the hospitals in Southern Maine and New Hampshire are full." Liz spread the old quilt across their laps. "Sit closer. We'll keep each other warm."

Liz put her arm around her. The cuff of her sweatshirt smelled of freshly cut onions, probably from making dinner. It smelled simple and homey and reminded Lucy of Erika's delicious soup. She wanted to cry. Liz seemed to sense the change and pulled her closer. "I've got you, Luce," she murmured, and kissed the top of her head.

They sat in silence, waiting, staring at the bright entrance to the emergency department. Lucy watched the light at the door until her eyes burned.

Liz's phone rang, which made them both jump. "Stolz," said Liz, and then listened for a long time, staring out the window at the hospital. "Uh huh," she finally said. "I'll tell her. Thanks." She tapped off the call and reached for Lucy's hand. "On the scan, it looks like a ruptured aneurysm.

It's in a part of her brain where they can't operate, and even if they could, they'd have to find a neurosurgeon, and there isn't time. The bleeding can't be stopped."

"What does that mean?" Lucy asked anxiously.

Liz pulled her close. "It means it won't be long now."

Chapter 22

The woman in her arms was trembling fiercely, so Liz held her tight. "It's okay, Lucy. It's okay," she murmured.

"No, it's not okay," Lucy said and began to sob.

Liz relaxed her grip because she didn't want to hurt her. Sometimes, she didn't know her own strength and inadvertently hurt people. She suddenly thought of the time she'd broken her father's ribs with a bear hug. She hadn't meant to hurt him, only to tell him how much, despite all the miscommunication and emotional absence, she loved him. She hadn't meant to defeat him in the wrestling match either, which she knew was a blow to his masculinity that he would never forgive or forget. He was already frail then, and wrestling with him was a mistake, but she was only fourteen and didn't know better.

It was easier to reach all the way back to her adolescence than to think of losing her best friend of forty years, her wingman. Erika had been with Liz through all her major loves, through all her professional successes and failures. She always had something wry and witty to say, even in the worst moments. She was there when Liz's father died so young, his body ravaged by war, his soul defeated by the ignominy of being on the wrong side of the conflict. Erika understood the guilt Liz felt, even though neither of them had been born when that horrible war had been fought. They'd inherited Germany's national guilt, the daughters of its collective shame. Erika's father had been spared military service because of poor hearing and because the country needed his brilliant, mathematical mind. The experience had been so horrible that Stefan always left the room whenever Liz and his daughter spoke about the war.

It was strange to be thinking of the war and their shared heritage while Erika lay dying, but that was what had united them beyond a common language, a shared proclivity toward their own sex, and a love for continental philosophy. Liz wondered if she would ever find another friend, someone who could speak to her on that intellectual level. Of course, Liz was an amateur philosopher, largely untrained, but Erika had never held that against her.

Liz was glad that Lucy was weeping silently because anything more demonstrative would open the floodgates of her own emotions. Lucy clung to her tightly, her fingers gripping her arm like pincers. Liz gently stroked Lucy's hair as if she were a child. It was fragrant from her hair rinse, a floral scent. Erika had told her that Lucy had been adding henna to touch up her fading red hair. She'd chosen a natural solution because Liz preached about the danger of commercial hair dyes, and Lucy took Liz's medical advice seriously. Lucy's hair felt silken under her fingers and warm. Liz pressed her head against her chest, and Lucy clung more fiercely in return.

Finally, the sobbing ceased, and Lucy sat up. Liz reached down for the beat-up box of tissues she always carried in the backseat along with the old quilt. She ripped out a handful and handed them to Lucy. The windows were beginning to mist over from their breath. The halogen lamps in the parking lot and the entrance of the hospital looked like fog lights through a mist.

"Are you warm enough?" asked Liz. "I can run the heat for a while."

Lucy shook her head solemnly. "I'm okay for now. You're keeping me warm."

That pleased Liz. "Maggie uses me as a heater in bed," she said with a smile.

"How long will it take before it's over?" Lucy asked. The anxious look on her face, dimly lit by the light from the parking lot, told Liz she dreaded the answer.

"Do you really want to know?"

"Yes, I want to be prepared."

"Hours, but not long. Given the size of the lesion, she'll probably be gone before morning."

Lucy looked stricken. Her face contorted as if she would sob again, but she got hold of herself and took a few deep breaths.

"She was an organ donor," said Liz. "I doubt they have the

capacity—because of the pandemic—to harvest her organs. She would have been sad over the waste."

"German efficiency," said Lucy almost bitterly.

"Yes, but also because she was one of the most socially responsible, caring people I ever met."

Lucy nodded and looked like she was going to cry again. "You were her lover too."

Liz coughed up a chuckle. "She told you that? It was just one time. An experiment. We were stoned."

"You smoked pot?"

"Didn't everyone in those days?"

"By the time I got there, all the deaths from overdoses took the shine off of drugs."

"But you did smoke pot? All musicians do."

"Yes, a couple of times. But smoking anything isn't good for the voice. It makes it raspy."

"Of course, and we must protect the voice at all costs."

"I want to stay," said Lucy, abruptly changing the topic, "…until the end."

"That could be all night," said Liz. She gripped Lucy tighter before she asked the hard question on her mind. "Have you thought about where you want to send her body when it's over?"

"No, I haven't thought about it," said Lucy impatiently. "When I woke up this morning, I never thought I'd be burying my sixty-two-year-old, healthy wife."

"With the pandemic, I'm sure the hospital morgue is full," Liz said as gently as she could. "They'll want to get her out of there as soon as possible." Liz raised her arm to glance at her watch. "It's late, but I can text Billy LaPierre to give him a heads up that he might have to come out tonight."

"Okay," said Lucy in a shaky voice. "If you think it's best."

"Erika wrote in her advanced directives that she wanted to be cremated."

Lucy gazed out the window. "I forgot that you're her executor. She trusted you. She loved you, Liz."

That defeated Liz's control. Tears sprang to her eyes, she pursed her lips hard, and sucked in air to help keep her emotions from overflowing. If she gave into them, they'd both be sobbing.

Lucy gazed out the window at the ED entrance. "I should have called you right away when she started complaining about the headache."

Liz gave her a little squeeze. "It probably wouldn't have made any difference. And who thinks of going to the ED for a headache, especially if you think you're healthy? If there were other symptoms, like blurred vision or numbness, Erika probably would have insisted on going to the hospital herself. She's no dummy."

"Why didn't you know about this? You're her doctor!"

"Aneurysms can lie dormant for years and years. Some people are born with them. Unless there are symptoms, no doctor would think of ordering a brain scan. It's not something you do just for fun. Scans can expose you to a lot of radiation. Plus, they cost a lot of money if you don't have good insurance."

"I'm beginning to hate our healthcare system."

"No more than I do." Liz took her arm back. "It's getting cold in here. Let me run the engine for a while."

"Okay," said Lucy uncertainly. She grasped Liz's hand and gripped it tight. "You'll come back, won't you?"

"Of course," said Liz opening the door. "Bundle up in the meantime."

Lucy nodded and pulled the quilt around her shoulders. Liz unlocked the driver's door and got in. She started the engine and let it rev a few times before turning up the heat to full blast. She redirected the vents to blow up to the ceiling. The radio screen lit up meaning a call was coming through the blue tooth, but when Liz saw the number, she quickly directed the call to her phone, in case it was something Lucy shouldn't hear.

"Dr. Stolz?"

"Yes."

"It's Chris Greenfield, the hospitalist in neurology. She flatlined a few minutes ago, but we put her on life support because she has so many viable organs for transplant."

"You found enough surgeons for a team?"

"Yeah, we did. Sounds grizzly but they don't have enough to do with all the elective surgery being canceled. Medevac is tied up with COVID transports, so everything will be directed locally. Mass General is sending up a special vehicle with transplant support equipment. They'll distribute the organs as needed to the other hospitals in Boston. The heart is a match for someone at Yale-New Haven. They've dispatched a private plane to Portland."

Liz glanced at the time. "So, we're talking about hours before it's over?"

"Yes."

"I know this is a lot to ask, but if we suit up, can we come in so her wife can say goodbye?"

"I don't know, Dr. Stolz. Since the surge, we're on lockdown, as you know." There was a long silence. "Oh, who cares? You can sneak in through the front doctors' entrance. Call me when you get there. I'll bring PPE."

"Thanks, Dr. Greenfield. You don't know how much this means to me."

"This is my personal cell phone. Text this number when you're at the door."

As Liz tapped off the call, she felt Lucy's hand gripping her shoulder. She reached over and patted it.

"What is it?" asked Lucy anxiously. "Is she gone?"

The question hit Liz like a punch. She sighed and turned around. "Technically, yes. She flatlined, and they didn't revive her because of her advanced directive. But Lucy, she was probably 'gone' when you found her. Her wonderful brain was already so damaged by the hemorrhage, the woman you knew as Erika wasn't there anymore."

"No!"

"I'm afraid so."

"No!"

"Yes, Lucy. Erika is gone. If there's some special prayer you say for the dead, now is the time to say it."

"Oh…" Lucy made a little whimper like a hurt animal.

"Come up front. We're moving to the other side of the hospital. The hospitalist is going to let us in so you can see Erika before they take her in for surgery."

"What surgery?"

"Get up here, and I'll explain."

Lucy shed the quilt and got out to move up to the passenger seat.

Liz reached for her hand and looked directly into Lucy's eyes. "They're going to take her organs for transplant. Most of them are going to Boston. Her heart is going to Yale."

Lucy blinked a few times as she processed the information. "That's fitting, I think. She loved Yale."

"Me too." She let Lucy's hand go. "Buckle up. We're moving."

Liz felt slightly nostalgic when she parked in the main doctors' parking lot. There were many early mornings when she'd had to hunt for a space here when she was still operating on a regular basis. Even now, she could probably do biopsies and mastectomies in her sleep, but the loss of sensitivity in her fingertips made her leery. The last thing she wanted to do was to injure a patient for the sake of her vanity.

"We have to be quick," Liz explained, "We won't have much time and we don't want to get Greenfield in trouble for his kindness. Do you have your prayer book or whatever you need?"

"I have almost all the rites memorized."

"Of course, you do. If you can memorize a whole opera, why not a whole prayer book?"

"Liturgy isn't opera," said Lucy in a pointed tone. Liz was tempted to start a debate about religious service being a form of theater, but she stopped herself because Lucy was already so upset.

At that time of night, the doctors' lot was empty, so Liz parked as close as she could to the entrance. She turned off the engine and texted Greenfield.

He was waiting when they came to the door. He waved through the glass before holding the door open. "On that cart against the wall are your gowns and masks. Here are your IDs. You have privileges, Dr. Stolz, so I just printed yours out. Then I found your chaplain's pass, Rev. Bartlett, so I could print yours too. Since you're both technically 'official,' I doubt anyone will try to stop us."

"Why do I feel like I'm in a spy movie?" Liz asked, tying her paper gown behind her back. Lucy was having trouble with the ties, so Liz helped her.

The staff elevator was just a few steps away. Greenfield pressed the button for the surgical floor. "They moved her down from neurology, waiting on the transplant team." He glanced anxiously at Lucy. "Thank you for donating your wife's organs, Rev. Bartlett. They'll save a lot of lives."

"I had nothing to do with it," Lucy replied. "It was her choice. She was a generous woman." Liz saw how Lucy was struggling to maintain her poise, but she was doing it admirably.

The elevator was glacially slow, but finally, there was a ring and it opened onto the lobby to the surgical department.

"I've got to go back upstairs," Greenfield said, holding the button to keep the door open as they stepped out. "Leave the same way you came in. There's a bin for used PPE by the door."

"Thank you, Dr. Greenfield. Thank you so, so much. I'm forever grateful," said Lucy. "Blessings on you for your kindness to me and my wife."

"There are so many people who can't say goodbye to their loved ones at the end. I'm glad I could help. I'm sorry for your loss, Rev. Bartlett." He gave Liz a wan smile before the door closed.

"Do you know where we're going?" Lucy asked anxiously. She shook her head, evidently correcting herself. "Of course, you know the way. What am I thinking?"

Liz pointed forward and they headed down the corridor. Erika wasn't the only patient waiting in the large room. A nurse looked up and frowned as she watched them come in. "Hello, Dr. Stolz," she said as the light of recognition dawned in her eyes. "Are you here for the harvesting?"

Liz thought quickly. If she said, 'yes,' she would have to explain why she wasn't heading to scrub. "No. Other business," she said vaguely.

The nurse scrutinized Lucy's badge. "I thought chaplains weren't allowed anymore."

"This is a special case," Liz said quickly.

The woman's eyes narrowed. She glanced from Lucy to Liz. The nurse wasn't buying it, but Liz gave her one of those imperious 'How dare you question me? I'm a surgeon' looks that always made people back down.

"Well, okay, but you can't stay long," said the woman. Her eyes were still suspicious, but she went into the hall.

Liz turned around. While she'd been running interference, Lucy had found Erika's bed. Liz yanked the curtain across to divide the bay and give her privacy. Lucy was murmuring softly. Prayers, Liz assumed. Lucy's green eyes looked up and searched her face. "Liz, will you say the responses with me?"

"Of course," said Liz, distracted by her quick evaluation of Erika's condition. She was grateful for Lucy's sake, that her wife's eyes had been closed when the bleed began. It was always unnerving to the family when their loved one stared vacantly at the ceiling. She resisted the impulse to check Erika's pupils. The monitors confirmed that the machines and equipment crowding the small space were the only thing keeping her friend's body alive.

"Just follow my lead," said Lucy, her hand reaching for Liz's. The other held Erika's. "God the Father…We both say, 'Have mercy on your servant.'" Lucy calmly went through the litany for the dying, and Liz found she could instinctively anticipate the responses as if she could somehow remember them from the last time she'd assisted Lucy in praying at someone's deathbed. At the end of her prayers, Lucy held Erika's hand and gazed into her face.

"I'll give you time alone," said Liz, ready to step away.

"No, stay, Liz," said Lucy, reaching for her hand. "You loved her too."

On the other side of the curtain, she heard female voices talking. "We can't stay much longer, Lucy," Liz whispered. "I don't want to get Greenfield in trouble."

Lucy nodded. She pulled down her mask and kissed Erika's pale forehead. "Goodbye, my love. You will always live in my heart." She laid her hand on Erika's cheek. Liz fought back tears, determined to be strong for Lucy.

As they exited the room, Liz saw two surgeons she knew talking outside the scrub room door. "Hold on a minute, Lucy. I want to talk to these guys."

One of men waved as she approached. "Liz Stolz, long time no see."

"Hey, Mike. Are you on the harvest team?"

"Yeah. Both of us."

"Oh, hi, Liz. We miss you around here. How are you doing?" asked the taller one.

"I've been better, like the rest of us. That's my friend, Erika Bultmann, who's up for harvesting. I'd appreciate it if one of you could give me a call when it's over and she's disconnected."

The surgeon's gray eyes were sympathetic. "Sure, Liz. I have your number, but you should stop at the desk and make arrangements for what to do with the body. The morgue is filled with COVID patients."

"I intend to. Thanks…and thanks for letting me know. Don't forget." She gave each of them a firm look. She had authority on her side, being older, and they all knew her reputation from the past, so she trusted them to pay attention to her request.

The shorter man keyed something into his phone. "I'm writing myself a note to remind me to call you. Give me your number, so I don't have to look it up."

The other surgeon gave her a pat on the shoulder. "Sorry about your friend, Liz."

She nodded her thanks.

Liz stopped at the nurses' desk to give them her contact information and Lucy's, as well as instructions for the disposition of Erika's body.

Lucy looked like a lost child when Liz rescued her, standing by the elevator. Neither spoke as they rode down to the first floor. They deposited their PPE in the bin near the door. As Liz leaned against the door to open it for Lucy, a blast of cold smacked her in the face.

"It's always overheated in the hospital," Liz said, "I used to sweat like a pig."

Lucy looked at her as if she couldn't make sense of what she'd said.

Liz clicked open the doors of the truck. "I'm taking you home with me," she told Lucy as she held the passenger door open for her.

"I'm okay, Liz. You can take me home."

"We'll swing by your house so you can get what you need, but you're coming home with me. I asked the surgeon to call me when they disconnect her. The nurses will call you, but there may be a delay. I want to be there for you when the end comes."

Lucy made a little sound like the whimper of a puppy. Liz reached in and hugged her. Lucy clung to her and Liz didn't let her go until her grip lessened.

"Thank you," Lucy murmured.

"Let's get you home."

Chapter 23

Maggie heard the door open downstairs and sighed with relief. She'd left the doors to the bedroom and the stairwell open so that she could hear when Liz arrived. Whenever Liz went out on call, Maggie could never really sleep until she was home again. Maggie lay in bed for a moment considering the paradox. She'd been telling a therapist she might want to end her marriage, yet she couldn't sleep until her wife lay in bed beside her. How did that make any sense?

Liz was speaking. Her voice carried. Maggie assumed at first that she was on the phone, but then she heard another female voice, higher and sweeter in tone. Maggie strained to listen, but she couldn't make out whose. The voices came nearer. They were coming up the stairs. Maggie got up. She put on her slippers and threw on a robe.

The light was on in the seashore room, and she could see two figures moving inside. Now, she recognized the female voice as belonging to Lucy, who sat on the bed, staring at her feet. Liz put a small carry-on bag on the stand near the closet and hung up a black suit.

Maggie came to the door. "I'm so glad you're home," she said to announce her presence. "How's Erika doing?"

One look at their faces told her all she had to know. Lucy's mascara had run, leaving dark rivulets down her face. She looked up mournfully. In her eyes was unspeakable pain.

"Oh, no," murmured Maggie. "Please, not that!"

Liz approached and hugged her. "She's still alive," she explained to Maggie. "She's on life support until they can remove her organs for transplant."

"Oh, God. No!"

Maggie sat down on the bed beside Lucy. "Oh, Lucy. I'm so sorry." She put her arm around her. "What happened? Was it her heart?" she asked Liz.

"No, her heart was healthy. A brain aneurysm ruptured. It was inoperable. According to the neurologist who read the scan, the brain damage was extensive and irreversible."

"How could this happen?" asked Maggie, hugging Lucy closer. "Liz, why didn't you know about this condition?"

"No one knew. Not even Erika."

"She had a bad headache tonight," Lucy said. "She went to bed early. When I came upstairs, she was unconscious."

"Oh, Lucy! How terrible! What an awful thing for you to see! I'm so sorry." Lucy covered her face with her hands and began to sob.

Maggie felt a hand on her shoulder. "Come on. She's exhausted and needs to rest." Liz got down on one knee to look directly into Lucy's face. "Lucy, do you want something to help you sleep?"

"I don't need anything. I'm okay," she said, wiping her nose with the back of her hand.

Liz grabbed a handful of tissues from the box on the bedstand and handed them to her. "I'm going to leave you a mild tranquilizer. You can use it later if you need it."

Liz left. Maggie heard her feet on the steps and knew she was heading down to her office to get her medical bag. She returned with some pills and a bottle of water.

"Is there anything else you need?" Liz asked, leaning on her knees, anxiously scanning Lucy's face.

Lucy looked up and shook her head. "No, thank you. You've both been so kind. I'll just take off my makeup and get into bed."

"I hope you can sleep. You look so exhausted," said Maggie, brushing the hair away from Lucy's eyes. "Take off your makeup and get some sleep. Do you need makeup remover? I'll give you some."

Lips pressed together to avoid more tears, Lucy shook her head.

"We'll be right upstairs if you need us," Liz said. "You know where we are."

Lucy nodded solemnly. "I'll be all right. Thank you so much."

Maggie rose and kissed the top of Lucy's head. "Try to sleep. You'll need your strength." She sighed, thinking of the many funerals she'd helped plan—her parents', the niece who had died of bone cancer in her twenties. The bizarre ritual of arranging with the funeral home to dress up a corpse that will ultimately end up in the ground. The pandemic had changed funerals, making them shorter, sometimes virtual. Maybe that was a blessing in disguise. She glanced at Liz, wondering how she could face another funeral. She'd already buried three close family members and a close friend in less than a year.

Maggie went back up to the bedroom. Liz didn't speak while she put on the knit pants and T-shirt she had flung off when Lucy had called. If necessary, Liz could be out of the house in five minutes. "In the old days, they could call you for a patient at any hour. Now, care is a community effort," Liz had once explained. "But the ability to wake up from a dead sleep and spring into action is like riding a bicycle. You never forget."

Liz was about to plug in her phone to charge when she changed her mind and tapped open a call.

"Who are you calling at this hour?"

"Tom Simmons. He's used to getting calls in the middle of the night."

Maggie got into bed and listened to Liz explain to the associate rector of Lucy's church what had happened. She always found out more when Liz explained things to others than when she told her. Maybe Liz assumed that, as her wife, she knew more than she did. Maybe she thought she wouldn't understand.

"We'll need to break the news to Stefan," Liz said to Tom in that even, almost monotone voice she used when she explained something medical. "I'm especially worried about him. He's been depressed since they locked down that senior residence."

"I play chess with him online," Tom's booming voice said. It was audible across the room even though Liz didn't have the call on speaker. "But it's not the same as seeing real people."

"I might bring him over to stay with us for a while…if he'll allow it."

"I'll support you in that," Tom assured Liz.

"Maybe I'll encourage Lucy to stay with us too. We'll see how she's doing tomorrow. She's still in shock."

"Erika was so healthy. I never would have expected it. I'll really..." Tom's voice broke. "I'll really miss her."

"Me too." Liz's voice was thick.

Liz ended the call, as she always did, without saying goodbye. She plugged in the phone and got into bed, where she lay with her hands behind her head, staring at the ceiling.

In the light of the nearly full moon, Maggie watched her for a while, knowing her wife was deep in thought, decompressing after being ripped out of a sound sleep and needing to perform. It was hard to imagine how someone could settle down to go back to sleep after something like that. Despite Liz's training, it had to be disruptive to her psyche. Maggie, whose sleep was disturbed whenever Liz got a call, tried to imagine what it was like to dash into your clothes and head out into a frigid night to face God knows what.

"How do you feel, Liz?" Maggie finally asked. "She was your friend for such a long time."

"It's not only the length of time. There were things we could talk about that no one else understands. We had memories of events we shared. Now, it's only me. Sometimes, I would forget the things we did together, but she would help me remember. Between the two of us, we could tell the whole story. Now, I only have half of it."

Maggie realized what she was trying to say. As precisely as Liz could speak about medicine or philosophy, when it came to emotions and ordinary things, she sometimes stuttered, not literally, of course, but she would stare into space, unable to find the right words. Maggie saw part of her role as Liz's interpreter, so that Liz could express her feelings to herself. The deeper the feeling, the harder it was for her to express.

"Come here," said Maggie. "Let me hold you. You must be devastated." She opened her arms. Liz nuzzled into her shoulder, her cheek against her breast. Maggie lazily stroked her hair. "I'm sorry, Liz. I know how much you loved Erika."

"She was my wingman," said Liz. "I could always count on her."

"I know. She was a good friend."

"The best."

"You should get some sleep. You have to work tomorrow."

"There are a couple of patients I have to see. I'll ask Cherie if she can pinch hit for me. Now that she's back from her honeymoon, I'm going to make her work for a living."

Maggie clucked her tongue. "What a horrible boss you are," she said smiling so Liz could hear in her voice that she was only teasing.

"I'm going to bring Stefan over at lunchtime. Tom too, if he's free. We'll tell him together."

"I'll make some quick breads. We have plenty of eggs. Maybe I'll make a breakfast casserole."

"Don't go to too much trouble. Nobody will have much appetite."

Maggie realized Liz was right, but in her mind, she was planning an impressive spread, including fruit salad. She pressed Liz's face closer to her breast. "Go to sleep now," she ordered.

Liz was asleep in no time. Falling asleep on command was a gift. Maggie could always tell when she fell asleep because her head became heavy on her breast. She'd need to ease out from under her or her arm would fall asleep. Liz stirred and groaned but instantly returned to a deep slumber.

Maggie curled into the fetal position and tried to empty her mind, but she kept imagining Lucy's horror at coming up to bed and finding Erika unconscious. Maggie had played many such scenes as an actress, trying to evoke the horror someone might feel, the unspeakable pain, but she still couldn't fathom it. Acting might try to imitate real life, but when reality bit, it bit hard.

It was some time later when a sound, a bone-chilling shriek, ripped through Maggie's dream. She listened carefully and identified the sound as a woman's voice wailing. She remembered that Lucy was downstairs, and that Liz had left all the doors open to the second floor. Usually, they only left them open when children were visiting without their parents. Again,

Maggie heard the shriek, followed by moaning like a wounded animal crouching in the dark.

"Liz," she called. She gently shook her arm. "Lucy's screaming."

"What?" said Liz. She sat up and listened. The moaning started again. "I'll go down and see what's going on." She flung off the covers.

Maggie rolled over, thinking, *you brought her here. She's your responsibility*, but that was petty and cruel, and Lucy was her friend too. "No, Liz. I'll go," she said, getting up. "You try to get some sleep."

"Are you sure?" asked Liz doubtfully.

"Yes. You have to work tomorrow. Go back to sleep."

Maggie put her robe on over her nightgown, but she couldn't find her slippers in the dark, so she went down the carpeted steps barefooted. She closed all the doors as she went so that Liz could sleep. When she arrived at Lucy's room, she listened outside the closed door. It was quiet now. Maybe it was okay, and she should go back to bed. Then the keening began again, a terrifying, feral sound that cut to the heart. Maggie knocked softly. When there was no answer, she opened the door. She found Lucy, sitting on the edge of the bed, hugging herself, and rocking back and forth.

"Oh, Lucy," said Maggie, sitting beside her. "I'm so sorry."

"They called. She's dead now. Really *dead*."

In Lucy's green eyes, Maggie saw the waves of grief and pain crashing on her soul. As she put her arms around her friend, she realized she had no words to say. She knew better than to tell a priest that her wife, whom she'd only married a year ago, was now with God, that it was for the best, that Erika was in a "better place." Lucy had once tried to explain why saying glib things like that was wrong, even more hurtful to the person who'd lost someone. Lucy, who'd led so many groups to help survivors of loss, was now one of the bereaved.

"Maybe you should take one of the pills that Liz left for you. It might help."

"No, I don't want to numb the pain. I want to feel it, every bit of it. I want Erika to know how much it hurts to lose her."

Maggie sighed and gently stroked Lucy's back. There were sniffles and sobs, but her presence seemed to have stopped the awful keening.

Lucy turned to her anxiously. "I'm sorry. Did I wake you?"

"Yes, but only because Liz left all the doors to downstairs open so we could hear you. They're closed now. She can't hear you." She brushed Lucy's red hair back and noticed it was fading, but not the abundant freckles over her face. If possible, there were even more of them. Without makeup, Lucy usually looked younger, almost girlish, but tonight, in her grief, she looked ancient. "What can I do to help you, Lucy?"

"There's nothing anyone can do. Just sit here a moment. Let me catch my breath. I'll be okay."

Maggie gave her a half hug. "You will be okay," she said firmly and gave her other shoulder a little shake to emphasize her point. They sat without speaking until Maggie felt chilled. Liz liked to keep the heat down in the bedrooms. She was her own furnace and hated to sleep in a warm room. Even more, she hated to waste fuel heating empty rooms. Maggie could get up and raise the thermostat, but she suddenly had a better idea.

"Why don't we get under the covers, and I'll stay with you?"

"You don't need to stay. I'm okay now. Really. It's just the shock."

"I know," said Maggie. "Come on. Let's lie down and I'll hold you."

Lucy sighed. "You don't have to. I'm okay."

"Lucy, sometimes, you're more stubborn than Liz!" said Maggie pulling back the covers, so Lucy could get in. Maggie was about to turn off the light when there was a knock at the door.

"The surgeon just called," Liz said. "It's over."

"We know," said Maggie. "They called Lucy."

"Oh, usually, they're not that quick." Liz came in and stood at the bedside. "Lucy, you should take the Alprazolam. It's a low dose, but it will calm you down."

"She won't take it. Go back to bed, Liz. I'll stay with her."

Liz frowned, looking doubtful. "You sure?"

"You need sleep, Liz," said Lucy firmly. "You have to work today, and so do I."

"No, you don't. I called Tom. He'll handle your duties tomorrow. Get some rest. You'll be busy today."

"Go to bed, Liz. I've got this," Maggie said. A moment later, she heard Liz heading up the stairs.

To Maggie's surprise, Lucy soon fell asleep. She was so still as she slept, obviously exhausted. Her arm around her friend's waist, Maggie listened to the rhythm of her gentle breathing until her mind began to float.

When Maggie awoke, her arm was still around Lucy. Neither of them had moved during the night. The winter sun was bright against the curtains featuring seashells and starfish. Lucy needed rest, so Maggie got up as quietly as she could. Liz was already gone, of course. She always opened the office on Fridays. Maggie wished she had found her slippers. Her feet were cold as she crept downstairs to the kitchen. She remembered that she had a pair of Crocs in the downstairs closet and put them on.

There was a note from Liz near the coffee pot. Maggie read it while she drank her coffee. Her efficient wife had arranged for Cherie to cover all her appointments after eleven o'clock. Tom would be coming for brunch, and Stefan had accepted her invitation. It was the last line that hit Maggie like a blow: "I called Billy LaPierre to pick up the body." At least, Lucy didn't have to worry about that.

Maggie thought back to the evening Liz had asked Erika whether she wanted to withdraw her power of attorney and medical proxy now that she was married to Lucy. Erika turned her pale eyes on Liz and replied, "absolutely not." How wonderful to have such a deep and enduring friendship, a friend you could literally trust with your life…and your death.

Maggie cut up the fruit for the salad and prepared the breakfast casserole. She put the blueberry breads in the oven before going up for a shower. After she dressed, she decided to let her hair hang loose to dry. On her way downstairs, she quietly opened the door to Lucy's room and saw that she was still sleeping peacefully. *Good for you*, thought Maggie. *It's probably the only peace you'll get for a while.*

While she waited for the bread to finish baking, she sat in the living room and read the paper version of The New York Times. Liz still subscribed to it, solely because Maggie preferred to turn real pages and fold over her newspaper like she used to when she rode the subway to NYU's uptown campus. At the memory, Maggie put the paper down. Liz was so accommodating, so kind. How could she even think of leaving her? "Because it's not enough," Maggie said aloud to herself.

"What's not enough?" a voice replied.

Maggie looked up and saw Lucy standing in the doorway. "Never mind. I was talking to myself. I do that a lot lately because no one else listens." She gave Lucy a firm look. "Get yourself a cup of coffee. You know where everything is."

"I should. I lived with you for months."

"How are you doing today?"

Lucy heaved out a sigh. "A little better." Her eyes glanced in the direction of the kitchen. "I read Liz's note. I hope you don't mind."

"I think it was meant for both of us."

"Your wife is as efficient as mine is…was." Lucy's beautiful face crumbled in pain.

"I'll get you coffee. Sit down."

They drank their coffee but shared few words. There wasn't much to say. Maggie finished the brunch preparations while Lucy showered. Tom arrived first. Maggie always smiled when she saw the twinkle in the big, affable man's blue eyes. As Tom's beard grew whiter, the more he resembled Santa Claus.

"Hello, Maggie," he said, bending to kiss her. "How's our friend this morning?"

"Shocked. Devastated…like we all are."

"Indeed, we are," said Tom, a look of sadness passing in his eyes. "Erika was an original. She always marched to her own drummer. She will definitely be missed." He looked thoughtful. "I wonder if Liz thought to call the college."

"She left a note," said Maggie, pointing in that direction. "She didn't say anything about that."

"I'll call the dean of Colby while we wait for Liz and Stefan."

"Be quick. They'll be here soon."

He went into the dining room to make his call. Maggie could hear his warm voice, but not the words he said. Lucy came into the kitchen, her damp hair tied back. She was wearing her clericals but no collar.

"You don't think you're going to work today?" Maggie asked.

"No, but I thought it might be a comfort to Stefan."

"Oh, yes, just the thing to comfort an atheist, two priests sitting at the table."

"You know what I mean."

"I do. It's scary how I can read your mind sometimes."

Lucy managed a weak smile. "I'm sure my thoughts are scary to everyone but me."

As Maggie put the casserole in the oven, she heard the front door open, followed by the sound of Liz's and Stefan's voices. Her insides went cold when she heard the old man ask, "Where's Erika?"

"Let's sit down, Stefan," said Tom.

Maggie wasn't sure she wanted to be a witness to this painful scene, but she felt obligated to support her friend. Lucy was sitting beside her father-in-law, tenderly holding his hand, while Tom explained what had happened in a calm, soothing voice. What an asset he was to St. Margaret's and to Lucy, his boss.

"Erika told me she wanted to be cremated," said Liz. "It's in a memo in her will."

"No!" shouted Stefan. "No fire!"

"But Stefan…" Liz began.

"No! You cannot imagine how it was in Berlin during the bombings. The people screaming when they burned alive. It was terrible. A nightmare! Oh, you cannot imagine!"

Maggie remembered the discussion when Stefan's wife died. He'd insisted on burying her because of his bad memories from the war.

"Please, Liz," he begged. "No fire. I don't want my Erika burned up in an oven." Maggie's heart went out to the old man. Although he was still hale in his nineties, he suddenly looked gray and frail.

"It is what she wanted," Liz insisted.

Lucy subtly shook her head in Liz's direction. "It's all right, Stefan. It doesn't matter now. Erika is gone. The living matter now. If you want us to bury Erika, we will."

Maggie watched Lucy's face, marveling over her kindness and ability to offer pastoral care, even in the face of her own unfathomable grief.

Chapter 24

$\mathbf{S}$am had never seen Olivia look so shaken. For the space of a moment, her skin paled to a gray tone, and she looked every one of her sixty-one years. "Good God!" she exclaimed. Sam put down her fork, as if it would help her pay more attention and strained to hear what the caller was saying, but she couldn't. "Yes, of course, I'll help in any way I can. But what can I do?"

Now, Sam was overwhelmed with curiosity. "What's going on?" she asked.

Olivia shook her head in Sam's direction and listened more intently. "Of course, I'll approve the use of town property for a compassionate use such as that. Tell Brenda to call me as soon as she can."

After Olivia tapped off the call, she stared at Sam with her penetrating blue eyes. "Erika Bultmann died last night."

"What! What happened? Was it a heart attack?"

"A cerebral aneurysm. Her heart was healthy. They took it for transplant along with other organs."

"I didn't know she was an organ donor," Sam said, "but she was always very pragmatic, despite people thinking her head was in the clouds." The fact of the death suddenly hit her. "God, I loved Erika. I'll miss her so much."

Olivia sank down into her seat at the table. She pushed her half-eaten breakfast plate away. "We'll all miss Erika. She was low-key, but you always knew she was there."

"Who was that on the phone?"

"Abbie Roberts, the church warden. Tom is scrambling to take over the rector's duties while Lucy is dealing with her loss. Abbie is stepping in to help both of them. That woman is amazing! We are so lucky to have her. Do you know she ran a fifty-million-dollar division before she retired?"

"No, but I know that would impress you." Sam grinned to soften the criticism.

Olivia made a face, but she didn't respond to the obvious dig. "We have all these super-competent baby-boomer women, who have retired. If we could only figure out a way to put them to work in the community."

"Oh, no," said Sam, rolling her eyes, "I feel another Enright project in the works."

This time, Olivia heard the insult and gave her a dirty look. "Finish your breakfast," she ordered. "We should see what we can do to help."

"What's this about Brenda?" asked Sam, picking up her fork.

"There's a police van with a partition that blocks air flow from the back. Emily is flying back from New Haven to be with her mother. She's been tested for weeks to make sure she's COVID negative because she was coming home for Christmas, but now she has to get on a plane. Erika was going to drive down to Yale to pick her up. Obviously, Lucy's in no shape to do it."

Sam mopped up her eggs with her toast. "Good thing we finished Lucy's Christmas present early, or Erika wouldn't have lived to see how much she loved it. God! Dying right before Christmas. My dad died on Thanksgiving weekend. Anniversaries like that make the holidays miserable forever."

"Lucy is one of the strongest women I know," said Olivia. "She'll get through this."

Sam munched on her last piece of toast and thought about Erika. It was one thing to bury the people of your parents' generation; another to bury one of your own. Erika was only two years older than Sam, and she'd always looked so healthy. She walked every day, ate right, drank in moderation except when Liz took out the single-malt scotch. She remembered joining one of their drinking bouts, which was how she met Erika, who used to spend vacations in Connecticut with Liz and Jenny "for a change of wallpaper," as she'd say. Sometimes, Jeanine would come along, and they'd all go down to New York to visit the galleries and take in a Broadway play. Erika's quiet support when Sam's firm pushed her out had cemented their bond. As always, she was philosophical: "You're not a has-been. Life is simply forcing you to explore a new path. Embrace the adventure!"

Erika certainly had more than her share. Her description of escaping from East Germany in the trunk of an old police car belonged in a spy novel, not real life. How many people could say they'd survived crossing the Berlin Wall during the cold war?

"You're thinking about her, aren't you?" asked Olivia, scrutinizing Sam's face.

Sam nodded. "Yeah, I am. I'll miss her accent. It was unique."

"I wish I'd had more time to get to know her better," said Olivia with a sigh. "She was certainly an original."

"Yes, she was."

"Mother Lucy is going to be a very wealthy woman."

Sam gave Olivia a hard look. "How do you know that?"

"The crash when the pandemic started shook Liz's confidence. Why, I don't know. For an amateur, she is exceptionally competent at investing, but when she agreed to let me help her manage her cash flow for her business, she suggested Erika consult me too. Erika hired me as her financial advisor, making her number four of my many clients. Woohoo!" Olivia waved her hands in mock excitement."Except for modest bequests to Yale and Colby, Erika left everything to Lucy. And Stefan was leaving everything to Erika. I don't know what will happen to that money now."

"Why does it always come down to money?" Sam wondered aloud. "That's how my mother kept a noose around my neck. She threatened to disinherit me if I didn't keep a low profile about being gay. So, I got back at her by earning plenty of money of my own. I refused to be blackmailed."

"Good for you, Sam. That's what I like so much about you. Your independence."

"Yeah? That's not what you say most of the time. You'd probably like me to move in here."

Olivia patted Sam's hand. "You will when you're ready."

"No, I won't," Sam protested, snatching her hand away. "I'm not giving up my house on the pond. That's my place. I love it there."

Olivia was obviously making a concerted effort to look patient. "All right, it's a wonderful place, especially after the work you put into it, but don't you want more from this relationship?"

"I don't know yet," Sam said. "We might be heading there, but not yet."

Olivia exhaled a long stream of breath. "Life is so short. Look what happened to your friend. Did Erika know when she woke up yesterday morning that it would be her last?"

"Life comes at you fast, but that doesn't mean that we should rush into anything. I like you, Olivia. I like you a lot, in fact. You're one of the best lovers I've ever had."

"One of the best…?" Olivia raised a dark brow. "That's all?"

"You're so competitive. Do you always have to be the best at everything?"

"Yes. It's important to always do your best."

Sam rolled her eyes. "Okay. If you want to know, where the bedroom is concerned, you are the best."

Olivia gave Sam's shoulder an affectionate pat on her way to the kitchen sink with her dish. "Come on. Let's see how we can help our friends. What can we do?"

"Maybe we can help call people to let them know."

"But we should ask Lucy first if she minds," Olivia said. "There may be some people she wants to call personally."

"Maybe we can look after Erika's father. We don't want that poor, old man to get lost in the shuffle. God. He'll be crushed by this. Despite all their sparring, which was just for show, he adored his daughter."

"We can cook for them," Olivia suggested.

"Oh, I'm sure Maggie is already cooking up a storm."

"You can never have enough food at a funeral."

"Did Abbie tell you the arrangements?" asked Sam.

"No, they're still figuring it out. Tom will conduct the service. Close friends, those of us in the testing program, will be allowed into the church, but with strict social distancing. It will be carried in a private Zoom link for others. Her students and friends at the College where she taught and Yale, where her father still has friends, will be invited. The burial will be private for close friends and family only."

"Burial? Erika wanted to be cremated. Even I know that. She was appalled that her mother wanted to be buried. She worried about embalming fluid contaminating the water supply."

Olivia shrugged. "I'm only telling you what I heard."

"I should call Liz. This will hit her hard. She and Erika were very close."

"While you do that, I'll take a shower. Can't waste the entire day…as much as I'd like to take you back to bed and have my wicked way with you."

"Go shower," Sam ordered, pointing in the direction of the stairs. After Olivia left, she got up to bring her plate to the sink and load the dishwasher. She realized her phone was ringing in the pocket of her sweatshirt. She yanked it out and glanced at the screen. "Hey, Brenda."

"You heard?"

"Yes, the church warden called Olivia. They're besties now."

"Jeez. Olivia is infiltrating everywhere. We better watch out, or she'll take over the whole town."

Sam laughed. "Too late. I think she's done that already."

"The old townies will only let her get so far before they stonewall her. I've been living here for years, and they still remind me I'm from away."

"It's that Brooklyn accent that creeps in every once in a while. You have to practice sounding like a Mainer."

"Ayuh," said Brenda. There was a long pause. "God! Erika! She can't be gone. I loved Erika."

"Me too," said Sam.

"We're going to have to step up now and help Lucy…and Stefan. Poor Stefan. He's devastated."

"You've seen him?"

"Yes, I was over there this morning. Liz has everyone at her house. You know, doing her town doctor thing and taking care of everyone. I insinuated myself into their brunch."

"Of course, you did," said Sam with a chuckle. "You never met a free meal you didn't like."

"I love my Cherie's cooking, but Maggie's is good too."

"I love her cooking too. Just don't tell Olivia." Sam put her feet up on the hassock. "I hear you're going to pick up Emily at the airport."

"Yeah, she's coming in this afternoon. I volunteered to do it, but we had to get Olivia's okay to use the police van for unofficial business. With the old town manager, I used to decide that kind of thing on my own, but Olivia pays more attention. She's been good to me. I don't want to get on the wrong side of her again."

"No, I don't blame you. I wouldn't either."

"Okay, Sam, you already know what's going on. I'll probably see you later. Are you going over to Liz's place?"

"Yeah, probably. I'm sure Liz is hurting, but you know her. She's playing tough guy and being stoic."

"I'm sure Maggie will make sure she doesn't get away with that," said Brenda. "She'll look after her."

"Hmm. Not so sure about that. We should go over and sit with her… Lucy too."

There was a long silence. "I bet LaPierre's funeral home would love to get the business Liz is getting at her house for free. Billy's been losing his shirt in the pandemic. Big funerals are banned. There's no money in cremations. No big, fancy casket to buy. You can transport a cremation urn in a car, so you don't even need to hire a hearse."

"Billy was losing his shirt before the pandemic. Those three-day wakes are so old school. No one can take that much public grief."

"But we used to do it all the time. We had a two-day viewing when Marcia died. It was stupid because most of our friends were still in New York and hardly anyone came."

Sam heard squawking in the background and realized it was Brenda's radio.

"Gotta go, Sam. Maybe I'll see you later at Liz's house."

"I'm going to call her now," said Sam, but Brenda had already hung up.

Chapter 25

Lucy had always liked the screen porch overlooking the garden. She had fond memories of sitting there with Liz and Maggie that first spring after she'd moved to Hobbs. They had taken her under their wing. Although they were completely open about being gay, Lucy hadn't said anything about her own sexual preferences. She'd only had one relationship with a woman before, and she wasn't in the market for a partner, so she didn't feel the need to make a grand announcement.

She was drawn to them because they were welcoming, especially Maggie, who shared Lucy's love of liturgical music. Maggie seemed overwhelmingly curious about the idea of a female priest. She'd stuck with the Catholic church until the pedophilia scandal. Lucy sensed she was looking for a way to return to the faith. She was shy at first about it and still parochially Catholic, but she'd gravitated toward St. Margaret's. Eventually, she'd joined the choir. When the elderly music director retired, Maggie had taken his place.

Liz, being Liz, was less subtle about what she wanted from Lucy's friendship. Liz was a fanatical opera fan, so her interest in a retired opera star was a given. She was also a flirt, which Lucy found flattering, but didn't take seriously because Maggie and Liz were happily married, or so Lucy thought at the time.

That was before Erika. They'd all met at the same time, after Lucy's first carol service at St. Margaret's. Then Erika disappeared back to Waterville, where she'd taught philosophy for thirty years. When she'd returned, it had all happened so fast, their connection, the growth of their physical passion, and then they were married, both dressed as brides, in a beautiful wedding at Lucy's church. Lucy had always wondered if they'd acted too quickly. Now that Erika was gone, she realized there had been no time to waste.

Lucy remembered them sitting on the same wicker love seat, where she now sat, after returning from that fateful visit to New York. Unwittingly Emily, the daughter Lucy had given up for adoption as an infant, had nearly broken up the budding relationship. That had been Lucy's experience of life—gain one thing and lose another, but in this case, it hadn't worked out that way, until now…

"You're thinking of sitting here with her," Tom said, tapping Lucy's shoulder.

Lucy patted the seat next to her, and he sat down. "How did you know?"

"Because I'm thinking about it too. The night of the cast party, she asked me to explain the requirements for Episcopal marriage. In her efficient, Erika-way, she was plotting the proposal, and wanted to have all her ducks lined up."

"I loved that about her…her efficiency. She never wasted any time."

"Good thing, too. Apparently, there was none to waste. Do you think we can have premonitions? I mean not as in prophecy, but in the ordinary sense?"

"Funny. I was thinking the exact same thing. In thinking back, I remember things Erika said that made me think she was getting ready. Strange, isn't it?" Lucy couldn't stop the sob that suddenly seized her.

Tom reached for her hand. "When you're a pastor, it's especially hard to be the one who needs pastoral care. What can I do to help you, Lucy? Would you like me to pray with you?"

Lucy gave Tom's hand a little squeeze. "I can't pray right now. I feel such a void in my soul. I can't connect with God or anyone, really. I feel numb."

"It's the shock. That's the worst part of a sudden death. Your mind doesn't want to believe it. The shock is the way it protects itself from unbearable pain. But you know all this. Probably better than I do. You're a licensed therapist."

"Like being a pastor, it's no special help when you're the one who's grieving."

"I see some of Erika's philosophical stoicism has rubbed off on you."

Lucy sighed and took back her hand. "I learned that before I met Erika. My life certainly hasn't turned out how I expected."

"Whose does? When you were young, did you ever expect to be ordained?"

"It never crossed my mind."

"Mom?" said a young voice.

They both turned around and saw Lucy's daughter standing in the doorway. Whenever Lucy saw Emily after a separation, she was struck by how much the girl, actually a young woman now, resembled her. The main difference was that Emily's eyes were blue like her father's, and Emily was also tall like Alex.

Tom patted Lucy's shoulder. "I'll let you talk to your daughter. We can catch up later."

Over her mask, featuring an Escher print, Emily stared at Tom as he left. There was no hostility in her direct look, only the undisguised curiosity Emily displayed around people she didn't know well. Her adoptive parents, religious people, had trained her to be polite, but they had never succeeded in teaching her not to stare.

Emily sat down on the love seat across from where Lucy sat. Her mother held her breath. Because Emily was on the spectrum, anything could come out of her mouth. Sometimes, her words were completely appropriate and sensitive. Sometimes, they were so off, that even Lucy, who heard all sorts of things as a priest or a therapist, cringed. Emily was holding a brightly wrapped box Lucy presumed was a Christmas gift. She put the box on the coffee table and slid it in her mother's direction.

"I needed money to buy you a Christmas present. I called Erika. She sent it to me by PayPal. I know it's not Christmas yet, but please open it."

Lucy reached across for the box, which had been meticulously wrapped. The bow was perfectly tied. The flaps of the wrapping paper were folded neatly into triangles exactly equal in size. Lucy looked up and smiled as she slid the box out of the wrappings. Emily was sitting with her hands neatly folded. Her blue eyes were focused elsewhere.

"Should I guess?" asked Lucy.

"No, Mom, just open it, please."

Lucy took the lid off the box and found a small pile of colorful, protective masks with sayings printed on them. The top one said, "Don't Make Me Use My Opera Voice."

"That's genius," said Lucy, smiling.

"Look at the others."

Lucy read off the sayings printed on the others: "I'm the Psychotic Soprano Everyone Warned You About," "Soprano, We Get High," "Singing Soprano is My Superpower." There was one with a treble staff and a high C that read "Soprano. No Problem for Me." The last two, Lucy could get away with wearing in public. The others, she'd have to think about, but she had to admit they were all ingenious. The gift showed incredible thoughtfulness.

"Thank you, Emily. These are wonderful. So creative."

"There were lots more, but I liked these the best. They remind me of you. You're both strong…and a little crazy."

Lucy laughed softly.

"I wish I could sit near you, Mom, and give you a hug."

Lucy could feel her arms involuntarily move, longing to feel that embrace. "I know, sweetheart. Me too. Soon."

"Aunt Liz says I'm negative, but I still have to wait. I don't want to make you sick."

Emily's beautiful, blue eyes clouded with disappointment. She looked like she might cry, so Lucy quickly changed the subject. "Was the plane crowded?"

"There were only two people. Me and an old lady. Liz said she will test me every day. I don't have to go back to school until January, so maybe I can hug you before I leave."

"Oh, I can't wait, Emily."

"I can't wait either." She took off her mask. "She said I don't have to wear it if I sit far enough away."

"That's better. I want to see your face."

Her beautiful features twisted in pain. "I'm sad, Mom. Very sad. I really liked Erika. I loved her."

Lucy felt tears coming on, so she simply nodded in reply.

"When I started looking for my birth mother, I had no idea I would get two moms. It was only for a short time, but I was very lucky to have two mothers. Some people don't even have one."

That sentiment defeated Lucy's ability to keep her emotions in check. She grabbed a handful of tissues from the box Maggie had set beside her and blew her nose.

"I made you cry, Mom. I'm sorry," said Emily, looking mournful. "Now, I want to cry too."

"Go ahead. Sometimes, it's good to cry. It lets the sadness out. If you cry and cry when it hurts, sometimes you use up all the tears, and then, you feel better."

"I'll cry later," said Emily. "When no one is looking. I cried after you called me at school. My professor asked what was wrong. I told him about Erika. He knew her from when she went to school there…and Stefan too."

"I'm glad there are people at Yale who still remember them. Did that make you feel better?"

"Yes, it made me glad that she wasn't forgotten. I don't want her to ever be forgotten." Emily curved her mouth into what for her was a smile. It was something she'd had to learn and to do consciously, so it was never completely genuine, more like a model's plastic smile. Her eyes were more successful in conveying her pleasure.

"Emily?" called Alina, Maggie's daughter. The small dark-haired woman leaned into the room. "The dining room is clear now if you want to get some food."

"Thank you," said Emily. "I'm starving."

"Go ahead. And after you eat, the kids want to watch a movie with you. The media room is so big you can sit far enough apart."

After Emily left, Lucy was glad to be alone again. The tears kept coming. She went through a stack of tissues. Fortunately, Maggie had also thought to give her a small trash can in which to deposit those she'd used.

"Lucy, why are you sitting all alone?" Cherie's voice. She couldn't know that solitude was a relief. Everyone wanted to comfort her with their presence. That's what people did when someone died. They showed up and said meaningless words of sympathy. Their good intentions were somewhat comforting, but trying to keep up a good front took such effort.

Cherie came in and sat down beside her. When she reached for her wrist, Lucy knew she was surreptitiously taking her pulse. Like Liz, her boss, Cherie was subtle about it, but Lucy could feel the artery depressed under her fingertips.

"Am I still alive?" asked Lucy, trying for humor. Her face ached from so many forced smiles, and she couldn't manage another.

"Not subtle enough, am I?" Cherie asked, gently returning Lucy's hand to her thigh.

"It's all right. I know you're all worried about me, but I'm okay. Really."

"It's such a shock. For all of us. We loved Erika."

Lucy dabbed her eyes with a fresh tissue. "Do I look okay? Not like a raccoon?"

Cherie grinned. She took the tissue out of Lucy's hand and did a little touch-up. "Now, you look okay. But don't worry how you look. No one cares." She put her arm around Lucy's shoulders and gave her a little hug. "Is there anything I can do for you? Do you want something to drink?"

Lucy shook her head. "Liz has been pushing so much water on me I can't stay out of the bathroom."

"It's important to hydrate at times like this."

"And here are my two favorite ladies," said Brenda. "Lucy, can you scooch over…just a bit, so I can sit down on your other side? I think my ass is still small enough to squeeze in."

"Do you think this little love seat is strong enough to hold the three of us?" Cherie asked.

"Now, that's insulting," Brenda said with a scowl. "Don't think because we're married you can say anything you want."

Lucy wondered if she had the emotional energy to put up with their good-natured banter, but she smiled weakly. They meant well.

"What can we do for you, Lucy?" asked Cherie. "You're always the one cheering up everyone else. It's hard seeing you hurting like this."

Brenda reached for Lucy's hand. "I know what to do."

"Hold hands?" asked Cherie, taking Lucy's other hand.

Brenda smiled and put a finger to her lips.

"Oh, I get it," said Cherie.

Lucy almost wept over the idea that her lesson had been learned so well.

Chapter 26

"The people need to see me," Lucy insisted. "They need to know that I'm okay, that I haven't abandoned them."

Tom rolled his eyes in Jeff's direction. Jeff made a funny face but not a sound, a good thing because Lucy had a good sense of humor, but she liked to be taken seriously. Disrespect could fire up one of her rare displays of temper.

Tom knew when he could push Lucy and when to step back. For such a good-natured person, Lucy could be surprisingly stubborn. She was the boss, which had always been clear, yet it was she who had pushed for the title of associate pastor when Tom would have been content to be her curate and spend more time at the beach. He'd been oddly touched by her insistence that he be paid as an associate rector, not that the salary was so generous. He'd made almost double as the rector of his historic parish in Connecticut. In a nod to his status, Lucy had insisted that he take over the rector's quarters when she moved into the beach house with Erika.

In Tom's estimation, Lucy made an impressive rector and leader of the parish. She always listened to everyone's opinion, no matter how harebrained it was. She let people appointed by the vestry do their jobs instead of micromanaging.

"Lucy, I just want you to know that I am here for you," Tom finally said. "I can take more of the load. This is a difficult time for you. It's been less than a week since you buried your wife."

"I know, but I need to get back to work. It's Christmas, and we're in the middle of a pandemic. People need to know their priest is there for them."

Tom sighed in resignation, knowing that arguing further wouldn't get him anywhere. As Erika used to say, quoting the Borg Queen, "resistance is futile." At the memory, Tom felt a lump rise in his throat. He cleared it, so no one would notice.

Erika had been a good friend, and, for a woman, a good lover—the only female lover Tom ever had. They'd parted ways amicably. Erika had left the math department before he did. She'd dumped theoretical mathematics in favor of continental philosophy. He hoped she had followed her passion. It had been hard to know at the time whether it had been rebellion against her father, the head of the math department, or genuine interest. After they'd lost touch, Tom occasionally saw notices of Erika's guest lectures at Yale, but he'd always been too busy to attend. He'd planned to read her books when he retired and reopen the conversations they'd begun decades ago. Now, it was too late. At least, Erika had books to her name. What did Tom have to show for all his years of study beyond his theology dissertation that was never published?

"I'll do the outdoor Eucharist this afternoon with the Christmas pageant. You take the midnight service on Zoom. I'll take the morning Eucharist tomorrow," Lucy said, summarizing what they'd decided.

"Whatever you say, Lucy," Tom said, trying to sound like a good soldier.

Through the phone, Tom could feel her reading his slight impatience. "I don't want you to think I'm pushing you aside, Tom."

He smiled and hoped she could hear it in his voice. "You're not. Everyone knows the midnight service is the big event."

"Make sure to wear the gold vestments. Those bespoke pieces are some of St. Margaret's greatest treasures. They need to come out of the closet once in a while."

"Will do, boss," he said, "but I'm finally out of the closet, thanks to you."

"Thanks to *you*," said Lucy. "It was brave, and I'm proud of you."

Tom smiled because Lucy never flattered. Her praise was always sincere.

"Merry Christmas, Tom. I'll see you later."

"Merry Christmas, Mother Lucy." He kept using that title, despite her shying away from it lately. He still liked to be called, "Father Tom," and didn't want to be the only priest in the parish clinging to the past. The older people in the parish seemed to prefer it, and Tom always believed in catering to his best customers.

"Are you going to stay here or in your miserable rectory tonight?" asked Jeff after Tom hung up from the call. It was hardly a choice between Jeff's spacious house in Webhanet with a view of the ocean versus a one-bedroom apartment in an aging building with indifferent heat.

"It might be good to stay at St. Margaret's tonight. Holidays are hard on people, and harder still since people can't travel to see their loved ones. Suicides and opiate overdoses are going way up. Someone might need me."

"You have a telephone, you know. Just bring your little priest bag along in case you need it." Jeff swung his feet around to the floor. While he was prone, Tom had been admiring both his flat stomach and the bulge in his soft sweatpants. He shaved his head now that he'd lost most of his hair. Tom found bald men particularly sexy. "Tony and Fred are coming over at three tomorrow. Will you be here by then?"

"I doubt I can make it that early. The outdoor Eucharist starts at two, but I'll be here soon after they arrive. We can't socialize with the parishioners after services, and it's supposed to be cold tomorrow, so it should be relatively early."

"Good, because I'm counting on you to cook the roast."

"I'll leave instructions just in case. It's easy-peasy. You turn on the heat on high for half an hour. Then you turn off the oven and don't open the door for two hours. That's it. I prepared the mustard crust. You just spoon it on before you put in the roast. Think you can manage that?" Tom glanced at his phone to see the time. "I'd better get home to make sure everything is ready for tonight and see if Lucy needs any help setting up for the evening liturgy." He turned to Jeff. "Thanks for being the camera man."

Jeff shrugged. "Hey, I started my career as a camera man. It's the least I can do."

"Sure you remember how? You spent the last three decades as a network exec."

"Believe me. It's not something you forget. Besides, if you can't operate today's digital cameras, you must be brain dead."

Tom visibly flinched, thinking of Erika so recently in that state.

Jeff was sensitive enough to realize his mistake. "Ouch, I'm sorry, Tom. I forgot. She really meant something to you."

"Yes, she did."

As Tom drove back to the church, he realized how much he was looking forward to the Christmas Eve services, especially the Christmas pageant performed by the children of the parish. He and Jeff had helped Abbie and the verger string the Christmas lights on the low branches of the trees in the churchyard. When no one was watching, he'd taken a break to say a prayer at the new grave where his friend lay. It was the first new grave in the churchyard in thirty years. Lucy had to get special permission from the health department to open the ground.

When they'd been planning the funeral, Tom wasn't sure at first that he'd be able to conduct the service for such a close friend. He'd considered asking one of the priests from the next parish to do it until he realized it would be his last gift to the only woman to whom he had given his body.

Lucy helped plan the service, which was simple and sweet. Maggie sang. Brenda, Liz, and Olivia volunteered to read. Liz eloquently eulogized her friend, breaking the somber mood by sharing some humorous stories. Even Lucy smiled. The entire service was carried online. Erika was beloved in Hobbs, but even more so by her students, past and present. The Zoom meeting hit the maximum of five hundred participants, so the college opened a link and streamed it on their website.

The memories put Tom in a somber mood as he drove back to the rectory to pack a bag to take back to Jeff's. He threw in his emergency kit, as he called it, the blessed oil for administering the last rites as well as small *Book of Common Prayer*. Tom took out his best, black suit, hung it on the back of the door, and carefully brushed the lint and dandruff off the shoulders. Even if no one saw it under his vestments, he wanted to look his best. After all, it was Christmas.

When Tom walked over to the church, he saw that people were beginning to arrive for the evening service. Lucy wasn't vested, but she had a knot of people around her. She was wonderful with the children of the parish. They all called her "Mother Lucy," proving to Tom's satisfaction that his instincts were right.

She'd given him a heads-up that she intended to preach on how brief the time was from Christmas to Easter, even though it spanned Jesus' entire life. The liturgical year, like life, was short, which was why it was so important to be in the present and celebrate the joys. Everyone would discern the not-so-hidden message behind this theme, but Lucy could be an eloquent preacher. No matter how dismal her topic or how painful, she always managed to sound a hopeful note, like a sublime high C at the end of an aria.

Tom picked out the most ornate of the antique, gold chasubles.

"I'm glad someone can wear that one. It's gorgeous, but much too heavy for me," Lucy said behind him, "and too long."

"It was clearly made for a fairly tall man," replied Tom. "Someone who cheerfully bore the weight of his ministry." He chuckled at his own pun.

To keep her feet warm in the snow, Lucy had on her black bearpaw boots. She wore double-weave black pants and a black parka.

"I see you're prepared for the cold," Tom observed.

"Yup. Even have my thermals on. I just hope I can get on my alb over all these clothes."

"Oh, you will. And if not, there are plenty of others in the closet."

They vested. Tom helped Lucy into her chasuble because with all the bulk under her vestments, it was hard to move.

"My mother always used to say, 'where there's a will there's a way,'" said Lucy. "It was nice of the Maine Dio-log to give us a plug for our outdoor services."

"From what I hear, you're the talk of the diocese. By holding these outdoor services, we're putting all the other churches to shame."

"I'm not looking for the attention…or the envy," said Lucy. "I just know how hungry people are in this dark time of isolation to see other people. Spiritual Eucharist is a great concept during the pandemic, but Holy Communion was always intended to be a physical connection between humans and the divine."

"I'm sure you'll cover that in your book on sex," said Tom, arranging his stole, and tying the cords of his alb over it. "I heard that Spangler agreed to supervise your dissertation. Lucky girl. He's the expert on the material nature of Christianity. Whatever you write, it will be mucho controversial. You probably couldn't get away with it anywhere but Union. They're so radical there."

"It is an approved Episcopal seminary," said Lucy in a prickly tone. Since the funeral, she was more reactive, which was completely understandable. Tom decided to change the subject.

"Erika told me she was looking forward to having two doctors in the house," said Tom. "Have you seen all the nonsense mocking Jill Biden for using her academic title?"

Lucy shrugged. "What do you expect from those people? Misogyny is rampant. Even the women hate women."

Tom clucked his tongue. "Lucy, Lucy. Not very charitable."

"Sometimes, I just have to speak my mind. I can't tell everyone what I think, but I can tell you."

"I'm honored you would say so," Tom said, and meant it.

Lucy glanced out the window to the churchyard. "The natives are restless. I think it's time to join the celebration."

The pageant featured live animals, a miniature donkey, a sheep and two goats. In New Haven, where Tom had been rector, such a folksy addition to the Christmas manger would be considered an affectation and a bit kitsch. Here, in Maine, people loved it.

"I'm going to take your lead on this liturgy, Lucy. After singing Wagner at the Met, you're the expert on blockbuster performances."

"Say a prayer this goes well after last year's run-away pig."

Tom laughed. "Yes, that was rather entertaining."

The pageant was as awkward and wooden as any Sunday-school play, but the older boys playing the shepherds read the psalms and epistle quite well. Tom's coaching on how to avoid sounding monotone seemed to have worked, but during the second reading, one of the goats released a strong stream of urine and bleated proudly afterward. Behind his black mask, Tom smiled.

It began to snow during Lucy's homily, which somehow made her reflections on birth, life, and death all the more touching. He perceived that Lucy's pace increased as the snow came down harder. By the time she removed the chalice veil, she had to dash away a little pile of dry snow. The flakes grew larger for a few minutes, but as Lucy approached the consecration, they almost miraculously stopped.

They made quick work of distributing Communion because the snow was coming down hard again. Lucy was dashing around to deliver the hosts while Tom and the eucharistic ministers gave out the Chinese restaurant containers of consecrated wine. By the time they had finished distributing Communion, the altar cloth was covered with snow. The goats started to bleat, and the donkey brayed in protest.

"I think we'll skip the exit hymn because of the weather," Lucy said and gave the blessing. "Merry Christmas, everyone! Don't forget, Tom will host worship at midnight."

Tom helped the verger collect the sacred vessels and take down the makeshift altar, a plastic table from the church basement. The warden was scrambling to get everything together. Lucy was rushing around the churchyard to wish as many people as possible a merry Christmas.

Tom shook the snow out of his hair when he got inside. With outdoor services as their only option to gather in person, of course, they would have a white Christmas. He glanced around, looking for Lucy but didn't see her. He caught Abbie's arm as she went by. "Have you seen Lucy?"

"I thought she came in already. Isn't she in the vesting room?"

Tom looked inside, but the room was empty. He looked out the window, but all the lights were off and the churchyard was empty.

He took off his stole and alb and hung them up, exchanging them for his parka. Christmas would be an occasion, if any, to wear his black dress coat, but in Maine, where most people only had one winter coat, it seemed pretentious.

By the time he dressed, he was becoming curious about Lucy's whereabouts. Surely, she should be here by now. Maybe she had slipped in before him and changed quickly. He glanced out the window into the churchyard again, but there was no one to be seen. Then he looked more closely and saw something that didn't belong—a small white mound. At the end was a black hat with a pompom. Moving on instinct, he ran, almost knocking down one of the shepherds waiting in the alcove for his ride home. The snow was slippery, and in his dress shoes, he had to watch his footing. He knelt in the snow and scooped the small figure into his arms. "Lucy! Lucy! Wake up!"

He pulled his phone from his coat and dialed Liz's number. "Are you still here?"

"Yes, I'm still trying to get out of this fucking parking lot."

"Come quick. Lucy passed out in the churchyard." To his relief, Lucy opened her eyes and gazed at him. She murmured his name. "She's awake now, but she doesn't look good."

"Can you get her inside?"

"I'll try."

"I'll be right there," said Liz. Tom could hear a large engine roar. He put the phone in his pocket. "Can you stand, Lucy?"

"Yes, if you help me up, please."

Tom practically had to lift her to her feet, but she was tiny and as light as a bird. He swung her arm around his neck and picked her up.

"Oh, Tom," Lucy protested, "I can walk."

"Never mind. It's freezing out here. We need to get you inside."

Liz saw them and dashed across the churchyard. She gave Lucy a quick, critical assessment. "Bring her in. We need to warm her up."

They attracted attention as they came through the door into the nave. "No need for alarm," Tom announced in his most authoritative tone, hoping to warn them off. "Everyone is fine." To Liz, he whispered, "Do we need an ambulance?"

"I don't think so. Let's get her to a private place."

Tom brought her into the vesting room and set her down on the bench. Liz took her pulse and checked her eyes. "Help me get her out of these damn vestments," she growled. Together, they undressed her down to her black parka. Liz stripped off Lucy's gloves and rubbed her hands. She inspected her fingernails. "No frostbite yet, but it can happen fast in this type of weather." She held Lucy's chin and looked directly into her eyes. "Lucy, what happened to you?"

"I went to Erika's grave to wish her a merry Christmas. I don't remember any more."

"You passed out. Did you hit your head?"

"I don't think so."

Liz yanked off Lucy's wool hat and tossed it aside. She inspected her forehead and scalp. Evidently satisfied there were no head injuries, she unzipped the parka. "Jeez, Lucy how many layers are you wearing?" she complained, unzipping the polar fleece beneath. "Good thing, too. They protected you when you were lying out there in the snow." Liz pushed the diaphragm of her stethoscope under Lucy's clerical blouse and listened intently.

"Should we call an ambulance?" Tom asked.

"No, I think she's fine," Liz pronounced with a frown. "Just exhausted and still shocky. I knew this was a stupid idea."

"She insisted," Tom said, sounding a little defensive. "I never should have gone along with it."

"It's not your fault. She's the boss, and you know how damn stubborn she can be."

Lucy made a dismissive motion and waved them off. "I'm fine. Now, everyone leave me alone! Please!"

"I guess she's okay," said Liz. "Maggie's got Emily. She's taking her to our house, and you're coming with me." Lucy opened her mouth to protest. "And no arguments! Do you understand?"

"I'd never dare speak to her that way," said Tom, smiling at having his battle fought and so easily won for him.

"I have science on my side."

"I have God on mine," said Tom with a little grin.

Liz grunted a half chuckle. "Come on, Lucy. Let's go."

"I'll hang up your vestments, Lucy."

"Thanks, Tom, and thanks for rescuing me. Too bad you can't rescue me from this tyrant." Lucy gave Liz a filthy look.

Tom laughed. "Yes, Liz, I think Mother Lucy is just fine."

Chapter 27

"I'm sorry I frightened you," said Lucy, reaching over the console to pat Liz's shoulder. "I thought I could manage the Christmas services. I really did."

"You did manage it. It was a beautiful service, and your sermon was poignant. There were people in the back crying their eyes out. But why did you go to Erika's grave? You know she's not there."

"It's strange. She's gone, but the grave is a place I can go to remember her. I know it's just her body, but it's the body I cherished. She loved me with that body. I loved her in that body."

Liz shook her head at Lucy's musings. She started the windshield wipers to push off the light snow and cranked up the defrost. "Burying people in the ground is bizarre. At least, if she'd been cremated like she wanted to be, she'd just be a pile of ash. She'd be released. Instead, she's trapped down there under all that earth."

"Did we make a mistake by giving in to Stefan?" asked Lucy.

Liz turned to her in surprise because she so seldom heard Lucy express doubt. "Stefan was hysterical over the idea of her being burned in a fire. I get that his war memories terrify him, but Erika's dead. What does she care what we did with her body? Hell, most of her organs are in Boston."

"Her heart went to Yale," said Lucy with a slight smile as if the idea pleased her.

"Knowing Erika, she would have liked that."

"You speak about her in the past."

"I don't believe in an afterlife." Liz looked over her shoulder to pull out of the parking space, ignoring the backup camera on the dashboard.

"Neither do I," said Lucy.

"Isn't that heresy? You're a priest! Today, you spoke of the resurrection at Easter."

"I don't believe in a fantasy afterlife where people sit on a cloud and talk to the angels. I think there may be some existence after death, but nothing like that. Some part of our personality might survive. Energy can neither be created nor destroyed. Sometimes, I can feel Erika nearby. She's probably listening to us right now."

"Yes, and she's probably saying you were a fucking idiot for going back to work so soon."

"She would never have called me something so awful, but she certainly wouldn't approve. She always cautioned me about burning myself out. One of the reasons I fell in love with her was how tenderly she took care of me before Tom came to help out."

"I'm glad you're coming back with me, and not only because I want to keep an eye on you, which you can be sure, I intend to do. I can use your help."

"What can I do?"

"Stefan's not doing too well."

Lucy let out a big sigh. "I was afraid of that."

"Can you imagine being ninety-three and losing your wife and your only child? The only child, who was all the family you had left in the world? We'll have to take good care of him, or he'll join them soon."

"That bad?"

"He's pretty despondent. I have to figure out what to do with him. Erika talked him into making me his alternate medical proxy and conservator. He'll be isolated in that retirement home. I can keep him with us. He's no trouble, of course. He entertains himself with reading and music and chatting with his friends online. He and Emily are working on the next great theorem. The only thing we have to do is feed him."

"But he's my responsibility now, not yours."

"Why? Because you're his daughter-in-law? Legally, that means almost nothing. I'm Erika's executor. That gives me nominal responsibility."

"I wasn't thinking of the legal obligation. I love Stefan."

"So do I. He and Helga were like second parents to me. Plus, I promised Erika I would take care of him." Liz glanced in Lucy's direction. "You too, you know."

She felt Lucy's eyes on the side of her face. "You don't have to take care of everyone, Liz. Let others help you."

She reached over and patted Lucy's thigh. "We can make a plan about how to handle Stefan. But first, we have to get you back into shape. You're like me. You'll give everything you have to help others and leave nothing for yourself."

They stopped at Lucy's house so she could pick up some clothes. While Liz waited in the truck, she looked over the house that Erika had remodeled. What had once been a cramped, old-fashioned beach cottage was now an architectural showpiece thanks to Sam. Modernized and enlarged, it was worth a small fortune. She wondered if Lucy had given any thought to whether or not she wanted to stay there. It was a big house for one person.

"I almost didn't come back," Lucy said when she got into the car. "I could refuse to allow you to kidnap me."

"Nah. I'm holding your daughter hostage."

"I'll report you to the police."

Liz laughed. "Yeah, complain to Brenda. I'm sure she'll come right out and arrest me."

"You talk about Olivia using her influence. You're just as bad."

"Thanks," Liz said in a proud voice. For reasons she couldn't explain, she liked to have her naughtiness praised.

But Lucy was quiet as they drove down Route 1, which was only wet, not snow covered, because of the traffic. Liz dared to glance at her passenger and saw that she was dozing. Evidently, her diagnosis of physical and emotional exhaustion had been correct. Finally, she turned into the long driveway that led to the house. The driveway hadn't been plowed, and the crunch of the snow under the wheels woke Lucy. She sat up and looked around.

"Sorry I fell asleep on you. I'm not sleeping well."

"I could give you something to help."

"I don't like to take sleeping pills. I have my home remedies. Golden milk works great."

"Watch out. The turmeric will stain your teeth."

"That's the one downside. I feel sleepy, then I have to get up to brush my teeth."

Liz pulled up to the garage. "You want to get out? I'm going to pull in the truck, so I don't have to shovel it out in the morning. It's a tight squeeze."

Lucy got out and pulled her bag out of the back seat. "Weren't you worried about sending Emily home in the same car with Maggie? I mean, with her cancer history?" Lucy asked as Liz looked for the right key on her ring to open the garage door.

"Nah, Emily's been negative for a week. Besides, Maggie got the real vaccine. So did you. So did Erika, not that it matters now."

"So, I can hug my daughter? Why didn't you tell me?"

"There's a remote chance you could be carrying the virus and give it to her. It's complicated."

"Did you get the vaccine too?"

"I did. But now, I have to catch up with our friends to vaccinate the ones who didn't get the real vaccine, only the placebo. I'm glad the company unmasked everyone so the test group can get the vaccine now that it's approved."

"Does that mean we don't have to wear masks anymore?"

"No, it means you probably won't have to go to the hospital or die from the virus. Until we achieve herd immunity, we still have to take the same precautions."

Although Lucy had a key since living there during the lockdown, she waited until Liz unlocked the door. Emily came into the mud room and called into the house. "They're here!" She flung her arms around her mother's neck. "Liz said I can hug you now!"

"Don't go overboard, Emily," Liz cautioned. "You can still give each other the virus."

"I don't care. I want to hug my mother."

Emily stared at Lucy's bag. "I brought clothes for you too," her mother explained.

"How long are we staying here?" Emily glanced at Liz for an explanation.

"Until your mother proves she can take care of herself."

Lucy gave her a filthy look.

"I'll take care of you, Mom," said Emily, stroking Lucy's arm.

"I'm keeping you at least until after Christmas," said Liz. "I have an enormous standing rib roast, and I'm counting on you two to help eat it. I was going to invite you anyway."

"But I have the afternoon service tomorrow," Lucy protested.

"No, you don't." Liz took Lucy's coat out of her hands and hung it in the closet. "I'm sure Tom will be happy to do it. Remember? That's why you have him." Liz sniffed the air appreciatively. The delicious aroma of Maggie's bouillabaisse cooking in the kitchen wafted into the hallway.

"What smells so good?" Lucy asked.

"Bouillabaisse. Maggie uses lobster AND shrimp. It's really good. She still believes in having fish on Christmas eve," Liz explained. "Some of those old, Catholic traditions will never die."

"I don't mind," said Lucy. "It's been years since I was a practicing Catholic, but I still fast during Lent, and I don't eat meat on Good Friday or Christmas eve."

"So, what happened to all those Catholics who ate meat on Friday before they changed the rules?" asked Liz. "Did they go to hell? Inquiring minds want to know."

Lucy smiled. "Of course, not. I don't believe in hell any more than I believe in sitting on clouds and talking to angels."

Liz guided Lucy into the living room with a hand at her back, but Lucy stopped short in the doorway. "Your tree is so beautiful!"

"I didn't feel like having a tree," explained Liz, adding wood to the stove, "but Maggie thought it would cheer us up."

Lucy sat down on the couch, and Emily, who hadn't let her go since she'd arrived, sat next to her. She leaned her head on her mother's shoulder and took her hand. "Don't worry, Mom. I'll take care of you."

Lucy kissed the top of Emily's head. "Thank you, sweetheart. We need to take care of one another now."

Stefan came into the room, looking a little more stooped than usual. As always, his pale blue eyes lit up when he saw his daughter-in-law. "Merry Christmas, Lovely Lucy."

"Merry Christmas, Papi," she replied, reaching for his hand. "You don't mind if I still call you that?"

The old man sighed. "Of course, not. You are still my daughter-in-law. And your little genius there is my one and only and *favorite* granddaughter. That will never change."

Liz jumped up to arrange the cushion at the back of Stefan's favorite chair before he sat down. He slowly lowered himself into it. "I'm very stiff today. It's the weather. They said it would snow. I've felt it for a few days, although the experts say it is a myth. Hah! What do they know? They've never been as old as I am." His pale eyes smiled as he took in the Christmas tree. "A beautiful tree. So big. Everything in America is so big."

"We do tend to overdo things," Liz conceded, pitching some logs on the fire.

"One time, when things were so bad in Berlin, and we had to wait in line for bread, no one could find any Christmas trees. I walked everywhere I'd heard there were trees. Nothing. Finally, I took the train out to Spandau, and there I found a tiny tree. The branches were so thin, they couldn't hold many candles, but I wanted my Erika to have a Christmas tree." His lined face suddenly looked so ancient. His pale eyes glistened with nascent tears.

"She's here, Papi," Lucy said. "She's enjoying the tree too."

Stefan turned his face and gazed at her fondly. "I'm glad someone still believes."

PART IV
THE DARK WINTER

Chapter 28

Olivia glanced around the tiled squares in the Zoom meeting. The faces of the vestry members, mostly older women and few men, looked grave while they listened to Lucy speak. Olivia switched to speaker view so that she could see the rector more clearly. She looked deadly pale and the bright red lipstick she was wearing, probably in an attempt to look cheerful, didn't help. She should have put on more blush to balance it, but that was probably the last thing on her mind. Lucy looked smaller than usual. She was petite but her personal magnetism always made her seem bigger than she really was. When she smiled one of her incandescent smiles, it lit up an entire room. Today, her inner light seemed dim.

How did the loss of a spouse, especially so soon after marriage, compare to other losses? Was it as painful as losing a child? That was the deepest loss Olivia had ever experienced, but her grief over Jason's death was tangled in her disgust at his behavior before he'd taken his life. When the girls were visiting at Thanksgiving, she desperately wanted to ask about the terrible secret, still holding out hope that the abuse charges might be false. But she'd taken Lucy's advice seriously because the last thing she wanted to do was to hurt those precious girls even more than she had.

"While I'm on bereavement leave, Tom Simmons will be acting rector of St. Margaret's," Lucy said. "I've spoken to the bishop, and he's in full agreement. Of course, all of you have the last word, but remember, this isn't a democracy." Her warm smile undercut the warning.

Abbie Roberts, the warden, said, "About time our expensive associate rector earned his keep."

Tom's eyes widened in mock offense. "I beg your pardon!"

Everyone laughed, but Olivia said, "Both of our wonderful priests earn their keep."

Tom basked in the praise. "It is an honor to assist Lucy in these difficult times. I pray to be worthy of stepping into her shoes."

"Maybe you could fit your big toe in one," Abbie said, keeping up the banter.

Olivia was glad for the humor because everyone looked so grim. The holidays had been hard enough for people without dealing with the staggering national death toll, growing larger by the day. Families were unable to gather, although some in the parish, especially those of a particular political stripe, continued to flout the CDC advisories and the governor's rules under the state of emergency.

Even the vestry members, who were the core of the parish, looked defeated. The loss of Erika Bultmann, their rector's most loyal supporter, had been hard enough, but news had spread of Lucy's collapse in the churchyard on her way to her wife's grave. What if Tom hadn't persisted in looking for Lucy and had gone home instead? How much longer could Lucy, in her weakened state, have survived in the cold? It had shaken up the church leadership to think they might need to bury another one of their own.

Lucy had never acknowledged how close she had come to freezing in the Christmas Eve storm. She'd treated the whole thing lightly and kept up a strong front, but in moments when she thought she wasn't being observed, Olivia could see the faraway look in her eyes.

The business of the meeting was done. Someone called for a motion to adjourn. It was obvious that everyone was ready for the meeting to conclude, but the banter before the link closed showed their reluctance to leave seeing their friends and neighbors. For some of them, this was the social highlight of the day, perhaps, the week! Olivia knew that feeling well. She'd spent the first winter of the pandemic in almost total isolation except for meetings of the town Republican party. As the Zoom window closed, she felt grateful for landing in Dr. Stolz's office, despite the pain of the urinary tract infection. It was Liz Stolz who'd sent her to Lucy Bartlett to justify prescribing tranquilizers. God certainly did work in strange ways.

Olivia decided to give Lucy a call and give her a pat on the back for having the good sense to step down during her bereavement. Not only did her actions show humility and care for her flock, but good leadership.

Olivia admired good leadership and thought about how much she admired Lucy's other qualities as she listened to the phone ring on the other end.

"Lucy, I want you to know I am behind you one hundred percent in this decision. It is the best thing for the parish and for you. A less confident woman couldn't do what you did."

Lucy sighed. "I wish it was confidence, but I'm just exhausted, and it's not fair to the congregation to keep pretending."

"Are you having trouble sleeping? I did too, after Jason died. I couldn't sleep for months."

"It's a pretty common symptom of grief," Lucy said, reverting to her professional tone.

"You should ask Liz to give you something."

"She has, but I prefer natural methods. I have my own recipes. I take melatonin. That usually works."

"You shouldn't turn down help when you really need it."

"I know, but I've seen too many people get addicted to medications meant to help."

Olivia laughed softly. "And I thought I was stubborn."

"Sometimes, stubbornness gets you through a hard time."

"You can say that again! But Lucy, dear, we all love you. How can I help?"

"Everyone's already been so generous. People know I can barely cook, so they've been sending me casseroles. Now that I have Emily at home, they're appreciated. That kid sucks in food like a vacuum cleaner!"

Olivia smiled. "She's a teenager and still growing."

"Oh, I hope she stops soon. It's hard for tall women, especially for someone like Emily, who already has…challenges. Her father was very tall."

Olivia heard something interesting in Lucy's voice when she mentioned the girl's father. Certainly, not a note of warmth or affection. Nobody ever talked about the backstory of how Lucy had become a mother and why she'd given up the baby for adoption. Olivia could certainly understand the career angle, but somehow that didn't explain it. Lucy was so kind. It never made sense that she could coldly give away her baby. Olivia desperately wanted to ask the father's identity, but this wasn't the time, especially not with Lucy such a mess.

"I have some pot pies I made from our Christmas turkey in the freezer," said Olivia. "I'll bring you one. That should be enough for you and Emily, even with her big appetite.

"Thanks, Olivia, but the freezer is full. Can you hold on to them until we work off the generosity of the women of the parish? I am grateful, of course. But I hate to waste food."

"Of course. Just let me know and tell me if you need anything, anything at all. I'm also happy to provide a sympathetic ear. As you well know, I'm familiar with grief."

"That's so kind, Olivia. Everyone's been so kind. Sam was here yesterday and shoveled in front of the garage and the path to the front sidewalk."

This was the first Olivia had heard of Sam's good deed. "She was there?"

"Yes, she's been here every time it snows. I appreciate it, but I can shovel my own snow. I'm not an invalid."

"Oh, that's Samantha doing her butch thing. Enjoy it and say thank you."

Lucy's silence made Olivia realize her statement sounded overly proprietary. "Samantha's such a good person," she added.

"She is," Lucy agreed, "and thank you for offering food. I may need to take you up on it. People are always helpful right after a funeral, but then they go back to their own lives and forget about the grieving survivor. It's the most common complaint I hear in my bereavement groups. In the beginning, everyone is there for you, but then they fade away."

"Well, your friends are not going to do that!" Olivia declared. "Of that, you can be sure!"

"I know. I'm so blessed in my friendships."

"Take care of yourself, Lucy. I'm sending a virtual hug."

Lucy again assured her that she was fine, but her tone suggested that her words were really meant for an audience of one. After Olivia got off the phone, she wrote a reminder on her phone calendar to call Lucy in a few days. While she did, she noticed that she had a text message from Sam: I made a pot of green chili. Want to come for dinner?

Olivia wrinkled up her nose at the idea of chili, although she had to admit that Sam's version was tasty. What intrigued her was the invitation. Sam seldom initiated a visit. Naturally, Olivia wanted to encourage this behavior, so she quickly tapped a reply: *Certainly. What can I bring?*

Nothing. Just you. I have a good wine for you to try.

That sounded promising.

Should I pack a bag?

Olivia's anxiety level spiked because it seemed to take a long time for Sam to reply.

Sure. If you want to.

What time?

Now's good. I'm done for the day.

Okay. Be there in half an hour or so.

Olivia smiled to herself and went upstairs to pack an overnight bag.

Sam's kitchen smelled good when Olivia arrived. Sam, in stocking feet, was standing at the island mixing a bowlful of batter. "Making a quick jalapeno cornbread to go with the chili," Sam explained. "The wine is in the refrigerator if you want to open it. It's a new pinot. Liz said it was good, and she never steers me wrong. We have our eight-dollar wine club."

"What's that?" asked Olivia, opening drawers, trying to remember which one held the wine-cork puller.

"It's a friendly competition to find the best wines under eight bucks. It used to be six bucks, but then all the wine prices went up, and we had to raise it."

"Ah, the ravages of inflation," said Olivia with a dramatic sigh. "It's why I always advise investors to have a sensible stake in the stock market. Of course, the pandemic hasn't helped. The distribution problems are still there. That's why food has gotten so expensive."

Sam stared at her, and Olivia realized she'd been giving a lecture. But

Sam shrugged and went back to mixing her batter. She dumped in a whole can of jalapenos.

"Piquant," observed Olivia.

"Something to spice up your night."

"You do that very well on your own."

Sam made a little bow in Olivia's direction. "Taste the wine and tell me what you think." She poured her corn bread mixture into a pan and slid it into the oven. She reached for the wine Olivia had poured for her. "I think it's pretty good."

Olivia swirled it in her mouth. "Dry for a pinot," she observed.

"Yes, I like that about it. I don't like my wines too sweet." Sam screwed up her face to demonstrate her disgust at the idea.

"And those songs about drinking a woman's sweet wine?" asked Olivia with a seductive smile.

"No, that's different," Sam agreed. "But don't get too eager. Let's eat dinner first. Shit. Forgot to time the cornbread."

"It can't be more than two minutes since it went in."

Sam grabbed her phone off the counter to set the timer.

"What's the occasion?" asked Olivia, helping herself to the corn chips and salsa Sam had set out.

Sam looked up from her phone. "What do you mean?"

"You don't usually invite me here."

Sam shrugged. "Just returning the favor. I don't want you to think I'm a freeloader."

"It would never cross my mind."

"No? I seem to spend a lot of time at your house."

"I like having you there."

"I know you do. To be perfectly honest, I don't usually invite you because you don't seem comfortable here. My bed is smaller. We can't shower together because my bathroom isn't big enough. You complain of the dampness from the pond..."

"It's no worse than living by the ocean."

"Then stop complaining."

Olivia took another swallow of the wine. Sam was right. The drier taste was appealing. "You didn't tell me you were shoveling Mother Lucy's driveway."

"Why would I tell you? It has nothing to do with you."

"You could shovel mine."

"You hire that kid to do it. I don't want to deprive him of the money, especially because he needs it, and you can afford it."

"Charity begins at home."

"Then why don't you come and shovel my driveway?" asked Sam, pursing her lips to hide a grin.

"Because it's a private road, and it has to be plowed."

Sam laughed. "Yes, I can't quite imagine you operating a plow truck."

"Don't pull your butch superiority on me, Samantha McKinnon. There are many things I can do that you can't."

"Such as?"

"Such as make a soufflé that doesn't collapse."

"Who would bother? What a stupid waste of time trying to keep hot air in some eggs."

Olivia gave her a dirty look. "There are hundreds of things I can do better, but I won't embarrass you by listing them."

"Good. Be nice for a change. If that's possible." Sam playfully pinched her rear to lighten the mood, but Olivia sensed the criticism was meant.

Chapter 29

Maggie had put all the glass ornaments away, carefully matching the shapes to the compartments in the storage boxes. Little Christmas, called the "feast of the kings" when she was growing up, was the traditional time to take down the Christmas tree. Unlike many people, she didn't believe in putting put up the tree at Thanksgiving and leaving it up until Valentine's day. Christmas was Christmas, a short season at the end of December, and that was that. She was glad Liz was in agreement, but lately, that seemed like one of the few things they agreed upon.

The coffee table was covered with special ornaments they'd bought over the years to celebrate their relationship. They usually featured a pair of animals, because same sex couples were seldom represented in commercial ornaments. Even the animal pairs were anthropomorphically male and female with exaggerated characteristics. The few female pairs clearly depicted innocent friendships and featured primly dressed mice drinking tea or old women laughing together, sexless and no threat to the culture.

When the ornaments were all removed and snug in their boxes, Maggie spread a painter's drop cloth on the floor to catch the needles. It was time to take the lights off, but where was Liz? Ten minutes ago, she had abandoned the tree project to return a patient's call via the Telehealth system. She was on backup today, so they must be busy in the office if they were calling her at home. She'd taken the day off because, as usual, she'd covered for everyone over the holidays.

Maggie considered taking off the lights herself, but that had been Liz's job since they'd put up their first tree, a division of labor they'd honored ever since. Impatient, Maggie switched on the TV to cable news. Everyone was so anxious about the election being certified because the outgoing president adamantly refused to acknowledge he'd lost. Steps in the process, such as state certifications that few people even thought about, were suddenly getting scrupulous attention. Today was congressional certification date. Some of the president's allies had already announced they would contest the certification of certain states. It wouldn't be the first time this political theater had played out, but it was the first time a president had refused to concede.

Maggie didn't follow politics as closely as Liz and some of her friends did, but even she'd lost sleep during this tumultuous post-election time, counting down the days until the new president took office. She'd often found herself awake in the night after a stress dream. Usually, she chewed some melatonin gummies and went right back to sleep, but sometimes she went online and saw how many of her friends were awake. As Liz had said, no one would sleep soundly until the new president was inaugurated. After four years of chaos, why should the end of this presidency be different? Maggie couldn't remember feeling consistent anxiety like this since her breast cancer had been diagnosed. It even eclipsed her worry over her biannual tumor marker tests.

Watching the roll call of the certification votes was boring until they got to the rebellious senators. The anchors were explaining what would happen now. No one expected anything more than the delay of the inevitable, a pointless frustration of a constitutional process. The details didn't interest Maggie, but she studied the anxious faces of the commentators for clues to how they really felt. Although they spoke reassuring words, they didn't look as sure as they sounded.

Suddenly there was confusion in the house chamber, but no obvious cause. The news feed cut to an exterior view where the president's supporters had gathered waving confederate flags and election banners in his support. The news ticker on the bottom of the screen only reported that the two houses of Congress had adjourned to their chambers to debate the objections of their members. Maggie could see that the barrier holding the protestors back from the entrance to the Capitol had been breached. It looked like some of the police were opening the barricades to the surging crowd. Was she seeing things?

"Liz!" called Maggie. "Liz! You've got to see this."

Liz came into the living room.

"What's the matter?"

"What were you doing?"

"Marinating the steak for dinner. What's the emergency?"

"Something's going on at the Capitol."

Liz sat down beside Maggie. Her eyes were riveted on the screen as the announcers described the growing crowd on the Capitol steps. Then the cameras switched to a group of protestors bashing in a window on the side of the building.

"Oh, my God! They're breaking into the Capitol!" Maggie couldn't believe what she was seeing with her own eyes.

"I fucking knew this would happen!" Liz said. "And you laughed at me when I bought all that ammunition."

"I laughed at you because you paid ridiculous money for it."

"There were shortages everywhere. You should have seen the empty shelves at Cabela's. All the online retailers were price gouging."

"So, what are you going to do? Hold them off by yourself? Are you crazy too?"

"I'm not going down without a fight," said Liz, looking furious. "That asshole down the street still has his signs up. If they were any bigger, he'd have to get a billboard permit! And the moron next to him with his black 'blue-line' flag. They don't give a shit about police lives. They're just racists, all of them!"

Maggie could see Liz's fists tightening. Maybe it wasn't a good idea to watch something so stressful. She knew Liz was still upset from Erika's death and, in characteristic Liz-fashion, wasn't showing any emotion about it.

"Jesus! Did you see that? That policeman just opened the barricades to the protestors. They're colluding with them!"

"Let's shut this off," suggested Maggie, picking up the remote. "You're getting too agitated."

Liz snatched away the remote. "No, I want to see what his scum is doing to our country. This is history!" Liz pointed to the screen where Congress members were shown crouching under their seats.

The voices of the news announcers sounded more and more alarmed as the scenes unfolded: "The protestors are in the Capitol building now. Here's footage broadcast from inside the rotunda." Gone was the even, professional tone the broadcaster had used only minutes before. They weren't even pretending any more.

Maggie needed a break from the tension, so she got up. "You want a cup of tea? I'm going to make myself one."

"No, thank you," said Liz. The words were polite, but her voice was surly and her face dark as she continued to watch the screen.

When Maggie returned with her tea, Liz was on the phone. It was on speaker, so Maggie heard every word. She recognized Brenda's voice.

"Yes, I went down to the break room to see what was going on. The guys had on Fox, but I made them change the channel to CNN. I got dirty looks, of course."

"Let me guess. The same people who refused the vaccine."

A huge sigh was heard through the speaker. "I don't remember exactly, but you're probably right."

"I warned you, Brenda, you have nuts right in your department."

"Listen, Liz. I'd love to hang and talk to you, but the state police are coming in on my squawker."

Radio voices were audible in the background.

"We're mobilizing," said Brenda. "In case the insurrection spreads to Maine."

"Here? Brenda, you've got to be kidding!"

"Can't talk now. Call you later."

Liz turned to Maggie with an amazed look. "They're preparing for the insurrection to spread."

"This can't be real."

"But it is."

Liz's phone danced on the coffee table as it rang. Cherie was calling.

Why did Liz bother taking time off? They never left her alone. Maggie felt resentful on her behalf, but surprisingly Liz never seemed to share the resentment. She simply saw it as part of her job. She frowned as she listened to Cherie describe whatever problem she was facing at the office.

"She's having chest pains? Who's not having chest pains? Have you seen the news?" Liz listened again. Her frown deepened. "Can't you monitor her? I doubt there are beds at Southern Med. It's worse than in the beginning of the pandemic." She rolled her eyes. "Okay. Use your best judgment. Call me back if something changes."

"Everything okay?" Maggie asked to show interest.

"Everything is never okay." Liz sighed. "Goes with the territory."

"What's going to happen?"

"With my patient? Or this insurrection?"

"Is that what you think it is, or is it just a bunch of his nuts going crazy?"

"Obviously, he told them to march to the Capitol. He hasn't called it off. They're revolting against the government and the peaceful transfer of power. Yes, it's an insurrection," said Liz gesturing toward the TV screen. "And where is the national guard? Don't tell me they didn't know this was going to happen. Even I knew!"

"You didn't say anything."

"You were scared enough."

"Liz, take the tree out. It will give you something to do with all that energy."

Liz grumbled, but she got up and unscrewed the tree from its base. Maggie went to open the front door, while Liz carefully pulled the tree out of the base. Holding it away from her body to avoid disturbing more pine needles, she carried it outside.

The distraction lasted all of five minutes. When they returned to watching the scenes flashing across the screen, they were mesmerized. A man, wearing buffalo horns, his torso covered with two-toned body paint, marched through the rotunda of the Capitol with a spear. The dazed look in his eyes suggested he was high on something, and he was howling at the top of his lungs. Was this a joke or was it real? Everything about the last four years had been so crazy, it was hard to know.

Liz got up and double-locked the front door, obviously leery of their radical neighbors still flying their Trump flag. Maggie heard her rummaging around in the hall closet and realized she was taking her pistol out of the safe.

"I'm going in to flip the steak in the marinade," said Liz returning to the room. "At least, that's something I can control." As she turned to leave, the outline of her pistol was clearly visible under her flannel shirt.

Chapter 30

Liz opened her eyes. It was too early for the alarm. The red numerals of the clock were flashing. She'd forgotten to replace the battery, so the flashing display meant the power had been off. It was on now, of course, because the generator had kicked on as it was programmed to do. Liz listened carefully and heard the hammering of portable gas generators in the neighborhood. But that wasn't what had awakened her. She realized that her phone was dancing on the top of her night stand. When she picked it up, she saw Lucy's smiling face.

"Hey, Luce," she said softly, getting out of bed. Her feet instinctively found their way into her moccasins. She yanked her sweatshirt off the closet hook and headed into the hall. "Is everything okay?" she asked, quietly closing the door to the bedroom where Maggie was still asleep.

"I'm so sorry to wake you. I'd hoped you'd be awake by now."

"Usually, I am, but today's my day off."

"Oh, I'm so sorry. I forgot!"

"It's okay. I don't expect you to remember my schedule," said Liz, heading downstairs. She switched on the light in the living room. She opened the stove and stirred the ashes with a poker to see if there were any hot coals. Suddenly, a dozen orange lights began to glow. Liz threw in the kindling, but she left the door ajar so the stove could draw air. "Why are you up so early?" she asked, sinking into the leather club chair near the stove.

"I'm usually up at dawn."

"But it's still dark out," said Liz, lifting the shade to look out the window. "Did your power go off too?"

"Yes, it's still out. That's why I called. I don't know how to start the generator."

"Didn't Erika show you?"

"She did, but I forgot. I'm not really good with mechanical things. Oh,

Liz, I'm so sorry I woke you, but I'm afraid I'll do something wrong. I remember you have to do it in a certain order."

"Well, yes you do. First, you have to take it out of the garage and push it under the deck. To start it—"

"Liz, I'm sorry, but I'm not going to remember, and it's getting really cold in here."

"How long has the power been out?"

"About three hours."

"Okay. I'll be there in a few minutes. Go back to bed and get under the covers. I'll let myself in with my key when I get there."

"I'll wait until you get here."

"Lucy, please, get into bed and warm yourself up. I'll ring the bell when I get there, so you can come out and see what I do."

Finally, Lucy agreed.

Liz turned on the coffee maker. She searched through the cabinet and found her blaze orange Cabela's travel mug. While the coffee brewed, she ran upstairs to get dressed, skipping the bra because she didn't want to waste time looking through the drawers.

"Where are you going?" asked Maggie, raising her head from the pillow.

"Lucy can't start the generator."

"Oh," she said and rolled over. "Be careful. I can hear the ice hitting the house."

Liz was glad she didn't have to shovel off the truck. She'd pulled it into the garage because gale-force winds had been predicted, and she didn't want a tree branch hitting it.

"Erika, I told you to get an automatic generator," Liz said aloud as she backed out the truck. "You were spending all that money on the remodel, why not a few thousand more?"

In her mind, she heard a voice as clear as if someone was sitting there: "I just wanted to make you say, 'I told you so.'"

"Gee, thanks. Next time, remind your wife how to start the fucking thing." *I'm talking to a voice in my head,* thought Liz. *I'm really losing it.*

Downed pine branches littered the driveway. One was so big that Liz needed to stop and pull it out of her way. Ice pellets pinged on the hood and roof of the truck. They stung her bare hands and glistened in the headlights.

"Oh, Lucy, if I didn't love you so much, I wouldn't be doing this."

"Yes, you would," said the voice in her head.

"Shut up, Erika," she said to the empty passenger seat as she climbed back into the cab.

The local roads were even more slippery than the driveway. Liz switched on four-wheel drive and turned on the fog lights so she could see better. The thought of her hot coffee sitting just an arm's length away was tantalizing, but she decided to wait to get to the state road, which was likely to be plowed and salted. She was relieved to get there and find it only wet but not slippery, but the wind blasts rocked the truck, reminding Liz to watch out for downed power lines in addition to fallen branches.

When she got to Beach Road, she saw that the salt marsh had flooded over the roadway. She slowed down as she drove through the huge puddle. "This is not good," she said aloud. When did she start talking to herself? she wondered.

"You're talking to me," said the voice in her head.

"Now, I'm really losing it."

"Liz, you lost it a long time ago."

Liz chuckled. *Now I'm being insulted by a voice in my head*, she thought.

"Tell the truth. You miss me," said the voice.

In fact, she did.

Liz pulled in front of the garage door. She still had the key from the practice room project. She opened the back door of the bay. Before she pulled out the generator, she checked the oil and the gas levels. There was a paper posted near where the generator was stored with a record of when it had last been started and the oil checked. Although Erika wasn't mechanically inclined, she maintained everything meticulously. The gas tank was full, which made the generator even heavier. Liz groaned as she lifted the handles to wheel it out to its space under the back deck. She wondered if

Lucy could even lift the machine, never mind push it up the ramp to get it above the flood line. "Erika, this was bad planning."

The wind whipped Liz's face as she adjusted the choke and prayed the battery had enough juice to start the engine. There were a few uncertain coughs, but it started. Liz breathed a sigh of relief. As she turned to plug in the cord, she saw Lucy standing there.

"Go inside," Liz ordered.

"I want to see what you're doing," Lucy insisted, hugging herself.

"Show's over. Go inside. I'm coming in too."

Liz followed Lucy inside and closed the bay door behind her.

"Come on," she said, heading to the basement door. "I'll show you how to flip the main breaker." Liz ran down the stairs, with Lucy behind her. She took her flashlight out of her pocket and navigated to the service panel. With effort, she shut off the switch to the main breaker. "Jeez, that's tight. I doubt you'd be able to throw it."

Lucy gave her an insulted look.

"It's nothing personal, Lucy. The mechanical world isn't designed for women and small people." Liz flipped the generator breaker. The basement lights went on and the furnace kicked in. "You should get about five hours out of the gas in the tank. We'll need to shut it down to refill it." Liz glanced at her phone. "I'll set a reminder to come back."

"You don't think the power will be out that long?"

Liz shrugged. "Who knows. The wind is still whipping around out there."

"Thank you!" said Lucy, throwing her arms around Liz's neck and hugging her. When Liz returned the embrace, she noticed that Lucy's hair, usually so fresh smelling, had an oily scent.

"Come upstairs. Now that I have power, I can make you a cup of coffee."

Liz sat at the kitchen table while Lucy prepared two cups of coffee. "I can survive without a lot of things, but coffee is not one of them," she said, putting a cup in front of Liz. She opened the refrigerator and took out a mostly empty gallon of milk. Liz glanced inside and saw that the shelves were bare.

"Looks like you need to go to the market," said Liz. "If you make a list, I can run up there and get some things for you."

"Don't worry about it. I'll go later."

"You're sure?"

"Yes, I can go this morning. Now that I'm on leave, I don't have much to do."

Liz poured a few dribbles of milk into her coffee to save some for Lucy. "Emily drinks a lot of milk," said Lucy idly. "I guess that's good for her. She's still growing."

"In fact, the absorption rate of calcium from milk isn't that impressive. It's a marketing myth put out by the Dairy Association."

"But it won't hurt her."

"Probably not…as long as she's not sensitive to lactose." Liz gave Lucy a long inspection. "Are you doing okay, Lucy? You look tired."

"I can't sleep."

"I can give you something for that," said Liz and took a sip of coffee.

Lucy shook her head. "I don't want to get started with sleeping pills."

"Sometimes, you need them. You know how stingy I am with prescriptions for tranquilizers and psychotropic drugs. I wouldn't recommend them if I didn't think it would help. I'll send a script to the pharmacy. You can pick it up when you shop for groceries."

Lucy smiled. Liz sensed it was to placate her.

"Lucy, you're getting too thin. You have to eat. You don't have an ounce of fat to spare. Are you eating?"

"I'm not hungry."

"Then pick up some protein drinks and force yourself. You need to keep up your strength."

"Okay," said Lucy, but she glanced away.

Liz heard a banging on the front door. "Who the hell could that be? It's not even seven o'clock."

"I'll get it." Lucy jumped up and headed to the front door. A moment later, Liz heard Brenda's voice in the living room.

"I came down to see the damage to Ocean Road and saw Liz's truck outside. Is everything okay here?"

"I didn't know how to start the generator, so I called Liz."

"I could have done that for you," Brenda said.

"I'm sure you could, but you're busy with police matters."

"But the town doctor's not busy, of course," said Liz, standing in the doorway.

"The roadway is flooded," Brenda said. "Good thing you have your truck, Liz. It's pretty deep for a car."

"I've got a Subaru. They're high off the ground," Lucy said.

Brenda gave her a skeptical look. "I've got to get back to work," said Brenda. When she tipped her campaign hat, water ran off it. "Sorry about that, Lucy."

"It's nothing. I'll wipe it up."

"See you later. Liz, I'd get off the island while you can. Come back after the tide goes out."

"Thanks for coming, Brenda," said Lucy as she closed the door behind her.

Liz gulped down the rest of her coffee. "I'll run up to Hannaford and pick up some things for you."

"No, Liz. I can do it."

Liz bent down to kiss her cheek. "Go take a shower while you have hot water."

"Is that a hint?" Obviously, she'd sensed it was.

Liz shrugged. "Is there anything you specifically need from the store?"

"Milk."

"That's obvious."

The ice pellets stung as Liz ran out to her truck. The waves were splashing high on Ocean Road as she headed out. The puddle on Beach Road had grown into a pond. It looked like they were going to have a king tide. She'd better get the groceries and get back before it hit.

The shelves of the supermarket were stripped as usual before a big storm. Fortunately, the customers always grabbed the white bread first and left behind the expensive multi-grain bread. Liz tossed a loaf into her basket and threw in a loaf of cinnamon-raisin bread because she knew Lucy liked it for breakfast. The only gallon jugs were whole milk. Liz added two bottles to her cart. She filled the basket with healthy vegetables and salad fixings. Then she went down the meat aisle and chose easy-to-prepare things like chicken thighs. Against her better judgement, she added some store-made, prepared meals to the mix. Lucy wasn't much of a cook on a good day. Maybe a meal that needed minimal preparation would encourage her to eat. In the fish department, Liz ordered stuffed salmon fillets that only needed to be heated in the oven. She stopped at the pharmacy, wrote out a script for a mild sedative, and waited for it to be filled.

By the time Liz had to cross the puddle again, it had become a surging river. She slowed to a crawl to cross it. She set the grocery bags on the garage floor behind Erika's car, giving it a sad look as she did.

Lucy, with her hair wrapped in a towel, opened the door for her. "Let me help you," she offered.

"I'll bring it in, but you'll have to unpack it. The water's rising fast. I hope the garage doesn't flood."

"Oh, me too. What a mess it made last time."

Liz hurried into the kitchen, carrying six grocery bags at a time. Lucy began unpacking. Emily had come downstairs and stared with sleepy eyes at all the activity.

"Hello, Aunt Liz. Thanks for turning the power on. It was so cold!"

"You're welcome, Emily," said Liz, emptying grocery bags and organizing items on the counter.

"Oh, good! You got the yogurt I like!" said Emily.

"I pay attention," said Liz. "Can you help your mother unpack? I need to get out of here while I can."

"The water's rising that fast?" asked Lucy, looking alarmed.

"Fast." Liz reached down and kissed Lucy on the cheek. "I'll be back in a couple of hours to put more gas in the generator."

Lucy hugged her. "What can I do to thank you?"

"Think about investing in an auto-on generator."

Liz remembered the prescription in her pocket. "Here," she said, handing the white bag to Lucy. She glanced at Emily. "I'll see you later. Keep an eye on your mother while I'm gone."

"I will," called Emily as Liz headed out the door to the garage.

As Liz drove home, she processed her observations of Lucy's state. She never liked to push patients, but Lucy wasn't taking care of herself. She tried to think of a way to encourage her, but she was reasonably sure she would get nothing but protests that she was fine. Why was Lucy so stubborn?

Liz realized she needed reinforcements, but who? Cherie was a good one. She was a shrink and could use her psychotherapeutic wiles on her fellow therapist. Tom could work his priestly magic. But the best of all was Olivia, who was so bossy, she would just bulldoze through any resistance.

Liz had formulated that much of a plan by the time she opened the garage door and pulled in the truck. She reached for the doorknob to open the door to the house when Maggie pulled it open." About time you got back. I was worried about you."

"The road to the beach is flooding."

"Yes, I know. I've been watching the local news."

Liz hung up her wet parka on the bathroom door by the hood. She sat on the bench near the door to take off her wet boots.

"Is Lucy all set now?" asked Maggie.

"I told her I'll come back in a couple of hours and refill the gas tank."

"Can't she even do that?" asked Maggie in an irritable tone.

"When we're not in the middle of a nor'easter, I'll show her how to do it."

"That's good. She needs to learn to fend for herself. You have better things to do," Maggie said in a sharp tone.

Liz looked up with surprise, but Maggie was already heading down the hall.

Chapter 31

January's snowfall had been at a record low. Sam was beginning to wonder why she had bothered to put the plow on her truck, but after the nor'easter hit, it had been one storm after another.

Sam plowed her driveway, then Liz's. Liz came out on the porch and waved. "You should go into business," Liz said, when Sam rolled down the window.

"Nah, I only do it for my friends and I don't need the money."

"Want some coffee?"

"I have some, but thanks."

Liz's driveway was long, but Sam had figured out how to make quick work of clearing it. After she finished, she headed to Lucy's house. She never bothered to plow there because the driveway was just long enough for a car to park. The one time Sam had tried to plow it, she'd spent more time waiting for the traffic to pass than she had pulling out the snow. Now, she took a couple of swipes with the plow and shoveled the rest.

Sam parked in the open parking space next to the garage and hopped out, only to realize she'd forgotten to bring a snow shovel. Lucy should have one in the garage, and Sam still had the key from the building project. As she trudged through the snow, she wondered if Lucy ever used the practice room they'd built. After all the planning and work that had gone into it, she certainly hoped so. Sam was worried when she found the garage door unlocked. Burglaries and home invasions were more likely in the beach houses than in other parts of town, especially in the winter when many were vacant. Sam tried to think of a tactful way to remind Lucy to keep the doors locked.

After kicking the snow off her boots, so she wouldn't track it in, Sam stepped into the garage. She was surprised to see the trash and recycling bins overflowing. Bags of trash and recycling stood piled nearby. *When was the last time Lucy went to the dump?* Sam wondered. *If it were summer, this place would stink to high heaven!*

The snow shovel was hanging neatly next to the roof rake. Sam admired how organized and neat Erika's garden tools were. The trowels were arranged by type and size. She noted that the shovels had even been sharpened. Erika had loved her garden, especially her roses.

Sam grabbed the snow shovel and headed out to shovel the walk. Fortunately, it was cold, and the snow was light. She was cleaning up in front of the garage doors, when one of them opened.

"Thank you, Sam. You're a gift," said Lucy. She was wearing worn sweats, an old Columbia sweatshirt and fuzzy slippers that looked like they could use a wash. She wore no makeup. Sam had never seen Lucy without makeup before, so she stopped shoveling and stared. She had no idea Lucy had so many freckles.

"Do you have time for a cup of coffee?" asked Lucy.

Sam had said that she would stop by Olivia's, which meant she didn't have a huge amount of time, but Lucy looked like she could use the company.

"Thanks, Lucy. Let me just finish up here, and I'll come in." She leaned on the handle of the shovel. "Do you mind if I take your trash with me when I go?"

Lucy gazed in the direction of the trash bags and let out a long sigh. "Yes, I guess I need to go to the dump. You don't have to take it."

"It's nothing. I'll just throw it in the back of my truck. I pass the dump on my way home. I probably can get most of it out of here in one load."

Lucy reached out and patted Sam's arm. "Thank you, Sam. That's so kind. Come in when you're done."

After Sam shoveled the steps to the porch, she hung up the shovel where she'd found it. She took off her boots and came in through the garage door. As she walked through the living room, the mess shocked her—dirty cups and papers on the coffee table along with an empty wine bottle. There was a bed pillow on the couch and a couple of polar fleece throws. *Was someone sleeping down here?* she wondered. When she went into the kitchen it was even worse. Empty frozen dinner boxes littered the counter top. The kitchen trash was overflowing. Erika would never keep her house like this. When Sam turned, she saw Lucy had been watching her reactions.

"I know. I need to clean up. I just don't get to it." She gestured toward the kitchen. "Sit down. I'll make you coffee."

Sam took an empty pizza box off the chair and sat down. "Lucy, do you need help? I'm not the world's greatest housekeeper, but I can help you."

"No, it's okay. I'll do it later," said Lucy, putting a cup of coffee in front of her. "What do you take in your coffee?"

"Just milk."

"Good. I don't know if we have any sugar left. Emily uses too much."

At the mention of Lucy's daughter, Sam looked around for clues to where she might be.

"She's still asleep," Lucy explained. "I used to sleep a lot when I was in college. But I always did a lot of late-night performances."

"Really? What did you do? Sing opera?"

"Sometimes. I also sang in a jazz club in the village. I like all kinds of music."

"Me too," said Sam, stirring some milk into her coffee. "I like opera too."

"I didn't know that."

"Liz used to take me along when Jenny wasn't available, which was often. Jenny is an obstetrician, so she missed a lot of performances. I was usually available at the last minute, so it worked out."

Talking about music seemed to relax Lucy. Her face looked less pinched.

"I wish I'd heard you sing at the Met," Sam said.

"My career there was pretty short. If you blinked, you missed it."

"Why was it so short?"

"My agent embezzled my earnings. He 'forgot' to pay my taxes." Lucy made air quotes around the word, forgot. "One of the producers was supposedly helping me work it out, but he had a hidden agenda."

"What was that?"

"Sex."

Sam made a face. "Don't they all?"

"Long story, short, I got on the wrong side of the politics, and I was forced out. That was after I got pregnant with Emily."

"So, you took him up on the sex?"

Lucy casually stirred her coffee. "No, he forced me."

Sam stared until she finally remembered to close her mouth. "Oh, shit, Lucy. I'm sorry. I had no idea."

Lucy shrugged. "Not many people know. It's okay. It was a long time ago. I've dealt with it."

Sam drank in silence while she considered what Lucy had said. "That's why you trained in martial arts," she concluded.

"Bingo," said Lucy.

Sam look up. "I'm not used to you like this."

"You mean without my collar? Just being normal?"

"I don't know if I'd ever call you normal, Lucy." Sam grinned.

Lucy suddenly found her coffee interesting. "Lately, I can't find the energy to act like Mother Lucy or even good, old Lucy. It takes too much effort. They say anger is one of the stages of grief. I guess I'm in the angry stage. Everything and everyone annoys me. Not you, of course, or any of my friends. You've all been so kind, but if I seem out of sorts, I hope you'll understand."

"I've never lost anyone as close as Erika was to you, but I think I understand."

Lucy reached out and patted Sam's hand. "Thank you."

Sam gulped down the last few swallows of coffee. "If you give me a bag, I'll collect the trash in here and bring it to the dump with the rest of it."

"I'll help you."

"No, finish your coffee. Just point me in the right direction." Then she spotted the roll of orange Hobbs dump bags on the counter. "How about recycling bags?"

"I've been too lazy to sort it. There are tall kitchen bags under the sink."

Sam found them and sorted the recycling, while Lucy filled the trash bag.

"I can take it out," protested Lucy, when Sam reached for it. "People keep trying to help me. I can manage."

"Lucy, let me," said Sam in a gentle tone because Lucy sounded so prickly. "You're always helping everyone. It's our turn to help you." She took the bag of trash out of Lucy's hands.

"I hope you're not just doing this because I'm a priest."

Sam made a face. "Hell no. In fact, that would be the last reason. I'm doing it because you're my friend, and that's what friends do."

Sam collected the trash bags and loaded them into the truck. Fortunately, the dump was between Lucy's place and Olivia's house. Sam knew Olivia would have a fit if she parked a truckload of trash in front of her house. The thought made Sam smile, and she was momentarily tempted to see what would happen if she did. Her better angels told her to unload the truck before heading to Gull Island.

On the way back, Sam called to tell Olivia she was on the way. "How is Lucy doing?" Olivia asked.

"She's living on pizza and Lean Cuisine, and the place looks like a bomb went off."

There was a long silence. "That's not good," observed Olivia, stating the obvious. "We need to do something."

"What can we do?"

"Let me think about it."

When Sam arrived, Olivia was making waffles. She was cooking up a storm, including two blueberry breads. "What's the occasion?" asked Sam, rolling up her sleeves to wash her hands in the kitchen sink.

Olivia nudged her with her hip. "That's what the lavatory is for."

Sam yanked off a paper towel and dried her hands. While Olivia wasn't looking, she snatched a waffle off the top of the pile and bit into it. "Good," she said with her mouth full.

"Can't you wait a few minutes?"

"No, I'm starving. I worked hard this morning and it's not even nine o'clock."

"Well, sit down, and you can have some waffles. Let me warm the syrup in the microwave." Olivia filled Sam's cup with coffee. "I called Ellie and asked her to clean Lucy's house."

"I'm sure Ellie can use the work, but will Lucy mind?"

"I'm sure she won't since I'm paying for it."

"That's very nice of you."

"You sound surprised. Sometimes, I'm nice."

"Sometimes, you are." Sam doused her waffles with syrup and dug into her breakfast. Olivia put a plate of bacon in front of her and sat down to serve herself.

"After Ellie works her magic over there, you and I will pay a call on the Reverend Lucille Bartlett."

"Shouldn't you warn her about this?" asked Sam between bites.

"Oh, I will. We'll bring over those frozen turkey pies she refused last month, and we'll do a little shopping. She needs to eat real food, not that frozen garbage." Olivia mocked a shudder. "How anyone can eat that plastic food is beyond me!"

"She needs sugar. Emily likes a lot in her coffee. She could probably use coffee too."

"Yes, we'll shop for essential supplies too." Olivia gave Sam a once over. "I want you to dress up a little to set a good example. You know, put on a nice top and a polar fleece instead of a sweatshirt. And put on a bra."

Sam made a sour face.

"You need a little lift, Samantha. You have beautiful breasts. Show them proudly."

Sam's face grew warm and she knew she was blushing, but Olivia wasn't paying attention. Her brain was working so obviously, Sam could almost hear the gears grinding.

"Lucy will resist charity," Olivia continued. "She's supposed to be ministering to us, not the other way around. So, we'll have to handle this strategically." Olivia frowned as she chewed. "I'll tell her we're coming for tea. That's why I'm baking the blueberry breads. I'll also make a lemon curd tart." Sam's mouth started to water. Olivia's lemon curd tart was her favorite after blueberry pie. "I'll amp up the formality with the tone of the invitation. She'll get the message."

"Sounds good. I guess I should go home and clean myself up a little."

"Oh, you have time. This won't happen until this afternoon. That will give Ellie time to get over there, and Lucy a chance to get her act together. Lucy is a performer. And she's a trooper. You watch, Sam. She'll rise to the occasion."

As Sam studied Olivia's determined expression, she had no doubt that Lucy would perform as expected.

Chapter 32

"But Tom, I know with your help, I can come back to work. I don't know if I'm able to handle pastoral counseling, but I can, at least, assist at worship."

Lucy studied Tom's kind, blue eyes. She could practically hear him weighing the pros and cons in his mind, but he looked sympathetic.

"Maybe you could, Lucy, but why put yourself under strain? We're managing fine without you."

"That's what I'm afraid of," said Lucy. She forced a smile to show humor, but she was serious about her concerns.

The chuckles in return were also forced. Lucy looked from Tom's face to Abbie's. She'd been a senior executive, accustomed to making hard decisions. She had the same expression as Tom's—sympathetic but resolute. Only Olivia was hard to read. Her piercing blue eyes were scrutinizing Lucy's image on the screen.

Lucy was glad she'd washed her hair and put it up. She'd also carefully applied makeup, including a strong shade of red lipstick, and she wore a clerical blouse and the last linen collar Erika had ironed before she'd died. Lucy almost wept when she put it on, but she stopped herself because she didn't want to wreck her mascara. Despite the great effort to show a professional image on the screen, below, Lucy was wearing jeans and her fuzzy slippers.

It had taken such effort to get herself together. Afterwards, she was ready to lie down and take a nap—a sure sign, if she was willing to acknowledge it, that she wasn't ready to go back to work. Other things had suffered. Despite the hiatus in her pastoral duties, Lucy was barely able to keep up with her theology classes, and she'd probably be late submitting her papers this term. The only thing that kept her going was the idea of letting Erika down after she'd encouraged her to write her book and pursue a PhD.

Both of the women in the meeting let their eyes wander, which let Lucy know they were waiting for someone to deliver a pre-planned message. She was disappointed when Tom began to speak. His female colleagues had defaulted to letting the male in the group speak for them. When Tom's face became especially kind, Lucy had a fleeting moment of hope before realizing it was merely to prepare her for bad news.

"Lucy, we've discussed this, and believe me when I say this was a hard decision for us to make, but we all agree you should take another month's leave. After that, we'll re-evaluate."

"But I'm the rector," Lucy protested.

"Yes, but we are senior members of your vestry, and in charity, we are offering you our best advice."

Abbie jumped in. "Lucy, we all love and support you. When I worked in corporate, we only gave a few days of bereavement leave, and it was a bad policy. When the managers came back from leave, they weren't at the top of their game. We often paid for our shortsightedness in medical or counseling bills. I hate to put it so bluntly, but if we give you the time now, in the long run, it will be better for you and the parish."

Olivia had been listening intently. Finally, she said, "Lucy, please listen to us. We all look forward to the day when you stand in the pulpit again. We just want you to take the time you need to heal and not force it. You can't rush these things, as you well know."

"Please tell us, you accept our decision," Tom pleaded in his most sympathetic pastoral tone.

"Do I have a choice?"

"Yes, of course, you do. But see this for what it is, our way of caring for our rector and our parish."

Lucy swallowed hard. She knew they meant well, and her collapse at Christmas was still fresh in their minds. Sam had probably told Olivia what a mess Lucy's house had been. There was no hiding in this town. "Thank you all for your advice," Lucy said. "I accept the decision."

"Thank you for trusting us," said Tom, sounding greatly relieved. "We're out of time, so let's end this meeting. Agreed?"

Lucy nodded. "Thanks, Tom. Thank you, Abbie and Olivia."

"See you soon," Abbie said in a hopeful voice and offered a warm smile.

The image on the screen collapsed, but Lucy stood staring at the red "meeting ended" notice. A lump came up in her throat. She tried to swallow it, but she couldn't. Her plan for climbing back into the saddle had just dissolved. *No, don't cry*, she told herself. *You will get through this.*

Then an email message notice flashed on her screen. It was from her friend in the Queer Youth Alliance, Rabbi Rebecca Morgenstern, so she opened it.

Dear, dear Lucy!

I just heard about Erika's death. I'm so sorry. Words are never enough, especially at a time like this. I said the Kaddish for Erika. She was among the righteous and the just. Know that I am holding you in my heart and praying for you. Please call me if you need anything. I mean it!

Much love,

Becca

Lucy felt like crying, but she found she had no more tears. She shut the laptop and plugged in the charger. The meeting had completely exhausted her reserves. She decided that she really needed a nap. She'd made a cozy nest on the couch. Although she'd tried several times, she couldn't sleep in the queen-sized bed without Erika. She felt lost in it like a tiny penguin adrift on an ice floe that had broken off from a glacier, and she was so cold without Erika's warm body beside her.

Sometimes, she put her face into Erika's pillow to see if she could still smell the woman she loved, but Erika was so clean, she never left any scent behind. Even her dirty laundry was scentless. Nevertheless, Lucy sometimes put on a polar fleece hoodie that Erika had worn, although Lucy swam in it and had to roll up the sleeves. She had already decided she would never wash it. Never. It was the closest thing she would ever have to having Erika's arms around her again.

Lucy pulled the fleece blanket over her ears. She closed her eyes and thought of Erika's warm body. Moments later, she began to doze.

"Yeah, Mom said she would give me her car, but she can't find the keys. She said she put them somewhere safe, but now, she can't find them."

"That used to be my car before I got the new one. I might have the concierge key in my desk. I'll look for it."

Lucy opened her eyes and realized that Emily, talking in the family room, had the speaker on, but why was she talking to Liz?

"I walked up to the supermarket, but it's a long way to carry a lot of stuff. I love pizza, but I just can't eat any more."

"I get it," said Liz. "Okay. I'll be by in about a half hour. I'm just finishing up my office hours. Thanks for calling me, Emily."

"I hope Mom's not mad at me."

"You did the right thing. Don't worry."

Lucy sat up. She felt betrayed. Then she told herself that was irrational. Her child was hungry, and she wasn't feeding her. She gave her daughter credit for asking for what she needed.

Emily came into the living room. "Aunt Liz is coming over."

"I heard," said Lucy, repositioning the elastic to get her hair out of her face. "Why didn't you tell me you were tired of pizza?"

"I did, Mom. You just gave me your credit card and told me to order something else."

"You could have ordered Thai food or Chinese food, or–"

"I could've, but I didn't know what you would eat. I want you to eat, or you'll get sick." Emily's eyes pleaded with her. "Please, Mom, I don't want to lose you too. I just found you."

Lucy's eyes filled. A single tear broke loose and rolled slowly down her face. "I'm sorry, sweetie. I promise to look for Erika's car keys again. I never drove her car, so I put them in a safe place. Now, I can't remember where."

"You've had a lot to think about," Emily said, impressing Lucy with her sensitivity.

Lucy tossed aside the covers and got up. "Help me tidy up in here a little. I don't want Aunt Liz to see this mess."

"I'm sure she doesn't care."

"Believe me, she does. Please bring the blankets and pillow upstairs. I'll get rid of these dirty cups."

Emily collected the bedding. "What do you want me to do with this?" she asked, holding out the linen collar. Lucy stared at it, realizing the button must have opened while she'd been asleep.

"Put it in our bedroom...my bedroom...on the dresser. Thanks, sweetheart."

By the time Liz arrived, the place looked fairly presentable. All the trash had been taken out and the dirty dishes were in the dishwasher. Erika had bought a fake narcissus plant in a clever bottle filled with clear resin to suggest water. Lucy placed it on the coffee table for cheer.

Liz brought in a blast of cold, fresh air. It smelled good compared to the stale smell of the house, which persisted despite the scented candles Lucy had lit in the kitchen. Liz hung up her parka on the coat tree and stepped into the room. Lucy felt her physician's eyes scanning her, assessing her physical state.

"How are you, Lucy?" asked Liz, taking her into her arms. Her hair smelled fresh and cold like outside. Her cheek was cool. Usually, Liz gave her a bear hug, but she was gentle this time. *Do I look that fragile?* Lucy wondered. Liz's arms lingered for a moment before she let her go.

Emily came into the room. "Hey, Aunt Liz."

"I called Audi. I found the key tag with the number in my safe. They're sending two sets, but I bet I can find Erika's keys if I look around. Did you look in Erika's purse?" she asked, engaging Lucy's gaze.

"I haven't. I can't go through any of her things. Not yet."

"How much you want to bet, the keys are in there, and there's a spare set in her desk?"

"I never thought to look in the desk."

"I'll go look," Liz volunteered. A few minutes later, she returned, dangling the keys. She handed them to Emily. "Go pack a bag for a couple of days. I'm taking you home with me." Emily glanced at Lucy, who reluctantly nodded her permission.

After Emily went upstairs, Liz took Lucy in her arms, hugging even more gently than before. "You're disappearing, Lucy. We can't have that. We need you in the land of the living. Erika would have wanted me to feed you."

While Liz stroked her back soothingly Lucy laid her cheek against her crisp, gabardine blazer. "It's going to be okay, Lucy" Liz whispered. "You're a strong woman, and you *will* survive this." Liz strengthened her embrace a bit. "I bought a whole salmon fillet. I'm going to make Erika's recipe with fresh dill and wilted greens and that rice pilaf you like."

"You're making me hungry."

"That's the idea." Liz let her go. "Now, pack a bag. I want to keep an eye on you for a few days."

"I'm all right."

"No, you're not. Maggie and I will take care of you."

"I don't want to impose."

"You're not. You're always welcome in my house."

Lucy went upstairs into the bedroom she shared with Erika. She found her overnight bag and threw clothes into it. She deliberately left behind the lacy red bra Erika had hung from the Christmas tree. She had to search for her laptop bag under the pile of dirty clothes on the chair.

When she came downstairs, Liz was wearing her parka, ready to go. "I turned down the heat and the hot water heater. I checked all the doors. Are you ready?" asked Liz, reaching for her bag.

"I can carry it," Lucy protested.

"I know you can but give it to me anyway." With a sigh, Lucy handed it over.

"I don't want to be enabled."

"We can argue about that later," said Liz, putting her arm lightly at Lucy's back to guide her out through the garage. It seemed so strange to see Erika's car gone.

"Erika taught her to drive," Lucy said sadly.

"Thank God. I'd be afraid to drive around Hobbs if you'd taught her."

Lucy tried to think of a witty comeback, but her brain wasn't working.

As Liz navigated to her house, Lucy surveyed the damage on Ocean Road from the big storm. This was the first time she'd been out of the house in weeks. In the meantime, a big chunk of roadway had washed away. Liz navigated around it carefully.

"Speaking as your doctor, I really want you to take better care of yourself."

"I will."

"Don't give me lip service, Lucy. I love you and I want you to be healthy. I think you should hire Ellie to keep house for you until you get back on your feet. Erika left you plenty of money. Her insurance paid off the mortgage, so you don't even have that to worry about. Ellie is great. She'll be happy to shop and cook for you. You've got to eat right, or you'll get sick."

"Liz, please don't lecture me. Emily shouldn't have called you."

"She did it because she loves you, Lucy. We all do."

"I know. I'm letting everyone down."

"Well, yes, you are. You refuse our support, and you're not taking care of yourself. We need you in this town. I need you. I just lost my best friend. I don't want to lose you too." Liz compressed her lips and stared at the road ahead. Lucy sensed she was desperately trying to hold back tears.

Lucy didn't know what to say, so she reached out and patted Liz's shoulder.

When they arrived at Liz's house, Emily was waiting in Erika's car. She rolled down the window as Liz approached. "Where should I park?" Liz pointed to a plowed area on the other side of the driveway.

Liz took Lucy's bag out of the back seat.

"Does Maggie know I'm coming?" Lucy asked.

"No, but I'm sure she won't mind."

Liz unlocked the front door. She waited for Emily to catch up with them. "Take any room you want," Liz said, "And take your mom's bag upstairs, please."

Liz directed Lucy to the living room, where she opened the wood stove to put on some wood. "It will warm up in a few minutes." Lucy sat down on the sofa, and Liz draped a colorful afghan around her. "My grandmother made this. When I'm sick or really tired I put it around me and I can practically feel her hugging me." Lucy snuggled deeper into the afghan to show her appreciation.

Maggie came into the room. Her smile lacked warmth. "Hello, Lucy."

"Thanks for having us, Maggie."

"You're welcome," she said. Her tone was anything but welcoming. "Liz? Can I talk to you in the kitchen?"

"Sure. Let me get the fire going, and I'll be right there."

The fire started to blaze. Liz left the door slightly open. "Keep an eye on this, Lucy. If any sparks fly out, close it."

Liz left, and Lucy heard loud voices coming from the kitchen. The door slid shut, which muffled the sound, but the angry voices persisted. Lucy pulled the afghan tighter around her and cringed.

Chapter 33

Olivia watched Lucy look around the house now cleaned and in perfect order thanks to Ellie. She knew that feeling of coming home after being away. Olivia's business had often taken her away from her New York apartment for weeks at a time. She remembered the experience of coming home to a place where the most familiar things suddenly looked strange. Even the air would feel different and the sound of the appliances. She watched Lucy taking in the details.

"This was always so much Erika's house," said Lucy, turning to her. "I never had much to add. I collected things when I traveled as an opera singer, but when I decided to become a priest, I got rid of most of them."

"Like going into the convent?"

"No, I wasn't taking a vow of poverty. I only wanted to put my past behind me so I could fully embrace my new life." Lucy paused at the photo showing the bombed spire of the Kaiser Wilhelm Memorial Church in Berlin. "I sometimes wondered why Erika kept such a sad memento of her past, but she, and all Germans of that generation, can't seem to forget the horror of that war. It's as if they need to remember that awful experience along with their parents."

"The sins of the fathers…" Olivia quoted.

"I don't believe in that," Lucy said, her tone slightly sharp. Olivia wrote it off to another effect of her grief. After Jason had died, Olivia had angered easily too. Sometimes, she took offense over nothing at all.

Lucy turned and smiled, obviously to make amends for being impatient. The smile nearly achieved the radiance it had before her wife had died. When Lucy had called to ask for a ride home, Olivia hadn't hesitated for a second. She'd been relieved to see how much better Lucy looked after being in Liz's care for a week. Lucy needed someone to drive her home because Emily had taken Erika's car with her when she returned to Yale. "Liz will hold me hostage as long as she can," Lucy had explained when she'd called that morning. "Maggie goes to an appointment on Saturday mornings. I can sneak away while everyone is out of the house."

"I know it was forward of me to have Ellie clean again," Olivia explained as she put down the groceries on the kitchen counter. "Sam lent me her key to the garage and told me the code to get into the house. I hope you don't mind."

"I appreciate it. Coming home to the rat's nest I made would be so depressing."

"You could consider hiring Ellie on a regular basis. She's very reasonable and reliable."

"Liz suggested the same thing, but I feel so guilty having another woman clean my house."

"That's how Ellie makes a living. There's no shame in hard work. And you're a busy woman, Lucy. You have a very important role in this community."

"I had a house cleaner when I traveled for my music engagements," Lucy admitted. "But of course, I couldn't afford it as a priest."

"Now, you can. Erika left you very well off. Spend her money. She left it to you out of love."

Lucy's face contorted, and Olivia feared she might cry again, but after a momentary struggle, Lucy pulled herself together. She nodded. "Yes, she did."

"Ellie did your laundry too," Olivia explained.

"Oh, no. There were some things I didn't want washed."

It took a few seconds for Olivia to understand. "I'm sorry. I didn't know."

"I had a hoodie of Erika's hanging on the back of the closet door."

"Then don't worry. She only washed whatever was in the laundry hamper or on the floor."

"She washed my underwear?" Lucy blushed. She had such a fair complexion, it was always obvious when she was embarrassed, no matter how much self-control she practiced.

"Yes, of course. She's used to that."

"I've never been such a pig," said Lucy. She smiled. "Erika would call me her little piglet when I enjoyed her food and ate more than usual."

"You *should* eat more, Lucy. You're much too thin."

Lucy took a deep breath. "I will, Olivia. I'm determined to prove that I'm all right. Maybe then, you'll let me have my job back."

"You can have your job back anytime. We've discussed it in the vestry. It's not our place to tell you what to do, but please take it easy, Lucy. When I lost my Jason, I tried to bury myself in work. Staying busy might block out the pain but only for a while. Then, it comes roaring back."

Lucy nodded. "Let me bring up my bags. Can you stay for a cup of coffee?"

"Sure," said Olivia. She watched Lucy head down the hall. "Ellie washed the bed linens too," she called after her.

Lucy returned to the top of the stairs to say, "That's so kind. I'm going to try to sleep there. I just couldn't before."

"One step at a time, Lucy. I'll bring in the rest of the groceries."

By the time Lucy returned, Olivia had stowed all the perishables in the refrigerator. "I would have made coffee, but I have no idea how to use that new-fangled coffee thingy."

Lucy laughed and filled one of the reusable pods. "Erika liked it because it's so efficient, but in the morning, I could drink a whole pot by myself. I kind of miss the smell of coffee brewing."

"So? Get yourself a regular coffee maker."

"I would, but Liz gave this to Erika as a gift, so it would be hard to get rid of it."

Olivia tried to think of a way to say what she was thinking without offending Lucy. "We all have a tendency, when someone passes, to preserve the details of their lives out of respect. What we have to avoid is making where they lived a museum in their honor."

Lucy looked reflective and a little hurt. "I didn't think that's what I was doing. I'm just not ready to give up the things Erika liked."

"You'll know when you're ready. My mother gave me my grandmother's favorite coffee cup after she died. In the beginning, I used it all the time. Now, I only take it out when I want to feel close to my grandmother."

"I don't have too many things from my family," said Lucy. "My father died young, and Mom moved into an apartment. She got rid of a lot of things I would like to have now."

"Things are nice to have if they bring back memories. When I sit out on the deck, I think of Jason and how he had to have that big house right on the water. When I moved in, I left many things the way they were, but the first thing I did when I moved in was to remodel the bedroom and bathroom, and I got a new mattress."

"Maybe I should do that, but Liz built the bed for us as a wedding present, and the mattress is nearly brand new. It's just that a queen-sized bed seems so enormous for one person."

"I wouldn't go with something smaller. You never know who'll land in your bed."

At that, Lucy blushed fully crimson.

"Oh, stop, Lucy. You're an attractive woman. Stunning, in fact. I'm sure when you finish grieving, people will be beating a path to your door."

If possible, Lucy's complexion grew redder. She turned away and opened the door to the refrigerator.

"Ah-hah," said Olivia. "There's someone waiting in the wings!"

"That's the last thing I'm thinking about."

"You're young, Lucy. Don't give up on love. You have your whole life ahead of you." Olivia changed the subject, realizing this one was making Lucy sad. "You have a lovely figure, but you could stand to eat a little more. All those prepared foods aren't good for you."

"I'll have to learn to cook first. My mother was a singer too, and she didn't have time to cook. Erika was trying to teach me, but she was one of those people who cook by taste…a dash of this, a pinch of that." Then she looked reflective. "I tried to get Erika to write down the recipes. Unfortunately, she didn't get far before she died. She said Liz knew all her mother's recipes too, and I could ask her."

"Liz is going to miss her friend."

"Oh, yes. They shared everything. Erika was her wingman."

"Her wingman?" Olivia had only heard that expression when Jason was a college boy. "You mean they went to bars together?"

"According to Erika, Liz was a favorite with the ladies."

"I can see that." Olivia imagined a young Liz Stolz striding up to the prettiest woman in the bar. "Liz has a surgeon's confidence…and arrogance."

"My experience is that arrogant people are often covering up insecurities."

"Maybe so, but if you play at it long enough, arrogance becomes a permanent character trait."

Lucy looked at Olivia in a way that made her think she was surprised by that insight. "Was that your experience?" she asked.

"Is that what you think, Lucy? That I'm arrogant?"

"Let's just say you have an overabundance of confidence." She grinned.

"That's a nice way to put it. But you're right. I had to learn how to look and sound confident, otherwise people run right over you, especially if you're a woman in a position of power."

"I understand."

"You do?" Now, it was Olivia's turn to be surprised.

"Yes, of course. It's not easy to be a female priest. Many conservative people think it's sacrilege. Never mind being a lesbian priest. That's sinful *and* a sacrilege."

"Forget those stuffy, old men. I think female priests are exactly what the Church needs."

Olivia glanced at the clock. "Would you like me to make you some lunch? That rotisserie chicken you bought would make lovely sandwiches, and you'll still have plenty for dinner. I'll show you how to make my signature chicken salad. I'll even reveal my secret ingredient."

"What's that?"

"A dash of curry. It gives the salad a lovely golden color and just a little heat." While Olivia rinsed her cup in the sink, an idea occurred to her. "Lucy, I could teach you how to cook."

Lucy's face brightened. "You would do that?"

"Certainly. You could come over and we can cook together. I'd be glad for the company. Sam often works late. We can start now, with the chicken salad for lunch. Finish your coffee, and we'll get to work."

Chapter 34

"Now that you'll be moving up to Scarborough, it will be a long trip for you to come to Portsmouth," said Gloria. "Wouldn't Zoom or telephone sessions be a better option?"

"I don't mind the drive," Maggie replied. "It's nice to see a real person for a change. I have Zoom fatigue."

"Many people do." Gloria studied Maggie, who squirmed a bit under the scrutiny. Gloria's eyes were always kind, but sometimes, it seemed they could pierce through her façade to her soul. After a pause, Gloria asked, "When are you going to tell her you're moving?"

"Today. She has a light day on Saturdays. The office is only open until noon."

"It must have been difficult holding on to the announcement so long."

"It was, but I wanted to wait until we had privacy in the house. Now, Stefan is back home in his residence and Lucy's gone. She called to say she was leaving today."

"How has your relationship been with her?"

Maggie shrugged. "It's more or less back to normal. But we'll never be as close as we were before the kiss."

"Why not? You said you forgave her, and you don't see the kiss as her fault."

"I don't, and I love Lucy, but I know that, as soon as I'm out of the picture, Liz is going to run straight into her arms."

Gloria gave Maggie a long, hard look. "You don't know that. Lucy just lost her spouse. She is a sensible person, and a trained therapist. I would be very surprised if she rushed into a relationship with anyone."

"True," Maggie conceded. "But I know she's interested in Liz."

Gloria sighed. "Why not see what happens? Besides, if you're moving on, why do you care what they do?"

"I don't want to care, but I do."

Gloria leaned her elbows on her knees and sat forward. "Maggie, are you sure you want to end the marriage? It sounds like you still have feelings for Liz."

"Of course, I have feelings for Liz. We've known each other for almost half a century. We've shared a bed and made love. We've gone through some difficult times together. I love Liz."

"Maybe you can convince her to work on the marriage through counseling."

Maggie rolled her eyes. "You don't know Liz. She's so stubborn about this. It will never happen."

"Did you ask her?"

"No."

"Why not?"

"Because it was hard enough to make up my mind. Now that I have, I don't want anyone to try to change it."

"I see." Gloria sat back. "Are you going to tell her when you get home?" Maggie realized Gloria was probably asking to prepare for fallout.

"She should be home by the time I get back. I already packed my bags and brought them to the downstairs guest room."

"You plan to leave right after you tell her?"

"I think it's a good idea. Liz has a long fuse, but she has quite a temper. I want to get away while she's still in shock."

"That's really not fair, is it?" Gloria gave her a long inspection. "You don't fear she'll be abusive?"

"No, Liz would never hurt anyone, but I remember when I confronted my ex-husband. He hit me. Just once. Then I threw him out."

"Maybe it's better to avoid projecting bad memories onto the present situation," Gloria advised.

"Of course, it is, but it's hard. I lived in fear of provoking Barry for a long time. I tiptoed around him for years."

"That sounds like a topic for further exploration, but let's stick to the present for a moment. It's probably best to tell Liz in as calm a way as you can manage. Can you do that?"

"I'm an actress," said Maggie with a dazzling smile.

"Yes, you are, and a good one, I imagine, but sometimes being authentic works better."

"I'll try," Maggie promised.

"I don't expect a call after you tell her, but I am here in case of an emergency. I hope it goes well."

As Maggie drove home, she anticipated the conversation with Liz with a mixture of dread and relief. The relief was stronger because she'd been keeping so many things from Liz, including the sale of the co-op in New York. Both Maggie's daughters knew about her decision. Sofia was shocked and sad because Liz had been instrumental in her career as an oncologist. Alina was worried because Liz was holding the mortgage on her condo. Her two daughters had become attached to Liz and considered her another grandmother. "Can we still visit her in Hobbs?" Alina had asked. "I'm sure the girls would miss her."

That question had made Maggie especially sad. "Of course, you can visit. Liz and I will still be friends." Maggie had mustered her most confident voice, but she wasn't entirely sure Liz would want anything to do with any of them. Then she realized she was being ridiculous. Liz was loyal to her friends, sometimes to a fault. After things settled down, they would find their way.

When Maggie came up the driveway, she saw Liz's truck and steeled herself for what was to come. She parked her car and leaned her forehead against the steering wheel as she gave herself a pep talk.

She was greeted by cooking smells. She sniffed the air and determined that Liz was making herself an omelet, a Spanish omelet, she guessed, from the smell of peppers and onions.

"Hey, sweetie," said Liz casually when Maggie came into the kitchen. She turned away from the stove to plant a quick kiss on Maggie's cheek. "Did you have a good…whatever it was you were doing?"

"Yes. How was your morning at the office?"

"Uneventful. Business is still slow. Hey, would you like this omelet? I can make another one for myself."

"No, you eat it. I'm not hungry now."

"Okay." Liz slid the omelet onto a plate and carried it to the breakfast nook. She opened her iPad and propped it up, so she could read while she ate. When Maggie pulled the bench across from her away from the table, Liz smiled and flipped closed the tablet. "Thanks for keeping me company while I eat."

"You're welcome. When you're finished eating, can we talk?"

"Sure. We can talk now if you want."

"No, enjoy your lunch. We can talk afterward."

Liz frowned, but she said, "Okay," and continued shoveling away the omelet. Maggie was still amazed that anyone could eat that fast. The good smell in the kitchen was tantalizing, but Maggie shut down her hunger. She didn't want to be distracted from her mission. Besides, it would be too easy to fall into the familiar pattern of eating together and the casual conversation that accompanied it. Liz finished the last bite of her lunch and drained her water glass. "All done," she announced. "Now, what did you want to talk to me about?"

"Let's go into the living room."

Again, Liz frowned. "Let me clean up the kitchen, and I'll join you there."

Maggie felt a shiver of anxiety at the conversation being further delayed. "Can't that wait? This is important."

"Maggie, you're starting to worry me. What's going on?"

"Come out and I'll tell you." Maggie went out and took a seat on the sofa. She heard Liz running water in the kitchen, probably washing out the frying pan. Maggie wondered if Liz sensed what was coming and was trying to delay it. No, that was impossible. She hadn't let on. She'd wanted to give Liz warning, but when her best friend died, she just hadn't had the heart.

Liz came out and sat in the club chair opposite her. She dried her hands on her jeans, leaving dark streaks starting with a wet handprint beginning at the knee and moving up her thigh. "What's going on?" she asked, looking puzzled.

Maggie forced herself to take a long, slow breath instead of sucking in air all at once, although she felt like she was suffocating. There was an odd ringing in her ears. She dismissed it and forced herself to concentrate. She assumed a neutral but pleasant expression. "We've been having a hard time lately."

Liz frowned and looked faintly suspicious. "Yes, we have. The pandemic has been hard for everyone."

"Liz, that's not what I mean. I think we should admit we made a mistake and separate."

The only sign that Liz had heard was her eyes suddenly blinked. Otherwise, she had on her doctor face, unreadable and imperturbable. "What do you mean…separate?" she finally asked.

"I want a divorce."

"What?"

"I want to end the marriage."

Liz just stared at her with an inscrutable look on her face. After an unending moment, she asked, "What made you come to that decision?"

"I'm not getting what I need from this relationship, and neither are you."

"What do you need that I'm not giving you?"

"Conversation. Attention. Acknowledgement that I exist!"

"What?"

Maggie stared at her. Was it really possible that Liz didn't see what to her was as plain as day? "You have time for everyone except me. If it's not your patients, it's this friend or that one. Stefan was parked here for weeks. You went to work and expected me to take care of him."

"Stefan entertains himself. He's busy writing the next great mathematical theorem with Emily."

"I had to feed him lunch."

"I didn't know that was such a monumental act. How hard is it to heat up leftovers in the microwave?"

"That's not the point."

"What is the point?"

"It's not working."

"Says who?"

"Liz, can't you see?"

"No."

Maggie rolled her eyes and sighed. "There's no hope for you."

"Oh, fuck. Do whatever you want." Liz got up. A moment later, Maggie heard her office door slam. This wasn't going according to plan. She let out a long slow breath while she considered what to do next. She got up and knocked on the door.

"What?!?" Liz called out.

Maggie opened the door. "I need to tell you I'm leaving."

Liz didn't look away from her computer screen. "You already said that."

"I mean today."

That got Liz's attention. "Where are you going?"

"I'm moving in with Alina."

"I'm sure that will make for tight quarters. Good luck." Liz's voice was completely cold.

"We've looked at a house in Scarborough, a mother-daughter. Her condo is on the market."

Liz's blue eyes bored into hers. "You talked to your kids about this before you talked to *me*?"

Maggie began to tremble. She could sense that below Liz's perfectly orchestrated calm, she was furious. "Yes," Maggie admitted. "I needed to make plans."

"That's right. You plotted all your moves before you threw out your ex-husband."

"Liz…"

"Forget I said that. The bastard deserved everything he got." Liz turned back to her computer screen. "Get out. If you're going to leave, just go."

"Liz, I still love you. I just can't be married to you anymore. Please try to understand."

"Whatever."

Maggie stood in the doorway. She wanted to go to Liz and hug her. She wanted to explain how much it hurt her to say that she needed to leave, but Liz looked so stony.

"Well? Are your bags packed?" asked Liz, looking up.

"Yes."

"Do you need help bringing them out?"

"No, I can manage. I brought them down from upstairs. They're in the downstairs guest room."

"I'll help you," said Liz in a voice that left no room for argument.

Maggie followed her to the guest room, where Liz automatically picked up the two heaviest suitcases.

"I have more stuff," Maggie said, "but this is what I need for now."

"I'm not going to change the locks, if that's what you think." Liz's smile was almost a sneer.

"I never thought that you would."

Maggie stood back and let Liz pack the luggage in the trunk because she took such pride in doing it efficiently. "Anything else?" Liz asked, her face still stony.

"For now."

Maggie reached out to touch Liz's arm, but she flinched away. "I think you should go," Liz said.

"I think you're right. Call me when you calm down and we'll talk."

"What is there to talk about? You've already decided everything."

"That's not true. We need to decide—"

Liz glanced at the house with a sad look. "Now, I know why you moved downstairs. It was wasn't your allergies. At least, you could have told me the truth about that!" She glared at her. Maggie could see she was working herself into a temper. She should leave as soon as possible.

"Goodbye, Liz. Let's talk later." She got into the driver's seat and started the car. In the rearview mirror, she watched Liz go up the stairs to the porch, where she stood with her arms folded.

Chapter 35

Liz watched Maggie drive down the driveway, the little plume of white vapor almost insultingly cheerful as it puffed from the tailpipe. She waited until Maggie's Subaru was out of sight before closing the door. Then she went into the living room and sat down to calm herself. The emptiness of the house was unnerving. Without the presence of another human for distraction, all the house noises seemed so loud—the refrigerator motor humming in the kitchen, the furnace kicking on from time to time, and the tick of the clock.

She glanced at the clock on the wall but decided it was too early to start drinking. "Where the hell are you when I need you, Erika?" she said aloud to the empty room. "I don't know what to do. This is the first time anyone's left me. I always do the leaving."

After she said it, Liz realized it wasn't true. Maggie had left her forty-seven years ago, and nothing had ever been the same since. Liz had punished every woman she'd ever met since. Loved them and left them, and every time she did, she punished Maggie, paid her back for all the pain and loneliness and for almost destroying her hope of becoming a doctor. She told herself she wanted love, but what she really wanted was to hurt them like she'd been hurt. She wanted to fuck them in every possible way.

Liz considered ways to numb the pain. She could finish mortising the hinges for the doors on Olivia's armoire, but that would require using a router with extraordinary precision. Liz wasn't sure she could muster the necessary control under the circumstances. She thought about doing it by hand, chopping it out, making precise cuts and then hogging out the waste with a sharp chisel and a mallet. She imagined it in her mind. She always visualized her woodworking tasks the way she'd once visualized her surgeries.

No, best to stay away from sharp edges. In her state of mind, she would surely cut herself. Liz imagined slicing open her flesh with a chisel, like she did when she was building the bed for her cousin. The chisel went deep. Fortunately, it had missed any tendons or nerves. Liz opened her hand to inspect the white line in her palm between thumb and forefinger. Jenny had sewn up the wound in the kitchen of the Connecticut house. She'd done an excellent job, but wounds like that could never be erased. The scars went with you to your grave.

Liz tried to nudge herself into an emotional response, but she couldn't make herself cry any more than she could when her mother had died. It was just one more thing. One more loss. One more death.

Maybe she'd have one beer. She went to the fridge and opened the drawer where she kept her beer. Maggie had always complained about Liz taking up a perfectly usable vegetable bin with her bottles of IPAs and lagers. Now, Liz wouldn't have to listen to her complaints. Maggie was gone, and she could do whatever she wanted. Small consolation for her marriage ending.

Liz picked through the bottles in the drawer before deciding she really didn't want a beer. The compressor went on, but still Liz held the door open. She stared at the pot of beef bourguignon Maggie had made for dinner the night before. She always made the classic Julia Childs recipe to perfection. On a shelf on the door was the special hot sauce Maggie liked for her recipes. Liz closed the door, so she didn't have to see all the things that reminded her of her life with Maggie.

Her eyes fell on the antique bottle full of small shells that Maggie had collected on the beach. Liz hated clutter. When she lived alone, her house was spartan. After Maggie moved in, watercolor paintings found their way to the walls. Family photographs covered the shelves. Maggie had softened up the place and turned it into a home.

Liz wanted to take pleasure in the idea that now she could get rid of all those little things that annoyed her, but all she could feel was a dull ache in her chest. Her mind went into hyper drive, wondering if it was her heart, before realizing this pain had no physical cause.

"Erika, I really need you now. Where are you!"

The voice in her head said, "Call Sam."

Why hadn't she thought of that? Liz fished her phone out of the pocket of her sweatshirt and tapped Sam's number.

"Hey, Liz. What's up?"

"What are you doing?"

"Refining a rendering for a client."

"Can you take a break and spare a few minutes for an old friend?"

"I'm kind of into this at the moment. Can it wait?"

"Please."

Evidently, Sam heard the urgency in her voice. "What's the matter?" she asked.

"Maggie left me."

A long silence. "Oh…my…God."

"Yeah…exactly."

"Oh, shit, Liz. What happened?"

"Hell, if I know. She came home from something this afternoon and made this grand announcement like she'd been planning it for months. She and her daughter had even looked at houses to buy."

"And you had no idea?"

"No. None." As she said it, Liz scanned her memory looking for clues. "I mean she's been complaining, but just the usual stuff. I don't pay enough attention to her. I should retire. I should cut back on my activities. I spend too much time with my friends…"

"Does she mean Lucy?"

"Maybe, but she didn't mention her specifically. I just think she wanted me…all of me, and I didn't give her enough, which is crazy. She knew when we reconnected that I had a lot going on in my life."

"But then she retired and didn't have as much to do. And you did tell her you were going to retire."

"I thought I would…I guess. Then as time went on, I just didn't want to. Being a doctor is who I am. I'd be bored."

"You'd be bored? You? Never." Sam sighed. "Want to come over?"

"Yeah. I have to get out of here. Too many memories. Everywhere I look I see Maggie."

"I'm sure that will be hard. All right. Give me half an hour to finish this and then I can hang with you until tonight."

"Hot date with Olivia?"

Sam chuckled. "None of your fucking business."

Liz grinned, but her mirth quickly vanished. "Okay. I'll bring over some beer."

"Forget it. I have plenty. I'll see you soon."

Liz changed and took a shower to make sure no germs from the office hitched a ride to Sam's house. She brought beer anyway. Her mother had taught her never to arrive empty-handed.

Sam looked comfy in old jeans with threadbare knees and a thick hoodie. "I told you I had beer," she said, holding back the door. "Come on in. It's nice and warm in the living room."

Although Sam's architectural style had been influenced by the mid-century modern greats, she'd always chosen comfortable furniture for her own home. She'd built the two Morris chairs and matching settee in the living room when she'd gone through her Arts and Crafts phase. As she sat down, Liz admired her friend's meticulous work.

"Your armoire for Olivia is pretty much done, but I'll let you install the hardware. Not my favorite thing."

"I'm glad it will be finished for her birthday. She's been asking about it."

"How are you going to finish it? French polish?"

"No, too much work. I'll use that recipe in *Fine Woodworking*. It looks the same. Besides, Olivia won't know the difference." Sam studied Liz with a frown. "You don't really want to talk about woodworking, do you?"

"Any subject but the obvious one."

"Tell me you're really surprised. I told you this would happen when you kissed Lucy last summer."

"You did. But that's not what caused her to leave."

"It's not?"

"No, she said it was time to admit we'd made a mistake, and we're not right for each other. And she's right. I love the outdoors. She complains about the bugs biting. I love to be out on the water. She gets seasick. She needs everyone's attention. Everyone wants my attention. We're opposites."

"Supposedly, they attract. How long have you known this?"

Liz shrugged. "In the beginning, everything was wonderful. Maggie wanted to do everything I wanted to do, even fishing. She didn't seem to mind having a houseful of people every summer. And she was busy with teaching and her shows. It was the pandemic that brought everything into focus. I'm sure our marriage won't be the only casualty."

"Liz, you sound very philosophical, but even Erika would call you on this. Were you surprised?"

Liz thought for a moment. "I knew she wasn't happy. She made that clear at every opportunity."

"At least, it's a clean break. No drama. I hate dyke drama."

"Me too. I'm so glad I insisted on a pre-nup and separate bank accounts. There will be some legal stuff, of course. I've been managing her investments. I have power of attorney, and I'm her conservator. She'll probably want to turn that over to her kids."

"Liz, you sound so calm about this, but I know you're not."

"It hasn't really sunk in yet. It helps to focus on the practical aspects. It makes it real."

"What about your feelings?"

"Oh, please, Sam. You're starting to sound like Lucy."

Sam laughed. "No way. But I know you. Once this hits you, it will hit you hard."

Liz drew a long, slow breath. "I don't know. I've had so many hits lately, I'm kind of numb. You know what I mean? How much can one person take?"

Sam looked thoughtful. "With COVID deaths hitting half a million, it's hard to focus on any one tragedy."

"Exactly. But you're right. It's early days. Who knows how I'll feel tomorrow?"

Sam got up. "You want a beer? I'm getting one for myself."

"Sure. Why not?" While Sam was gone, Liz put her feet up on the ottoman. Sam's place always made her feel at home because it had been designed to perfectly fit its owner's needs and tastes. Sam had made no compromises for other people. Liz decided she needed to get back to what really mattered to her. No more letting women try to "soften" her environment, like Jenny's quilts and Maine kitsch in the guest rooms. It was time for that to go, along with Maggie's memorabilia.

"What are you thinking about?" asked Sam when she returned with the beer.

"Getting rid of Maggie's junk…and Jenny's. I want my home to be mine again."

Sam snickered. "Just wait 'til Lucy gets her hands on your place."

Liz turned to her with a fierce look. "Sam, you're my friend, and I love you, but keep your fucking assumptions to yourself."

"Okay," Sam replied warily. "Sorry, Liz. I didn't mean to offend you. I won't mention Lucy again."

"Good. Don't."

PART V

ASH WEDNESDAY

Chapter 36

Tom watched the rector's face carefully. He could understand why she wanted to meet privately. Maggie Fitzgerald had been a prominent member of the parish in addition to her role as music director. She gave back her salary to the church because she and her wife were wealthy. They would have to pay whoever replaced her. In addition, Maggie and Lucy were close friends. All of those aspects made the situation more delicate than usual.

"Scarborough isn't far from Hobbs," said Tom. "Would Maggie consider staying on temporarily?"

"It's a forty-minute drive," Lucy said. "That's pretty far, even for Mainers."

"But we're not worshipping in person, so what difference does it make? She could join our Zoom and Facebook Live services remotely."

"Actually, I was thinking of having an Ash Wednesday service in the church yard."

"How did I know you were going to say that?"

"Because great minds think alike." Lucy smiled one of her solar-flare smiles. Tom basked in it, relieved to see Lucy looking like her old self. Her color was better. She'd put on a little weight, which was good because she'd been gaunt. "Well? What do you think?" she prodded.

"It depends on the weather, of course."

"Of course, but I feel it's really important to be out there where people can see us. It's been such a dark winter. So much death and isolation. People are desperate for human contact. We've been vaccinated, so we're lucky, but so many people are alone."

Tom chuckled softly. "I know better than to argue with you, Lucy. You're like a force of nature. If you don't win them over with your arguments, you irradiate them with your atomic smile."

Lucy winked. "Love is my secret weapon."

"As it should be…for all pastors." Tom smiled and circled back to his original suggestion. "Should we ask Maggie if she would be willing to continue?"

Lucy's auburn brows bent toward the bridge of her nose. "Tom, I have a confession to make."

"Formally? As a priest? Should I get my stole?"

"I'm not looking for absolution. I've already repented, but I think I need to tell you what's going on."

Tom adjusted his posture to look more receptive. He uncrossed his legs and put his feet flat on the floor. "Go on. I'm listening."

Lucy looked pensive for a moment, as if she couldn't figure out how to begin. "I feel partially responsible for the breakup of Maggie's marriage," she finally said. "I had a small part in it, but it may have been what pushed her over the edge."

Tom felt uneasy, but he kept his expression absolutely neutral. "You don't have to tell me all the details."

"I want to tell you because I'd also like your advice." Lucy's smile faded and she looked grave. "Liz Stolz and I have been attracted to one another since we met. Erika once asked if I was interested in Liz, but I didn't tell her the whole truth. Maybe because I couldn't face it myself. For a long time, it was just sexual banter and flirting."

"Yes," said Tom, sitting back in his chair. "I've observed you two at play. It can be quite amusing."

"Last summer, it became more. I invited myself along when Liz was going fishing. I didn't have any hidden agenda. I just wanted to see what it was like. My father used to take me fishing. We were having a great time being out in her boat. Everything was fine until Liz kissed me."

Tom squeezed his hands together tightly, his little trick to avoid reacting.

"Before I pushed her away and reminded her that we were both married to other people, I responded to the kiss. I responded because, at that moment, I wanted her."

"Oh, dear," Tom finally said.

"But that's all that happened. One kiss. One time. At first, neither of us said anything to anyone, but Maggie guessed and confronted me. Once Maggie knew, I felt I had to tell Erika too. I didn't want it to come back to her from another source."

"Wise. How did Erika react?"

"Surprisingly, she was very casual about it. She wasn't jealous or upset. She even gave me permission to sleep with Liz. I was shocked."

"That sounds like Erika. Remember she was trained in philosophy to be reasonable about everything and raised by that atheist, Stefan Bultmann. He was quite the womanizer himself."

"Stefan? My father-in-law? That sweet, little old man?"

"He wasn't always sweet or old. When I was his graduate student, he was a handsome man in his early fifties with intense, blue eyes. Even I found him attractive. I doubt he ever cheated on Helga. He adored her, but I wouldn't be surprised to know he had very liberal ideas about marriage."

"Prior to our marriage, Erika had open relationships."

"We all did at one time. Liz as well. But that's all I will say about it."

"I know that Liz also felt free to roam in her previous relationship. I want to say now, before you and before God, that I often wished I had taken up Erika on her offer."

"Is what you feel for Liz more than sexual attraction?"

"Yes. We have a deep, romantic friendship. We love each other, but before the kiss, I never acknowledged that I am in love with her."

"I see. Now that she'll be free, do you intend to start a relationship?"

"No, I'm not ready for that, and Liz needs to deal with the fallout from her divorce."

"But if the time were right?"

"I don't know…"

Tom raised his brows. "I think you do know."

Lucy nodded. "We'll see." She focused intently on Tom's eyes. "I won't insult you by saying this has to remain strictly confidential, but I loved

Erika, and other than that one kiss, I was completely faithful to her. I don't want any shadow on her memory."

"Of course, not. And Lucy, you can love Erika and still love Liz. You can be sure I'm not one of those clergymen who has all the answers, but I do know one thing about human love: it's complicated."

"Yes, it certainly is," said Lucy with a sigh.

"Lucy, accept God's love and the grace to find your way…with or without Liz." He frowned as he considered all that he'd heard. "I think you're right. Given the history, let's let Maggie join the parish in Cape Elizabeth. She probably wants a fresh start, and so do we."

"I'm glad you agree. Thank you, Tom, for listening."

"My pleasure. Thank you for trusting me."

They concluded their meeting with a prayer. Tom went upstairs to change out of his suit and collar. As he put on his sweater, he thought of Liz. She and Maggie had given him the fine cashmere pullover the first Christmas after he'd moved to Maine. It had since become his favorite. He said a silent prayer for the broken couple. He realized he missed their company. He especially missed talking to Liz, whose wit reminded him of Erika's. After he finished dressing, he found his phone and called Liz's number.

"Thomas!" said Liz brightly when she answered. "How are you?"

"I'm well, Liz, but I was wondering if you could use some company."

"Funny you should say that. I'm on my way to the Irish pub to pick up a shepherd's pie for my dinner. I was thinking how nice it would be to go in and eat it at the bar for company. Of course, with the COVID restrictions, that's out of the question. But I could pick up something for you and we could eat at your place."

"Oh, I haven't had a good shepherd's pie in ages. Yes, please pick one up for me too."

"Roger that. How about some Irish poutine to go with it?"

"What's that?"

"You know the French-Canadian dish poutine? French fries, cheese curds and gravy? This is similar, but it has Maine cheddar, bits of home-cured corned beef, and curry gravy."

"Sounds intriguing. I'm game."

"And I'll bring some Guinness."

"Excellent. I can't wait!"

Tom whistled an Irish tune as he set two places at the kitchen table. As much as he enjoyed the company of Jeff and his friends, he missed the intellectual engagement he'd shared with Erika and Liz. Of course, when Liz was in her relationship with Maggie, he didn't want to intrude. The same with Lucy and Erika. But now that Liz was single, he could be more forward in proposing invitations. The idea cheered him as he searched through his CD collection for Irish music. He found a disc of Celtic fiddle music and inserted it in the CD player. It never mattered to him that people might consider him a dinosaur for owning such antiquated technology because the sound was so much better.

While he waited for Liz to arrive with their dinner, Tom tidied the living room. He wasn't the sort of bachelor who turned his living space into a dirty nest. In fact, he set aside time for house cleaning every Wednesday after he'd finished writing his sermon, confining the most onerous tasks of the week to one day.

He heard the downstairs door close firmly and the sound of footsteps in the hall. He opened the door and sang out, "Hey, Liz. Thanks for making deliveries."

"Hah, now you're forced to eat with me."

"I can't think of anything I'd rather do tonight."

"Good. Let me take the bags into the kitchen and put out the food. Do you want to eat in their containers or use real plates?"

"Oh, let's be civilized," said Tom, opening the cabinet and taking down some plates. "You seem to know your way around this place."

"When Lucy lived here, I spent some time here, mostly fixing things. I replaced that faucet," she said, nodding toward that the sink.

"Lucy is lucky to have loyal friends like you."

Liz turned and looked at him suspiciously, but then went on to unpacking their food. "We need to eat the poutine first. Then if we still have any appetite left, we can eat our real dinner. Good idea to use plates and prevent contamination of the leftovers."

"Only you would think of that."

"Well, I am a doctor. I think of such things. Speaking of which, I used sanitizer, but nothing works as well as good old soap and water. Mind if I use your sink?" Tom watched her vigorously washing her hands like she was scrubbing for surgery.

She opened a container holding French fries slathered with a golden gravy. "Here taste," she said, holding it out to him as she snatched a fry for herself. "Doesn't get better than this."

Tom regarded the pile curiously. "It looks like a heart attack waiting to happen."

"Oh, it is. Just take your cholesterol meds tonight and you'll be fine. However, this is a special treat. Not for regular consumption."

"Yes, doctor." Tom sampled a fry, tasting the delicious curry sauce dotted with flecks of corned beef. "Oh, my word! This is obscene!" he exclaimed. "How have I never had this before?"

"Told you so," said Liz, bringing it to the table. "Now dig in and let's eat it before it gets cold. It's disgusting when it's cold."

Tom chuckled. "Thanks for the warning."

They made pigs of themselves and demolished the pile of fries in no time. "You can have the last one," Tom said gallantly.

"No, you. It's your first time. It's yours."

Tom was so enjoying Liz's company, he wondered why he hadn't thought of this before. His mind invented excuses. He told himself he hadn't wanted to look conspicuous about checking on his friend. Even worse, Liz might think he was trying to minister to her, which would make her furious.

Liz cleared away the container from their appetizer. "How about we split a shepherd's pie? You can have the other for dinner another night." Liz didn't wait for an answer. She divided the contents of the container onto two plates. "Not as picturesque scooped onto a plate, but who cares? Maggie was always big on presentation, but it's just us tonight."

Tom heard the longing note in Liz's voice when she said her wife's name. "You miss her, don't you?"

"I do. When we weren't arguing, I enjoyed her company. The house is very quiet." Liz placed a dish in front of Tom and sat down at her place.

"Is there any possibility of a reconciliation?"

Liz sighed. "It doesn't sound like it. She's decided it's over, which means it's over."

"But you're not sure?"

"It doesn't matter what I think. I never even had a chance to protest. It was presented as a done deed."

"You could ask her to reconsider. Perhaps counseling…"

"No counseling, damn it! You and Lucy!" She glanced up. "Sorry, Tom."

"No offense taken. But Liz, sometimes it does help. You've gone through a lot this year. You lost your mother, your dearest friend, and now your wife. The pandemic has been a special burden on medical people…"

"I'm managing, Tom. I'm pretty resilient." Liz raised a brow. "I hope you didn't invite me over to minister to me."

"I wouldn't dare."

"Lucy didn't put you up to it, did she?" Liz asked, giving him a hard look. "She should know better."

"No, no, she had nothing to do with it. She doesn't even know we're getting together. It was totally spontaneous. I got the idea to call you when I put on this sweater, which I love, by the way, and wear all the time."

"It looks nice on you. Good color for you. Maggie picked it out."

Again, Tom heard the faint note of longing when Liz spoke Maggie's name. "Liz, I want you to know I'm here for you if you need a sympathetic ear…not as a priest…or counselor…but as your friend."

"Good to know, Tom. And I will return the invitation because I enjoy your company. Now that I'm single again, I'll have more time to visit with my friends." She glanced at his plate. "What do you think of the shepherd's pie?"

Chapter 37

Olivia's breath caught after the video chat window opened on the screen. "Oh, Liz, you look terrible!" The woman, who always seemed to have boundless energy, looked like she hadn't slept for days. Her healthy summer tan had long since faded, and her winter complexion without makeup was sallow. The blue eyes returning Olivia's inspection lacked their usual spark. "How are you doing?" Olivia asked in a gentler tone.

"I'll admit it. It's a hard adjustment."

"Have you talked to her?"

Liz shook her head. "Only about business matters—transferring power of attorney to her daughters…things like that." She managed a weak smile as if to prove she remained undefeated by the strain.

"How are you managing?"

"I lived alone for years before Maggie showed up. I'd forgotten how much work it takes being alone. Doing the simplest things is harder, even making dinner after coming home from work. I used to be so efficient at living solo. I suppose married life made me lazy. I never realized how many things Maggie did for me…for us."

"Yes, it's so much easier to live as a couple. There's always someone to drop you off when your car is serviced or drive you home from a root canal." Olivia sighed. "What can I do to help?"

"As I said, I'm sending Maggie to you to manage her investments. She sold her co-op in New York. The proceeds far exceed what she needs to buy that house in Scarborough. It's a big sum to invest, especially for someone who's never managed that kind of money. Lately, she's been acting like my advice is an intrusion. Better it should come from someone else."

"Don't take it personally. She probably wants to assert her independence."

"I've never tried to tell her what to do. I only made suggestions."

"I know, Liz, but Maggie is in strange territory. It may have nothing to do with you. She's probably trying to prove to herself that she can manage without you."

Liz looked thoughtful, then sad. If they were in the same room, instead of talking through video chat, Olivia would have offered her a hug.

Liz took an audible breath and composed her face, now looking all business. "I'm going to transfer all Maggie's financial files in a secure, encrypted link. After you've downloaded everything, I'll destroy the link and the files. Promise me you'll take good care of her, Olivia."

"You know I will, Liz." She grinned. "If I don't, I know I'll have you to answer to."

"You better believe it. Send me a text when you finish downloading the files."

Olivia smiled at the picture on her screen after the video chat ended. Her wallpaper was a silhouette of her granddaughters against the sunrise on the beach. The capture had been a perfect moment at a perfect time in their lives. That was the best we could hope for, mused Olivia, magical moments of joy and the happy memories of them. Otherwise, life was mostly hard work and struggle.

But the story of Maggie and Liz was one of the saddest Olivia had heard in a long time. Two young lovers, torn apart by a mother's religious homophobia, reunited after forty years. One contracts breast cancer and her lover, a famous breast surgeon, not only cares for her medical condition, but marries her. Now, the magical love story had come to an end. Olivia was a cynic about most things, but oddly, she still believed in love.

An email from Liz landed in her phone with a ping. Olivia opened her laptop and began the download. Time estimate: ten minutes. Instead of staring at the screen while she waited, Olivia left her office and closed the door.

Sam was sprawled out on the sofa, watching a women's soccer match broadcast from Scotland. Olivia nudged over Sam's feet, so she could sit down.

"How's Liz?" asked Sam, her eyes fixed on the TV screen.

"She looks like hell."

"I'm not surprised. She told me she's only sleeping three or four hours a night."

"That's not enough. She needs to get more rest."

Sam grunted. Obviously, the soccer match was more interesting than the conversation.

"I think Liz still loves Maggie."

"I'm sure she does. That doesn't mean they should be together."

"You really don't believe in romance, do you?"

"I believe in attraction…in sex. Friendship and loyalty mean more to me than romance."

"So, be a good friend and invite Liz over for dinner."

"I don't know if that's a good idea."

"Why?"

"Isn't Lucy coming tonight for her cooking lesson?"

"I thought they like each other."

"They do. That's the problem."

Olivia knew that if Sam had been more engaged in the conservation, she never would have let that slip. She decided to test her hypothesis. "So, they like each other too much, is that what you're saying?"

Sam continued to stare at the screen, providing Olivia with her answer.

"Samantha, I'm inviting Liz over for dinner. You should be more supportive of your friend."

Sam rolled her eyes and slipped down on the couch. "I'm not going to argue with you, Olivia. You're going to do what you want anyway."

"Come on, sit up." Sam didn't move. Olivia wasn't surprised. Sam was often stubborn. "Why don't you invite Liz?" Olivia suggested.

"It will mean more coming from you," said Sam without taking her eyes off the soccer match.

Olivia decided that Sam was right, so instead of texting when the download of the financial documents finished, she telephoned.

"What's the matter?" asked Liz. "Didn't the files transfer correctly?"

"Oh, yes. Everything's fine. I'll look them over tomorrow. I called to invite you for dinner. Too often when people break up, their partnered friends shun them, as if divorce were a kind of contagion that can be spread."

"Sometimes, a difficult relationship can be a mirror, and that scares people," Liz replied. "I've heard that some people fear the newly single person might try to steal their partner."

"You'd have to be pretty insecure to think that."

"Perhaps, but people do. But you don't have to worry. Sam and I have been friends for over twenty years. We've never even thought about falling into bed together."

"You're too much alike," observed Olivia. "Come to dinner."

"What can I bring?"

"Nothing, but if you must bring something, bring wine. White. We're having chicken."

They settled on a time. When the soccer match ended, Sam finally got up from the couch. She came into the kitchen where Olivia was setting out the pans and ingredients as if she was producing a cooking show. Everything was staged carefully, lined up in the order it should be used or added to the recipe. "You're really taking these cooking lessons seriously."

"If Lucy learns how to cook tasty and attractive food, maybe she'll eat more." Olivia split off exactly six cloves from the head of garlic, making sure they were approximately the same size, and added them to the lineup. "If Lucy wants to catch another mate, she should learn how to cook."

At that, Sam snorted with laughter. "What century are you living in? Lucy is beautiful, and she sings like an angel. She doesn't need anything else. And who says she wants another partner? She never married before she met Erika."

"She didn't have time during her opera career. Besides, she was a late bloomer."

"Like you?"

"I wasn't a late bloomer. I've known since college that I prefer women. I also knew that I needed to marry a man for my career."

Sam gazed at her for a long time. Olivia could feel her judgement as surely as if she had spoken it aloud, but all she said was, "I think I'll take a shower before your guests get here."

"Good idea," Olivia agreed.

After Sam left, Olivia took out the parsley and inspected it. She was about to wash it when she decided that should be part of the lesson. Everything was arranged by the time the doorbell rang. Olivia looked at her phone and saw the video feed of Lucy standing outside the door. She obviously knew she was on camera, because she smiled sweetly. Olivia unlocked the door remotely.

"Come in, Lucy," said Olivia through the intercom. "I'm in the kitchen getting ready for our lesson. You can find your way, can't you?"

Olivia realized that Lucy probably wouldn't know where to put her coat, so she headed to the door to meet her. She opened her arms for a hug. As she scooped up Lucy, and her arms went fully around her, Olivia was reminded how tiny the woman was.

"It feels so good to be able to hug someone," Lucy said. "Thank you so much for making time for me."

Lucy's simple expression of gratitude made the effort of putting together these cooking lessons worthwhile. After Olivia let Lucy go, she looked her over from head to toe. Her red hair had faded even more since Erika had died, but her makeup was perfect as might be expected of someone who'd spent a good portion of her life on the stage. She was wearing a heather-green cardigan over a blue top that exactly matched the blue threads in the heather. As Olivia had often observed, green was Lucy's color. It was such a relief to see her looking so put together.

"Come in, dear, and let's get started. I've chosen a meal that can cook quickly, but there's some preparation involved."

Olivia explained why it was important to chop the ingredients to a uniform size, so they'd cook evenly.

"Your knives are so sharp," Lucy noticed after taking a few cuts. "I have to be careful, or I'll cut myself."

"Well, be careful, but if you hurt yourself, our friend, the doctor, will be here momentarily."

Lucy put down the knife and turned to her with wide eyes.

"You don't mind, do you? I invited her because she's been looking so sad lately."

Lucy's emotional reaction lasted only a moment before she recovered her composure. *How good you are, Mother Lucy,* thought Olivia. *You must have been brilliant on the stage.*

"Of course, I don't mind. It's kind of you to include her. I only hope my dinner turns out to be edible."

"Oh, it will. I'll make sure of it."

Olivia admired Lucy's perfect profile as she continued to mince the garlic as she'd been instructed. She wondered whether to bring up the topic of Lucy's interest in their mutual friend. Then she decided it might offend her, and Lucy's recovery was still fragile. Besides, it was really none of her business.

"The meal we're making is a variation of the classic French dish, persillade," Olivia explained. "I've adapted it for a sheet pan cooking style so we can cut down on the dishes to wash."

"Anything that minimizes cleanup is good with me," Lucy said with one of her brilliant smiles. Then the doorbell rang, and Lucy visibly flinched. Fortunately, she'd paused the motion of the chef's knife.

"That will be the good doctor," said Olivia. "Are you all right here while I get the door?"

"Yes, I think I can manage that much."

Olivia washed her hands and quickly dried them on a dish towel before heading to the door. To Olivia's relief, Liz was looking better than when they had talked on the phone. She'd put on some makeup to cover her pallor and done her hair, scrunching it into its usual, deliberate messiness.

"I'm a few minutes early. I hope you don't mind," she said.

"No, come in. We're busy with prep, but you know how that is." Olivia took the bottle of chardonnay out of Liz's hand, glad that it was chilled, and pointed to the hooks in the hallway as Liz wiggled out of her coat. "Come into the kitchen. You know the way."

Olivia deliberately stood back to watch the reaction of the players when they saw one another. Liz suddenly stood straighter, but her hands found their way into her pockets. She had something to hide. Lucy's smile when she saw Liz was so radiant it could have melted an iceberg. She turned up her face for a kiss. Liz looked hesitant at first, but she landed her lips carefully on Lucy's cheek.

So, thought Olivia, *my instincts are correct!*

Chapter 38

Maggie found Liz sitting on the screen porch reading on her iPad. Everyone was desperate for spring after the long winter. Although it was still cold, Maggie had gone for a walk on Scarborough Beach before coming down to Hobbs to pack. It was beautiful, but so different from the familiar terrain of Hobbs Beach or the rocky shore of Gull Island. She was looking forward to learning some new geography.

She stood watching Liz, who, as usual, was so absorbed in what she was reading, she didn't notice Maggie standing on the other side of the glass. The propane stove was burning brightly. Although the early March sun was bright, it was too chilly to sit on an uninsulated porch without heat. As it was, Liz was wearing a heavy sweatshirt. She finally looked up when Maggie opened the door.

"You don't have to hang around while I pack," Maggie said. "I'm not going to steal anything." She smiled to show she was joking, but Liz didn't smile.

"I never thought you would. I'm here in case you need help."

"I think I can manage. I'm mostly done. I sorted the Christmas ornaments as you asked. I left the ones we bought together in a separate box. I didn't know what to do with them."

Liz shrugged. "Take them if you want."

"You never liked them."

"That's not entirely true. I liked the sentiment behind them. Commemorating another year of being together…and you being cancer free."

Maggie swallowed hard because she felt her throat thicken. "Maybe I should take them. You'll just throw them out."

"I won't. I'll just leave them in the box until next Christmas. Then, I'll decide."

"I'll take them," said Maggie decisively. "They mean something to me."

"Okay."

All their negotiations about how to split up their common goods had been equally amicable. If anything, Liz had been overly generous in giving away the things they had purchased together because she didn't need them. She'd had a fully furnished, complete household when Maggie had moved in. Maggie had rented her New York apartment furnished, so there was little merging of their personal items. Not that Maggie had much. Her one-bedroom in the Village was tiny. "Microscopic," Liz always called it.

"Can I help you bring out boxes to the container?"

"There's not much. I'll take home what I packed today. There's not much room left in the container. Luckily, the closing is next week."

"It was nice of the sellers to let you move in so fast."

Maggie shrugged because the quick closing had nothing to do with kindness. The owner's husband had died of COVID, and she was moving to Arizona to live with her daughter.

"Thanks for not bringing the kids like last time," Liz said. "It's still hard for me. They look so sad when you drive away."

"They'll get used to it. They like having grandma there all the time. Believe me. They take full advantage of it."

"Baking cookies all the time?"

"Among other things. There are still things they like to do with Grandma Liz."

"I hope you'll let me spend time with them."

"Of course, I will. They love you. I love you too, and I hope we can remain friends."

"I need some time."

"We both do," Maggie agreed.

Liz finally closed her iPad and sat up. "Are you sure we can't work this out?"

"It's a little late for that."

"But we never really talked about it. You just marched in here and made a grand announcement: 'I want a divorce!'"

"Well, you never talk to me, or I would have told you sooner."

"I do talk to you. I've always talked to you."

"Not about the things that really matter. You'd tell me about the Rotary meeting and who's doing what in town. How mad you are that the vaccine plan left out the small practices when they could be on the front lines. When did we ever talk about us?"

"So, you had to leave to get my attention?"

"I guess so. Nothing else worked."

"Well, maybe we should talk about us."

Maggie sighed. "It's too late, Liz. And maybe we shouldn't have married. I know you proposed out of kindness, and we married, but not necessarily for the right reasons."

"Who cares what the reasons were? We made a good pair. We loved each other."

"We still love each other. At least, I still love you."

"You're making my argument for me," said Liz with that earnest look in her eyes. It reminded Maggie so much of the young Liz she'd met in college forty-seven years ago. It was so hard to refuse Liz when she looked at her that way.

"Just because we love each other doesn't mean we should be together."

"But if we try, maybe we can find our way back to where we were."

"We can't go back, Liz. We can only go forward. You say that all the time."

Liz now had that sad, puppy-dog look that made Maggie want to kiss her. It made her heart hurt to see her in such pain. "Liz, we're not right for each other," Maggie said gently. "We can't give each other what we need."

"Like what?"

"I need conversation. I'm a social person. I need to see your face and hear your voice. I need to hear you say, 'I love you.' I need to hear you say those words every day."

"I tell you every day that I love you."

"You did. But I wanted more than a mumbled, automatic saying like a pre-recorded message, but something you really mean."

Liz frowned and looked thoughtful. Maggie imagined she was examining her conscience to see if the accusation rang true. She had to give Liz that. She might be self-absorbed, but she was always fair. If she was wrong, she always admitted it.

"Liz, I need more attention than you can give me. You're so busy with this, and busy with that. You're a busy person. You just don't have time for me."

"I could make more time," Liz said in a small, hopeful voice.

"You could try, but Liz, you're doing things you love, and they help other people. Hobbs would probably fall apart without you."

Liz scowled. "That's an exaggeration."

"Yes, but really, Liz, are you willing to give up all those activities to spend time with me?"

"Maybe some of them."

"Really? You'd resent me if you did. And when we got married, you promised you'd retire, and we'd travel."

"We did travel. It's not my fault the pandemic shut everything down."

"But you still haven't retired. You kept promising soon, soon, but soon never came."

"I'm not ready to retire," Liz admitted.

"I know you're not. And it's good that you want to contribute. I miss that sometimes."

"You could go back to teaching."

"No, I've had enough. I'm focused on directing now, and I want to spend time with my grandchildren."

Liz had the familiar, reflective look that meant she was processing information. Then she sighed and looked away. "I guess I have been pretty neglectful."

"I don't think you did it deliberately. You were just living your life. That's all."

"I've heard the list of what I'm not providing. What aren't you giving me?"

"Liz, you know what I'm not giving you."

"What?"

"Sex! You need a lot of sex. We've always been mismatched that way."

"The oophorectomy and the tamoxifen depressed your libido. I know that. I've tried not to be too demanding."

"I can't even pronounce that word. The joys of living with a doctor. But it's not just physical, Liz. Even before the operation and the drugs I never had the sex drive you have."

"I don't believe that. When we first got back together, you always wanted sex."

"Everyone's eager in the beginning. And sex was the only thing that blotted out the anxiety after we found out I had cancer. I needed you to make love to me because it comforted me and made me feel safe."

"Why didn't you tell me these things before?"

"I've only found out some of them since I've been in therapy."

"You're in therapy?" asked Liz in surprise.

"Yes, every Saturday morning."

"So, that's where you go. I was beginning to wonder if you were having an affair." Liz grinned, but Maggie's heart skipped a beat. Maybe it was time to tell the truth.

"I also found out in therapy that I'm probably not completely gay. I'm probably bi."

"But you told me you only slept with men because that's what you were supposed to do. You said you only married Barry because you wanted to prove you were straight."

"That's what I thought. But you can't be married for twenty-five years and have sex with someone and not have some feelings for them. I find sex with a man exciting."

Liz took a deep breath and sat back with a dark expression on her face. Her brows were knit in a frown. "But you said you love women now."

Maggie knew she couldn't leave without telling Liz the truth. "I didn't want to tell you this, because I thought it would hurt you, but I had a fling. It was after you and Lucy had your little kiss on the boat."

Maggie could see a flinty look forming in Liz's eyes. Maybe this wasn't such a good idea.

"What do you mean, you had a fling?"

"There was a young actor at the State Theater. Very handsome."

"You had an affair with a man?" Liz's eyes flashed blue fire. "You *fucked* a man?"

"Yes, it was stupid. I wanted to hurt you like you hurt me when you kissed Lucy."

"You *fucked* a man?" Liz repeated. Despite the calm look on her face, her complexion had darkened. Maggie felt a cold finger of fear poking her in the back. *I need to get out of here*, she thought, watching Liz's face darken.

"You *fucked* a man because I kissed Lucy?" demanded Liz in an accusing voice.

"Yes. Because you betrayed me."

"I kissed her. I didn't *fuck* her. And I never kissed her again." Liz stared at her. "Who was this guy? That little moron you kept talking about? Brad What's-his-name?"

"I'm not saying. It doesn't matter."

"You're a bitch," said Liz. She jumped up and walked out of the room. Almost ironically, she carefully closed the door to the porch as she left. Maggie listened carefully to see if she could figure out where she was headed. Then she heard her feet on the basement stairs.

Maggie knew she should leave. She still had stuff to pack, but it was nothing important and could wait until another time. She went into the hall and saw Liz heading out of the house with her tactical bag over her shoulder and the canvas bag she used to carry her range gear. Maggie hurried to the front window and watched as Liz put the bags into the passenger seat of her truck and roared down the driveway.

Maggie's heart was pounding as she tried to decide what to do. Liz would be furious if she called the police. Besides, they probably wouldn't do anything. The red-flag law had been voted down. Maggie opened her favorites and tapped Lucy's number. The phone rang and rang. Fortunately, Lucy finally picked up.

"Maggie? It's so nice to hear from you."

"Lucy, this is an emergency. I told Liz about the affair, and she just rushed out of here with her pistols and gun stuff. I don't know what she intends to do."

"Did you tell her the man's name?"

"No, but she guessed. I talked about him a lot last summer."

"You don't think she'd try to harm him?"

"No, she wouldn't hurt anyone. At least, I don't think so. And Brad went back to New York, so she'd never know where to find him."

"Did she threaten you?" Lucy asked in an anxious tone.

"No, she just roared out of here with all her guns."

"Okay. Stay calm. You should probably leave in case she comes back. I'm going to call Brenda to tell her what's going on."

"Let me know, please. I don't want anything to happen to Liz…or anyone else."

"I know, Maggie. And I will get back to you. Now, let's get off, so I can call Brenda."

Chapter 39

Lucy tapped off the call and got up to close the door, instructing her admin to route all her calls to Tom. Before Jodi could answer, she shut the door tight. Her heart was hammering. She was sure Liz wouldn't hurt anyone, but guns were dangerous. They terrified Lucy despite the ladies' gun class she had taken with Maggie the first year she'd arrived in Maine.

Liz had been the instructor and Lucy remembered thinking what a good teacher she was for a class of women terrified by guns. Liz didn't try to take away their fear. If anything, she'd reinforced it with her lectures on safety.

As she tapped Brenda's number, Lucy remembered Liz putting her hands around hers on the pistol to show her the correct way to position her fingers. "Finger on the slide, not the trigger," Liz had said and given her that endearing, slightly off-center grin. "And watch your stance." Lucy had jumped like she'd been goosed when Liz put her hands on Lucy's hips to encourage her to crouch deeper.

Lucy's mind raced as she waited for Brenda to answer. "Come on, Brenda!" urged Lucy, "Pick up! I really need you."

Finally, she heard Brenda's voice. "Lucy, is it urgent? I'm in a meeting."

"Yes, Brenda. It's important."

"Hold on a minute. I'll be right back." The call was muted. Lucy sat down to calm herself, but she drummed her fingers on the desk while she waited.

"Okay. I had to excuse myself and find a private place to talk. I'm in my office now."

"Liz and Maggie had a disagreement. Liz left the house with her guns and ammunition."

"How did you find out?"

"Maggie called me."

"I thought they were parting on good terms."

"Maggie told her something that made Liz really angry."

"What did she tell her?"

Lucy scanned her conscience. Maggie had confessed the affair to her as a priest, and Lucy was ethically bound to keep it a secret. "I can only say someone's life could be in danger."

"Oh, fuck. Did Maggie sleep with a man?"

How could she know? wondered Lucy, but then realized Liz had probably told Brenda how Maggie's heterosexual past infuriated her.

"Does Liz know who the man is?"

Lucy knew she was now in so deep, she had to tell Brenda the essential details. "Apparently."

There was a long silence. "Well, I don't think we really need to worry. Liz wouldn't hurt anyone. I mean, if she needed to defend herself, she would, but she would never hunt someone down to kill him."

"Then, where did she go with all those guns?"

"Probably to the range to blow off some steam. I do that myself from time to time. It helps when you're really angry to plink some targets." There was another long silence. "You're not worried she'd hurt herself?"

"No, Liz has enormous ego strength. Sometimes, it's over the top, but it's within the normal range. Plus, she's psychologically well-attuned. She'd direct her anger appropriately outward."

"That's my read too," said Brenda. "So, let's all calm down. I hope Maggie left when Liz did. I wouldn't want her to be around when Liz comes back."

"I told her to leave. Hopefully, she listened to me."

"Well, Lucy. What do you want me to do? Do you want me to go look for Liz? She's a big girl. I'm sure she can take care of herself."

"I'm worried about her mental state. I need to know she's safe."

Lucy heard a long intake of air as Brenda sighed. "I already turned the meeting over to one of my captains, so I guess I can go look for her."

"May I come along?"

"All right," said Brenda in a patient voice. "Are you at the rectory?"

"Yes."

"I'll be there in a few minutes."

Lucy gathered her things in her bag and shoved her laptop into its case. She'd already decided she wouldn't be coming back today.

Jodi glanced up with surprise when Lucy, wearing her coat and carrying her bags, stood at her desk. "I have to leave for an urgent appointment," Lucy explained. "Direct any business to Father Tom. If it's a client, and it's an emergency, ask them to call Cherie Bois."

"Yes, Mother Lucy. I will." Jodi's eyes were anxious, but Lucy realized they were reflecting her own anxiety. "Is there something I can do to help?"

"No, thanks. I have to go. Have a good rest of the day."

Lucy went outside to wait for Brenda, but the March wind was brisk and drove her back into the alcove to shelter from its gusts.

She was surprised to see Brenda pull up in her truck. "I don't want to create a stir by driving a cruiser down the road to the range," she explained as her passenger climbed into the truck. Lucy cursed under her breath because she was wearing a skirt and still found it impossible to climb into the truck modestly. Brenda gallantly averted her eyes while Lucy yanked the skirt down and straightened the twisted hem.

"Lucy, I don't mind doing this, but I think you're overreacting, Liz is a sensible person. She would never risk her medical license by getting on the wrong side of the law. That said, if my wife cheated on me with a man, I don't know what I'd do." She sighed. "Why is it worse when they cheat with a man?"

"Because you're on a level playing field with another woman, but not with a man," Lucy explained.

"What was Maggie thinking?" asked Brenda, shaking her head. "She knew that would drive Liz crazy, and why would she tell her? That's just stupid." Brenda glanced at Lucy, who just shrugged. "You know. You're just not telling me."

"You know I can't tell you, Brenda."

Brenda grinned. "You're some piece of work, Lucy Bartlett."

The banter with Brenda had helped Lucy calm down...a little. What reassured her was Brenda's relaxed attitude, but Lucy would be glad to see with her own eyes that her worries were unfounded.

Brenda turned onto the dirt road leading to the range. Lucy had only been there one time before, when she'd taken Liz's firearms class, but she recognized the dilapidated homes set back from the road. They looked like something out of the movie, *Deliverance.* Lucy almost expected hillbillies to come out with shotguns.

When they reached the gate, Brenda rolled down her window and cocked her ear. The sound of gunfire could be heard in the distance…a few shots, followed by a series of rapid-fire bursts. "Well, someone's out there shooting." Brenda got out to use her electronic pass card to open the gate. She drove through but had to get out again to close it.

"I could have done that for you," said Lucy, "I wasn't thinking."

"I understand. You're stressed. You can get the gate on the way out."

Lucy breathed an enormous sigh of relief when she spotted Liz's truck parked at the end of one of the shooting bays. They had to pull past the concrete barrier to see Liz, standing downrange. There were four shot-up targets in tatters on the backer board. The ground was littered with spent targets.

"She's shooting off a hell of a lot of ammunition, and there's a shortage, so that's expensive."

"Why is there a shortage?"

"Looney tunes are buying it up after the insurrection…for and against," Brenda explained. "It's even hard for law enforcement to get ammo. I went to Cabela's the other day. The shelves were completely bare."

"That's crazy," said Lucy.

"Yes, it is." Brenda narrowed her eyes as she watched Liz through the windshield. "Do you want to get out and talk to her?"

"Yes, I do." As Lucy slid out of the truck, her skirt rode up nearly to her crotch. "Shit," she said, yanking it back down. She heard a chuckle before Brenda closed the driver's door.

Lucy followed Brenda to the old picnic table at the end of the bay. The shooting continued, a few shots, then multiple bursts. "She's just emptying one magazine after another," Brenda said loud enough to be heard over the shooting. "Like I said, she's blowing off steam. Hell, she's not even aiming, just firing."

"How can you tell? The bulls-eyes are full of holes."

"Liz is a better shot than that," Brenda explained. "She's deadly."

"Can she hear us?" Lucy asked raising her voice to match the volume of Brenda's.

"Not while she's firing. Those hearing protectors are electronic. They turn on when shots are fired, off when she's not, so she can hear people speaking. We'll have to wait until she needs to reload."

Finally, the shooting stopped.

"Liz!" called Brenda. "Liz!"

Liz put the gun down on the table and pulled off her earmuffs. "What the fuck are you doing here?" she asked, frowning at Brenda. "I'm not doing anything illegal."

"We're just watching," said Brenda, folding her arms on her chest. "Your aim sucks today, Liz. You need to line up your sights better."

"Thanks for the advice, but I don't need it. Now, get out of here and take the priest with you," Liz said, glaring at Lucy. While Liz headed back to her shooting position, Lucy pulled out her tab collar and stuck it in the pocket of her coat. This situation was volatile enough. It didn't need more triggers.

"You're wasting a lot of ammo, Liz," Brenda called. "You could donate it to the Hobbs PD. We could use it."

"Forget about it. Buy your own ammo. That's why I pay taxes."

"Liz," called Lucy, "Liz, please stop. I know you're angry, but please stop."

Brenda gave Lucy a sharp look. "Don't get in the middle of this, Lucy. Just let her blow off steam."

"Get her out of here, will you, Brenda?"

"I will, but it's almost sundown. You know the rules. No firing after dusk."

Liz turned her back, evidently unimpressed.

"Liz!" Lucy called. "If you come home, I'll make dinner for you. I learned a new recipe from Olivia. I'll make it for you."

"Why would I want to eat with you after you called Brenda on me? Did Maggie call you? That fucking bitch!"

"Yes, she called me. She was worried about you. Now come home, and I'll make dinner for you."

Liz stared at the ground. In the sharply angled afternoon sun, the spent cartridges glittered. They were everywhere. "I have to rake up the brass."

"What does that mean?" Lucy whispered to Brenda.

"She has to rake up the spent cartridge casings. Good range etiquette, and you know Liz. She always follows the rules."

"Your house or mine?" Liz called to Lucy as she got her gear together.

"Your house. I have to pick up a few things first, and I'll meet you there."

"Good move," said Brenda softly. "Get her home and keep her there."

"Let's go," said Lucy. "Drop me off at the rectory, so I can get my car and pick up dinner makings. I want to get to Liz's place as soon as I can."

Brenda nodded. "See yah, Liz. We're heading out now."

"Good!" Liz flipped her middle finger at Brenda and grinned.

"Try to stay out of trouble," Brenda called back.

"Don't worry, Lucy. She'll be all right," Brenda said as they rode back to town.

"Everyone's struggling right now," Lucy said.

"You can say that again."

After that, they were silent. Brenda dropped Lucy off at the rectory. "Good luck with her," Brenda said as Lucy took her bag out of the back seat. "Call me if you need me." She raised her fingers to her forehead in salute.

Lucy made a mental list of things she needed from the supermarket as she headed home. She'd decided to pack a bag in case she needed to spend the night. After all the times Liz had kidnapped her and brought her home, sitting with her friend on this dark night was the least she could do.

She raced through the supermarket, tossing the items she needed into her basket. She stopped in the fish department because she planned to make Olivia's recipe for white clam sauce using frozen, chopped quahogs. She'd make a spicy Arugula salad with tiny tomatoes and shaved Parmesan and heat up a roasted garlic ciabatta.

The big, gray truck wasn't in the driveway when Lucy arrived, so she was hopeful she'd beaten Liz home, but when she let herself into the garage with her key, she saw it was parked inside. She had keys to let herself into the house, but out of respect, she rang the bell.

Beer bottle in hand, Liz opened the door. She lifted Lucy's overnight bag into the house, then took the supermarket bags as well.

"Pull your car in. With these high winds, a branch could come down on your nice SUV." She tapped the button to open the bay door and disappeared with the bags into the house.

It felt strange to pull her car into Maggie's space, but Lucy told herself it was just bad conscience and let it go. By the time she came into the kitchen, Liz had unpacked her grocery bags. "I see you intend to make white clam sauce, so I set out the stock pot and a pan for the sauce as well as a salad bowl. I left the clams on the counter to defrost," Liz explained. "I also opened some wine for you. A rosé. I didn't know what you were going to cook, so I hedged my bets. It's in the fridge." Liz opened a cabinet and set a white wine glass on the counter. "Do you need help?"

"We have some time," said Lucy, glancing at the clock on the wall. "Why don't we just sit and talk for a while?"

Liz gave her a suspicious look. "Whenever a woman says, 'let's talk,' I know there's a hidden agenda."

Lucy held up her hands, showing her palms. "I'm innocent…for a change."

Liz narrowed her eyes. "I trust you, Lucy. I don't know why."

"Maybe because I'm a priest?"

"You know that means nothing to me," Liz replied bluntly. Lucy nursed a tiny hurt at that remark as Liz headed out of the room. "Help yourself to wine."

Lucy found the open bottle of rosé in the refrigerator. The cork had been carefully replaced after it had been extracted. When she returned to the living room, she saw that Liz had switched from drinking the beer from the bottle to a glass. Hopefully, the nod to social convention meant she had calmed down.

"What did Maggie say when she called you?" Liz asked, casually pouring the beer.

"She said she was frightened because you ran out of here with all your guns."

"First of all, I didn't run out of here. I walked like a normal person. Second, I didn't take 'all my guns.' I only took three of my favorite pistols. She's so fucking dramatic."

Lucy steadily held Liz's gaze. "Why did you need guns at all?"

"Because I was angry, and I wanted to shoot something."

"Maggie?" asked Lucy in her calm, therapist's voice.

"No, of course, not. And not even the dickwad she fucked either. Ammunition is expensive. I wouldn't waste it on them. They're not worth it."

"But you don't mind wasting it on targets?" asked Lucy smiling because she knew she was deliberately trying Liz's patience.

Liz took her feet off the hassock and sat up. "I have no sense of humor tonight. Don't try your shrink's tricks on me."

"I'm just making conversation."

Liz sat back again. "Maggie is a bitch. She slept with a man to spite me because I kissed you. She did it knowing it was the one thing…the *one* thing that would end our relationship. Obviously, that was her intention."

Lucy focused on the minerals in the coffee table in the hopes that Liz couldn't read her thoughts from her expression.

"*You knew!*" accused Liz, leaning forward to scrutinize Lucy's face. "She told you, didn't she?"

Lucy met her gaze, but remained silent.

"It was told in confidence and you're not at liberty to say," Liz continued. "Am I right?"

Lucy merely shrugged.

Liz stared at her beer glass. "Fuck this. I need something stronger. I'll be right back."

When Liz returned with a full bottle of single-malt scotch and a whiskey glass, Lucy had a bad feeling. "Maybe I should start dinner. We can eat early. The pasta will help absorb the alcohol if you're intent on a bender."

"I don't have any specific plans," said Liz casually, "but suit yourself."

Lucy went into the kitchen. It was only four o'clock, not outrageously early for dinner. She defrosted the pint of chopped clams according to Olivia's instructions. While the microwave hummed, she searched the kitchen for an apron. She found two hanging on the back of the pantry door and chose the shorter one. Tying it behind her back, she realized it was probably Maggie's and felt a little funny putting it on, but grease stains always showed on her black shirts.

Liz came into the kitchen as Lucy was filling the stock pot with water. She flipped on the light over the stove. "I'm sorry I'm being so unfriendly. I appreciate your attempt to look after me. I truly do."

Lucy flashed a smile in her direction. "I just want to show off what I've learned from Olivia."

"How long have you been taking cooking lessons from her?" Liz asked.

"Not long. She says she's trying to fatten me up. That always makes me laugh. It reminds me of the parable of the prodigal son. The fattened calf." Lucy put on the stock pot to boil. She ripped apart a head of garlic. Liz handed her a chef's knife, and Lucy crushed the garlic with the heel to make it easier to peel.

"I'm impressed," said Liz, leaning against the refrigerator with her arms folded on her chest. "Olivia is doing a good job teaching you."

"Wait until you taste it. It's amazing."

"You're amazing," said Liz in a seductive voice.

Lucy nudged her with her hip. "Liz, I'm a newbie cook. I get nervous when people hover. I'll call you when it's ready."

"All right," said Liz. "I'll turn on some music in the living room. What would you like?"

"Some easy Jazz?"

Liz bowed. "Yes, Madam. Your wish is my command." She took her bottle of scotch and left.

It still stressed Lucy to watch all the pots doing something at the same time. She panicked when she realized she didn't remember where the colander might be to drain the pasta, but then she glanced into the sink and saw it. She had a brief moment of panic when the minced garlic was just beginning to brown, and the timer for the pasta went off at the same time. She remembered Olivia's instructions and stayed calm.

Liz came in, took out dishes, and began to set the table in the breakfast nook. "You don't mind eating here rather than in the dining room?"

"Not at all. Erika and I used to eat in the kitchen all the time." Liz brought the pasta bowl and salad to the table. Liz snatched the bread out of the oven and set it on a breadboard. She set a breadknife beside it.

"Well, I hope it's good," Lucy said. She closed her eyes to say grace, while Liz scooped out pasta into their bowls.

Liz closed her eyes as she savored Lucy's meal. "Delicious," she said. "I must get your recipe."

"It's Olivia's."

"It's yours now. No two women ever cook the same. That's part of the pleasure."

"Erika said you know all of her mother's recipes. Will you teach me how to cook them?"

"Of course," said Liz.

Lucy was pleased that the meal was tasty. The conversation despite the previous tension was relaxed. Liz chased her out of the kitchen to clean up. When Liz finished, she brought Lucy another glass of wine. Lucy watched with worry as Liz poured herself another glass of scotch. She'd had to tuck Erika into bed after a few of Liz's scotch-and-Nietzsche nights, and it wasn't a pretty sight.

"Would you like to watch a movie?" Liz suggested.

"No, I'm enjoying just being here with you. I enjoy your company."

"Me too."

"That's such a funny expression," mused Lucy. "Literally, it means you enjoy your own company. Or when someone says, I love you and you say, 'me too,' it really means you love yourself."

"That's good, right?" asked Liz and drained her whiskey glass. She instantly refilled it.

"Yes, it's good to love yourself."

Liz moved to the sofa next to Lucy. "I love you too," she said. "I've loved you since the first moment I laid eyes on you." She leaned forward, and Lucy knew she was going to kiss her.

"Liz, I'm not ready for this," Lucy warned gently. She put her hand up, ready to hold her back.

"Please…" Liz begged.

"No, not tonight. You're too upset. It's been a bad day for you."

"You keep fending me off. This time, I won't take 'no' for an answer."

The intense blue eyes moved closer. The lips pressing against hers were fierce. Liz's fingers gripped her shoulders so hard, they hurt.

Lucy's body moved as it had been trained. The coffee table flipped over, spraying the beautiful minerals in the cavity on the floor. The wine glass shattered. The bottle of whiskey overturned, pouring the hateful brown liquor on the floor.

Lucy was surprised to find herself holding Liz's arm twisted behind her back.

"Lucy, you're going to dislocate my shoulder," Liz warned in a pained voice. "Let me go. Please."

Lucy looked down and saw what she'd done. She didn't want to hurt anyone, but why was she here again with someone pushing her where she wasn't ready to go?

"Lucy, please let me go," Liz asked again, this time in the perfectly rational tone one might use with a difficult child.

Lucy released her. Liz snatched up the glugging bottle pouring out expensive whiskey on the floor. She dashed into the kitchen and returned with a roll of paper towels to mop up the mess.

"I need to go," said Lucy, trying to remember where she had left her bags and realized Liz hadn't moved them from the hallway.

"I'm sorry, Lucy. I forgot," said Liz collecting the shards of glass gingerly. "I had too much to drink."

"That's no excuse, Liz. Take some responsibility!"

"I'm sorry," Liz repeated. "I would never hurt you. I love you."

"Then act like you love me!" said Lucy in a furious voice and headed to the door.

Chapter 40

Liz knocked on the front door and stood back. Eventually, Lucy peeked through the space between the blinds and the window sash. When she finally opened the door, she was already wearing her coat-length parka and the black hat with the pompom that she wore for outdoor services.

"Let's go for a walk," she said, stepping out on the porch. She pulled the door shut behind her and locked it.

"It's pretty cold out here," protested Liz, her breath coming as vapor.

"It's good for us to get fresh air. You say that all the time. I walk nearly every morning at dawn."

"Not using your practice room much?"

"It reminds me too much of Erika."

Lucy wiggled her fingers into her gloves. Dressed all in black, she looked like she was heading to an official Episcopal event instead for a walk on the beach. "Are you wearing your collar too?" asked Liz.

Lucy gave her fierce look. "Don't be funny," she warned. Obviously, she wasn't in the mood for Liz's anticlerical humor.

"Okay," said Liz, raising her hands in surrender. "I'll try to be on good behavior."

"Good idea. Especially after last night."

"Yes, that was bad."

"Come on," said Lucy. "Let's go down to the beach." Lucy set a path for the beach access.

"I'm sorry," Liz said.

"Liz," said Lucy in a firm voice. "I don't like sexual aggression except when I invite it. I was raped. Don't you remember?"

"I remember."

"When someone is too aggressive, I get panicky. I don't want to hurt you, but you know I can."

"You wouldn't hurt me," said Liz in confident tone.

Lucy looked at her sharply. "Don't test me!"

Liz eyed her cautiously. They continued to the beach in silence. Lucy reached for Liz's arm. "Liz, I love you, but it's too soon for sex. I'm not ready and neither are you. Maggie just moved out. I'm not going to be your revenge fuck or your rebound relationship or any kind of relationship that's not about *us*. Do you understand?"

"You're not going to make me wait until marriage like you did Erika?"

"I didn't make her wait."

"No, Erika told me about the mercy fuck after her mother died."

Lucy flung off Liz's arm, and she walked off with determined steps. Liz hurried to catch up with her.

"Sometimes, Liz, you are such an asshole. Don't you know when to shut up?"

"I'm sorry."

"Just shut up."

"Lucy…"

"Shut up, or I'm going home, and you can talk to yourself."

Liz thrust her hands into her pockets and walked silently beside Lucy, stealing glances in the hope of finding an opening to speak. Then Lucy stopped abruptly.

"Don't test me, Liz. I have a temper too." Liz looked at her warily. Lucy took off her glove and reached out her hand. Cautiously, Liz took Lucy's small hand. Despite the glove, it was cold. Liz pulled it into the pocket with hers.

"It's cold," said Liz "We should probably go back."

Lucy nodded. She took her hand back and put on her glove. "Liz, you make it so hard for me sometimes. I love you, but if you think I'm going to put up with your mischief like Maggie did, you are very mistaken."

"So, there is hope for a relationship?"

"Maybe. I'm not making any promises. Let's see how things go. I'm willing to spend time with you to find out, but not if you keep putting the moves on me. I need time. I'm still hurting…really hurting. Can't you understand?"

"I do understand. Of course, I understand."

"And your wife just left you. Don't you dare think you're going to fill the void with a sexual relationship with me. That's not going to work."

"Don't shrink me, Lucy."

Lucy stopped, grabbed Liz's wrists and yanked on them. "I'm not shrinking you! I'm loving you! Can't you see?" She let go and raised her eyes to heaven. "Why can't you let people love you?" Lucy marched toward the beach entrance.

Liz was glad they were heading back. Even in her pockets, her hands were feeling numb. Finally, they reached the house, and Lucy opened the door to the porch.

"Come in and warm up for a moment. I'll make you a cup of coffee." Lucy didn't sound very friendly, so Liz wasn't sure she wanted to take her up on the invitation.

"Is it safe?"

"Liz, please be serious for a change. Yes, it's safe. Come in." Lucy turned the key in the lock and leaned on the door. She hung her coat on the coat tree along with her scarf and hat. Liz stood there. "Well? Take off your coat."

Liz hung her parka on an empty hook and followed Lucy into the kitchen.

"Sit down," Lucy ordered. Liz pulled out a chair from the kitchen table and watched Lucy fill a coffee pod. "You like that super-dark coffee that Erika liked," said Lucy. "I can't drink it. It's like mud."

"I'll take it off your hands if you don't want it anymore. It will just go stale in the cannister."

"No, sometimes I just take the lid off and smell it because it reminds me of her." Lucy put down the pod and the spoon. Liz saw the bright tears running down her cheeks. She got up and turned Lucy gently by the shoulders, surprised when she fell into her arms without resistance. She stroked her silken hair while Lucy cried. "It's okay. It's okay," she soothed.

"It's not okay, but eventually, it will be." She nudged Liz away and resumed filling the coffee pod. "Be patient, Liz. I'm worth waiting for."

"I'll try to be patient."

"Don't try, Liz. Just do it!" Lucy's green eyes were still brilliant from the tears. "You're worth waiting for too. And I'm willing."

Lucy looked so beautiful, despite her nose being red from the wind and the wisp of red hair standing up in the back from static electricity. Liz felt a tender ache deep inside. "May I kiss you?" she asked in a whisper.

Lucy stared at her, but not in a way that made Liz think she was angry or disapproved.

"Please," Liz begged. "Let me kiss you. Just once."

"All right. Once."

Liz took her in her arms and kissed her softly. Lucy's lips parted the way they had on the boat on that hot July evening. Cautiously, Liz tested the invitation and found Lucy's mouth was warm and sweet. They stood there at the kitchen sink kissing like they could never get enough of one another. Finally, Lucy came up for air. She gave Liz a little nudge and went to the refrigerator to get the half and half for their coffee.

"If you ever wonder if I'm interested, remember that kiss," Lucy said, her head in the refrigerator.

"Oh," said Liz. "I'll never forget it."

Also by Elena Graf

THE HOBBS SERIES

HIGH OCTOBER

Liz Stolz and Maggie Fitzgerald were college roommates until Maggie confessed their affair to her parents. When Maggie breaks her leg in a summer stock stage accident, she lands in Dr. Stolz's office. Is forty years too long to wait for the one you love?

THE MORE THE MERRIER

Maggie and Liz's plans of sitting by the fire, drinking mulled wine, and watching old Christmas movies get scuttled by surprise visits from friends and family.

THIS IS MY BODY

Professor Erika Bultmann, a confirmed agnostic, is fascinated by Mother Lucy, the new rector of the Episcopal Church, especially when she discovers Lucille Bartlett was a rising opera star before mysteriously disappearing from the stage.

LOVE IN THE TIME OF CORONA

Police Chief Brenda Harrison shows an interest in Liz's biracial PA, but first Cherie needs to get past her loathing for all law enforcement since a state trooper shot and killed her sister.

THIRSTY THURSDAYS

Liz Stolz initiates Thirsty Thursdays, a weekly cocktail party on her deck, so her friends can socialize safely during the pandemic. Pretentious, overbearing Olivia Enright pursues Liz's friend, architect Sam McKinnon, and tries to push her way into the tight-knit group.

THE DARK WINTER

Erika hires Sam to build a sound-proof practice room for Lucy. Fortunately, the early Christmas gift is ready before tragedy strikes. As the women of Hobbs pull together to help a beloved friend deal with her loss, the dark winter brings tension and realignment in their small community.

SUMMER PEOPLE

Melissa Morgenstern, a high-profile lawyer from Boston, is spending the summer with her widowed mother. She's doing some trust work for Liz who introduces her to the attractive Courtney Barnes, Hobbs Elementary's new assistant principal. The arrival of Susan, Lucy's ex, complicates her deepening relationship with Liz.

STRANDS

Cherie hears her biological clock ticking and would like to start a family. When a shocking tragedy creates an opportunity for her and Brenda to become parents, their friends need to step up to make it happen.

THE RECTOR'S WEDDING

The sudden opportunity for Lucy to return to her singing career throws everything in her life into doubt—her vocation as a priest, her settled life in Hobbs, even her upcoming marriage to the woman she loves.

THE VANISHING BRIDGE

Rev. Susan Gedney tries to rebuild trust after her humiliating exit from Hobbs. Bobbie Lantry always needs to rush away to take care of mysterious elderly woman. They need to share their secrets, but do they dare?

EXTENDED CAPACITY

A small town in Maine wakes up thinking it's just another winter day, but a tragedy has been set in motion by dark secrets from the past and an unfortunate series of recent events. The horror that every town fears is about to come to Hobbs.

RIP TIDE

After the tragic shooting at Hobbs Elementary School, people are trying to get back to normal, but the town and its inhabitants will never be the same. Healers Dr. Liz Stolz and Rev. Lucy Bartlett are used to binding up the wounds of others, but in this book they are hurt by the unintended consequences of their actions

THE IMPERATIVE OF DESIRE

A coming-of-age story that takes a brilliant aristocratic woman from La Belle Époque through a world war, a revolution that outlawed the German nobility, and the roaring twenties to the decadent demimonde of Weimar Berlin.

OCCASIONS OF SIN

For seven centuries, the German convent of Obberoth has been hiding the nuns' secrets—forbidden passions, scandalous manuscripts locked away, a ruined medical career, and perhaps even a murder.

LIES OF OMISSION

In 1938, the Nazis are imposing their doctrine of "racial hygiene" on hospitals and universities. Margarethe von Stahle has always avoided politics, but now she must decide whether to remain on the sidelines or act on her convictions.

ACTS OF CONTRITION

After the fall of Berlin, Margarethe is brutally assaulted by occupying Russian soldiers. Her former protégée, Sarah Weber, returns to Berlin with the American Army and tries to heal her mentor's physical and psychological wounds.

About the Author

Elena Graf has published four historical novels set in twentieth-century Europe. Two of the titles in the Passing Rites series have won Golden Crown Literary Society and Rainbow awards for best historical fiction. In addition to her historical series, the author has written a series of contemporary novels set in Maine. She pursued a Ph.D. in philosophy but ended up in the "accidental profession" of publishing, where she worked for almost four decades. She lives in coastal Maine.

Find out about events and new books at her website, elenagraf.com. You can write to Elena at elena.m.graf@gmail.com. Or find her on Facebook.

Elena is a member of iReadIndies, a collective of self-published independent authors of Sapphic literature. Please visit our website at iReadIndies.com for more information and to find links to the books published by our authors.